TWO GIRLS.
ONE DEAD. ONE DISAPPEARED.
WHICH ONE OF THEM IS LYING?

How could things have gone so wrong between Syl Jameson and Viola Harrison?

Syl and Viola are like sisters growing up in the small, stifling town of Love Hill. Though they are as different as light and dark, they connect. And for Syl, Viola's family is a warm refuge away from the unaffectionate place that Syl calls home. But the reality is Syl can get a little needy and jealous. Viola can get a little toxic. And, like everyone in Love Hill, they have secrets. Eventually their friendship is bound to snap.

One night, it comes to a crashing end. Syl is found dead behind the wheel of Viola's car, and Viola is nowhere to be found. Lucky for Viola, dead girls don't talk. Or do they?

In this enthralling dual narrative, there are two sides to the story. Which girl's version to read first is up to you. Whatever the choice, the truth will reveal itself in the end.

This is a work of fiction. Names, characters, organizations, places, events, and incidents are either products of the author's imagination or are used fictitiously. Otherwise, any resemblance to actual persons, living or dead, is purely coincidental.

Text copyright © 2023, 2025 by Sandra J. Paul

All rights reserved.

No part of this book may be reproduced, or stored in a retrieval system, or transmitted in any form or by any means, electronic, mechanical, photocopying, recording, or otherwise, without express written permission of the publisher.

Previously published as *Dead Girls Don't Talk* by Hamley Books in Belgium in 2023.

Published by Skyscape, New York

www.apub.com

Amazon, the Amazon logo, and Skyscape are trademarks of Amazon.com, Inc., or its affiliates.

ISBN-13: 9781662531897 (paperback)
ISBN-13: 9781662531903 (digital)

Cover design by Mumtaz Mustafa
Cover image: © Alexia Feltser / ArcAngel

Printed in the United States of America

Dead Girls Don't Talk

VIOLA'S STORY

What if you were accused of killing your best friend in cold blood?
Viola may be on the run, but she's determined to tell her truth.

When she gets the chance to tell her side of the story to the one person who might believe her, she takes it. She wants the world to know about Syl, who she was and why she's now dead.

But will the world believe her? Syl can't defend herself, and Viola is known to have lied before. Yes, Viola can spin a tale like no one else.

**If you choose to go with Syl's version of events, please turn to page 1.
If you decide to go with Viola's, please go to page 169.**

PROLOGUE

What a mess. What a terrible, terrible mess.

Viola's car lies in ruins against the tree that broke in half. Her beautiful new Toyota is beyond repair. Ruined. Destroyed. Shrapnel. It's odd, really, that metal and glass can create such artwork.

Yes, the car is ruined. Just like I am.

The moment I regained a sense of what had happened, I could *feel* that this was absolutely, horrifyingly wrong.

Dead. I. AM. DEAD.

Seventeen, going on eighteen, and gone. Destroyed.

A body beyond fixing.

I was killed and left behind in that car.

And Viola is gone.

THE DEAD GIRL SITTING ON THE CROOKED CHAIR

Annie Jones sits on the same comfortable couch I'd been using twice per week when I was still alive. It's an act that surprises me. She usually takes the chair sitting on the other side of the coffee table, the one with the tattered upholstery and springs that creak when she sits down.

She waves me toward the chair, even though she can't see me. "It seems fitting that you take it."

I sit down. The springs don't creak when I do, and the upholstery doesn't bend under my nonexistent weight. I don't feel the fabric beneath my fingertips, nor do I really touch the chair. I can't. It still feels comfortable, though, being here, in this familiar room, with Annie as my only lifeline to what I've left behind.

Annie moves a heavy standing lamp across the carpet and sets it up so that the area around the chair is lit.

I don't blink; the light doesn't bother me. It's like it's not even there.

"There," she says. "Much better. Now I can see you."

"You can?" I say, surprised.

"Yes. I can't explain it, but now I can catch a glimpse of you. You're vague, though, as if you're a shadow made of colors. I know you're not really there—or at least not your physical form—but it's as if I can see your soul."

"That must be strange."

"It is."

"Aren't you afraid of me?" I ask, curious. "I am, after all, the proof that your ability exists."

"No. There was never a doubt in my mind about that, and you know that I have some experience with situations like this."

"Yes, and it seems that us being here in this odd situation is the very proof of that too."

Annie pours a glass of water from the bottle that is sitting on the coffee table, but she doesn't drink. She's obviously nervous, even though she's trying to hide that from me.

If the situation were reversed, I would be nervous too. I *was* when I first walked into this room nine months ago, asking her for help. Before that day, I had never set foot in this house. I'd only seen parts of her home on Instagram, where she freely shares photos and videos of her life.

When I walked into this room nine months ago, I had looked curiously at the tattered chair I'm now sitting on, because it seemed so out of place in her otherwise-modern renovated house. The piece of furniture didn't seem to fit in at all with the rest of her carefully selected things, unless it was some sort of statement about combining the old with the new. Her house has white walls and lofty ceilings, and colorful drapes that stand out against the stark white, falling gracefully from top to bottom. You could eat off the floor, with its clean beige tiles.

Not a single object feels out of place. Even the books on her shelves are obviously deliberate choices, though they're not the types of reads that an average person would choose. Science and psychology are entwined with rare editions of classic literature. All organized by genre and then by color. If I still had one, I would bet my life on the fact that she hasn't read one of them.

Being a social media influencer and writer may bring in the big bucks, but it doesn't bring in the warmth that I generally crave when connecting with people. I never clicked with Annie, not once, but I still returned to her like a moth to a flame. This is a cold place, just like she is.

But truth be told, she is the only one I can turn to right now, so we're stuck with each other.

Annie Jones was born and raised in Love Hill, like I was, and is a cold and emotionless product of this town. She has plenty of old money and a lot of ambition, and she's not afraid of flaunting both. As an influencer, her life is a social media extravaganza—devoted followers accept every word she says, and sponsors pay her handsomely for it. She wrote a couple of books about the paranormal, sprouting from her own experiences—which, I suppose, I can now confirm are true. She's extremely popular, and she has tons of emotional baggage that makes her even more endearing to the outside world.

During those nine months that I came by on a weekly basis, Annie became like a mentor in the craziness of my own existence. She was my confidante during the psychological trip and led me through my personal war zone. She didn't help *that* much, to be honest, but it was something. I distrusted her and could never shake the feeling that she might use my story for her own benefit.

But when I walked into that study nine months ago, looking for *something*, and saw that crooked chair, I felt drawn to it. In some ways, that chair was the reason I kept returning to this house, this room. Even now I can't explain what I felt. Annie saw me gazing at it that first time, and she smiled as she ran her hand over the wood. It was a tender gesture, as if she loved that chair more than life itself.

"I will never part with this thing," she said.

"Why not?" I had asked, my voice sounding crooked and tattered, just like that chair.

"Because it was my sister's. She still uses it sometimes. She likes to put her feet up on the coffee table, even though I tell her all the time that that's not how I raised her."

Annie's words had a deep emotional impact on me. The chill that ran down my spine was quickly replaced by something more surreal, a form of acceptance for the odd situation we found ourselves in. There we were, Annie Jones and I, talking about her dead sister, as if it were all so damned normal to accept that the deceased weren't gone yet.

It should have surprised me, but it didn't. It felt right somehow.

That chair is the reason why I am here today. "Do you talk to her?" I had asked on that first day.

"I do."

"What about your parents? Do you see them too?"

"I was too young to realize the nature of my gift when they passed away," Annie said, and she suddenly didn't sound so cold and distant anymore, if only for a moment. She sounded as if she was still mourning her losses.

"What happened?"

"Nothing," she said. "Because I didn't act on the signals they gave me. I didn't know anything about death or how to deal with it, so I pushed away all the signs. I regret that every day. It would have made my life easier and their passing more acceptable."

"And you know everything about death now?"

"Enough to be able to communicate with my sister."

Annie Jones had lost her parents and her sister in less than four years. Her parents died in a boating accident, right here in Love Hill. A stupid tourist-caused incident. Annie was eighteen and took custody of her sister, until the girl died under tragic circumstances too. She fell out of a tree when she was only twelve years old. People went crazy for less, but Annie? She picked up the pieces and moved on, or at least it seemed that way to the outside world. Now that I saw her for who she really was, I realized she hadn't moved on at all, or her sister wouldn't still be here.

"Do you miss her?" I asked.

"More than I can ever express."

"Where is she now?"

"Oh, she's sitting right next to you on the couch."

I looked aside, but nothing happened. I couldn't see her. I wouldn't know how to do that. And I regretted not having the gift. I would have given an arm and a leg to be able to see the one I'd lost, if only for a few moments.

Annie smiled. "She says it's good to see you here. If you feel uncomfortable sitting with her, we can move to another room, or I can ask her to leave."

"That's fine. I don't mind," I found myself saying.

Annie smiled, her eyes fixated on a spot next to me. "She asks why you're not afraid of her."

"I don't know," I'd said.

"Your mind is open for this, I can tell. It's interesting. You're not faking your lack of fear."

"Why should I be?" I asked.

"You're right, there's no reason to be afraid. Besides, she won't be around for long, anyhow. She's finally fading away."

"What do you mean by that?"

"Her time's up. She's been keeping me company for a while. She felt that I needed it, after all I'd been through. She said I needed that extra bit of comfort, and she has taught me how to communicate with spirits. But now that I'm doing fine and can stand on my own two feet, she'll be leaving me. It's high time too; she's tired."

"So you haven't been faking all of that stuff on your socials?" I blurted out. "I always thought it was a load of crap, to be honest."

Annie laughed. "No."

"You're a conduit, right? You get messages from the dead."

Annie didn't laugh this time. "If you believe in such a thing, then yes, maybe I am. Or at least, I might be when it comes to my sister, because so far, she's been the only one I can see. I do feel them, and I'm waiting for the moment when someone else will be able to communicate with me. If that moment ever comes."

Annie leaned forward and placed a gentle hand on my wrist and looked at me with the concern of a mother, even though she was not that much older than I was.

"I'm not sure if this is going to work. You're the first one to ever walk into my house, begging me for help. I haven't done this before, so you'll have to forgive me if I fail."

"I have nothing left to lose," I said. "So let's get on with it."

We never spoke about her sister again. Except for that one moment, several weeks later, when she told me that her sister was gone. She was sad about that.

I did come to realize that I didn't like Annie much. She was an opportunist, cold at heart, and eager to learn, to thrive on my sadness and despair. She spoke about me on her socials without naming me. But everyone in town knew it was me she was talking about.

A month ago, I gave up on Annie after a long and lengthy argument with her. I'd told her to go to hell. Had shut the door to this very room. Had sworn I would never come back.

And now I'm here, taking her sister's seat. The irony of it does not escape me.

"Are you okay?" Annie asks, and then she smiles sadly. "I guess that's a stupid question to ask a dead girl. What I meant to say was—"

"How am I holding up now that I'm dead?"

"Yes, I suppose that's what I wanted to ask you. It's an odd question, I know."

"I think I'm okay," I say. "I don't know, really. It's the first time I've died. No reference for this kind of thing. No going back, that's for sure. There's nothing to go back to— my body is gone." Even if all this was a fluke somehow and I was meant to go back to my former human form, I knew I wouldn't be able to do so. It's as if I never existed at all, and it's odd to think that soon I'll be gone from this room too. The fading that Annie spoke of has already begun. I can feel it; it's the one thing I *can* feel. It's like a tugging at my soul, a warning that I won't be here for long, like her sister. Whatever holds me here has already started pushing me away too.

"Why are you here, Syl?"

"I don't know that either."

I think about Viola and know that this is a lie. I'm here because of her.

"Syl?"

"Viola, I think," I blurt out.

"You came to me because you need to find her?"

I shake my head. "No, I know where she is. I won't be able to communicate with her. She's beyond my reach."

"You know where she is?" Annie says, surprised. "Everyone is out there looking for her. Can you help?"

"No," I say. "It's not up to me to find her. I don't have time for that."

"Then why did you come to me?"

"You know why. You're the only one I can talk to."

"Do you want me to pass on a message to your parents?"

I think about that question.

"No."

"Then maybe you just feel the urgency to tell me your story. This might be all you need to do in order to move on."

"What is there to tell?" I say with a shrug. "I died tonight. I was killed in a car crash—you were there, you saw me dead. And yet I'm still here. Why is that, you think? Why *am* I still around?"

"Because you have unfinished business to address," she says.

"Isn't that a cliché?"

"I don't know," Annie says. "Why else would the dead still linger, if not to tell their story?"

"What would be the point? It won't bring me back."

"But it might relieve you of the pain you're feeling right now."

That's true, I think.

Annie leans back. "Well, there obviously *is* a reason why you're still here, and we don't have much time, so let's get started. Let's start at the beginning."

"And where might that be?" I ask.

"Your fairy tale."

"My . . . fairy tale?"

"Yeah, the story of Syl and Viola. The one that everyone in town believes in."

I laugh. "I'm not so sure if I would call that a fairy tale. It used to be when I was young and oblivious."

"And you've grown up since then?"

"Yes, unfortunately."

Annie doodles on her notepad. "Okay. Let's talk about tonight, then. Why she did what she did."

"You mean, why she killed me?"

"Did she kill you?" Annie asks. "Is that what you're saying? Because right now, nobody's even sure what happened in that car. There are those who believe you were behind the wheel."

"I wasn't. She moved my body."

Annie frowns.

"Why would I lie?" I say. "It's not as if I can be punished for it. I'm already dead."

Annie doesn't reply.

"She drove that car, but I don't know if she did it on purpose," I say. "I do know that she abandoned me after the crash."

"And you still feel nothing? No anger? No hate toward her?"

"No. I have no emotions left. They died with me."

"Do you know *why* she might have left you?"

"Yes."

"Are you willing to share that with me?"

I lean forward. "Do you want to hear the whole fairy tale, even when it turns dark? Are you prepared for what I have to say, even if it's not what you want to hear?"

"Yes. I'm curious how you perceive your situation. I wanted to ask you if I may share this tale with the rest of the world?"

"How would you do that?" I ask.

"I could record everything and put it on socials. Everyone would go crazy."

"Why would I want that? They wouldn't even be able to see me. And you know how we parted. It wasn't exactly fun to be mocked."

She doesn't flinch. "The situation is different now. Maybe they'll be able to see you, maybe not. Maybe just a few people, maybe all of them. In that case, the joke's on me. But I do know this: This is your one and only chance to get your story out there, Syl. I'm offering you an opportunity, but it's up to you to grab it."

"And make you even more famous than you already are on social media?" I state.

She smiles. "Or have people lock me away for talking to an empty chair."

"True," I say.

"Look, this could bring justice to you. Viola's still out there, and she did awful things that she should be punished for. Don't you want that?"

I think about Viola and say nothing.

"Listen," Annie says, leaning forward again as if she wants to grab my hand, only realizing then that she can't. "You can trust me. You know that already, or you wouldn't be here. You chose to show yourself to me; I didn't ask for this."

She's right about that.

"Okay, then," I say. "Record it—but no filming; that would be pointless. See what happens, if you can catch my voice on tape. Make notes, for all I care. As long as you do something with my story later on. Just remember that people might not believe you."

"What do you want me to do with your story?"

"Tell my parents. Tell the world."

"I swear I'll do what's right," Annie says. "Why don't we start with the crash and how it was for you when you realized that you had passed away, and then move on to what happened before? Would that make it easier?"

She places her cell phone on a stand in front of our two seats. The light is still quite bright. Annie makes sure that I'm in sight, whatever that might mean to her.

"Ready when you are," she says.

"Ready."

She starts recording our conversation.

"All right, then," I say. "I will tell you everything about my unhappy ending. Hope you're ready for it."

I close my eyes and tell her the story of my death, and what happened afterward, while her phone records my tale for the world to hear.

PART ONE: THE BALLAD OF SYL JAMESON'S DEATH

CHAPTER ONE

Viola was with me when we crashed. It was her car, her precious Corolla, that still smelled new because she hadn't used it much. Her mom had given it to her; she was going to take it to NYU with her. It was an expensive hybrid model, modern, with a dashboard that resembled a cockpit. So many features and buttons to push that anyone would be distracted while driving.

Viola liked dance music, '90s or Tomorrowland-festival type stuff. Hard, thumping techno beats that would rage through the car as we moved at high speeds over dark roads with narrow lines and sharp curves.

She would sometimes turn up the volume, and it would feel as if we were cruising alone, with nothing but a DJ encouraging us to go even faster. We wouldn't speak, and I would try to ignore the sharp undertones of the music while gazing outside. I didn't have a car of my own, not after last year, and she would always be the driver. She was a control freak and wouldn't have let me drive anyway.

Tonight we weren't listening to anything that even remotely resembled a crushing, thumping beat. In fact, she had turned off the music the moment we'd gotten into her car. We had been arguing, and the car's speed had increased by the second. We spoke fiercely, fought, discussed, snapped. Cried, or at least I did—I don't remember seeing tears coming from her. Then again, she wasn't the teary-eyed type. Never had been. She was always harsh, cold, serious, and argumentative.

We were complete opposites, which had become painfully clear over the past two years, when we started drifting apart. She hardly cared about the things that kept me up at night.

She liked to argue about everyday things. Love Hill and its residents. Things she felt were inappropriate. She talked a lot about our parents, about how they had ruined our lives. She openly discussed my life and what I had gone through, but she always avoided talking about last year's tragedy.

When I brought up the subject tonight, she became really upset. She didn't like how I saw things differently than she did, and she wouldn't accept the fact that I was angry and sad and . . . ready to tell the world the truth.

"Let it go," she snapped. "All of this is your fault, anyhow. You've done this to yourself."

"No, I didn't."

"Yes, you did, and if you don't shut up about it now, I'll make your life a living hell."

"That won't work with me anymore," I said. "I'm tired of your threats and antics."

"Well, I'm tired of you being such a bitch. I'll be glad to see the last of you when we're finally on opposite ends of the country. I've had it with you and your ridiculous sense of justice. Get over it already. It's over and done with, and nobody's the wiser. Why stir up trouble now?"

"I can't forget about it. I won't," I said. "I want it out in the open. It's eating me up."

"Bullshit. You just want to get rid of your own guilt."

"Am I not entitled to?"

"No."

"I'm not like you," I said. "I'm not mean or vengeful. I want to lead a decent life without guilt overwhelming and suffocating me every single day of my existence. I'm done with you. Our friendship is over."

She didn't speak again. Her hands clutched the steering wheel, her knuckles were white, and I could see the stress displayed on her face. She sped up.

And I got scared. I realized I had to get out of that car and away from her. The past had torn us apart, but that was nothing compared to what my words had done tonight.

"You're going to kill me, aren't you?" I asked.

And that was the last thing I ever said.

CHAPTER TWO

Viola's car is beyond repair, and so am I.

Even if a thousand experienced doctors were here to try to keep me alive, they would be unsuccessful.

I am dead.

That is quite something, really. Almost fascinating. Ironic too.

I was supposed to major in premed at Stanford. I wanted to become a trauma surgeon, to save people who came into the ER all shattered and beyond repair. Only the best of the best would be able to save them. Ironically enough, I had wanted to be that person.

I had envisioned myself leaning over someone being brought in from a car crash, digging my elbows deep into blood and tissue while trying to figure out how to fix all the broken bones and torn arteries.

And there I was. Here I am. A victim that no doctor would be able to save. My body is sitting in the driver's seat. She must have done it. I wasn't driving her car—never had, never wanted to. Never in my life would I have sat behind that steering wheel, gazing at all those fancy features, not knowing their uses.

There are sirens in the far distance. Police, EMTs, and fire trucks are headed this way. They will be too late. No one to save here. Trauma surgeons won't be able to fix this broken girl.

I notice my body lying crumpled in the car. Trapped between the seats and dashboard of Viola's Toyota, shattered into a million pieces, only held together by the skin that surrounds my bones. Crashed, shattered, bruised, battered, trapped. Seventeen, no longer going on eighteen. That will never happen now.

I'm standing next to her car looking in on myself, and I barely recognize my own body. My face is all messed up. My eyes are open, my skull cracked. Brain matter leaks through my bloodied and twisted long, ruined hair. My arms, legs, feet, and pelvis are obviously smashed. Internal bleeding is drowning my organs.

The moment the car crashed into that tree, my heart stopped. Or it could have stopped the second my head smashed into the dashboard and my skull cracked open. Or when I was thrashed around, hitting the window, the door, the dashboard.

Smoke billows from the hood of the vehicle, but the car is not yet on fire. I realize this won't take long now, that the flames will consume my body.

For a moment I wonder if I am not entirely dead, despite my broken, open eyes and the fact that I can see brain matter seeping through my cracked skull. Perhaps there is still a bit of life in me and I am in limbo, lingering between this world and the nether, waiting for that miracle trauma surgeon to save me, which would end up being a worse fate than if I were to just die. I would be a vegetable until the end of my days.

This is better. This death, whatever it may be. Unless I'm supposed to stay here forever, that is.

My death was inevitable, come to think of it. The perfect ending to a life that wasn't even supposed to be.

I've always known my parents didn't want me. I've felt it from the moment I could retain memories. I could feel it in the way my mom barely acknowledged me, often ignoring me, as if she wanted to show me the hard way that I was not supposed to be part of her life.

I don't know why she didn't just terminate her pregnancy. Often I would think that would have been less hard on me. I wouldn't have felt, experienced, realized that I was not meant to live.

Of course, I've always known why she wouldn't have had an abortion. Living in a place like Love Hill means existing in a glass house, where people know everything about you and every moment is examined to such detail that it would have been impossible to keep it a secret.

I was my mother's daughter. I came from her womb. There was no doubt in anyone's mind that I was my father's natural child. I was his spitting image, from the eyes to the chin, the nose, and the ears. I resembled him.

I was their daughter for sure, but the love I was supposed to receive from them was nonexistent. It had never been there.

I wonder how they will feel about me now.

CHAPTER THREE

I wasn't wearing my seat belt at the moment of impact, even though I had been strapped in before. I had unbuckled it, thinking that the best thing to do to escape Viola's wrath was jump out, believing also quite naively that she would slow down when she noticed, but the car hadn't slowed down at all.

I never saw the tree, didn't feel the impact to the car or to me. The world turned dark in the blink of an eye. There was nothing that gave a warning sign against the collision, or what came next.

There was no pain, just oblivion. Until I regained some sort of consciousness as I stood silently by the car and realized that I was dead but not gone. And that Viola had left me there after recognizing what she had done.

I don't know why I'm here. This could be some twisted sense of humor coming from whatever divine entity that is supposed to carry my soul into the next world. Something is trying to tell me that I shouldn't move on without the truth being revealed. What if I am supposed to do things I can't do when I'm dead and gone? Whatever reason there is, I need to figure this out.

I lean into the car and study myself. I guess I should be repulsed by the sight of my corpse, trapped awkwardly in that car with its broken limbs and twisted skull, but I'm not. I don't mind seeing myself in death at all. It's like watching someone else, like being witness to a gruesome movie where the victim is on graphic display.

I don't feel emotionally attached—it's like I feel nothing at all anymore. There is no pain, physical or emotional. I can't sense the wind blowing through the trees on this dark night, or the pebbles stuck beneath the thin soles of my shoes. I did feel them before I stepped into that car, too much in a hurry to pry them out from the gaps in the tread.

I touch the car but can't feel the metal. I touch the leather seat but can't feel the fabric beneath my fingertips. I know what it should feel like, but it's as if it's not there. I touch the fabric of the coat I'm wearing in death and don't feel it. I was cold when I got into that car, but now there is no sense of warm or cold at all. My dead form's clothes are torn, but mine aren't.

When I look at my "ghost hands," I see no broken skin. My legs aren't fractured, and are hidden beneath jeans that have not been damaged. My face doesn't feel smashed, and my hair looks like it always does.

I can't say the same for my dead form. I touch the already cold skin, but it's like I can't feel the human frailty at all. It's like there's nothing to touch. Like my fingertips are made from some strange fluid substance that bounces back, like liquid metal. As if I'm floating on air and can't even sense the wind that is undoubtedly here on this frigid and stormy night.

Sounds mingle; sirens are approaching fast now. I debate what to do next. Staying here seems to be the only thing I can do, really. If I leave, I'll need to start my search for Viola, and I'm not ready for that yet.

I hear noise behind me—a cry and a hiss. Someone trying to catch air while attempting to compose herself. When I turn around, I see her. Annie Jones. Of course. Of all people I had expected here, I somehow knew that it would be her. She's stumbling over to the car; her eyes are fixated on the wreckage.

She trembles and looks as white as a sheet, as if she's the one who just passed away. She looks right at me. I freeze and gaze back at her, daring her to see me, remembering her words about her sister, whose spirit was still lingering in her home study. I challenge her to see me, too, but she doesn't. She's trying hard to look away from the vehicle and my body, but fails miserably.

Death has an odd impact on people. They want to pretend that it doesn't exist, but at the same time they realize it cannot be ignored at all. I know exactly how she feels. Today, one year ago, I was *her*. I was standing right here, looking death in the eye too. It was awful.

I should feel sorry for Annie, but I can't. I'm emotionless. She holds a hand in front of her mouth as she approaches the vehicle and stifles a scream. So many memories must be overwhelming her. It almost feels like death is a constant in her life.

I said goodbye to Annie about a month ago to focus on my departure for Stanford. I had been working hard all year to get there, to get high scores on my SATs, to keep my grades up. I told her I would not come back, and she was sad about that.

"We've made such good progress," she said. "Why say goodbye now? We've still got a few weeks before you go."

"I don't have time, and I'm not interested in being used anymore," was my cold statement.

She figured out, at that moment, that I had seen her posts about our conversations, even though she had always assumed I wasn't on social media.

"I'm sorry," she said. "I didn't mean to—"

"To have people mock me? Tell me to my face that I'm an idiot?"

She didn't say anything else, and let me go.

I pushed her out of my mind to focus on Stanford. I visited campus twice on my own, signed up for a dorm room, filled out all the necessary paperwork, cleaned out my bedroom—which meant I was living out of boxes for half the summer—and was mentally prepared for a new life there, where no one knew me and I could be a regular student for once. I wouldn't have to endure the sad gazes and the accusing stares, and I would not have to return to Love Hill ever again.

I thought of ways to tell my mom that I wouldn't come back for Thanksgiving or Christmas. Even spending the holidays alone was preferable to an impersonal Christmas dinner with the three of us, and an expensive gift that was supposed to replace the lack of attention and love. The only person I would really miss seeing was our long-term housekeeper, Marie, whom I loved dearly, but we planned to be in constant touch, and she promised to fly over to visit when she could.

My parents would have been relieved over my absence. They hated the holidays. My dad always worked on Christmas Day. As soon as he could, he was out of the house, living his own life again. Drowning himself in work was the only way to forget what had led him to this point in his life.

My mom would be happy to spend Christmas watching movies and pretending to be warm and cozy under a blanket while munching on all the things she didn't allow herself to taste all year. This was the one day she would permit herself to eat more than vegetables and grains. My dad's absence meant he would take all the bad memories with him, but also that she wouldn't have to pretend to love him. She had done that for most of her adult life, but this past year, she no longer bothered.

Annie Jones is talking to someone on her cell phone, I'm guessing a 911 operator. This must be why the sirens are already so close. Not because of the smoke billowing from the engine or because other drivers saw the wrecked car as they passed by. This is a quiet route, and one only takes it when one needs it, but Annie does, every single day of her life. She lives just down the road, in her parents' house, with the tattered chair in her study.

"I think she's dead. No, I *know* she's dead," she says, speaking in a hoarse, emotional voice. "No, she's alone."

She looks up suddenly, flinches, turns around, and looks me in the eye without really seeing me. She *can't*. She's confused. She trembles.

"Syl?" she says, dazed.

"I'm here," I say softly.

I know she can hear me. Her eyes open wide, her hands shake, and she nearly drops her phone when she hangs up while the operator is still speaking.

"Syl. Oh my God. I can't see you, but you're here, aren't you? Say something."

"I'm here," I repeat. "I'm standing next to you."

She takes a deep breath.

"I *am* a conduit," she whispers.

She has a million questions and so do I, but then I hear something—a strange, sharp sound that makes me look up and *feel* that something's off. The smoke has turned black; a hissing sound pierces the air. Danger lingers around her.

"Annie, run!"

She looks at the car and realizes at the same moment I do what is happening. She sprints away over the slippery surface, back to her own vehicle. She kneels beside it, her hands covering her ears, just as the Toyota explodes.

When it happens, I don't feel a single thing. The car, with my body still inside, is blown to smithereens, and I still feel nothing. No change in me, no white light or soft voices dragging me to eternal bliss. I'm still here, and so is Annie, hovering behind her own vehicle. She will have nightmares about this for the rest of her life, I'm sure.

"Are you okay?" I ask.

She looks up, dazed, with fear in her eyes, but she seems unharmed. She sits up and stares at the wreck. I'm standing between her and the burning car. The flames brighten up the area.

"I'm okay," she says. "Oh my God, I can see you standing in the light."

I look at her, surprised. She doesn't elaborate, but from the way she sounds, it seems she was never able to do that with her sister.

"You can?" I say. "How do I look?"

She smiles. "Like an angel, but without the wings."

I can't help but laugh. Perhaps all emotion is not gone just yet.

CHAPTER FOUR

I don't believe in divine intervention or a god that somehow lingers over our world, watching and protecting us. Never have, never will. Not even when my soul is waiting for something.

I didn't see a bright light. Didn't hear an otherworldly voice. I was alive one minute and dead the next. And I expect that "death," whatever that is supposed to be, will come and take me away at any given moment.

That's what's supposed to happen, right? People are expected to move on. But that's not what happens, not even when the car explodes in my face and I feel nothing of the heat and flames, or the smoke that is now circling high in the dark sky.

I'm here and so is Annie, but she is human, and I am dead. She's also feeling the rain that starts to pour down on us. I can't feel it at all, but she can. When it starts coming down in buckets as vehicles move toward us, she doesn't flinch. She waves at the fire trucks and the ambulances and the cops who have arrived at the scene. There's nothing more to save, not a single ounce of hope left for me, which is obvious in all its ugly facets, of course, but that doesn't mean they won't try to salvage as much of the scene as possible. And there is a possibility that the car might explode a second time.

I imagine someone like that pathologist from that television series where they investigate bones showing up to piece together what is left of my body, for whatever good that would do. It's obvious what happened:

Car crash. Explosion. One person inside the vehicle. The flames are out quickly, thanks to the fire department and the rain, and then the cops start investigating the wreck, placing yellow tape around the whole area. In the meantime, it keeps raining with a vengeance, as if the gods themselves are weeping along with the people who might actually mourn me.

Annie obviously doesn't tell anyone about her conversation with me, or the fact that I just saved her life. She is taken away to a waiting ambulance, where she tells her story while they deal with her wounds.

"Syl Jameson," Annie says. "She was already dead when the car exploded."

"Are you sure it was her?" a cop asks when one of his colleagues carefully removes the license plate of the burned vehicle and matches its registration to Viola. "This was not Syl's car. It was Viola Harrison's."

"Viola wasn't in the vehicle, it was Syl."

"You're positive about that?"

"I am."

"So she was alone?"

"Yes."

The cop clears his throat.

"Syl was sitting behind the wheel, and Viola is not here. So we must assume that Syl took the car without Viola knowing it."

"Viola drove," I whisper, and Annie doesn't flinch. She looks both men straight in the eye.

"Syl would never drive that car."

"Why not?"

"Because she didn't drive. Everyone in town knows. Syl hasn't driven since—you know, what happened last year."

The cop holding the license plate makes a humming sound and shares a glance with his colleague.

"I'm telling you that she would not drive that car," Annie insists. "Viola must have been with her."

"Then why was Syl in the driver's seat? And where is Viola now?"

"She put me there," I whisper in Annie's ear. "She took off because she was scared. She wants to blame my death on me."

"I don't know. But I do know that Syl would not drive that car," Annie stubbornly repeats.

"Hmm."

Again, that humming sound. It annoys me. The cops don't say much more to Annie, who remains seated inside the ambulance, out of the rain that is now slowly starting to subside. I decide to follow the cops—Jensen and Smith, I read off their tags.

"Damn," Jensen says, wiping the rain off his face.

"You think she was right about the not-driving part?" Smith asks.

"Everyone in town knows that Syl Jameson doesn't drive anymore. So that can only mean Viola was driving, and she put her own best friend—who was already dead—behind the steering wheel to make it look like she was alone, then took off. This is pretty bad."

"Obviously," Smith says. "But look, the whole scene does *look* like an accident. She must have been in shock; why else would she take off like that? They were best friends, right? We have to track her down fast, before anyone else does."

"Do we treat this as an accident?" Jensen asks.

"You don't think it was?" Smith says, surprised.

"Can we tell for sure? What if she did this on purpose? They might have had a fight. She might have pulled at the steering wheel, crashed her car against that tree to end both their lives. Or deliberately crashed it so that Syl would not survive."

"That seems like a stretch."

"Look at the wreck, the seat belt, the tire tracks," Jensen says. "The forensic team will see this too. That girl didn't slow down whatsoever; there are no skid marks or brake trails. She drove her car into that tree in such a way and position that the brunt of the impact was taken by Syl's body. The driver side is unscathed; she may not even have a scratch on her. What if she crashed her car on purpose?"

"There's only one way to find out," Smith says. "We need to find this girl fast."

"And how are we going to do that without alarming the rest of this crazy town?" Jensen asks. "You know what they're like. They'll be like vultures, scavenging for prey."

The cops sigh at the same time, which would have made me smile if circumstances were different. This was spot on.

Jensen writes down the license plate number. "We'll keep her identity a secret for as long as we can."

"As if that'll work." Smith frowns. "The paramedics already know, and they love to gossip. Remember what happened last year? They'll tell others; I'm sure they've already done so. That's how this town works."

"Hopefully, we'll have enough time to find that girl before anyone else does," Jensen says.

"What about Syl's parents?"

"Leave them to me."

More cars approach the scene—official vehicles as well as townspeople. In the center of all the buzzing activity is the burned wreckage of Viola's Toyota. People get out and start walking toward the area despite the yellow tape that should be holding them back.

We all know that the truth never stays hidden for long in Love Hill. It's only a matter of time before everyone here will find out why Viola killed me. And maybe that's not such a bad thing.

CHAPTER FIVE

A small white truck parks itself among the other cars, and people come running out with cameras and phones. The local press. Vultures. I debate between going back to Annie Jones or staying here to listen to what these creeps have to say.

"Officer Jensen! Is it true that Syl Jameson died here tonight?" a woman in a gray suit shouts. I recognize her as Joan Lind, the local reporter and town gossip, who lives for drama and unethical means of getting to said drama. People avoid her, unless they have a score to settle with someone else. Then she suddenly becomes the town's most interesting person to have a chat with.

Jensen and Smith share a glance and a sigh.

"No comment. Adam, can you please get rid of them?"

Another police officer walks over to the camera crew and talks to Joan with a grave look on his face. The reporter and her camera operator are pushed back behind the yellow tape, much to their frustration.

"You have no right to stop us!" she shouts. "It's our duty to report this to the public."

"Shut up!" someone in the small crowd yells.

"Have some respect for the dead. This is a crime scene," another person says, which shocks the crowd.

"A crime scene?" Joan responds, aiming her cameraman at the person talking.

The police officers, standing at a short distance, obviously realize the urgency of the matter. If it hadn't become clear by now, this conversation pushes them to hurry up their investigation. "We should call her parents *now*, before they find out from someone else," Smith comments.

"I'll take care of it," Jensen says. "Get those people out of here. The forensic crew will be here any minute, and I don't want people hovering nearby to catch a glimpse of the car and the girl. Just move them away, okay?"

I know what he means. I've seen what is left of me in that car, and it's not a pretty sight.

"Will do," Smith says.

Jensen and Smith part ways. While Smith walks over to the crowd and asks them to leave, Jensen reaches for his phone, calls the police station, and requests my father's address and number.

Don't bother, I want to say, but of course he can't hear me. Something tells me that my parents already know and are on their way. Everyone here is aware of the fact that the only heir to the Jameson throne has tragically passed away. Which means that one bystander, or several, have already taken out their phones. It's only a matter of minutes before my parents arrive.

I don't know what to do next; I still have no clue how to leave this mortal coil. Finding Viola won't do me any good. She won't be able to communicate with me, nor I with her. I look at Annie sitting in the ambulance, and realize I have been given a gift. If I can communicate with her, she can talk to Viola and pass on the message. But what would I even say?

Hey, you killed me, but I just wanted to let you know that I forgive you and understand why you did it. Yep, that'll work.

My thoughts are interrupted by another car arriving at the scene, grabbing everyone's attention. Two people rush out of the vehicle and run toward us. The woman is stopped by Jensen while Smith runs over to the man, who screams my name as if he cares about my fate. My parents.

I look at them in wonder, and for one startling moment, it's as if they can see me too. My mother looks like she's seen a ghost, but blinks, shakes off Jensen's grip, and walks right through me.

My dad looks like he's ready to fall apart at the seams. He's different from how I've always known him, emotional and distraught. He screams and shouts and clutches Smith tight, who is standing between him and the vehicle, preventing him from running toward the car and seeing something so gruesome that it would give him nightmares for the rest of his life.

My dad weeps. My mom almost collapses where she stands. And I can't help but think that they *did* love me a little bit. Here I am, believing I've always been a burden on their shoulders. What if I was mistaken all this time?

"Is it really her?" my mom asks, and her voice breaks. "It is my daughter?"

"We're not sure yet, but yes, it does appear so," Jensen says. "Ms. Annie Jones identified her. She saw her before the vehicle—"

My mom runs to Annie Jones. I tag along.

"I'm so sorry, Mrs. Jameson," Annie says, in tears.

She says this before my mother can speak, and that's the moment my mom seems to realize it's true. It's the first time I feel something too. Sorrow. Sadness. Regret. Pity. "No," my mom says. "Please tell me that it wasn't my Syl. Please tell me you're mistaken. It can't be! It has to be Viola."

"I'm so sorry."

My dad is there, too, and he holds my mom tight. It took my death to reunite them as a couple, I think sadly. What a price to pay.

"Was she alone?"

"Yes," Annie says. "Viola's gone; they believe that she was driving and are looking for her. I told them that Syl would never drive someone else's car."

A change hangs in the air. My dad turns toward the cops with balled-up fists, and his voice is harsh, rough, and dark.

"What happened to my daughter? Where the hell is Viola? Did she do this to Syl? Tell me what is going on!"

His words come out as growls. Jensen looks desperately at Smith, but before he can speak, a third cop in a fancier uniform arrives. The police commissioner. He's a big shot around town, and he's friends with my dad.

"Alex," he says, placing his hand on my dad's shoulder. "I'm so sorry. If there's anything I can do, I will do it, but this is not the time nor place to talk about Viola. We've got it under control. Concentrate on your wife right now. She needs you. Let us help you."

My dad is obviously not in the mood for pity and sympathy. He looks at the commissioner angrily, brushing off his grip.

"Don, please tell me that you are doing everything you can. Where is Viola? Did she kill my daughter?"

"We are figuring this out, Alex. You know me; I'll get to the bottom of this. As soon as I found out about the accident, I jumped in my car. How did *you* find out so quickly?"

"This is Love Hill."

"Of course." A sympathetic smile appears on the commissioner's face. "I know you're grieving. Why don't we take you home?"

"Not a chance. What happened to my daughter?"

"We don't know yet."

"Was Viola here?"

"We really can't say, Alex."

"Is she at the hospital? Was she hurt?"

The commissioner clears his throat. "We don't know."

"What do you mean, you don't know? Where is she?"

"We're trying to find her as we speak. Several of my people are out there looking for her. We'll find her."

"So she *was* in the car?"

"We have every reason to believe that she was. But we don't know yet for certain if she drove."

Jensen and Smith are obviously surprised that the commissioner knows all of this—but hey, this is Love Hill, like my dad said. Nothing surprises anyone around here.

"Don't give me that, Don," Dad says, and the volume of his voice increases. "My daughter would never have driven Viola's car, and you know it! She hasn't gotten behind the wheel of any car in a long time, not after what happened last year."

"Alex, you need to calm down," the commissioner shushes. "We are doing our best to determine the cause of the accident. Right now, there is nothing you can do. Why don't we take you to the police station? We can talk about Syl then. Not here, where everyone is eager to listen to our conversation."

I follow my parents as they are led away from the scene by the commissioner. God, how I hate that guy, especially after last year's tragedy. I remember every detail of what he did to me vividly. I remember him treating me as if I were a suspect. I remember him asking me sensitive questions, if I had something to do with *her* death.

"No!" I said, knowing he didn't believe me. He only let me go because I was my father's daughter. Truth be told, I wouldn't have believed me either.

CHAPTER SIX

I've never been seriously ill. I haven't broken a single bone in my body, have never visited a hospital. All I know from hospitals is what I learned from other people or on television. Hospitals are places to avoid, unless you really have to be there.

My parents stand near a group of police officers who are doing their utter best to comfort them without really knowing what to say. Behind us, others work the scene, people in white suits who look like they are exploring the remains of the car.

My dad doesn't want comforting. He wants justice. He wants to know where Viola is; it's the only thing that matters to him. He's angry more than sad. The cops must sense that, too, because they have stopped consoling him.

"Other people are looking for her," Jensen says. "Did the girls have any specific places they would go to when together?"

"Not particularly," my mom says. "I'm not sure if she would go there anyhow. Not when she's facing time in prison."

"Why would she be?" Smith asks curiously.

"She hurt my daughter. Left her. Killed her."

"We don't know that," Jensen says. "You have to be careful with these accusations, Mrs. Jameson. We don't know the whole story yet."

"Even if it *was* an accident, she left my daughter in that car to die. Syl could still be alive right now, but she didn't do anything."

"We believe Syl died on impact." Smith speaks softly. "Ms. Jones said she was—" He doesn't say it out loud.

"Listen, people do crazy things when they are traumatized," Jensen continues. "Viola might be in shock, out here in the night without any recollection of what happened to Syl. That's why we need to know where she could be. The commissioner is on his way to her house now."

"Good, then stop asking us about it," my father barks. "Do you know how we feel? No, you don't. No one does."

He turns around and leaves them there, and then he moves his hands to his face and shakes while my mom hugs him tight.

"It's okay," she whispers. "It's okay, it'll all be okay. I'm here."

"We lost her," Dad says.

"I know."

For the first time since I can remember, my parents stand together in a display of grief I didn't expect. I place my hand on my dad's shoulder, and he suddenly looks up and shivers.

"What is it?" my mom asks.

"Nothing," he says.

"I feel it too," my mom says. "Like she's still here with us, watching us."

My mom looks over her shoulder. I smile and reach for her wrist. She doesn't shiver or move. She doesn't feel it. My hand feels strange on her skin too. I can't feel her warmth or the strength of her arm. It just lingers on her, without really touching her.

"We first need to figure out what to tell the cops," Mom says.

"What is there to tell? She died. She's gone. That's it."

"We know where Viola is."

"No, we don't," Dad says sharply.

"They'll start asking questions about her and Viola. They will want to know why Viola—"

"Stop." Dad raises his hands. "We don't know anything, all right?"

"Are we going to lie about Syl?"

"We'll lie all we need. I won't have my daughter's name being dragged through the mud after her death."

"Viola won't hesitate to do so. She'll put all the blame on our child, and we won't have any defense against it," my mom says softly.

"Then let's pray they don't find her," Dad says. "She could take off and never be found."

"Is that your answer to this mess?"

"Yes."

"They will figure this out, you know. Then they'll find out what really happened last year. And that will be the end of our reputation," Mom tells him.

"We are not to blame for hiding Syl's secrets. No one is. Every parent would have done the same thing." Dad looks around at the people and the camera in the far distance. "I don't want to discuss this any further. Drop the subject, all right?"

The moment of sweetness between my parents is long gone. They are enemies again, torn apart by the secrets they've been keeping for so long. Only, one of those secrets came out two years ago: the one about my father's hidden feelings toward one particular man. That one ruined us all.

"We didn't do the right thing back then, and this has already cost us dearly. We've ruined Syl's life."

"No, we didn't," my dad insists. "This accident is not our fault."

"Yes, we did, Alex. And today, the loss of our daughter is the result of that. She is gone; we will never get her back. We should have told the truth when we had the chance."

"That wouldn't have solved anything," Dad says.

"It would have shown her that we cared enough."

"She never came to us for help."

"Because we pushed her away. We should have been there for her, but instead we chose to ignore the fact that there was a problem."

"She was doing a lot better," Dad says. "Ever since she started focusing on Stanford, she became more herself again. I thought we were getting there. She obviously wanted to leave this town as quickly as she could, and I supported her decision."

"That was not enough," my mom says, and I couldn't agree more.

This last year has been a living hell. I wish I could say that my life was improving, but it wasn't. I threw myself into my books and work and Stanford, but it was never enough. I lived, survived, focused, tried to forget. Tried to be happy again, but failed miserably. Suffered, cried in secret in the confines of my bedroom, tried to find solace in trivial things. Failed miserably again. Accepted many losses; survived them too. Until now.

"This town killed our daughter," my dad says.

"Or we did," Mom mutters. Which was also an undeniable truth.

I turn away from them and walk over to the ambulance, where Annie is now being released and ready to go home.

"Do you need a ride?" a female police officer asks.

Annie shakes her head. "No," she says. "I'm fine."

She looks at the camera crew and the woman doing an interview, and sighs. We all know what is happening there: The reporter is presenting something that will not reflect the truth. I would bet my life on it. But that's what they do. They omit the truth and make a story of their own to fit their greedy need for drama and excitement. I know—the same thing happened to me a year ago, when they made a story out of something that wasn't even partially true.

Vultures.

Annie rolls her eyes and moves away, avoiding the limelight. She walks over to her car, where people immediately circle around her. She waves all questions away, gets into her car, and then hesitates before she closes the door. I'm already inside. The door was open, and I slipped in before she did, moving over to the passenger seat while wondering if anyone would be able to see or sense me.

Annie waits for a moment before putting the key in the ignition. People make way for her, and she backs her car out of the area, past the cops and the press and the curious people still arriving in droves.

"Are you still there?" she asks when we're driving. Her house is just a mile off the road. It won't take long to reach her study with that crooked chair.

"I'm here," I say.

She doesn't reply, but I can tell she has a smile on her face. Oh yeah, she's already enjoying this.

THE DEAD GIRL AND THE PARENTS WHO DIDN'T LOVE HER

"Are you okay?" Annie asks after a long silence that follows my description of what happened after my death.

She doesn't comment on my mixed feelings toward her, which I have expressed openly. She doesn't care that I feel like she's using me. I guess she's used to people saying that about her, because it's true. No denial, just a clear view of how she perceives life and the people around her.

I sit quietly on her dead sister's tattered chair and realize I can still cry. Tears drip down my face and onto my hands. But unlike human tears, they don't feel warm to the touch. I just can't feel anymore. It's like the emotion itself has evaded me.

"Yes," I say. "I'm fine."

I wipe my hand across my face and see the glistering of water on my fingertips. It's gone in an instant, as if it never existed.

"You can still cry."

"I guess."

"That's amazing."

"Did your sister never cry?" I ask.

"My sister couldn't feel any emotions," Annie says. "She always said that she was looking at someone else's life without playing a part in it anymore. That she went to her own funeral and saw the casket being lowered into the grave, but it didn't affect her at all."

"Because we don't take anything with us to our graves," I say. "No soul, no emotion."

"Why do you think that is?"

"I don't know. I do know your sister and I are the exception to the rules of death. I don't believe that everyone sticks around."

"That'd better be right," Annie says, smiling softly. "I can't imagine seeing millions of souls in this room."

Annie still doesn't look at her phone, and I wonder how many people will believe her recording once they get to hear this. Will they even be able to hear me? And if they do, will they believe that I am indeed a paranormal entity, or that it was all a setup? Or, which I believe more than the first scenario, will they remain oblivious to everything I have to say and only hear Annie talking to herself? This conduit thing might work for her, and not the outside world. In that case, they would think *she* was batshit crazy for talking to an empty chair.

But *if* they can hear me, the world will go nuts. The ultimate proof of paranormal existence—how crazy would that be? Annie would either be a hero or a witch. They've burned people for less.

Annie obviously doesn't mind, one way or the other. She has a certain look in her eyes that makes it clear to me she's enjoying this moment. Whatever happens next, she'll deal with later.

"It must have been rough seeing them like that. Your parents, I mean," she says, bringing me back to the conversation.

"It was," I say, contemplating my answer. "And at the same time, it wasn't. I don't feel anything, really."
"What about pain?"
"You mean physical pain?"
"Yes."
"I don't have any. I didn't feel my death. I don't feel anything at all."
Annie rubs her hand over her face. She's obviously tired, as it is the middle of the night. She doesn't talk about going to bed, though. She would be crazy to do so, given this opportunity.
"Are *you* okay?" I ask.
"I'm fine."
"Do you want me to take a break?"
"No. Are you— How long do you think you still have?"
"I don't know," I say. "It doesn't matter."
"It does to me," Annie states.
"Why?"
"I would like to know the whole story before you leave."
Well, she *is* honest, I must give her that.
"I'm not sure there is much more to tell," I say. "I died. That's it. I'll take the rest of it to my grave."
"Don't say that, Syl. Of course there is a lot more to this story. We haven't even scratched the surface. You haven't spoken about the things that led up to the accident."
"You mean that you don't know the story about Viola and me yet," I point out. "Or why things are so difficult between my parents and me."
"Yes. Your parents acted strangely tonight. I know you've mentioned this before, that they don't really care about you. But how can that be? All parents care about their kids. Why would your mom willingly accept that Viola killed you?"

"Because it's the truth," I say. "Viola had her reasons to get rid of me. I don't blame her for what she did. She acted on impulse, even if she then tried to put the blame on me. Which failed miserably, of course. Any idiot could tell it was a setup."

"What reasons are those?"

I smile as I stand up while making sure I'm still in the light that Annie put in place in order to see me. I wouldn't want to ruin her moments of grandeur. I can *feel* the urgency radiating from her. Oh yes, she's very much enjoying this.

"She hated me," I say. "Well, she hated me in the end. She didn't before, until we turned sixteen. Then everything changed."

"Why?"

"Do you always ask so many questions?"

"I'm curious about the two of you. When you were— well, when you came to me earlier this year to talk about the mess you were in, you talked about her now and then, but never in such detail that I could grasp the relationship between the two of you. Now that you're here and we're doing this, I'd like to know the whole story."

I nod at the phone. "No, you want a scoop."

She doesn't deny that.

"Tell me something, Annie. After all the discussions we had when I was still alive, why would I share the rest of my story with you? Why would I want to harm my parents and Viola, and leave them with a legacy of sadness and disgust? I don't want to see them hurt. I loved them."

"Even when they ignored you?"

"Yes."

"But why, Syl? Why give them all of your affection, even after they killed you?"

"My parents didn't kill me."

"They did."

"How?"

"They drove you into the arms of others who didn't care about you. That's why you were killed tonight. All of the events have led to this moment, and you are the victim of their ignorance. Don't you want to see them get what they deserve?"

I look her in the eye. "You weren't kind to me either. You used me for your own benefit. Why should I trust you more than them? At least they gave me everything I needed, but what did you have to offer?"

"Please," Annie says, getting up from her seat. "You chose *me* to talk to tonight. You and I have had a bond from the day we first met. You came to my house and asked me for help, and I gave it to you, even if I did do things that you didn't like. *You* chose to go with me tonight and to confide in me. Why would you do that if you didn't want to tell your story to me?"

"I want to move on. To do so, I think I need to do this. But don't think for one moment that you were my first choice. If I had options, I wouldn't have come here," I say.

She flinches for the first time. I've struck a sensitive chord.

"Why, if you hate me so much, did you come to this house for nine months, without missing one single session?"

"Because I was hoping, against my better judgment, that you would be able to give me answers about my loss. In the end, you never did. I wanted you to find the connection I so desperately needed, but you were just a con artist like everyone else."

Again, Annie flinches.

"That is true," she admits. "I was never able to connect with you, and I'm sorry for that. This—what is happening to us now—is unique. You are only the second spirit I have ever spoken to besides my sister, and the proof that I have not been crazy during the entire time I believed her to be with me."

I look at her. "Are you telling me that you weren't sure your sister was around? That you believed it was all in your head?"

She smiles. "Yes."

"Well, I could have told you nine months ago that it wasn't. Even I could feel her presence."

"I know, but that wasn't enough for me," Annie admits. "I have doubted my own abilities and beliefs for a long time now. Even at this very moment, I'm wondering if I didn't just bump my head when the car exploded and am in a coma right now."

"You aren't," I say. "I'm here."

"Then please confide in me. Help me figure this out so you can find your peace." I sit down on the chair again, but this time, it almost feels as if I can touch the upholstery.

I want to sense the fabric, pinch my skin, feel something.

"You grew up in this town," I say. "Do you hate it as much as I do?"

"This town isn't the easiest of places to live in; I know that," Annie says. "I've seen and heard so many things, and it's often hard to figure out what the truth is."

"Do you know what kind of rumors circulate here?"

"Yes."

"Do you know about the big scandal involving Mr. Harrison?"

"Yes."

"Do you know the details?"

"Not really. Just what the rumors said about him."

I look at my hands.

"You asked me about the fairy tale of Viola and I earlier. Our friendship."

"Yes, I did."

"Were we friends, though? Why should two girls, with nothing in common except for their birth date, be friends? It all turned out to be bullshit in the end. Yes, we were born on the same day at the same hospital, and we slept next to each other in the nursery, or so it is said. Those brief moments might have seemed to announce the start of a new lifelong friendship, but honestly, that friendship was never meant to be from the start. It was nonexistent."

"Isn't that harsh?"

"No, it's the truth. I mean, our parents weren't friends—or at least, our mothers weren't. They couldn't stand each other. Our dads did occasionally connect for drinks, golf, or racquetball. But to call them friends? Nah."

"So you're saying that the two of you were friends by connection, but not really by heart?"

"Yes."

"Why weren't your parents friends?" Annie asks.

"My mom was already messed up before I came into this world, and Viola's mom was sweet, kind, and sensitive. My mom was arrogant, stubborn, and had a strong will; all of this steered her in a single direction: to show this town that she was a lot more than just the rightful heir of influential people. She never stood a chance in life. I don't blame her for making the decisions she made, even if it messed her up."

"You and I also come from this town, and we're not screwed up," Annie says.

"Aren't we? Isn't everyone who lives in this toxic place? Love Hill isn't exactly an example of a perfect town, is it?"

"I don't believe that we are all screwed up. Why would you think our town is so poisonous? I mean, we know we have our difficulties, but are they really that different from other towns'?"

"I'm sure of it. You know what this place is like, how people love to hate each other. How they can't stand if someone is doing better than them. The gossip, the way they love to stab each other in the back. The fake behavior at whatever party-of-the-week they're holding, the manner with which they show fake concern but are glad that whatever is happening isn't happening to them. This town reeks of old money, and they hate each other for it."

"But is that really everywhere?"

"Think back to the events of the past few years. Of course it is. I'm living proof that it is. My death is. If my former best friend can abandon me like this, what chance do the rest of you stand to survive this hell?"

Annie seems concerned. I don't think she really wants to discuss the impact this place has had on me, but to get to know me and understand what I'm saying, she has to accept a couple of simple facts. I know she doesn't want to; she never did when I was still alive and came to her for help. Even then, she never believed me. She thought I was exaggerating the facts, that I loved to tear Love Hill apart because I was leaving for Stanford soon and not planning to come back. But she loves this town, and so she steers the conversation in a different direction.

"What about your mom, then, Syl? She's CEO of a successful business, collaborating with your dad. You guys live in a gorgeous house, have plenty of money. Yes, your parents came from old money, but they earned more than they inherited in the first place. That's good, isn't it?"

"If you call being overambitious *good*, then yes," I say.

"Your mom does what a lot of CEOs do. She works eighty hours a week, gives everything she has for her company and her staff. She's highly appreciated for that."

"I don't despise my mom for being so successful," I say. "Like I said: I don't hate her, and I'm not upset with her. I love her. But the truth is that she loves that company and her job more than she ever loved me."

"How can you be so sure?"

"Because she told me. She told me that I was an accident. *An unforeseen challenge*, that's what she called it. I wasn't supposed to exist. She had never planned on having kids. Isn't it ironic that she didn't want her children to go through what she did and ended up doing the exact same thing?"

"That's awful," Annie whispers.

"If I was still alive right now telling you all this, I would feel sad and abandoned. Those were constant feelings in my life. But the thing is, I also understood where she was coming from, even now. She grew up with parents who cared about themselves first, who worked just as many hours as she does now. How could she have loved me, when she didn't know how to feel love in the first place?"

"But your parents love each other, don't they?"

I smile. "Of course not. They stay together because it's convenient and suits their purposes. A marriage formed from the desire to succeed."

"You mean their business?"

"Yes. That's the one thing that keeps them together. My dad uses my mom because she's good at what she does, and she uses him to keep up her image of the perfect couple. It works for them."

"Come on, everybody is capable of loving," Annie says. "Only the worst psychopaths cannot love or care about another person. Are you telling me that your parents are evil?"

"No, but they are narcissists. Always have been. Their lack of love towards other people is one of their special traits. And yet, they are both capable of love—with the right people, that is."

"What about your dad, then? Does he love you?"

"I don't know," I admit.

Annie is flabbergasted.

"I'm sure he tried to. I'm sure they both did. But did they succeed? Nah."

"You are pretty harsh, Syl."

"Don't I have the right to be? I think that Viola's birth, on the same day at the same hospital, came as a gift to my mother. When she met Mrs. Harrison and noticed how this woman seemed to be a natural-born mother, she must have decided to learn from her. Or to use her when she needed help."

"You grew up with nannies; you mentioned that once. So how did Mrs. Harrison fit into all of this?"

"My mom hired nanny after nanny. They were all sweet and kind, but they weren't mothers. My mom didn't change her lifestyle whatsoever, she didn't cut back on her working hours. She just continued living her life, and when she came home at night, I would already be asleep. When one of my nannies took time off or went on vacation, my mom would turn to Mrs. Harrison for help, who would take care of me, no questions asked. My mom pushed the friendship between Viola and me because it was easy for her that we were close friends. It gave her an excuse to drop me off at the Harrisons' without feeling guilty."

"Mrs. Harrison became a surrogate mom."

"That's right."

"I get it," Annie says. "Your mom realized that her daughter was lonely, and so she encouraged her child to hang out with the girl across the street. It made it easier for her than having her daughter staring at her with those big eyes, pleading for love she couldn't give her. Am I right?"

"Yes. Until a time came where I was never allowed to go into that house again."

"But you still stayed friends with Viola."

"Yes. She still came to our house, but I couldn't go to theirs anymore."

Annie frowns, trying to deal with this added information about my mother. She now saw her as the woman she really was—a coldhearted, selfish creature, who destroyed the lives of the people around her without so much as a wince.

"What happened six years ago?" Annie says.

I smile. "What caused the rumors to start."

"What do you mean?"

"Later, Annie. I will talk about that later. But first, I think I should tell you about my special relationship with Viola. That's what you're waiting for, right?"

"Yes," she says, not even flinching.

Annie doesn't hold back her desire to find out all there is to know about Viola and me.

I don't blame her. If I were the alive one, I would be curious too.

PART TWO: THE GIRLS WHO WERE BORN ON THE SAME DAY

CHAPTER SEVEN

"Are you coming with me?" Viola asked.

I looked up from tying my shoes and gazed at the clock above the door. We'd just had practice, I was tired, and to be honest, I didn't really feel like spending my evening at Viola's—but as always, she insisted, and I caved.

"Sure," I said.

"I need some input."

Of course. I knew Viola needed help with her math and that this was the reason why I'd been asked to go home with her after school. But I didn't mind, even though I had plenty of work of my own.

Going with her meant being with the people I liked the most, which was nicer than being stuck home alone, apart from our housekeeper, Marie, that is. I sent Marie a text that I would be home late and walked alongside Viola to her mom's waiting car. Mrs. Harrison was friendly as always and gave me a warm hug.

"Are you staying for dinner?"

"Sure. Thanks."

We drove to Viola's house while my best friend chatted loudly about Steve, calling him everything except a god. She couldn't stop going on and on about his gorgeous eyes and hair, and I rolled my eyes, sighing loudly.

"Seriously?" I said. "You're fifteen and in love? Come on, Viola. That's a load of crap. You can't be in love at our age."

"Why not?"

"Because we're kids, and love is overrated."

Mrs. Harrison laughed.

"You should listen to Syl, hon. Believe me, you'll have plenty of time to love someone and get your heart broken. Don't worry about all of that now."

"That's very dark, Mom," Viola remarked.

"But it's what happens to many people, honey, trust me. Just wait a while longer before you head in that direction. You're already growing up too fast. I want you to enjoy your years in high school without having a broken heart."

Her words made me curious, so I looked at Mrs. Harrison through the rearview mirror. I was sitting behind her and Viola, watching the road as I always did. I was learning how to drive, and since she was the only person I spent time in the car with, I wanted to see how she did it. It wasn't really that hard: focus, keep the foot on the right pedal, and just go, making sure you don't wind up in a ditch. Easy-peasy.

"Have you ever had your heart broken, Mrs. Harrison?" I asked while Viola occupied herself with sending text messages to Steve.

"Of course. It happened in high school, I was seventeen. The cutest boy in school didn't glance at me once; he ignored me through the entire year. And I hated him for it. But what I really wanted was for him to look at me like he did Denise."

"Denise being . . . ?"

"The queen bee, of course. Gorgeous, rich, smart. She had it all, and then she had that boy too. I thought it was so unfair."

Viola rolled her eyes, but I smiled. I could imagine Mrs. Harrison like this. I really could. The thing was, Viola couldn't. Even at this age, I could tell she didn't care about other people like her mom did, or like I did. I cared too much, found myself too busy thinking about what others said or did, or how they would react to things *I* did. I hated that, but I couldn't help it.

"Anyway," Mrs. Harrison said. "Don't mind me, that was a long time ago."

"Yeah, the Dark Ages," Viola muttered. I thumped her. She made a face. Her mother laughed and then became serious.

"Just watch what you do, okay? Things can get nasty in the town from hell. You'll learn someday."

I was surprised. This wasn't the first time Mrs. Harrison had commented on Love Hill, but the nickname was new. I always thought she was one of the few people who didn't really seem to think badly of our town. I was wrong.

"I'm sure Syl will watch out for me," Viola said.

I would. Viola and I were good friends. Sometimes we got along well, sometimes there would be arguments. We had different opinions and totally different characters.

Looking back on it, I think we were both too lazy to find other people to connect with when we were younger, but as years passed at an alarming rate, that started to change. Especially lately, with Viola looking at boys, while I didn't care about them; there were changes lingering in the air.

Apart from her interest in other people, there were days Viola barely spoke to me, usually when I had said something she didn't like. So I avoided saying things she didn't like. It was a lot easier that way.

"Why do you always agree with me?" she'd asked me a couple of weeks ago, out of the blue.

"I don't," I had replied.

"Yeah, you do."

"I just don't like conflict."

"And I do?"

"Yes, sometimes."

She hadn't denied it.

Our houses were right across from each other, and I could even see theirs from my bedroom window. We had a few other friends—or at least she did, but none who came to her house much like I did. I had no one else, I wasn't that good at making friends. She would make them for the two of us, and then I would tag along. That worked out perfectly fine for me, so I let her make my decisions.

She was the extroverted one, I was the quiet one who liked to study. Over the years, this hadn't changed. She was the girl who would end up organizing parties, while I would be sitting in a corner reading a book. She would be the one wearing the extravagant dresses, while I'd be hanging around in sneakers, jeans, and a plain T-shirt. This was our future; I was sure of it. We would grow old together like this.

Viola always took care of me, even if she didn't want to. She would tell me she was going to this or that place and not invite me, but in the end, she would always wait to see if I was tagging along. Her friends knew I would come too; there was always room for me, even if I spent that time sitting in a corner reading or scrolling through my phone.

She had never traded me for another girl, but one day, she would do so for a boy. That day, however, had not come yet.

CHAPTER EIGHT

I knew every nook and cranny of Viola's house because I'd spent every spare minute there for as long as I could remember. It was my home away from home, a beautiful house I could go to whenever I wanted.

My fondest memories were of their home, where I sat at the kitchen table, surrounded by the smells of tea and cookies, of homemade food, of flowers and herbs. Their house was fun. It was warm and welcoming, and the walls were painted in cream and beige colors, and they had big paintings that radiated color through the living areas. It was soft, that's how I would describe it: a soft, colorful, warm, nice-smelling house, unlike mine, which was cold and colorless. What a difference, as if we were part of two different worlds.

I hung around their house all the time, spent more hours there than I did at home. Mrs. Harrison called me her adopted child, had a place set at the table for me. More often than not, I ate there, my nannies happy to have some time off to do their own thing.

"You're always welcome here," Mrs. Harrison said.

"I know," I said, "but I just wish I would be welcome at home too."

Viola and I were besties back then; we couldn't spend a single day without contacting each other. Even though we were as different as day and night, both in appearance and in behavior, we connected, and that connection went further than just friendship.

"Your parents are weird," she said when we hung out in her room at night watching television. "Why don't they care about you?"

"They do care; they just don't show it."

"That's stupid."

"I know."

"I care."

"I know."

"You can be my sister. We can ask my parents to adopt you."

I laughed. "I don't think mine will be happy about that."

"Why not? They don't care, remember?"

"I still don't think they will want that. Besides, I'm not sure if I want that too."

Viola pushed herself up and looked at me. "Why?"

"Because they're still my parents, and I have nothing to complain about."

"Well, if you ever decide to come and live here, there is plenty of space in the attic. You can run away and live there! That would be amazing. I could bring you food and things to do, and nobody would know. Don't you think your parents would be sad if you really did run away? It could make them see that they love you, and then they will come around and be real parents."

"You read too many books," I said, but she'd made me laugh. She gave me hope, which made it even worse during the summertime, when I was forced to stay at my house. During those weeks when Viola and her family were on vacation, I felt lonely and sad. Because unlike most people, my parents hated vacationing. They've never grasped the concept of rest. Out of the question.

"Why don't we ever go away?" I asked my mom some time ago. They were always working, and I had the house to myself—apart from Marie, that is.

"Because vacation is boring."

"And working isn't?"

"No, it's not."

"But why do other people go on vacation, then?"

"Because they're idiots. What's the fun in reading books or sitting on a beach with a cocktail? It's a stupid waste of time."

"What about visiting cities or museums?" I pushed on.

"Everything that costs money is ridiculous. Stop pressuring me. Go do something useful." My parents' lack of interest in traveling had an impact on me. I had never been anywhere. All that I knew of this country and the rest of the world was what I had learned from books and television.

Viola's parents were totally different. Her dad worked hard, but he also liked to take time off with his family. I was jealous of that, and mostly sad too. So when one day in June, Mrs. Harrison offered to take me on vacation with them, I was stunned. They had never asked me before. Why that year and why all so suddenly, I still don't know, but looking back on it now, I believe she felt that Viola and I were growing apart, and this could be our last chance to spend some quality time together.

My parents didn't need much persuading, probably because I only told them a week before and they were too busy with a new project.

"We're going to have an amazing time," Viola said. "You'll love it! We go to the same place every year, and it's like a second home to us."

That second home turned out to be a quaint little place called Westport, which wasn't even that far away from Love Hill, but it still felt exotic to me.

To this day, I still hold fond memories of that trip. It was the best week of my life, in so many ways. Westport was a beautiful, colorful oceanside town. The moment we got there, I felt at home. People knew Viola's family; they were called by their first names and greeted like old friends. "So good to see you again!" people chanted, before looking at me. "Oh, who is this beauty? Did you adopt her?"

Mrs. Harrison laughed. "It almost feels like that. This is Syl, Viola's best friend."

It was the first time I really felt part of a normal family, enjoying a long-overdue vacation. When we walked around town, I couldn't help but notice the many extraordinary couples who strolled the streets. Same-sex couples were holding hands; sometimes several of them walked the streets together. They were all kind and friendly and wore rainbow T-shirts that seemed to shine brightly in the summer sun. It made it feel as if we were vacationing on a different planet. No one in Love Hill walked around like that. It was absolutely amazing.

We talked about it back at the hotel, how open people were here about who they were, and why it was not an issue. It felt like a whole new world to me after witnessing the narrowmindedness of Love Hill with its conservative values.

"Most of the people in our town simply don't get it," Mr. Harrison said. "They don't want to know about how the people live here. They would call it evil—blasphemy, even."

"But why is it so difficult in Love Hill? We're in the twenty-first century, but it seems like our town is stuck in the past."

"Because sometimes people don't like to see other people being happy with who they are. It's that simple."

I didn't understand. Why were we supposed to exist in a town like ours when there was so much more freedom elsewhere? Why did my parents choose to stay there? The answer was simple: Because they were part of that same judgmental community.

I wasn't. I would never be. I couldn't be.

Later that night, when we were in the adjoining hotel room and Viola was in a deep sleep, I heard her parents talk.

"Maybe we should move," her father said. "It's pretty obvious that Love Hill isn't the town we want to spend the rest of our lives in."

"You're kidding," Mrs. Harrison said, obviously upset. "Why do you want to leave? We've built a life there."

"Because I hate every moment there," he said.

I could hear sadness in his voice. Mr. Harrison was a nice man who always spoke softly. He never became angry or upset. He worked hard and earned a lot of money, but unlike my dad, he still had plenty of time to spend with his family. This week in Westport had shown me what I had been missing my entire life in so many ways. For the first time, the blanket of depression I'd been feeling in Love Hill was shaken off. Here, I could be myself. I could enjoy the company of people who weren't the same. People who thought differently. Viola's parents were spending more time with me than my own parents, and they had that same open-mindedness I was looking for in others. I could talk to them about these things. The more I thought about it, the more abnormal it felt to live in such a cold home, with people who didn't seem bothered that I was so lonely.

Mrs. Harrison had always been like a mom to me, but now that I'd gotten to know Mr. Harrison, I realized he was a wonderful dad. I hated that he wasn't mine. We shared the same interests, like superhero movies and comic books. We argued about who was the strongest hero, and he found it funny that he adored Batman, while I was crazily in love with Thor. We ate pizza and ice cream, often not in that order. I felt like a kid again, even though I was turning sixteen soon. I wasn't a kid; I never had been. I had to fend for myself in so many ways, but here, for a while, I could let go of all that.

"If we leave, you'll ruin Viola's life. She loves it there. And look at Syl. That poor child needs me," Mrs. Harrison said. "She is so lonely. Her parents are awful. She's not able to be who she wants to be."

"Her dad isn't awful."

"Alex's just as absent as Elisabeth is, but nicer. *She* just uses people," Mrs. Harrison said.

Mr. Harrison spoke after a long silence. "You're right. Moving away might not be a good idea. How about I speak to Alex about Syl and ask him to spend more time with her? He needs to get to know her."

"He doesn't know anything about her. You think that'll help?"

"We're friends. I can casually bring it up during golf. Maybe he can do something about it."

"Just be careful what you say. He's conservative."

"I won't bring up certain topics."

A silence followed where I tried to contemplate what he would tell my dad.

I hated going back home after that vacation. Westport, with its vibrant population, already seemed like a distant dream, like something that had happened to other people. I was forced to go back to my old life, but at least there were things to look forward to.

Little did I know that I would never see Mr. Harrison again. When I came to Viola's house to hang out, he was always at work. Two months later, in September, he was gone. He'd announced that he would move to Los Angeles, and he left Mrs. Harrison and Viola. And that changed everything.

CHAPTER NINE

Love Hill. I guess, to understand why things are the way they are around here, it's important to know what this place is about. It's a terrible nickname for a loveless town. Nobody even remembers where it came from, but everyone uses *Love Hill* instead of its real name: Lovell. We don't even have a hill, so that name was ridiculous to begin with. But calling this town a place filled with love is stretching it too far as well.

Love Hill is a small community with a population of a little over two thousand, a place where ignorant people move to unknowingly because it looks beautiful and serene, with a cobblestoned town square that is centered around one of the oldest churches in the country, quaint brick houses, and a couple of museums focused on the Revolutionary and Civil Wars. This town endured both. And of course, we have a beautiful harbor, where every local has a boat to show off their wealth.

The whole area has been the center point of a lot of difficult periods in our American history. Facts our history teachers love to go back to, even though thousands of people have lost their lives on the very soil the town is built on. Thanksgiving is quite a big deal around here, but so are Christmas and Memorial Day.

It's a very Christian-oriented town, which is hell for those who don't feel the same way. As far as I know, nobody owns a gun, except for my dad, who has one stashed away. There has never been a shooting, but that doesn't mean the people here are saints.

I guess on the outside, Love Hill resembles a typical American small town, with the difference here being that people are knowingly cruel to one another. But all that stays within the confines of our homes. Tourists have no clue what hides behind the redbrick walls that form our beautiful town square or exquisite mansions. They don't know that our mayor looks down on everyone who is different from him. We've never had a female mayor or people of color in significant positions.

Everyone's friendly toward the tourists because they indirectly help support the extravagant lifestyles of those who are trapped here. Outsiders don't stay long enough to experience the ugly truth behind those beautiful walls. Newcomers who decide to move here usually don't take too long to figure out that it takes a lot of effort to adapt to Love Hill's bizarre culture and its hierarchy, which has been in place since our town was founded in the late 1600s. The town revolves around power, money, and appearances. Divorce is uncommon.

"Have an affair," they say, "but keep it under wraps." When leaked, a scandal is quickly swept under the rug. Couples like my parents prefer to live in strained relationships and go to counselors who teach them how to survive loveless marriages. A counselor in Love Hill is not meant to bring couples back together—more like to teach them how to survive.

Not caring about anything is quite easy if you think about it. It allows people to focus on their everyday routine to keep up with the ambitious and ridiculous standards Love Hill expects of its citizens. Maintaining this self-inflicted facade also means that superficial reactions to tragedies have become the town's DNA. It means not thinking about whatever happened or why. It means focusing on what to wear at a funeral instead of wondering why that funeral was needed in the first place. It means trying to outdo each other on flower arrangements, even if they hardly have a bond with the deceased. But hey, the most beautiful flowers get the most attention, so why not invest?

It seemed as if funerals were the most important social event of the year. Like when Annie Jones's parents or sister died. Especially with the sister, there were tons of flowers.

Weddings were other big social events, of course, as were birthday parties. Whether it be for adults or kids, most people relied on event planners to create the perfect celebration. But sometimes parents did it themselves, like Viola's mom.

Until we were sixteen, we shared a birthday celebration at her house. Our birthday fell in November, so it was usually cold outside. My mom always refused to organize anything. She felt it was ridiculous to have a party in our house for a bunch of kids who would wind up destroying half her property. So she happily accepted Mrs. Harrison's offer to host the annual party at her house. She had plenty of time and a lot of creative ideas, so it felt like the perfect match. My mom wrote her a big check for the expenses, and that was it.

I remember Viola as a hardheaded—and often quite difficult—child. She would have tantrums, especially when it came to those parties. Months in advance, she would freak out about the details. When upset, she would snap or pull at other kids' hair. She demanded attention and always got it.

Before Mr. Harrison's departure, she was a daddy's girl. He was the only one who could really control her and calm her down. After he left, her erratic behavior increased to a point of unbearableness, even for me. I found myself escaping to the confines of my own home whenever it became too much. Which became the standard instead of an exception.

The problem was that Viola was never her mommy's little girl, but after they were left to their own devices, she had no choice than to turn to her mother. She needed to reconnect with her to get things done her way. She put a plan in motion to get her dad back home, something she needed her mom for. Mr. Harrison was the one who earned all the money, while Mrs. Harrison didn't have a job, and Viola had become accustomed to a high standard of living.

"I want him back," Viola said over the phone when she called me after he had left. "I hate this mess. I hate my mom. She barely looks after herself anymore. I *need* my dad back home to stop the madness.

I need to find out where he is so I can head over there and demand answers. I can't *stand* living like this. Mom is so depressed."

"I'll help you find him," I promised. "Get this thing sorted out."

She snorted. "How? You can't even find your own phone in your bedroom."

True.

"How can you track him down if my mom doesn't even know where he is?" she demanded.

"I can ask my dad."

"He won't care. Nobody does."

"They were sort of friends, weren't they?"

"They went golfing together. That doesn't count."

"So how do your parents get in touch?" I asked.

"They don't. He's been shutting himself off ever since he left. They are no longer on speaking terms, with the whole affair thing and all."

"Who do you think it is?"

"I have no idea," Viola said. "And how the hell did he meet her? He hardly ever traveled for work."

I thought about our vacation in Westport and the way her dad had sometimes looked at other people. He had this way of observing situations. He may have met someone there, and maybe he was now living with that person in California. That was the only logical explanation. Whatever had happened, nobody knew the details.

Viola stayed home from school for two weeks. When she came back, she looked pale and exhausted. Her dad hadn't returned; she still hadn't spoken to him. But there was defiance in her manner and fierceness in her gaze. She dared all the kids to mock her, to give her a reason to physically fight back. They never did.

CHAPTER TEN

On the first day Viola came back to school, we sat on the bleachers behind the football field and watched the seniors practice. We often came here after lunch, just to hang out and chat. Sometimes other friends came along, but usually it was just the two of us. Even though we were gradually growing apart, Viola clung to this habit of ours. Those were the rare moments I was still important to her.

Mr. Harrison had left eighteen days ago, which seemed like forever to me. I couldn't imagine what that must have been like.

"How are you?" I asked cautiously. "Are you okay?"

"If you can call this 'okay,'" she said, making a face. "I hate my mom right now, I really do."

"What? Why?"

"She's constantly overbearing and sad. I can't stand it. It's like my dad died or something. I don't understand why she won't just head out to California to get him back."

"Did you ask her?"

Viola sighed. "Several times."

"Why won't she go?"

"She says she doesn't know where he is; he refuses to tell her. All she knows is that he's staying somewhere in downtown LA, but that's it."

"There have to be ways of finding out—it can't be that hard," I said.

"I know. But honestly, that won't do much good. My dad will never come back, and even if he did, it would never be the same. Plus, my mom is focusing all her attention on me now, to the point where it's simply becoming an unbearable situation."

"What do you mean?"

"She won't allow me to leave the house on my own. She wants me to give up lacrosse and tennis. She wants to keep me close. I'm almost sixteen, Syl! I'm not a child."

"But why?" I said, surprised. "That won't change what happened to your dad, so why is she so overbearing?"

"She tells me that she doesn't want to lose me too. But to be honest, I'm tired of arguing with her about it," Viola said. "It's horrible at our house. It's just so quiet now—well, except for her crying. Which she does all the time. Sometimes I just turn up the volume on the TV so I don't hear her sobbing."

"Is he really gone forever?" I asked carefully.

"Yep. He sent her a long email saying he wants a divorce. He plans on selling the house and his current business, and wants to move permanently to LA. He says Love Hill sucks up all his emotional energy and he can't stand living here anymore. My mom sent back an email, pleading with him that we could move, too, but he didn't even respond. I don't get this, Syl. If he was unhappy here, then why not ask us to come with him? I would leave tomorrow."

A coldness ran through me when she said that. Leaving me felt like the worst thing that could happen, but of course her family came first. She would not hesitate to kick me out of her life. I could offer to go with her at some point.

"You should tell your mom," I said softly.

Viola shook her head sadly. "I don't know this man anymore, Syl. He's no longer my dad. Whatever is going on, it's clear to me now that he doesn't want me in his life anymore. I must have done something terrible."

"No!" I said. "Of course you didn't."

"Then why did he give me up so easily?"

I thought about the man who had taken me to Westport, who had loved the same movies and talked about books and had bought me ice cream because I wasn't allowed to have it at home. I could not believe this man would do this to his own daughter, but he had. He was doing it right now.

I hugged Viola tight.

"This sucks."

"Yeah," Viola agreed. "And the worst part is that I don't know who the woman is that made my dad leave. How crazy is that, Syl? He was having an affair right here, in this town, and she broke his heart. That has got to be the only logical explanation. She drove him away after turning him down, and when he wouldn't relent, she must have started those rumors out of revenge. Her name is still a secret, but his was smeared all over town. Why is that, you think?"

My genuine, naive surprise made Viola smile.

"My dear, sweet Syl. You really have no clue about anything that goes on in this town, do you? That woman, whoever she is, must be powerful enough to shut people up, including my dad. She must have a lot of influence around town. She must have extorted whoever wanted to bring this out in the open. She might have known something about him that would damage his business or us. Whatever it was, it must have been important enough for him to abandon us without blinking an eye."

How come I hadn't heard about this? Then again, I *was* naive and always out of the loop when it came to things like that. Viola always said I was the last one to find out anything about anyone.

For one moment I thought about my mom, one of the most powerful women in this town. But when and how would she even have an affair, when she was working eighty hours a week? Where would she find the time?

"I think it might be her," I said softly. "Powerful, someone he knows. Someone who could drive him away."

"It's not your mom," Viola said after a while. "Trust me, I have gone through all the potential candidates, but no one fits the bill. I've been asking around, but nobody tells me anything. All those hypocrites at church obviously know."

"Perhaps it's better that you don't know," I said. "What would you do?"

"I don't know. I can't even imagine my dad seeing someone else. He was always so sweet to my mom. When would he even do this to her? It's all bullshit. It could all be a ridiculous cover-up."

"You're saying that the rumor of him having an affair was created deliberately in order to explain why he left?" I said.

Viola tapped me on the nose. "Right on."

"Why would they even do that?"

"Because the truth is often less dramatic."

"Meaning?"

"My dad could have walked out because he hated Love Hill, just like he said in his email. End of story."

I wasn't sure which scenario I found most believable: him leaving her mom for another woman, or him leaving because he hated this place. Why, then, would he not take them with him? Why leave like that, without any warning or explanation? No, it didn't add up.

"We should start organizing our birthday party," Viola suddenly said, catching me off guard.

"What?"

"Our birthday. Why not celebrate it like we always did? Life goes on, right? It's already the end of October."

"I'm not sure, Viola—"

"Come on, Syl, don't be a party pooper. My dad's gone, and I want to move on. I want to have a party, and my mom will happily organize it. It will take her mind off things. Besides, we only turn sixteen once."

I smiled because that was what Viola said every year.

"Okay . . ." I said. "But we could do it at my house this time? I can't imagine your mom wanting to do this now, under these circumstances."

"I'll ask her tonight," Viola said.

The next morning, Viola opened the front door to their house upset and gloomy. Her mom was sick again.

"I'm sorry," she said as we walked at a steady pace to school. "She wants us to spend my birthday alone at the house, without any other people there. No double party this year. I'm really sorry, Syl."

"That's okay," I said. "I'll do something at home, then. I'm sure my parents won't mind spending it with me. It's on a Sunday."

I went home that night mentally preparing myself for a nonexistent birthday party. I wouldn't ask my parents for anything; I never had. It would be a dreadful day, but if I knew that up front, I could accept it already and move on.

Little did I know that the days that followed—and in particular, that birthday—would never be forgotten, but for all the wrong reasons. Had I known what was going to happen, I would have moved to Los Angeles myself to avoid the pain I was about to feel.

CHAPTER ELEVEN

My sixteenth birthday was a day that I mentally marked as the beginning of *the Change*. Because everything really did change after that day. Looking back on it now, I only realized how much after those changes were already in place. Some came fast, others happened gradually. But all for the worst, except for one.

It was Sunday, and I hated having to spend this day at home and not at school, where I could at least pretend to be normal. Every Sunday morning, my parents would eat breakfast together and then separate. My dad would spend his day working as always, hardly even taking a break for lunch, while my mom had some cultural engagement she would attend. She usually ate elsewhere for both lunch and dinner, and would come back late in the evening.

They hadn't said a single word about my birthday, and there would be no cake, no presents, and no festive mood. No *sweet sixteen*. I had deliberately "forgotten" to mention there wouldn't be a party at Viola's this year and instead had made my own plans. I was going to leave the house around ten, head out to the local movie theater, and catch at least three movies. My lunch and dinner would consist of popcorn and hot dogs, and I was okay with that. The longer I could stay away, the better. They would be none the wiser, believing that things were still normal.

Marie was living in the guesthouse behind the main house. She did the cleaning, the cooking, and the caretaking, and she treated me like an adult. We got along well. She was the only one my mom trusted.

With my parents being gone so much, Marie could have had it easy. The house was never that messy, and half the time she only had to prepare a meal for the two of us. Since I wasn't that picky about food, I ate whatever she cooked, whether it was a local dish or something she used to cook for her two children, who lived in another state.

Marie's company was nice, but it didn't feel as cozy as it did with Viola's mom. Marie was the only one I had told about my birthday plans.

"You should tell your parents that you won't have a sweet sixteen party," she had said.

"Why? It's not like they care."

Marie was convinced my mother did care about me, and that my dad only pretended to ignore me because he had no clue how to treat kids. Which I found ridiculous.

"Your dad still has time to get to know you," Marie had said. "Maybe you should try a little more too."

"Too little, too late," I said. "Not interested."

"You are an amazing girl, Syl, and one day, they will see that too," she'd said.

"Probably when they need me to take over their business or something."

"Harsh love is still love."

"I prefer not to be loved, then," I'd told her, ending the conversation.

The truth of the matter was that I was yearning for them to tell me that they had made no plans and would spend the day with me, but that wouldn't happen. They were so self-absorbed that there simply was no space for me. They hadn't even realized I hadn't spent a single day at Viola's for weeks now, nor had they commented on Mr. Harrison's odd departure. After sixteen years, you would think I was used to their lack of interest, but it still hurt to realize nothing ever changed, not even on this special day.

My parents' relationship had been more strained lately. They'd had a fight a couple of months ago, but I didn't know what it was about. The fight had increased my concern about my mom having done something to hurt my dad. It was palpable in every move and gesture they made, in every forced, too-polite conversation and their choice of words.

We were sitting at the breakfast table when Marie came up to me and gave me a present. A box, wrapped in beautiful paper, that had come from an expensive shop downtown that I loved.

I looked at the box, stunned. Marie had given me a Christmas present in private, and another small gift she'd found one night when I was so sad I thought my heart would break. She would bake and wrap the cupcakes, cake, or whatever she had created in a box, which I would later find in my backpack during a break. She always went about things discreetly, as I did with her. I had given her a bracelet for her birthday.

This morning, as if to challenge my parents, who were sitting at the table with their phones in front of them, she placed the wrapped box next to my plate, which was stacked with pancakes with maple syrup, raspberries, and whipped cream. My parents had not gotten the same food.

Surprised, I unwrapped the box, and out came a small bottle of my favorite perfume. The brand was quite expensive, and I had ogled it at the shop before deciding to go with another brand. I couldn't believe she had found out and bought it for me.

"You're growing up fast, so I thought you might like this," she said.

"Marie, this is way too expensive!"

"No, it's not. It's my token of appreciation for your friendship and care," Marie said. "I love having you around; you make my life fun."

I could feel my mom's piercing eyes on me. She didn't say anything. Neither did my dad. But Marie's words must have cut right through them. I gently opened the perfume box, took out the bottle, and tried it. The smell I had loved so much at the store embraced me at once.

"I love it," I said, and gave Marie a hug.

"I'm so happy you do," she responded. "Now, eat your pancakes before they get cold."

Marie blatantly ignored my parents, who were doing their utter best to pretend everything was normal, and I ate every bite of those pancakes and left the kitchen, clutching that bottle as if it were worth a fortune. This birthday could be the best one yet.

In my bathroom, I smiled when I thought about my plans to go to the movies. About what I had said to someone special I was hoping to see there. I used the perfume again, and immediately I felt stronger and more powerful, as if that scent gave me strength and self-esteem.

I looked at myself critically, not liking what I saw. Does anyone, really? Lately, I had developed physically. More chest, more figure, strong arms and legs, slim but not skinny. I had some meat on my bones, and I was glad I wasn't super skinny and could eat all I wanted without having to put myself on a diet.

I had started noticing minor changes. The child in me was gone. I had started having feelings for someone at school. Someone I really liked. I just wasn't sure that these feelings would be reciprocated. I didn't talk about it, kept everything I felt to myself. To be honest, I was freaking out about the potential lack of interest coming from the other side, and the extreme consequences that a rejection would have on me. Time would tell, but no matter what would happen today, I would be happy at the movies.

I applied a touch of makeup, which the nice lady at the store had helped me with. I changed into skinny jeans and a T-shirt, took a pair of worn sneakers from my closet, and chose a light sweater in case it would be cold in the movie theater.

I had just finished applying some light eye shadow when the doorbell rang, immediately followed by loud banging. Marie rushed to the front door, probably thinking there was an emergency. I walked over to the top of the stairs, surprised to see Mrs. Harrison standing there.

She came into our house with a crazy look in her eyes I had never seen before. She was no longer the woman I had known up until that point. Her hair was mussed, and even at a distance, it seemed as if she hadn't taken a shower in weeks. She wore wrinkled clothes and wasn't wearing any makeup. Was this really the same woman who took such care of her appearance, even if only to take us to school?

Viola was nowhere to be seen. Mrs. Harrison had come alone, and she was acting crazy.

"Where is she?" she shouted at Marie.

"Who?" our housekeeper asked politely.

"That bitch, of course."

She looked up and noticed me standing at the top of the stairs, and for one long moment I thought that I was the bitch she was referring to. But then my mom walked into the hallway, and Mrs. Harrison immediately forgot about me. Marie was still present, obviously unsure of what to do.

"You can go, Marie," my mom ordered.

Our housekeeper turned around and fled down the hallway, but I remained where I was.

My mom was oblivious to my presence.

"I hope you're proud of yourself," Mrs. Harrison snapped. "I really, really hope that you will spend the rest of your days feeling regret over how you killed my husband."

My legs shook; I had to sit down. My mom grew pale. She trembled before composing herself.

My dad, who had walked into the hallway behind my mom, gasped.

"Felix is dead?" he slowly asked.

My father looked so pale and distressed suddenly, that I wondered for a split second if he was on the verge of having a heart attack. My dad and Mr. Harrison had spent some time together playing golf and racquetball, but it wasn't as if they had been the best of friends.

Viola's mom seemed to collapse into herself. She started shaking and her voice broke. Her tears fell onto the carpet. My mom looked at the wet spot with clear disgust written all over her face. I could just imagine her making a mental note for our cleaning lady to sanitize that carpet.

"He's gone. My Felix is gone," Mrs. Harrison wailed.

"How?" my dad asked.

"He jumped or fell in front of a car in downtown LA. The cops are still investigating. Why don't you tell me what you think happened? Did he cross the street in front of that truck on purpose, or was he too preoccupied to see it coming?"

Mrs. Harrison gazed at my mom with a disdain I had never seen on anyone before. It wasn't just aimed at my mom, though; her disgust was meant for both my parents.

"Emily," my dad began, but she raised her hand, silencing him.

"I hope the two of you are proud of yourselves. You killed him. His death is upon you, and I pray with all my heart that not a single day will go by without you realizing what you have done to us."

With those words, I could see the sheer shock written on my father's face. He crumpled and searched for support, but my mom refused to acknowledge him. She remained as cold as ever.

"We didn't kill him," she said. "This was a terrible accident. What makes you think he would do this on purpose?"

"Like you don't know," Mrs. Harrison said sharply.

"Of course I don't. We haven't spoken to him in weeks, not since he left Love Hill. Why would you even put this upon us?"

Mrs. Harrison snorted loudly while she wiped away her tears. My mom's words had a reverse effect on her, that much was obvious.

"You keep on telling yourself that, and one day you'll believe your own lies," she said. "I hope you can live with yourself. I can't stand the sight of you any longer. You stay away from my daughter, you hear? I never want to see *your* daughter at my house ever again. If any of you as much as approach my driveway, I'll tell this whole town about what you did. We're done."

Mrs. Harrison turned around and walked away. The front door remained wide open, until my mom closed it and looked my dad in the eye while she smiled, as if this was all one big joke. There was something in her gaze that scared me. I knew my mom could be a coldhearted woman, but this? No, I had never seen her like this before.

"Well, that was that, then," she said. "Problem solved." And left my dad alone in that hallway.

He looked up and only then seemed to notice me standing on the stairs. For the first time, I saw something like sadness in his eyes. He acknowledged me, but mostly he seemed afraid.

"Did you hear everything?" he asked.

"Fuck you both," I replied.

The words came out of my mouth, and I startled myself. Never had I spoken this way to my parents, who didn't believe in swearing and showing such disdain. But I knew that I meant it. I wanted them to go to hell. For the first time, I started believing that we were, in fact, already there. That this whole existence of mine was one bad dream. That I might have been reborn in hell for something I had done in a previous life. Why else would I have such weird parents?

I left him standing there, walked back into my bedroom, shut the door, and started weeping. My gut feeling that my mom had had an affair with Mr. Harrison had been right. She had slept with him, and then she had driven him away, and my dad knew about it. Why else would this be happening right now?

I didn't leave the house to go to the movies. Instead, I locked myself in my room.

Hours later I walked into the kitchen, expecting to see Marie there. My dad was sitting at the kitchen table in front of the same newspaper that had been open to the same pages this morning at breakfast.

"Where's Marie?"

"She's gone," he said, looking up briefly. "She left."

"Left? Where?"

"I don't know."

"You're lying!"

"I'm not," Dad said helplessly. "She's just gone."

"She didn't leave. She was fired," my mom said, walking into the kitchen, as if she had been waiting for me to show up. "You're sixteen now; it's high time that you start taking care of yourself. You don't need a housekeeper anymore. A cleaning lady is more than enough."

"You can't just fire her!" I yelled.

I ran to the guesthouse. It was empty. Marie had left without saying goodbye to me. My mom wouldn't have allowed her to, as punishment for giving me that perfume. Marie had been told to leave immediately, just like that, as if she hadn't spent several years in this house taking care of me.

I ran back to the house and just lost it.

"You're the worst mother in the world. Why did you even have me when you seem to hate me so much?"

"I don't hate you. I just don't have time for drama."

"You never have time for anything. You're taking away everyone that is dear to me. Why? Does it bother you so much that I love other people more than I love you?"

She stood frozen. And then she slapped me in the face. I was in shock, realizing that this was the first time in ages that she had voluntarily touched me. She seemed as startled as I was.

"I'm sorry," she said.

"Go to hell."

I ran outside and stopped in front of our house, looking at the cars passing by and the people walking down the street with their dogs and their children. Some people in this town seemed to lead normal lives. I envied them for their closeness.

I had lost everything today. Mrs. Harrison, Viola, Marie, Mr. Harrison. He would never return now. He was gone. My heart went out to Viola, to the heartache she must be feeling. I dug out my phone, planning to call her, only to realize that this was the worst thing to do right now. I sent her a text.

> I'm so sorry. Please tell me what I can do to help you. I want to be there for you.

Her message came back five seconds later.

Nothing. Have a great birthday.

I couldn't go back to that house, to those people whom I disliked so much. Only Marie had made my life bearable. And now she was gone.

I walked back inside, where I found my mom in the kitchen, busying herself with tidying up the kitchen table.

"You're going to bring Marie back," I said. "And not only that, you are going to give her a raise and additional holidays."

She looked at me as if I had sprouted two heads. "Why would I do that?"

"Because if you don't, I will tell this entire town about your affair with Mr. Harrison and how you drove him to suicide."

"The town already knows," she said sharply. "You're bargaining with the wrong chips."

"All right, then," I said. "I'll make sure that the whole town knows how you treat your own daughter. How you have never cared one bit about me. How you drove me into the caring arms of Mrs. Harrison and then repaid her by screwing her husband. I will make sure that everyone knows who and what you really are."

Mom turned pale. The satisfaction I felt dizzied me.

"You would never dare to go against me."

"No? Like you said yourself: I'm sixteen now. You can no longer treat me like a child. Try me."

"This is still my house, and you will live by my rules."

"Don't worry, Mom," I said. "You don't have to start pretending that we suddenly get along. You live your life, I will live mine. And soon enough, I will leave this house for college, and you won't have to worry about me any longer. I'll be out of your hair, and your life. You will never have to bother with me again. *If* you bring Marie back, that is. And only *if* you keep her on for as long as she wants."

My mom looked defeated. For the first time ever, I was winning. I had kept my mouth shut my whole life, had accepted and tolerated their disinterest in me. But not anymore. Now we were to play by my rules.

"Okay," she said. "I'll give her a call."

"And give her a raise. And extra vacation days."

"Anything else?" Mom asked, gritting her teeth.

"A car would be nice too. For her and for me. We can share it. She would like to go visit her children. Just a small one is good enough, one that will get her around. I don't want her carrying her groceries any longer."

"And you are willing to share one with her?" my mom asked.

"Sure. Well then, that's it for now. I won't be back until late tonight, so have a good rest of the day. I will celebrate my birthday elsewhere. I expect Marie to be back by the time I'm home."

She didn't comment. She didn't try to stop me. She didn't make a move or a nasty remark.

She let me go, just like that.

I felt as light as a feather and high on victory when I left the house again and walked to the movie theater, six blocks away. If I hurried, I would still make it on time for the matinee.

When I reached the entrance, my heart lifted for the second time. Despite all the drama, the loss, and the tragedies, this really had turned out to be the best Sunday ever. Standing in front of the building was the one person who made me forget my misery. Who had been waiting for me patiently. A smile lifted my spirits.

CHAPTER TWELVE

I was an idiot. How could I even think that me standing up to my mother would change everything? Nothing changed. In fact, things only became worse.

When I came back home that day, Marie was back, cooking as if nothing had happened. She was very quiet, though, and I couldn't shake the feeling that my mom had had a serious, threatening discussion with her, but she wouldn't say. Nobody talked about it ever again. Marie knew she had me to thank for her job, the vacation days, and the pay raise, and she doted on me with delicious food cooked especially for me.

My biggest surprise came a couple of days later, when my dad took me to a car dealership and told me I could pick one out for myself and one for Marie.

"I thought we were sharing," I said.

"No need," he assured me.

"Budget?"

"Just choose the cars."

I picked two medium-size models. Sturdy, modern cars that would be comfortable and felt safe. We picked them up a couple of weeks later; Marie had tears in her eyes. I hugged my dad awkwardly.

"Well, it's normal for a father to buy presents for his daughter, right?" he said.

I didn't comment. I felt it was more normal for a father to hug his child now and then.

If I had thought that would be the beginning of a new understanding between us, I was mistaken. After that day, my parents avoided me even more than they had before, but I do believe now that it had nothing to do with me and more to do with themselves.

Marie and I were alone at the house constantly now. Most of the time, my parents avoided each other. The unit they had been in the past when it came to their business, relationship, and me was gone. They slept apart, dined with different people, circulated in other crowds. They started publicly leading noticeably separate lives. They no longer notified each other about their plans, nor did they care that people on the outside had started noticing the distance too. They had finally become a couple like so many others in the #Townfromhell. They were only sticking together for practical reasons; the facade was gone.

My mom was now openly being chastised for her affair with Mr. Harrison. Even in church, there were mentions, mostly when the priest started discussing the ramifications of marital betrayal. During his sermon, he looked straight at her, talking about how people got hurt when adultery was considered a common good.

As for me, I started getting used to being even more free than I had already been. And I started enjoying it. With them gone, Marie and I had the house to ourselves. Our housekeeper never did anything to hurt me or make a comment that would rattle me. We were happy in our own way, her and me. We had fun, played music, added color and flowers to the rooms, made the house seem lighter.

Those months after my sixteenth birthday, I spent a lot of time in our garden but also met up with new friends I had made at school the previous year. I was used to my independent existence and never told my parents where I was or who I was with. I had grown accustomed to the changes in my life, which seemed to prepare me for a new existence away from Love Hill.

I don't think my mom ever forgave me for talking back, but she did seem to like the fact that Marie was still around to take care of me and the house.

And then there was Viola. Viola, who was no longer my best friend but also no longer the person she used to be. She was an angry, aggressive shadow of herself. Our friendship became something that was quite different from what it had been before that day.

Mrs. Harrison kept true to her word: I never saw the inside of their home again. Not the one they were living in at the time of our sixteenth birthday, nor the smaller place they moved to after we turned seventeen, which was located on the other side of town. We only saw each other at school now, and not in a pleasant way.

After the events at our house, I still naively held on to the idea that nothing had to change between Viola and me, despite what her dad and my mom had done. I was determined to remain friends, assuming Viola felt the same way. As it turned out, she didn't. That Monday morning, after the birthday I'd ended up spending with someone else, I had to go to school on my own. It was a ten-minute walk, and the weather was still unexpectedly warm for November, so I didn't really mind. It did hurt when her mom's car passed me by on the street without a wave from Viola, or an offer to give me a ride. I felt ridiculously upset. Why was I being punished for something our parents had done? It only made me more determined to regain her friendship.

But somehow, deep down, I already knew that would never happen. That crucial year, I learned that loss came in different ways. It wasn't just Viola whom I'd lost, but the one person who mattered more to me than anything in life.

THE DEAD GIRL AND THE GIRL SHE LOVED AND LOST

I swallow away sadness as I look at my hands but not at Annie Jones, who became very quiet during my tale. I could tell she felt sorry for me, that she didn't really know what to do or say.

"Are you okay?" she asks, like she did before. As if those three words are the only ones she could decide upon to show how much she cares. I think she really did start caring during our conversation. Somewhere along the line, she turned from a selfish influencer looking for the ultimate story into someone who genuinely cared for the subject of that story. Her hand reaches out for me, but of course she can't touch me.

"We don't have much time left. You're fading," she remarks.

"What do you mean?"

"The image of you is different. It's like you're still here, but not as clear to me as you were before. I think time's running out quickly now."

"It probably is," I say. "What time is it?"

"Around four a.m."

"You should get some sleep."

"No. If I do that, we'll waste precious time. But if you don't mind, I'm going to grab a quick bite to eat."

She walks into the kitchen while I remain seated on the chair with the light still shining on me, because I know she won't be able to see me if I move around the room. It's not as if I can drag that light with me, so I'm bound to this position.

"Can I ask you something?" she calls out from the kitchen.

"Shoot."

"Okay, so you've told the story about your mom and Mr. Harrison, and how this caused his death. But why would Viola be angry at you? You were her best friend. And what happened after that birthday? You said that you spent an entire year getting used to not having a decent relationship with your parents, but what about Viola?"

"Ah, but that's the next part of the story," I say. "Patience, Annie."

She comes back to the study with a plate with two peanut butter and jelly sandwiches, which makes me roll my eyes.

"You should pay more attention to what you put in your mouth," I say. "That's not good for you at four o'clock in the morning."

"Why not? It's not like PB&J is going to kill me."

"Funny."

"I try to be."

She sits down again and takes a big bite from her first sandwich, and I try to remember what that tastes like. I used to have peanut butter and jelly sandwiches myself, but not frequently. I was a health buff, loved to eat poke bowls and loads of fruit.

"So tell me. What do you want to hear next?" I ask. "I'm guessing that you want this story told sequentially, right? We just went through the disaster of my sweet sixteen, so I assume you want to hear about how Viola and I broke off our friendship and then later on rekindled it?"

"Of course I do. But I'm also curious about what happened last year, and what led to you becoming a weekly visitor here. I think that it's time to address that issue too."

"Then we need to go back again in time," I say. "Because what happened last year was only the result of what occurred years ago."

She takes another bite of her sandwich, eagerly showing her interest again.

"Okay, then. I need to tell you something about myself first. Something important. Something that only one other person in this world has really known."

She stops eating and wipes her mouth with a napkin. "What are you talking about?"

I look at my hands, and even though I can't feel nervous anymore because I'm dead, I *am* itchy. This secret could have gone to the grave with me, but then the rest of the story would make no sense at all. I just can't *say* it out loud. Annie looks at me curiously, and then she smiles broadly, without flinching or seeming repulsed.

"You underestimate me. Do you really think I hadn't guessed there was more to you seeking a psychic connection with a good friend that you lost? I know why you came to me."

"Viola..."

"She hurt you badly."

"Yes, she did. I fell in love with someone and she hated me for it."

"Hang on a second. Are you telling me that Viola killed you because of the feelings you had for someone else?"

"Yes, indirectly she did."

"But she had her own boyfriend."

"Yes, she did."

"Then why would she be jealous of you?"

"Because Viola is exactly the type of person this town creates. She thrives on the tragedies of other people. Ever since her dad, she seeks satisfaction in others having it worse than her. She wasn't happy, so she didn't want me to be either. She tried to break us up."

"But why?"

I shrug again. "Do you remember the funeral last year? The social event that it became?"

"Of course."

"Do you remember that white wooden casket, how it was covered with hundreds of flowers? White roses and lilies, and a touch of red here or there that stood out against the wood and looked like blood? And the purple ones? I had bought those, had ordered them especially because the florist didn't carry them. That was my way of showing the world that the person in that casket meant everything to me, and when we put that body in the ground, my heart was buried too."

Everyone in town tried to figure out who had sent those purple roses. Nobody knew, and the florist kept it to himself at my request. I didn't want people to know they were mine, not after what they had all accused me of.

Annie does not react to my words. She can't, because she was at fault, too, back then. She, too, had belonged to the fake group, had been socially punished for it. After the funeral, where a lot of people had said a lot of sweet things about the deceased, the whole town went to the cemetery to show their final respects. Up until that moment, it seemed like a decent enough burial. But even as the casket was still being lowered into the ground, it already became apparent that a large group of people were moving on mentally.

I heard whispers going around about a party later that night. Only four hours after the funeral everyone in town had wanted to be part of, there was supposed to be a huge party at the lake. Despite the tragic circumstances, it was not canceled.

The party organizer was Matt Hanks, son of the CEO of a start-up that had been picked up by some influential people back in the late nineties. Matt had sent a message to all the invitees saying we had to move on. I was disgusted when the party went viral. Thousands and thousands of people were watching the livestreams on Instagram and TikTok. Love Hill was trending.

#Tragedyisnottheend #Wewillsurvive #Thinkingofourlostone #Lovehillmourns

Partygoers got drunk and blabbered on and on while they were being filmed, not even realizing that thousands of viewers were commenting, wondering how these people could be so cold. Online, the party was trending, but not in a good way.

#Alovedonedeservesbetter #Justiceisnothere #Thetownfromhell #Partyfromhell

Every single person at that party was laughing and drinking the night away. I wasn't there; I was disgusted by the whole thing. I haven't spoken to a lot of people in our town since that night.

The parents spent that evening at the cemetery talking about their lost one while listening to the loud music coming from the adjacent house. They wept while I locked myself in my bedroom that night, far away from the disgusting social media uproar.

The hashtags stayed viral for a long time, and the parents of those who were present tried everything they could to take all the footage offline, but they failed. Even now, there are still a lot of videos out there, and every time I accidentally come upon one, my stomach churns.

"My funeral won't be so intense," I say. "Nobody will celebrate my life."

"You don't know that," Annie says. "Your death is just as tragic."

"Oh really?"

"Yes, really. Viola will be found, and she will be punished for what she did. This will go viral, too, believe me. And if not for her part in this, then for this conversation we are having."

"You do know that people hate me for my part in what happened last year? I was there that night, and I was blamed for it until the moment of my death, even if I couldn't prevent it from happening. I will be remembered only for that, so why would anyone mourn me? Up until today, there are still people out there wondering if things could have been different. I've wondered about that, too, more than I care to remember."

"This is not on you, Syl. You know that," Annie says fiercely.

"No? Every single day, I regret getting behind the wheel of my car and allowing this to happen."

"This could have happened at any time, any place. You know what happened that night, Syl."

"I know," I say impatiently. "A spontaneous coronary artery dissection. A tear formed in a blood vessel of the heart that caused sudden death."

"Yes. SCAD. You looked it up. You know you couldn't have prevented that from happening."

"Couldn't I, though? Some people believe I had been driving erratically, or we had been in a fight, causing the stress. Others say that I should have driven to the hospital straightaway, instead of stopping at that open space. That doctors could have worked their magic."

"You know that isn't true. The doctors confirmed that it happened in a split second."

Hearing Annie say those words reminds me of all that I went through that night. It's been a year, but it was something I would have carried with me to eternity.

"I think I know now why you are still here," Annie says. "You came to find a way to connect beyond death with the one you loved, to apologize and find peace. But what if the only person you still need to forgive for what has happened is you?"

I shake my head softly. "No. That's not it. There is another person I need to forgive. Someone who was just as involved as I was."

Annie shoots up from her seat. I realize I have finally given her what she was looking for.

"Viola," she whispers. "Was she there?"

Yes. Viola. Who was there that night, a fact I have concealed for a year. Viola, who never cared about a single person her entire life.

Viola, who killed someone, and got away with it.

PART THREE: THE GIRL WHO STOLE MY HEART

CHAPTER THIRTEEN

Going back in time to a moment where Viola was still just Viola. Always a friend, and much more than that. Family. A sister from a different mother. My bestie. Until things started to change in my mind, and she was no longer my sister but someone else close to my heart. When she became gorgeous, precious, amazing Viola.

For a very long time, I believed I was supposed to be with her for the rest of my life. Looking back at the situation now, I can recall only how stupid I was. What did I know about life and love? Nothing at all.

I can't remember the first time I started realizing that I felt more for my best friend than just friendship, but I do remember falling in love with her during that week in Westport. That week was the sum of all the emotional moments I'd shared with Viola. I was searching for a new step in our relationship, but instead, I received nothing but heartache.

I don't know why or how that change in feelings happened, but it probably had something to do with the almost hypnotic atmosphere that hung in the air, or the fact that in Westport, it was quite normal for two women to hold hands and kiss in public without having to fear repercussions. I had never seen that in Love Hill, and it almost made me giddy after ignoring my own feelings for years.

Even though there was magic in the air in that place, I am certain, even now, I was born gay and that this wasn't a whim brought on by the location and the people. It had already been there lingering inside me, when I looked at the girls in my class more than the boys and daydreamed about them in a way that Love Hill townsfolk would find inappropriate. My feelings only grew after that vacation; it became my secret.

I knew Love Hill wasn't exactly the best place to live when you belong to the LGBTQ+ community, which made it even harder for me to find kindred spirits. Everything had to stay closeted, or face repercussions. I could not imagine the priest doing to me what he had done to my mom, who had been publicly cited for her adulterous choices. If the priest were to find out that I liked girls, he would not hesitate to humiliate me too.

Yes, we were living in the twenty-first century. Yes, loving girls wasn't really that big a deal anymore. Yes, people came out of the closet all the time. But we were still living in an extremely religious town, where people were scrutinized for having another opinion or mentality. Until that vacation in Westport, I had never thought of myself as being different from most others. After that day, it seemed as if it was the most logical discovery I had ever made about myself.

Viola and I were sitting on the beach at some point, just the two of us. She was wearing her colorful bathing suit with a summer sarong over it, gazing out over the ocean. I sat next to her in my bikini, feet in the sand. Her parents weren't with us. This was the first time the two of us were alone.

"I wish this would last forever," I said, leaning into her. She wrapped her arm around me. I could feel her warm skin against mine, and it felt as if this was *the* moment I could express my feelings to her.

"I know," she said.

"I don't want to go home." My voice was hoarse and emotional. "Not ever. I want to stay here forever."

She looked at me, surprised. "Why? This isn't real life, you know."

"I know, and that's the hardest part. Even going back to the hotel, to your parents, is hard when I want to spend my time with you."

"I don't get it," Viola said, and she sounded unsure of how to answer.

I had to do this. It was my one and only chance. I had to grab the opportunity, or I would chicken out forever.

"I don't want to ever *not* see you," I blurted out. "I want to be with you forever. In every way."

She let go of me, just like that. Her touch slipped away; she shot up and was on her feet in a second. She pulled the sarong over her chest, reached for her sandals, and started walking away without saying another word.

That night, she wouldn't look at me, wouldn't speak to me, wouldn't spend the evening by my side. She just walked away and left me at the hotel. I spent the rest of the evening with her mom on the couch in the suite, watching some lame movie, until Viola walked in with her dad, said good night, and went to bed. She had obviously been crying. Her dad kissed me on the forehead and said that things would be fine. I wished I could believe him.

When I ultimately went to bed hours later, feeling I could no longer postpone going into that room, Viola lay in bed on her side, not facing me. I knew she was awake; I could feel the stress lingering over her.

"I'm sorry," I said. "I really am. Please forget what I said."

She didn't pretend not to hear me. She sat up and switched on the light. Her expression was a mix of sadness and pity. I hated the way she was looking at me. I stood in the middle of the room, unsure whether I should undress myself quickly and put on my pajamas as I had done every day before today. But now there was this giant elephant in the room. I started gathering my things, planning on changing in the bathroom.

"I'm not what you're looking for," Viola said while I had my back to her.

"I know," I muttered.

She got out of bed and placed her hand on my arm.

"I'm sorry. I didn't mean to be so insensitive and rude. I was caught off guard, I guess."

I looked at her with tears in my eyes. "It's okay. Just . . . please stay my friend. I will never say things like that again."

"But it's okay to say them. You just need to know that I don't feel that way about you."

"I know," I said. "Steve."

Viola smiled. Steve. Nice, decent, trustworthy Steve. The boy who had stolen her heart.

I walked into the bathroom feeling a little better, but I knew there was a thin line between a shallow conversation and a dramatic explosion. She could misinterpret everything I said from now on. How was I supposed to deal with that?

She already was someone to reckon with—explosive by nature, angry about things others didn't care about, spoiled to a point that, if things didn't go her way, she would just blow up. Add this, and I wasn't so sure we would survive.

But the next day, as we were walking on the beach, she poked me and pointed at a girl about our age walking on the beach.

"Isn't she your type?"

I was flabbergasted, and then I smiled. "No," I said. "I like a different type."

"Like who?"

"Some girls at school; it varies. It's hard to explain."

"Well, the moment you figure it out, let me know and I'll help you find the perfect one."

And that was it. The moment Viola gave me her support, forgave me for my mistake. I thought—against better hope—that this would be it. That she understood who I was and would have my back. That she didn't judge me for who I was.

How wrong I was.

CHAPTER FOURTEEN

Viola was not the kind of person who forgot things easily. I could sense a certain distance growing between us that summer, even though neither of us mentioned that particular conversation again. She stayed distant throughout the drive home, moved closer to the window and hardly spoke. Maybe she did it unconsciously, but to me, these were signs that she was scared of me.

Right after we returned from vacation, Viola started hanging around with Steve a lot more. She stopped texting me daily, and I stopped coming by their house. Her mom and dad might have noticed, but they didn't comment on it, nor did Mrs. Harrison make any effort to ask me what was going on.

The rest of that summer, I barely saw Viola. She was clearly avoiding me, and there was nothing I could do about it. To fill that void, she used Steve. Perhaps that was the reason why her parents never contacted me. They might have believed this was normal; a girl falling for a boy didn't have time for anything else, not even her best friend.

Steve had already been in our lives—we'd grown up together. He had been in our classes from an early age, which was quite normal in a small town like ours. When we were younger, he was part of our gang of friends, though we had grown apart naturally as we got older.

Steve and Viola had been hanging around last year, but they weren't serious about each other. They just grew closer again, and it had been fairly obvious to everyone that he had his eye set on her. Viola hadn't shown much interest, until now. She was using him, but he had no clue.

Steve was a nice guy, didn't act like the typical arrogant jock. He was just Steve, goofing around with his friends, making jokes, and pulling pranks on teachers. Everyone liked him, including me. How could I not? He was so likable and easygoing, and Viola had caught his attention. She wasn't the most attractive girl in school, but she had something that made people look twice. Steve wanted to be with her, but she clearly didn't want to spend time with him. She ignored him, even at the summer dance. Until suddenly, she fell head over heels for him—or so it seemed.

When the summer had started, even before we went to Westport, she changed her mind about him and later on called it a fun game to toy with his feelings.

When we got back, things changed. She went out with him all the time, and she started ghosting me. Classmates started inviting the two of them to parties as a couple. They were always together.

I gathered my courage and decided to talk to Viola before the start of the new school year, to find out if our friendship could ever go back to normal. But before I even crossed the street, I saw her and Steve in her driveway. There was Viola, turning sixteen in three months, kissing Steve in a way I had never seen before. I knew this was far more than just a fling now; it was getting serious. Jealousy struck me like a sledgehammer and knocked me backward against the wall of my own house.

The next day, *I* started ghosting *her*. I sent her a text message, telling her to leave me alone and that we were through. I removed her from my phone, blocked her number and emails. And yes, she reacted just the way I knew she would. She saw me on the street, and I walked away. She came over to the house, and I didn't answer the door. Marie told her I was out with friends while I stood behind the door and listened to her politely requesting to see me.

That evening, she came back. This time, I did open the door and looked at her coolly.

"What do you want?" I said.

"I need to talk to you," she said, and she had tears in her eyes. "I'm sorry. I'm sorry that I ghosted you, that I ignored you, that I treated you like I did. I was— I needed time to think about everything."

"Oh?"

"Yeah, and I—well, I realized I don't want to lose you. You're my best friend and I screwed up, and I'm sorry."

I was shocked by her words, and startled that she would actually come over and apologize so genuinely. It was the first time Viola had taken the time to show me that she cared, and even though part of me knew this was all for show because I had shut her out of my life, I craved being with her again. I couldn't imagine one day at school without her. I couldn't imagine ignoring her forever.

"Okay," I said. "I forgive you."

She looked up. "Just like that?"

"Yeah, why not?"

She didn't hug me. She didn't show affection. She just smiled. "Are we going to school together in the morning?"

"Sure. I'll be at your place around eight."

"Good, my mom will be happy. She misses having you around the house."

Ah. So that was it. Her parents had come to realize that things were off and had started asking questions. By the time Viola had turned around and walked off our driveway, I was regretting having caved in so quickly.

The next day, sitting in her mom's car, Viola acted as if things had never changed between us. She talked about her dad, about our new year, about the school, about the teachers—but she never mentioned Steve once, nor did she ask me how I was doing or what I had been up to all summer. She might not have liked the answer.

I pushed away all my doubts and decided to forgive her. By the end of that day, it felt as if we were old friends again, but we both knew that it was just a facade. It didn't feel right anymore.

That feeling continued in the weeks that followed. She was with Steve now, but she was also still my friend. We got along. We spent time on the bleachers, discussing random things. I helped her with her assignments. She pretended that everything was normal. But all that time, the feeling that something was amiss stayed.

Weeks later, after her dad left, she dropped me again. I remember that last conversation about her dad on the bleachers clearly, as well as her saying that we wouldn't be spending our sweet sixteen together. That was the last time I spoke to her thinking we were still friends. After that, it was all over.

I believe up until this day that she apologized with the sole purpose of punishing me for blocking her and trying to free myself from her. Nobody said goodbye to Viola like I had done. That late-October morning started off normally, even though Viola was cold and distant.

She barely spoke, and neither did her mom. We had different classes but had agreed to meet by the lockers for lunch. We walked into the cafeteria together, but after paying for her food, Viola spotted Steve sitting with his friends. Or maybe it had been set up like that.

He beckoned her closer with a broad smile. There was only one open seat at their table, so it was obvious I wasn't invited to tag along. Viola made no attempt to make room either. Her look of disdain and the sly smile on her lips when she brushed me off showed me that this was her revenge. My heart sank; I felt small and belittled.

Steve hugged and kissed her in front of everyone. Loud whistling followed. Kids clapped their hands while teachers reprimanded them to stop. And I stood there, in the middle of the cafeteria, unsure of what to do next. Steve didn't see me; he barely realized the hurt I was feeling.

I sat down at the first table I came across with an empty seat. Tears blinded my vision. I pretended to occupy myself with my food while trying to ignore a very triumphant Viola, who had finally gotten her revenge.

"Well, that was a long time coming," a voice said next to me. I looked over and saw Lila Jenkins gazing at me.

CHAPTER FIFTEEN

Lila Jenkins. Cute, adorable, well dressed, smelling of modest perfume and rose shampoo. Nothing more than a classmate, no close or dear friend. We barely knew each other.

Her mom ran a successful wellness center and knew all the gossip in town. People talked a lot when they were relaxing in bubble baths or being massaged. Her dad ran a golf club my dad and Mr. Harrison often frequented.

"Cat got your tongue?" she asked, her face as straight as an arrow.

"I'm sorry, what?"

"I said that it was pretty obvious that Steve and Viola would connect at some point, don't you agree?"

"I guess," I said, without looking at the couple sitting at the other table, which caused Lila to study me with a frown on her face. I noticed that the others at the table were curious too. I wasn't close to any of them; they were Lila's friends. I usually sat with Viola and a couple of other girls.

"Isn't she supposed to be your best friend?" one of the girls at our table asked.

"She is," I muttered.

"You don't seem happy about her and Steve," someone else said, and I could feel their interest piquing.

"Of course I am," I said hastily. "Why shouldn't I be?"

"Everyone wants to be with Steve," a third girl said, while Lila's eyes were still fixed upon me. "Jealous, maybe?"

"Not me," I mumbled under my breath, realizing this had been a mistake, in a town where everyone seems to have an opinion on everyone else.

"I'll find another place to eat," I said softly, standing up with my tray.

"Hey, don't. Please stay." Lila placed a hand on my arm.

Her touch was unexpectedly warm. I looked at her and then at the others, who started eating again without looking at me. The conversation turned in a different direction, as if someone had flicked a switch.

"Come on, stay," Lila repeated. "You look like you could use a friend."

I sat down again, all appetite lost, but I focused on my salad anyway. I didn't look at her once. The buzzing of people's conversations was like being trapped in a beehive. I hated the amplified noise, noticeable only when I wasn't talking myself. Someone was showing some video at another table. Viola and Steve were laughing, and it felt as if Viola's voice came through all the mingled sounds.

"Are you okay?" Lila asked after a while.

"Why do you ask?"

"You haven't touched your food, and your fork has been hanging between your plate and your mouth for an eternity."

I gazed at the fork and the greens on it and realized I hadn't eaten anything. I lowered it and shoved the tray away. People were leaving. The table emptied and there was just the two of us now. A quick glance behind me proved that Viola and Steve were also gone, his friends in tow. Well, it was clear now where I stood. She didn't even bother asking me to come with them. I picked up my phone and debated blocking her number for a second time, but didn't.

"No, I guess I'm not okay," I said.

Lila gave me a slight elbow bump. It was meant to feel supportive. I looked at her, realizing that tears were dripping down my face. She gave me a tissue.

"Don't worry about it. I know what it feels like to be pushed away like that. Happened to me last year. My so-called best friend started seeing this guy. I was forgotten. She came back six months later with her tail between her legs. The moment I told her to go to hell was probably the best one of my life so far."

I laughed. "Serves her right."

"Oh yeah." Lila smiled. "Don't worry, you'll get your revenge someday. I guess we should say that, for now, you should be happy for them. Steve's a nice guy; he will treat her right."

"I guess."

"And you know what they say about these things."

"What's that?"

"Once you start a serious relationship with someone, there's no room left for others in your life. So I'm guessing you'll have to live with the fact that your Siamese twin has cut herself loose from you and will move on."

I couldn't help but laugh, because it really did feel that way.

"You're right," I said. "It's going to be hard, though. Even though I have doubts about us being Siamese twins."

"You were. Everyone at school knew it. And in many ways, that makes it even harder. Wanna go for a walk?"

Lila stood with her tray in her hands. I looked around, expecting her to have asked this question to someone else, but it was aimed at me.

"Me?"

"No, your clone. Of course you."

"Sure, I guess."

I picked up my tray and followed her outside. She didn't head in the direction of the bleachers, fortunately, but chose a bench in the park, where she sat down and stretched her legs. I noticed something was off about her.

"Are you okay?" I asked.

"Yeah, why?"

"You look a bit pale."

"I'm always pale," she said. "Part of my condition."

"The heart thing?"

She smiled. "Yeah, the heart thing."

"How serious is it?"

She shrugged. "I can't participate in any sports or get too excited, because my heart is so fragile due to those arteries being messed up. It's not good for me to get wound up about things, so I basically never do. I get therapy to deal with emotions and such, just to make sure that I don't unexpectedly get excited about things that could literally kill me. In a couple of years, I will most likely have major heart surgery."

"That sounds terrible," I said, surprised at the gravity of her situation. "Am I bothering you with my questions?"

"It's okay. I don't mind talking about it," she said. "Usually, I wind up not doing fun stuff with people because they know about my condition and then don't want to damage my already fragile physical state. I'm not made of china, you know. I won't break. I just have to be careful about what I do. It sucks being the one on the sidelines all the time. Sometimes I dream about moving to another town where no one knows about this and they won't bring up the subject all the time. Or where people won't offer me a hand as if I'm totally helpless."

"I can't even begin to imagine," I said. "It does seem that we have a few things in common. I'm constantly standing on the sidelines too. Not due to illness, but because of my parents. They isolate me in many ways."

"Now you've made me curious," Lila said. "Tell me more."

"You don't want to know, trust me. I wouldn't even know where to begin."

She gazed at her watch. "I do want to know. We still have twenty minutes before the bell rings. Why don't you give it a shot?"

I took a deep breath and started talking about my life at home, about Viola's nice parents and the amazing vacation in Westport. I ended with the upcoming birthday that I would be spending alone.

After I had finished and she reacted by muttering, "Damn," she placed her hand on my wrist and patted it.

"Looks like you could do with a new friend. And I have an idea to make your birthday less gloomy."

She smiled and leaned over, squeezing my shoulder. Again, that touch. Again, that warmth; it made my heart leap. That was the moment I pushed Viola out of my mind and became focused on Lila. Just like that, I had found a new friend. Wonderful, lovely Lila Jenkins.

CHAPTER SIXTEEN

On my—rather dramatic—sixteenth birthday, Lila stood waiting for me at the entrance of the movie theater. I was ten minutes late, out of breath, and upset about the whole Mr. Harrison thing, believing I had missed my golden opportunity to get to know Lila better, even though, deep down, I had not expected her to show up for the matinee. She had said she'd catch a movie with me. The whole thing had been her idea.

"You like movies and you hate being home, so why not have a movie marathon on your birthday? I can join for one movie, maybe more. How does that sound? They're doing a *Lord of the Rings* trilogy marathon like they do every year. It's usually pretty full. You like *Lord of the Rings*, I hope? Everyone loves it."

"Of course I do."

"Good. Then that is what you should do. And if you don't like it, you can find other movies, I'm sure."

The thought was too absurd to be real. Why would Lila, who barely knew me, spend her Sunday morning with me at the movies? She had her own friends and life; she didn't need anyone else. But there she was, a radiating light in the darkness, bright as the light of the elves Frodo had brought with him, which chased away all the gloominess. She had even brought a gift.

"You look great," she said, hugging me before giving me a small box. "Just a small thing for your sweet sixteen. Happy birthday! How are you?"

"Good," I said, determined not to speak about the situation with Mrs. Harrison and Marie. "You?"

"Doing very well, thank you. Ready to go in? The movie will start in ten minutes."

We walked in together, bought popcorn, and took our seats in the middle of the theater. There was a crowd, like she had predicted. More than half the theater was filled with people from different ages. I recognized some kids from school; other people were a bit older. Some were in their fifties and sixties.

"Everyone loves Frodo." Lila smiled, noticing me looking around.

I quickly unwrapped the present. In the small box lay a beautiful necklace with a small stone.

Silver, like all my other jewelry.

"It's gorgeous!" I said loudly, causing people to look at us. "Sorry, it's beautiful," I whispered. "You didn't have to do that. This must have cost a fortune."

"It's a fake stone. I'm not going to buy you precious gems on our first date," she said laughingly.

I became quiet, unsure of what to say. It felt as if the world had come to a standstill.

What did she say? Did I understand her right? I was shocked into silence.

"Here, let me put it on for you."

She took the necklace from me, unclasped it, and placed it around my throat. She lingered on the back of my neck, pulling aside my hair as she locked it. And nope, I was not mistaken. Her hands touched my skin a lot longer than they should have. Every single touch radiated like flames scorching me.

"There," she said when the fake gem rested on my throat. "Perfect for you, just as I thought. You look gorgeous."

I tried to find the right words to say, and then the lights went out and the music started, and before long, we were living and breathing Middle-earth, traveling to the world of the hobbits. But I found myself stuck in our own world, consciously aware of Lila sitting next to me, eating popcorn. Laughing when it was funny, cringing when it became intense, whispering to herself when things were happening that endangered the main characters. I tried to focus, and failed miserably. We didn't speak throughout the whole thing. For almost three hours, I wavered between wanting to enjoy the movie and wanting to reach for Lila's hand to hold.

When the movie was finished, she got up and stretched her back.

"Hungry. Need to pee. Come on."

She took my hand and pulled me up, and yes, there it was again, that hot, burning touch that made me forget everything. I felt things I shouldn't be feeling, and I just wanted to kiss her so badly.

I shook my head lightly, grabbed my things, threw the empty popcorn tub into the trash can, and walked outside after her, into the theater lobby. Several people were waiting in line for hot dogs, while others were buying sodas, candy, and popcorn. The line for the bathroom was fortunately not that long. We walked into the bathroom and choose two stalls next to each other.

I sat down with my head resting between my hands, trying to come to my senses. Was this really happening? Was I here with this gorgeous girl, who seemed to be attracted to me? Or was I imagining it all, like I had done with Viola? I couldn't risk making the first move again— just *couldn't*. Going through this a second time would emotionally kill me. No, I had to get it together and realize this was all in my head. It had to be.

No one in Love Hill acted on their feelings toward people of the same gender. No one. It just didn't happen. I could not even imagine kissing another girl. Didn't know what it would feel like. It just would not happen.

I flushed and walked out, and there she was, standing by the sink, washing her hands vigorously. I smiled, washed up, and looked at her.

"When are you going to say something?" she asked.

"What do you mean?"

"Haven't I given you enough hints by now?"

"I—"

"In school, during our lunch breaks, in between classes. I've said stuff I never say to anyone else. Never. You are the first one I'm saying these things to. The first girl I've ever given a necklace to. I've touched you several times—I even called this a date. And you didn't even react."

I was flabbergasted. "I thought I was imagining it," I whispered.

Now she looked stunned. "You mean to say that all this time, you've kept your feelings to yourself because you thought I wasn't serious?"

"Yeah."

Lila started laughing. She moved forward, and then her hand was on my face, her fingers stroking my hair. "You are so adorable, Syl. So freaking cute."

Standing alone in the bathroom, I took my chance, leaned forward, and kissed her. Right there and then, I took the first step toward something that would be considered blasphemy in our town. My mind went numb, my brain melted, and I refused to think about the possible consequences if I got this all wrong. But I didn't. She opened her mouth and returned the kiss. When we released each other, out of breath, she gazed into my eyes.

"Want to forget about parts two and three and go have a bite to eat somewhere quiet?"

"Oh yeah," I said. "That sounds good. But only if we can finish watching the other two at some point."

"I have a big TV in my room and a Netflix account."

"Sounds perfect."

Lila grabbed my hand, squeezed my fingers, and pulled me out of the bathroom. But by the time we walked back into the lobby, we had let go. Because even though things had changed between us, they would never change in Love Hill.

CHAPTER SEVENTEEN

Sometimes you just feel it when things are exactly how they should be. It was like that with Lila and me. For the first time in my life, there was someone listening to me, someone who thought the things I had to say were interesting. We talked about our lives quite a bit. She was happier than I was, or so it seemed. She had a good relationship with her mom and dad, both hardworking, decent people.

Lila had a half sister whom she saw now and then, the product of her dad's first marriage (his wife had passed away from cancer), and she had a large family and many friends. She was close with her cousin, who was a bit of a quirky person, and she was into meditation and self-help. The medical issue was an unfortunate matter (her words, not mine), but it was something she could live with. She had accepted that this would be a part of her life and saw it as a challenge but not an issue.

She wanted to study economics and step into the world of accountancy. She was good with numbers. She had this dream of working alongside her parents in their businesses, supporting them wherever she could. She already did now and then. She had a natural talent for it. The combination of meditation and an analytical mindset worked perfectly well for her. "It may not seem like the most interesting job in the world, but doing the books for my parents won't stress me out. I know I will never be able to have a normal life or have a full-time job, but I won't be one of those women who are dependent on their well-earning partners."

I laughed. "Like so many others here."

"Yep. I don't want to stay in Love Hill my entire life. Maybe someday, though, I'll decide to move away and work on the next bestselling novel from home, in a quiet house on the beach somewhere, where I am surrounded by warmth and waves and tourists enjoying themselves."

"A beach house in Hawaii?"

"Yeah, something like that."

"What would you write about?"

"Girls like us. People who have to hold back because of their surroundings."

"That would be amazing."

Lila and I spent that entire birthday afternoon talking about everything. I told her all about Viola, Mr. Harrison, and what had happened that morning, and she listened sympathetically, with her hand on mine, which she only pulled back when the waitress came to take our order.

"Your friend Viola is not exactly nice to you, is she?"

I shrugged. "I'm used to it."

"She's not my type of person."

"How would you know?" I said, feeling a need to defend Viola. "She has her good days too. I don't want you to think or talk badly about her."

"Is she still your friend today?"

"I think so."

"Then let me ask you this question: Is she your friend because you want her to be or because she really is?"

"She really is."

"Then why aren't you over there right now?"

"What?"

"Her father passed away, and you're sitting here with me. Why are you not there?"

"She doesn't want me there."

Lila frowned. "Listen, Syl, it's none of my business, and truth be told, we barely know each other, even though I've had my eye on you for ages."

I blinked, surprised.

"I've seen how Viola treats you. This didn't start with Steve, you know. The distance between you two has been there for a long time. She's been gaslighting you. She's been treating you like her appendix, like something that she needs to tag along. Everyone at school knew it, and a lot of people were wondering when you would break free of her. We all like you, but many of us don't like her."

I blinked again. "Was it really that bad?"

"Oh yeah. We all saw it, and a lot of us felt sorry for you. But sometimes you need to figure out for yourself what you want."

I flushed. "Is that why you're here today? Because you pity me?"

"No! I'm here because I like you. I've been interested in you for a long time, but you know how it goes around here. I couldn't show my feelings for you, and honestly, I figured you weren't interested. I knew that you liked girls—girls like us feel that sort of thing—but I was sure you were deeply in love with Viola."

"I thought I was too," I confessed. "I told her so, and that's when she started avoiding me."

"Because girls like her are scared of girls like us. She thinks we're incapable of having a regular friendship—which is bullshit, of course. It's the fear of the unknown. You can't blame her. Growing up in this town is hard enough as it is, let alone when you're gay."

"I know," I said with a sigh.

I was surprised and scared, but also excited. The moment we said those words, we both seemed to realize we were admitting to each other that we shared the same feelings. That we were, in fact, contemplating the possibility of starting a relationship. That we were willing to take that risk, despite what others would have to say about it.

"Are you bisexual?" she asked.

"No. You?"

"Nope." She smiled. "I don't plan on marrying some guy or ignoring my feelings as I get older. No, thank you. I'll find that house on the beach, and I will never share it with a man. I hope to share it with someone like you."

I exhaled a breath of relief, which I didn't even realize I'd been holding until Lila started laughing.

"You really are afraid that this is all a dream, aren't you?"

"Oh yeah."

She glanced around, saw that no one was looking at us, leaned over the table, and quickly kissed me.

"I like you," she said. "And I already like being with you. Can't we just live in the moment and see where this leads?"

"I'd like that," I said.

And that was exactly what we did in the months that followed.

To the outside world, we were new best friends who had found each other, who liked hanging around together. Who had a lot of common ground.

We started sharing friends. Sometimes we hung around with her crowd, who happily embraced me as Lila's new bestie. Sometimes we sought the company of the crowd I used to share with Viola too. They still liked having me around, even when Viola wasn't there. She was mostly with Steve now, and everyone accepted that.

Lila and I loved hanging out. We liked the same movies, spent hours at her place watching marathons of the classics (*Scream, I Know What You Did Last Summer, Pulp Fiction*), but also spent hours bickering about new series on television that we loved or hated (*Stranger Things, Fargo*, whatever was new that week). I had this thing for serial killer stories, and she was into climate change documentaries.

We both had a passion for fantasy and sci-fi. The lamest movies made us laugh until tears rolled down our cheeks.

When at her place, in the confines of her room, we could hug and kiss and know that we were an item. But when her parents were around, we acted as if we were friends only. I didn't tell Marie about her, even though I was certain that she knew. My excitement was palpable as I told stories about her, I'm sure. My parents didn't have a clue; they were ignorant as ever, and I wanted to keep it that way.

Months flew by. My boring life was no longer dull. Every day was one to look forward to. Christmas became one of the best times ever. Lila came over to our house all the time during the holiday period and we spent it with Marie, watching cheesy Christmas movies for hours.

Spring came quicker than it normally did. We were joined at the hip, and for a while, it seemed as if things would forever stay that way. We lived in the moment, just like Lila had suggested, and I enjoyed every second of it.

Until, of course, Viola came back into my life with a vengeance.

CHAPTER EIGHTEEN

Viola had one skill that made her stand out: She used people's emotions against them without giving it a second thought. She was able to convince others that their tragedies weren't so bad, and that hers were the worst.

She also didn't hesitate to use her own emotions to get things done. After all, *she* had lost her father. *She* had been lied to. *She* needed therapy. *She* needed pity and sympathy and help. Never other people. Of course not. Not even Steve, who had been her steady boyfriend for eight months now.

In Viola's mind, only one thing mattered: herself—and Steve took the brunt of it until he could no longer put up with her antics. After a major blowout, he finally dumped her at the end of the school year. By that time, he had turned into a shadow of himself.

They had seemed like the perfect pair on the outside. Both attractive, smart, and willing to do anything to make their relationship work. However, they reminded me a lot of my parents in many ways, and I truly believe that if they had held on throughout the years, they would have become exactly the same.

But fortunately for Steve, he started figuring out that being in a relationship with Viola was not exactly a gift, that he would have to withstand a lot of storms if he stuck with her, something he wasn't willing to do.

After that particular lunch break way back in October, where Viola had shunned me and publicly chosen to be with Steve, she never once left his side. She was a leech. His friends had to put up with her; her friends hardly saw her anymore. She claimed him twenty-four seven.

Steve started neglecting his assignments, barely showed up for practice, and didn't seem to care about anything except for her. Viola reined him in and held on to him, probably—knowing her—terrified that someone would step in and sweep him away.

I read a lot of books about psychotic and narcissistic behavior, and she checked all the boxes. And Steve enabled her behavior. He was so in love with her that he was blind to her flaws, like I always had been. He just didn't seem to care about anyone's opinion.

During those months, I was hanging out all the time with Lila, and she was all over Steve.

We were done, and had been for a while now. I'd had enough of being treated like a useless object. Besides, she had Steve now.

Steve became her beacon of light in the darkness she went through after Mr. Harrison passed away. Their relationship became a lot more intense. She was no longer treating him like dirt, but seeing him as a means of support. This was the role Steve took on, and he did it well.

For months after Mr. Harrison's passing, it seemed as if stability had finally settled into their relationship, but nobody outside of Steve knew the dark secret Viola carried with her during that time. That all came to an explosive reveal at the school's summer dance in June.

I went to the dance with Lila, of course, but not as a couple. We were an item, but still without anyone knowing, or at least not mentioning it. I was pretty convinced that some kids—or maybe all—knew about us. How could it remain hidden when we were constantly together?

Lila and I had a good time, danced and laughed and had fun with other people. It was an amazing night, one I will always think of fondly. Due to her medical condition, Lila couldn't dance all night long, so we sat and talked. Our feet touched beneath the long tablecloth, and sometimes we held hands under the table too.

"I don't want to stay for too long," she said. "Can we go out for ice cream?"

"Sounds great," I said. "How about a movie too? There's a midnight screening of *Poltergeist*. Wanna go?"

"Oh yeah."

We loved going to the movies because it gave us the opportunity to sit close and hold hands. We had made a habit out of going into a theater at the last minute and choosing a row with little to no people in it. Then we would wait for the lights to turn down before holding hands. Sometimes we would sneak in a kiss. I loved those moments.

So there we were, sitting at that table at the summer dance, getting ready to leave, when suddenly Viola walked over and plunked down in the empty chair next to me, smiling radiantly at me while ignoring Lila.

Viola had a Coke with her, but I could smell immediately that there was something off about it. My dad drank whiskey every night; I knew the smell all too well. But there was another scent I couldn't place.

"Are you drinking?" I asked.

"Drinking? Only a Coke," she said, lifting her glass. "Cheers, ladies."

She drank, and when she did, her hand shook. I was shocked. This couldn't be Viola, who was always in control of everything.

"She's smoking too," Lila mentioned casually. "And I don't mean cigarettes. Don't you smell it?"

That was the scent I couldn't place. Some of the older kids at school smoked joints, testing their boundaries. They usually went to the bleachers so that no one would notice. I had never tried it; it didn't interest me at all.

"My God," I whispered, watching Viola drink her whiskey-Coke in one haul. "Are you crazy?"

"Nope. Just sad."

"Why are you sad?" I asked, stepping right into her trap even though Lila had reached for my hand. I knew she was trying to tell me to back off and not fall for Viola's bullshit, but of course I was doing exactly what my former best friend had wanted me to do.

"I'm sad because everyone dumps me all the time. You. My dad. Steve. Not even my mom likes me these days."

She seemed bleary eyed, and I could tell immediately that this was not the first time she had been drinking. There was something in that expression that told me the whole story. Small details came back that I had been ignoring: Her leaving for the bathroom all the time while in class, causing our teachers to groan. Her scurrying off to the bleachers, albeit with Steve, probably to drink and smoke. Her no longer eating in the cafeteria. Her losing weight. I had seen her swaying before on the school grounds. She chewed gum all the time.

"How long have you been drinking?" I asked.

She waved her hand and ignored my question. She reached out for me, tried to touch me. I shot up; my chair fell over. Lila was on her feet, too, and she pulled me away. It felt as if I had been stung by a bee.

"I want us to be friends again," Viola slurred. "Please, Syl. I love you. I can't go on without you."

I didn't reply.

"Stop ignoring me, Syl! I exist!"

Her words hung thickly in the air. Around us, people were watching. The music was still playing, and there were a lot of kids on the dance floor, but all attention had been drawn to us. She didn't even speak loudly; she was barely able to say the words. But there they were, like bullets on their way to shoot me down.

"Go to hell," I said. I turned around and left the dance with Lila by my side.

The following Monday, we found out that Steve had finally dumped her a couple of days ago after months of misery and tragedy. He'd had enough of her drunken antics, of her addictions. Nobody blamed him. He just didn't know that his actions would mean the end of my happiness too.

THE TALE OF POOR MR. HARRISON

It starts coming together now, and that's what Annie is feeling too. She is very quiet, and I can tell that she's sad because she knows what's coming next.

"It's important that you know the whole truth about Viola's dad before I get to the point where she ruined my life," I tell her.

"Her dad?" Annie asks, confused.

"Yeah. And my mom."

"But I know what happened between them. What didn't you tell me before?"

"Something very important. I've told you about how my mom thinks and feels, how status and prestige are so important to her. How she thought my dad would never betray her. Until one day he did."

"Your father? What are you talking about? Your mom was the one having the affair with Mr. Harrison."

"That's the whole thing. It was my dad who fell in love with someone else, but he didn't fall for a woman. He fell for a man."

"Mr. Harrison," Annie says. "Oh my God. And nobody knew?"

"They hid it well. But me? I should have seen it right from the start. The annual vacations to Westport, the way Mr. Harrison longingly stared at men as they held hands. I think he wanted to live like that, but he was afraid to. I know how that feels, so I'm not judging any decisions that he made."

"But your dad?"

"He liked both men and women, and I'm convinced that my mom knew this. Maybe she ignored it for years, or maybe she didn't want to know. Whatever the case, she didn't do anything about it, convinced he had chosen her. Until the rumors started to spread about Mr. Harrison having an affair with someone powerful in town."

"And in a town like ours, no one even considered the possibility that this someone could be a man."

"Exactly. My mom had to realize at some point that the rumors were referring to my dad, which meant she had to find out if they were true. Since my dad liked men, too, and often went golfing with Mr. Harrison, she put two and two together easily. She found out they were meeting in some dingy motel miles away from Love Hill, often staying there overnight. Perhaps that's what pissed her off the most. All this time, she believed my dad was out of town because he was closing a deal with a major telecommunications company, which could mean a large expansion of their business. My dad did broker that deal, but it didn't take as long as he claimed."

"How long did this go on?"

"I can't say for sure, but I'm guessing months. My mom immediately knew that this was a serious relationship and that she risked losing everything. If my dad decided at some point that he wanted to leave her for this man, he would leave town and she would lose the house, the company, and the money that she felt was rightfully hers. But most of all, she would lose every ounce of respect she held so dearly. There were plenty of people out there who wanted to see her fall flat on her face. No, she couldn't have that, not in her town. So she came up with a plan. One that would ultimately end up indirectly causing my death."

"Let me guess," Annie says. "Viola found out, too, during that time you guys no longer spoke."

"Oh yeah. But only when her dad was already dead. My mom did something horrible. She had photos, phone records, and screenshots of text messages. She dropped all these pieces of evidence in my dad's lap and confronted him with the truth."

"Your dad must have been shocked."

"He was. 'I want you to break things off with him,' she told him. 'And if I don't?' he said. 'Oh, I won't ruin you, but I will destroy him, his precious wife, and their ignorant brat. I will tear apart their lives and all they hold dear. They have a lot more to lose than we do.'"

"Terrible," Annie whispers.

"Yes, because he knew he had no choice in the matter. He caved quickly, like he always did. My mom figured that the church would forgive her for her infidelity, but they would never forgive my dad for his, so she decided to take the blame and make my dad sound like a saint for putting up with her betrayal."

"But in return, Mr. Harrison had to leave town," Annie remarks.

"Yes. If not, she would make all the evidence public, which would destroy the family. The next day, she contacted Mr. Harrison and told him to meet her at the same dingy motel. For Mr. Harrison, there would be no doubt in his mind that she knew the truth. My dad had already called to warn him. And Mr. Harrison responded."

"He admitted that he had a thing with your dad?"

"Yes. He said he wanted to leave his family for my dad, that he wanted to move to California and start a new family with him. That he was tired of living a closeted life in Love Hill."

"And then your mom used all of her emotional blackmailing skills to tell him what this would do to his wife and daughter, right?"

"Exactly. She showed him the photos and threatened to put them on the internet. Mr. Harrison still loved his wife and his precious daughter, so it would not have been that difficult to convince him that they would stand to lose everything. My mom must have realized she had hit his soft spot. Despite all of this determination to abandon his family, Mr. Harrison obviously realized this would mean the end of them. He didn't want that."

"So your mom persuaded him to move to California on his own and start a new life there, far away from your dad, right?"

"That's right," I say. "And when he still didn't cave in, she told him that my dad had chosen his business over him. That he wasn't there himself because he didn't want to sacrifice everything. Which was true, because otherwise, he really would have been there that day."

"Awful," Annie says. "This is really bad."

"It is. My mom's words must have hit home hard, because two days later, he left. A few months after that, the night before Viola's sixteenth birthday, he was killed by a car while crossing the street in LA. Nobody will ever know if he caused that accident on purpose. Viola's mom told her the truth on the day of the funeral. She had always known that Mr. Harrison loved my dad. She must have put two and two together too. Because that day, my birthday, she didn't come to accuse my mom of adultery. She came to blame her for chasing away Mr. Harrison."

"How did you find out the truth?"

"My mom told me a few weeks later. She said that I had the right to know, but I believe that she was afraid Viola would tell me herself. She had figured out that Mrs. Harrison knew the truth, and so she knew that the secret might come out."

"That was decent of your mom to do."

"Was it? I think she did it to drive a wedge between me and my dad. She wanted me to know that he caused all of this so that I would be more lenient towards her. She created the exact opposite."

"Because you are gay too."

"Yes. I can't for the life of me understand why my dad, as an adult, would have chosen a pathetic marriage over his one true love. He could have come out."

"You hid your relationship with Lila too," Annie remarks.

"True, but we weren't adults. I had already made plans to leave Love Hill forever. Lila was planning to apply to Stanford too. We were going to share a room together. We had it all figured out. And then I told my mom I was gay."

"How did she react?"

"She looked me in the eye and said, 'Of all the things you could have inherited from your dad, this is what he gave you to deal with? I feel sorry for you.'"

Annie looks stunned. "I'm so sorry, Syl. That's rough."

"It was, but not as rough as her ignoring everything that came after. My mom has always been good at pushing away bad things, like her husband falling in love with another man. Like me growing up lonely and hungry for affection. Like Viola changing after that day, or the relationship between us taking a nasty turn. Viola coming after the one person I loved. When Viola took her anger out on me the moment she got the chance, my mom didn't intervene. And it was her fault, all of it. She indirectly killed that man."

"What do you mean? What happened?"

"Viola was devastated when she learned the truth. She became this angry, upset, nasty version of herself that I couldn't understand. Her anger built up gradually, and she started lashing out at me after Steve broke up with her, because I wouldn't go back to the way things were. He took the brunt of her wrath, and once he was out of the picture, I became her target."

"But why? How could she be mad at you? You had nothing to do with it."

"I know," I say. "But it does make sense. She had lost her father, while mine just continued his life as if nothing had happened. It seemed unfair. I don't know what I would have done in her position. I understood the anger, the pain, and her reaction."

"So you put up with it."

"Yes, I did. At the expense of my relationship with Lila, who didn't get where I was coming from."

"Was Viola drinking when she drove tonight?"

I smile sadly. "She was always drinking. But ironically enough, tonight she wasn't. This was one of the rare moments that she was sober. I guess that makes my death even worse. She knew exactly what she was doing."

"Can you tell me what she did tonight? What really happened in that car?"

"I will," I say. "But first, you need to know what happened on the night Lila died."

PART FOUR: THE STORY OF THE UNSPEAKABLE TRAGEDY

CHAPTER NINETEEN

I read this story once about a couple who had been together for over fifty years and did everything as a team. They sang and performed as a duo, they traveled, they had the same hobbies. They basically spent every waking minute together. They simply could not live without each other.

When the woman unexpectedly died, the man passed away in his sleep less than a month later. She had been sick for a while, but he was as strong as an ox his entire life, even at the age of seventy-five. They said he died from a broken heart, that he couldn't exist without his wife.

It must be so extraordinary to love someone so much that you would end up dying from a broken heart. I'd assumed the story of this couple was wildly exaggerated, never believing that people could actually pass away like that, but today, I know what it feels like. I didn't die in my sleep from a broken heart, but I came close. First when Viola had started ignoring me, then when I lost Lila. My heart shattered from the guilt of what happened to her.

I can honestly say right now that I have not lived a full life in three hundred and sixty-five days, and if I had existed beyond tonight, I would probably not have lived a complete life for as long as I existed. And the one person to blame for that is Viola.

When Lila told me that I had been gaslighted by Viola, I had no clue what she was talking about. It felt strange to even consider the concept that I had, in fact, been manipulated into mistrusting my own emotions and feelings, but in many ways, this was exactly what she had done. Not just to me, but also to Steve and her own mother as well.

Viola always knew what she was doing. She manipulated me every time we spoke, or when she came back to "apologize" and then shunned me a second time, knowing how much that would hurt. She did all this on purpose, and she did it again when she came back once more and dumped all her issues on me. Over the past year, she had tried to do it multiple times. She would send me text messages when I was with Lila. She would call me in the middle of the night. I'd answer the first few times, and then I switched off my phone.

When we were in school—her with Steve and whoever was left of his friends, me with Lila and friends of our own—she would sometimes just show up at our table, wanting to talk. More often than not, the subject would be me, and she'd weave these tales about stuff we'd done when we were younger.

She ignored Lila blatantly. In her eyes, my girlfriend—*friend* to her—simply did not exist. I knew this was her way of telling me she still had control over me, and I fell for it. Every time she texted, I would sit there nervously, not knowing what to send back, until I couldn't stop thinking about it.

She would send nasty messages too.

I know that you're messing around with her. Wonder if she knows what a bitch you are?

Or:

You have no heart. One day you love me, the next, you love her. What is it? You can't have both.

Or:

You broke my heart. How could you do that to me? Stop ghosting me! Pick up your damn phone.

I never told Lila about any of these messages. I made sure that all the notifications on my phone were off and had blocked Viola, which didn't stop her from getting new numbers and still reaching out to me. I tried to reason with her one night, when I couldn't stand it anymore, and went knocking on her door, demanding that she stop (she wasn't there, and I couldn't do that to her mom, who already hated me and wouldn't have believed me).

One day at school, I walked up to Steve and told him everything, showed him the messages, and pleaded with him to help me. He frowned, told me he would deal with it, and that was it. She stopped texting me. Whatever he had said had worked, and I was willing to believe I would be safe, thanks to him.

I never told Lila anything to protect her, but that night at the summer dance, she realized what Viola had been doing. I could tell by her reaction to Viola's words.

"Stop ignoring me. I exist!"

That night of the summer dance, when Viola interrupted the magic, Lila and I left. We didn't go out for ice cream, nor did we see the midnight showing. We went home—her to her place, me to mine.

It was the first time since we'd become friends that there was distance between us. I had never imagined that this could possibly happen. Lila was so different from Viola in every single way, but the feeling of loss was exactly the same.

Viola sent me a text before we'd even walked out of the gym. I found that out later, when I checked my phone and saw that she had used someone else's number.

We need to talk. Please don't ignore me.

Lila started walking faster through the parking lot. She had picked me up in her mom's car, a really cool MINI. She was obviously upset. She was moving faster than she should, which caused her to start breathing faster. I knew all the telltale signs by now, how it sounded when she was overexerting herself. I could tell she was on the verge of losing herself in this stressful moment, forgetting what she was dealing with, which meant she would get exhausted and could simply pass out.

"Hey," I said, catching up to her. "Stop running. Don't do this."

"Don't do what?" she snapped.

"You're angry."

"Yes, I am!"

"Don't be," I begged. "Come on, Lila, nothing happened. Nothing's changed between us. I won't go back there."

"You already did." Lila turned to face me while tears streamed down her cheeks. "Why is it that every single time she sends you a message, you take out your phone and then start brooding over a reply? Did you really think I wouldn't know? Never in all these months have I complained about the way you work yourself up to a point that all the fun is gone in whatever we're doing at that moment. I know what she's doing to you, and I hate that you feel you have to hide it from me."

"I'm not—"

"Do me a favor and stop lying."

"Okay," I said. "Yes, she's been bothering me, but I'm so used to doing things on my own all the time I didn't feel it necessary to stress you out about it. I'm sorry, okay? I didn't mean to lie."

"You felt it necessary to withhold information from me because you felt I couldn't handle it physically and mentally, is that it?"

"Yes," I said softly.

Lila snorted. "You know what? I was wrong about you. You really are like all the others, and probably even worse. Here I was, thinking I could finally have a normal relationship with someone, and then it turns out that *you* are the worst of them all."

"I wanted to protect you."

"I don't need protection!"

"You're getting worked up as we speak. Don't you get it? I need to keep Viola away from us."

"You don't need to do anything," she snapped, and I saw a version of Lila that reminded me so much of Viola that it scared the hell out of me. This whole time I'd been thinking my girlfriend was the complete opposite of my former best friend, when in fact, they were pretty much the same. Didn't they say that people often sought out the same character traits in different relationships? She clutched her chest and walked over to her car, and I felt a sudden desperation not to let her go. I couldn't shake the feeling that she might not be alive in the morning if she went home like this. She would be lost to this world. I had to get her calm again.

The moment she reached for her car door, I slammed it shut. She looked at me with an irritated scowl. I was getting more desperate by the second, horrified by the possibility of losing her like this.

"Lila, I'm sorry! I really am. I care so much about you. Please don't go. I love you."

She calmed down, and suddenly I was in her arms and she was shushing me. I leaned against her, listening to her breathing and her heart. Her arms were around me, her hands ruffled my hair.

"You love me," she whispered.

"Yeah, I do."

"I love you too."

I smiled through my tears. "You do?"

"Always have. It's okay. I won't leave you, I promise. I'm sorry."

When she let go of me, it felt as if my heart had once again been ripped out, only to be put back in place. This was the most important person in my life, and I had almost lost her because of Viola.

"Let's go home," she said.

Lila was calm again, and I could feel a peace descending on her that had not been there before. I got in on the passenger side, and she drove in silence. But I couldn't get calm. For the first time, I'd been confronted with the fact that Lila's life was at stake. Before this moment, I had never really understood that, and now it scared me to death.

CHAPTER TWENTY

The summer was extraordinary in all facets. First, there was the unexpected peace and quiet that followed the school dance. Viola had called in sick the last couple of days of school. Nobody knew what was going on, exactly, but according to rumor, her mom had found out about her drinking and had sent her to a rehab center. I didn't know if that was true, but I sure hoped that it was.

Regardless, we didn't see her for a long time.

Lila and I never spoke of the incident in the parking lot again. She called me in the morning and apologized for going through the roof like that. We agreed to talk about it later, but we never did. During lunch break there were a lot of things to do, and after school, there were parties. Everyone was celebrating the upcoming summer. The weather was amazing, people were in cheerful moods, and we just wanted to feel free for a while.

In the days that followed, Lila became herself again. She was that happy, optimistic girl I had come to love so much, and I started feeling better and letting go of my fear of losing her. What stuck with me, though, was an urgency to never withhold information from her again. It was my fault she had gone off the rails like that. I had lied, not her. I vowed never to upset her again, to make sure she would never be endangered again. Now that I knew what anger did to her body, I would make sure she never had a reason to be mad at me.

We spent the entire summer together, either at her place or mine. We met with friends; went to parties; enjoyed lingering by the pool, going to the movies, or making day trips. I didn't mind doing most of the driving, as she was always dependent on her mom's schedule. She pitched in for gas and would often buy our lunch, even when I told her she didn't have to.

That summer was the best one I'd ever had, even better than that one week in Westport. When I started thinking about that, I felt homesick. So one day, on a whim, I asked her if she would like to go to Westport for a couple of days. She smiled because we both knew how free people were in that town.

"I would love to go somewhere with you," she said, "but I'm not sure my parents will allow it."

"We can at least ask, right?"

"Sure."

So she asked her parents, and to our surprise, they said yes. It was only a two-hour drive, so in case of emergency, we could drive back easily. To this day, I am not sure if her parents even realized why we wanted to go there—or maybe they simply didn't want to know—but her mom called and talked with the small hotel's owner about us checking in on our own and booked a room for us with her credit card.

I was counting on the fact that Viola would never go back to Westport. This was the time for us to be ourselves, without anyone spying on us. Lila loved every single minute of it. Those days with her are in my heart forever.

When we came back, we had to prepare for the next school year, which was starting in ten days. We had been invited to a party at Georgina's house, one of the girls from the group we usually hung out with. Feeling rested and ready for our senior year, Lila and I went.

When we got there, there was already a big crowd. The place was packed. People were lingering by the pool, more were in the house. Loud music was playing, and you could barely hear each other. They had hired a local DJ, and the mood was amazing.

Lila and I enthusiastically greeted the people in our regular crowd and found a place by the pool. There was a huge vegetarian buffet set up with delicious food. I went to get two plates for us, but when I got in line, I felt a tap on my shoulder.

There she was: Viola. Sobered up—or so it seemed. I was shocked to see her. She wasn't carrying a beer or a whiskey-Coke, and her eyes were clear. She wasn't high, she didn't smell like liquor, and she seemed a bit like her old self again.

"What are you doing here?" I blurted out.

"I was invited. How have you been?"

"Fine."

"Are you with Lila?"

"Yes."

"Good, I want to apologize to her."

Oh no.

"You've done enough damage as it is," I said sharply. "Please leave us alone."

"Syl, I'm serious. I messed up. I came to tell you I'm sorry, and then I'll be out of your hair. Part of my program is that I need to face what I've done, and that also means apologizing to the people I've harmed, like Steve, Lila, and you."

"No, thanks," I said. "I don't want to be part of your plan to redeem yourself. Please get out of my face."

Of course there was a crowd around us, and I could tell they were listening in on the conversation. They had no clue about all the things I'd been through with Viola, so of course they only saw me refusing to accept her apology. I grew impatient, thinking of Lila outside by the pool.

"Just leave us alone, okay? You want to apologize? Fine, I'll relay the message. But get this: Every time Lila sees you and gets worked up, you're basically endangering her life, and I'm not willing to risk that. So consider yourself forgiven."

Viola's lower lip twitched and she was shaking. And I felt myself melting for her, like I've always done.

"I'm sorry, okay?" I said, softer this time. "I just don't want to risk hurting Lila."

"I understand," Viola said. "I apologize. I hope you'll accept that."

"I do. Thanks."

Viola moved away. Someone behind me said, "That was amazingly brave."

It was. It really was. But I wasn't going to be fooled again. With Viola, there was always a reason why she did things. Selfish, egocentric reasons. This time, I wouldn't fall for them.

I went back to the pool and gave Lila her plate. She was sitting in the shade in her T-shirt and shorts, with her sunglasses on, unaware of what had just transpired. I knew I had to tell her before Viola showed up by the pool. The evening sun was setting, and soon it would be dark out. The music was turned up; people started dancing on the lawn. Most had left the poolside by now, but we stayed put.

"You were gone for a while," Lila said, looking at the plate of food. "That really looks delicious."

"Extra cheese on the side," I said, then hesitated. "Viola's here."

"Is she, now?"

"Yeah."

Lila smiled all of a sudden.

"You already knew," I remarked.

"Oh yeah."

"You were testing me."

"Yep."

I punched her gently. "You are evil."

"No, just having fun."

"You're not jealous or upset?"

"Nope."

I started eating and Lila did the same, and as we sat there, enjoying that delicious food, I started realizing that the blowout we'd had right before summer had been the best thing to push this relationship into one of blind trust. I had been stupid withholding the truth from Lila earlier.

"I'm sorry I didn't tell you about her last year," I blurted out.

"I'm sorry that I blew up in your face," she said. "You were so scared; I'll never forget that moment. I don't know what came over me."

I smiled. "I do. You were jealous and possessive."

"And that scared you."

"Actually, it made me feel really wanted. Even if you became this crazy fury that didn't want to share me with someone else."

We were whispering because of people nearby, still cautious about how people saw us, too aware of the fact that Love Hill's spies were everywhere. We were still just best friends hanging out, planning on going to Stanford together and sharing a room.

"You are amazing, do you know that?" Lila said.

"Nope. But if you keep on telling me, I might start believing you someday."

"I'll do my best not to withhold any compliments, then."

The last two people traded the pool for the lawn, and we were alone now, looking at each other as the sun went down at last and lights brightened up the area. Several light bulbs shone, dancing on cords over the entire area. The DJ was playing from the patio; the music was loud and infectious. Everyone started to dance except for us. We held hands and kissed.

It was just perfect, this very moment. It was amazing, the sum of all things that had led up to today. I couldn't believe my happiness, couldn't trust that everything would stay the way it was, but hoped it would grow by the day. This was my life now, and I was living it to the fullest, with a lot of good things to look forward to.

I felt happy and excited for the upcoming year. One more year, and then we could really live together in a dorm room, just the two of us. It was a prospect I was looking forward to so much. It made everything else bearable. I couldn't stop kissing her.

"And here we are," a voice said.

Even before looking up, I knew it was Viola. Of course it was her.

CHAPTER TWENTY-ONE

If I had ever had the slightest hope that Viola had changed during her rehab stay, it was shot down by the way she was looking at us. A sly smile appeared on her lips. She had been drinking between our confrontation at the buffet and now. It was obvious, since she didn't have a soda in her hands.

"So," she said, "how have you guys been doing?"

Lila remained seated by the pool, blatantly ignoring Viola. I should be doing the same, I knew that. But this was Viola, and I still had a soft spot for her despite everything. I got up so that we were at the same height and I wouldn't feel so small.

"Good. What are you doing here?"

She ignored my question. "You two are together?"

"We are an item, yes," I said. "But that's none of your business. You have nothing to do with my life anymore, so I suggest you move on."

"It is my business now. You two, huh? Since when?"

"Some time," I whispered.

"How long, Syl? Since you came on to me? Or earlier than that?"

"That is also none of your business," I said, feeling trapped.

"Come on, we used to be best friends, and you didn't even bother introducing me to your lover. That says a lot, doesn't it?"

"We are not—"

I stopped, gazing at Lila, realizing my mistake. Viola kept on pushing, and I kept on answering like I always did, feeling the all-too-familiar urge to defend myself, even though I *knew* that this was exactly what she wanted.

"Come on, we're old friends. Don't act this way. I apologized, didn't I? Why are you so mean to me?"

"Just go, Viola."

"I don't think so."

She took a soda, sat down by the pool, and looked Lila in the eye, who still hadn't said anything and was probably doing her best to stay calm. I sat down, too, and squeezed Lila's hand in support, but she quickly let go.

"So tell me, how's life treating you?" Viola asked.

I didn't reply.

"Come on, Syl, don't be like that. I offered you a truce and you accepted it earlier, but now you are treating me like a pariah again when all I offered is friendship. Why can't we be friends?"

Lila finally spoke. "You don't know the meaning of friendship. You're an abuser."

"I'm— Excuse me?!" Viola tilted her head and looked at us with disdain.

"You heard me. For years you've been treating Syl like garbage, using her for whatever you could. You never treated her with respect; you don't give a damn about her."

Lila coolly looked Viola in the eye, and for the first time, I saw her flinch. Oh yes, Lila stood up for me and Viola didn't know how to react. Someone had finally confronted her with her behavior, and she obviously didn't like it.

A nervous smile appeared on Viola's face. She looked at me with a mix of sadness and disgust. I had never seen her like that before, and I didn't like it. Couldn't bear it. Several events from the past flashed through my mind, things that had happened between us that were *not* upsetting or sad. That had been good. Like that week in Westport, or all the evenings I had spent at their house, feeling loved and welcomed.

All the moments in her bedroom watching movies together. The casual talks about whatever subject was on our minds.

Not everything had been bad, but a lot had also not been good. The many, many moments she took my toys and threw them away. And later on, how she took my homework and copied it without a single hesitation, without asking, sometimes getting me into trouble. The moments that she stood me up because I wasn't important enough. The times she actually mocked me in front of other people because I wasn't vocal enough. The times we went to parties and she mingled with people and I felt abandoned and sad. How she had treated me when she got together with Steve, after we'd found out about our parents having an affair. The many, many times she had made me feel small, stupid, and unworthy of being her friend, which I had ignored for far too long.

All that came back, too, and I realized I had always found reasons and explanations for her behavior. But not anymore. Viola Harrison was a spoiled brat, and I was done with her mistreating me.

"I thought we were friends," she said.

"No," I said. "Friends treat each other with respect and value their boundaries. You never did. Please go away."

"I'm hurting, Syl."

"Then find help elsewhere. We're done."

"You were always there for me."

"But you never were for me," I said.

Viola stood and looked at Lila, who kept on defying her with a look in her eyes that told Viola she'd had her chance with me and blown it.

Viola coughed and looked at me again.

"I came here tonight to tell you that I love you. It took me a long time to realize this, but I am in love with you. I was ignoring my feelings, like my dad had been, but I don't want to make his mistake. Syl, I want us to be together."

I was stunned. Lila gasped. My legs trembled when I stood up to face her. All these feelings raced through me like a high-speed train, and I felt weak and dizzy. If she had told me this one year ago, I would have been the happiest person on Earth. But now, it felt as if my world was collapsing and dragging me under with it.

"*Fuck you.*"

"Syl, come on!"

I took Lila by the hand, grabbed my bag, and walked away from the pool while the music continued to blare and people danced on the lawn. This was the second time Viola had ruined it for us, and I'd had it.

Out of the corner of my eye, I saw Viola following us.

"Syl, listen to me! I know things. Lila is not who she says she is. You're being fooled. Syl!"

"No!" I screamed, turning around and shoving her. "Stop ruining my life!"

"I'm not. I'm protecting you. Ask her what the truth is. Ask her!"

"You're crazy."

"No, I'm not, I swear. You have to trust me on this. We used to be friends. Did I ever betray you?"

I thought of all the times Viola had done good things for me, and then of all the times she had ruined it all again with her big mouth and her antics. Her selfish behavior was not forgotten. I couldn't trust her for the life of me, not after all she had done.

"Yeah, right," I said. "Just leave us the hell alone, or I swear I'll punch you so hard, you'll remember it for a long time."

"Syl, come on, it's me! Please hear me out, for old times' sake. You owe me that much."

"Leave. Us. Alone!" I screamed.

She was stunned and stopped going after us. I tried so hard to ignore what she had said, but there it was—that doubt she could create so easily. It had already started nagging at me. Of course it did. This was Viola, after all, and she always did this to me.

Lila was not who she said she was? Ask her about the truth? What the hell did she mean by that?

CHAPTER TWENTY-TWO

We sat in my car, Lila and I. I drove, she was quiet. We left without telling anyone we were going. I didn't think anyone would care. The party was still going at full force. In fact, it had just started. We could hear the music thundering, even from inside the car, with the radio playing a Justin Timberlake song.

I didn't know what to say, didn't know how to react. I was confused by everything that had just happened. Who the hell did Viola think she was? But most of all: What did she mean by what she'd said about Lila?

My overthinking mind went haywire. I went back to the first time I'd really spoken to Lila, then to what had happened at the movies, the things she had said. She had admitted to having her eye on me for some time. The moment we started hanging out, there'd been a connection. But didn't that happen with a lot of couples? What was wrong with that?

What was Viola talking about?

"Are you okay?" Lila finally asked.

"No."

"I'm sorry that she ruined our evening again."

"Me too."

"You're wondering what she was saying about me, why she would say that nonsense about me fooling you, aren't you?"

"Yes, I am," I said, focusing on the road. I was glad that driving gave me an excuse not to look at her.

"I don't know why she said that. I have no clue."

But there was something. I could hear it in her voice, could sense it in the way she reacted. She wasn't calm at all; she was nervous as hell. She was lying. For the first time, I realized she was holding things back too. Why did I always end up with people who lied to me through their teeth and felt they could get away with it?

"I know you're not telling me everything," I said.

"I am. I'm not lying."

"Now you are. I know you well enough by now to know when you're telling me everything and when there are things you don't want to share. What is it, Lila? What does she have on you? You might as well tell me now, because I am going to find out."

She placed her hand on my arm, but I didn't react to her touch. Something was broken between us. Tears rolled down my face; I rubbed them away viciously while speeding up. I didn't want to spend another moment in the car with someone who wouldn't hesitate to lie to me and kept on doing so despite my request to tell the truth. "Does it have something to do with her?"

She pulled back her arm, obviously taken by surprise by my remark.

"It does, doesn't it? She knows something about you, or maybe the two of you have a shared secret that I should be aware of. What's going on, Lila? Tell me the truth!"

"I can't. I won't."

"Why not?"

"It's— You wouldn't understand."

"Won't I? Why not? Is it that horrible that you would keep it from me? Is that why you didn't want Viola near me? She knows your secret, and you're terrified that she's going to share it with me, aren't you? Tell me!"

"Syl, you're speeding. Please slow down."

I was unconsciously pushing my foot down on the accelerator. We went faster and faster, but somehow I couldn't slow down. My heart raced, and I was getting angrier by the second. Was this how my world would always be? How I would continue to have relationships? Then I might as well end it now.

"Everyone in my life betrays me," I said. "My parents, Viola, you. Who's next?"

"Syl, I swear I didn't betray you. Please slow down. *Please!*"

I couldn't, not while the anger was growing inside me and I felt like I was going to burst out of my skin.

"I want to know the truth," I said. "Tell me now, or I swear I'm going to stop this car, ask you to get out, and you can go home on foot. I really don't care one way or the other, what's going to happen to you. I thought we were friends, Lila. Partners. I thought you loved me. But friends don't lie to each other."

"You did. Several times."

I laughed bitterly. "I *knew* you were going to use that at some point. But you know the difference between you and me? I did it to protect you. You're doing it to serve your own purposes, whatever they are."

"I swear that I care about you," she said, and started crying.

A car came from the other side, swerving over the road. Someone checking their cell phone or something, I'm sure. I honked the horn, and the car made another swerving gesture, this time to return back to their side of the road. The situation calmed me down instantly. I slowed and stopped the car on the side of the road, in a large, open area where kids from Love Hill often came to hang or make out.

Lila unbuckled and escaped from the car while I sat shivering like a leaf. I seriously contemplated leaving her right there, but my anger had dissipated and I only felt sadness. I turned off the engine, got out of the car, and looked at her as she stood there with her arms clutched over her chest.

"I want to know the truth," I said calmly. "If you really care about me, you will tell me right now."

"I'll lose you," she whispered.

"That will depend on the level of lies."

She sat down on a rock next to the large tree that had been there forever, and didn't look at me but at her feet.

"Viola asked me to date you."

I immediately saw red.

CHAPTER TWENTY-THREE

"*What* did you say?" I yelled, staring at Lila in disbelief.

"You heard me. Last summer, Viola came to me. We went out for ice cream and had a long talk about you. She said that you two were good friends once but that she was moving on and was afraid you wouldn't forgive her. She was looking for a replacement for her, so she asked me if I would be interested in you. She knew I was gay, knew that I liked you and would be interested. She said I was your type and you would fall for me, no questions asked."

I was stunned. I stood in that wide-open space, looking at Lila and suddenly seeing a whole new person.

"Look," Lila said, finally able to look me in the eye. "It wasn't as if this was an assignment or anything. I did like you before she even asked. It seemed logical to me that she would do this. I actually believed she had your best interest at heart. It was only later on that I started to realize she was manipulating you and everyone else. Her own friends told stories about how badly she would treat you when things didn't go her way. Or how nasty she could be. I didn't really know her that well, and when she invited me for that ice cream, explaining her plan, I didn't even realize that she wasn't doing this for your benefit, but for her own."

"Did she tell you I had a crush on her?" I asked hoarsely.

"No, she didn't. I had no idea until you told me that day at the diner. The more I spoke to you, the more details emerged, the clearer it became to me that she really was that nasty creature others took her for.

By that time, I was already falling head over heels for you and realized I couldn't tell you the truth. You wouldn't believe I wasn't her patsy, or that I didn't do this because I felt sorry for you."

A lot of things were falling into place now.

"We didn't really have that much in common, did we?" I said, referring to our movie nights and tastes in music and TV series.

"No. I actually like different things. She told me all about you, gave me a lot of details. And when the moment arose that day during lunch break, when you chose that seat next to me, I used that to get into your good graces."

"But why? Why would you do that? What did she have on you? Did she blackmail you?"

"Yes. She threatened to tell the world about me, which meant my life would become miserable in this town."

"How did she know?"

"She saw me kissing another girl at school about six months before you and I met. She said she wouldn't tell anyone to protect us, but when she called me that day, she used it against me. She threatened to tell and ruin our lives, mine and that girl's."

"So you allowed her to do this to you?"

"Yes, and I have been ashamed every day since. But you have to believe me when I tell you that I really love you and this wasn't a lie. The moment you and I started hanging out, I knew she had done me a favor. When she hooked up with Steve and sort of left us alone, I was so relieved. Then I found out how she was harassing you, so I went to her. She just smiled and said that she could do whatever she wanted."

"She showed her true colors, then."

"Yes." Lila stood and took my hands in hers. "You have to understand the other reason why I did this, Syl. Nobody in their right mind would date me. People have been avoiding me like the plague. But then you came along, and you didn't care about my disease. I was so happy that Viola did this to you, because it meant getting to know this gorgeous girl—inside and out—that I cared about more than life itself.

You mean the world to me, and it would break my heart if you told me to get lost from now on. But I would understand because I've lied and betrayed you. If it were the other way around, I would be angry too."

"That's just it, isn't it?" I said softly. "I can't trust you again, Lila. You've lied to me for eight months straight. You should have told me back then, not now. Would you ever have told me if Viola hadn't forced your hand?"

"I don't know," she admitted.

"Our relationship started on that lie. Here I am, having to find out that you are not the person I thought you were. You lied to my face, you made things up as you went along, going on information Viola fed to you. That's not okay, do you understand that? I can't just move past this and forget it ever happened."

"I know," she said. "I really do understand."

"Then give me the time and space to think things through. I can't just pretend that everything's fine when this is hanging over our heads."

"What are you going to do?" she asked, obviously afraid.

"I'm going to take you home. I don't want to see you in the next week or so. When I'm ready to talk about this, I'll let you know."

"You're going to leave me," she whispered, "aren't you?"

"I don't know."

She reached for my hand again, but I shook her off.

"Don't push me away," she pleaded. "*Please*, Syl. Please don't do this."

"I'm not doing anything except giving myself the time that *I* need, without looking at what others need," I said sharply, for the first time in my life defending my own rights. "You owe me this much. I need time to myself, don't you see? I'm fed up with all the lies. I'm going home. Get in the car; I'll take you. Or you can walk, your call. At this moment, I really don't care what you choose."

"I love you."

"How can I be so sure of that?" I snapped.

"You know that what we have is unique."

"Then you should have found another way of getting closer to me! She used you, don't you get that? Just like she used me for years. She's come between us, like she always does. She's ruined it."

Lila started panicking, I could see it in her whole demeanor. She was erratic, agitated, her mind and body racing, her thoughts all over the place. But was this real? My own mind raced. The high-speed train was now crossing the countryside at the velocity of a futuristic model only seen in movies.

I thought back to the school dance, remembering this exact same behavior. She must have been so afraid that Viola would spill the beans in her drunken mood. Had she used her medical condition to get me out of there? Was any of this even real? Her mom never talked about it, nobody at school seemed to comment on it. Nobody treated her like she was different. God, had she lied about this too?

Everything seemed to come together like the pieces of a complex puzzle, and I suddenly realized I didn't trust her anymore. If she had been lying about everything else, then would she lie about her medical issues too?

She knew perfectly well how far she could go in terms of sports and activities. She had been on long beach walks. If I hadn't known that she was fragile, I wouldn't have seen it. How could I ever distinguish the real Lila from the fake one?

She sighed, took a deep breath, and clutched her chest. And I only saw what Viola had put inside my head: the lies.

"Stop this," I said harshly. "Your tricks won't work on me."

"I can't," she whispered, clutching her chest.

"Lila, *stop it*! I'm taking you home *now*."

The moment I realized that her reaction was not fake was the moment she lost her life. Just like that. She fell forward, slumped to the ground—didn't say another word, didn't make another sound—and died.

CHAPTER TWENTY-FOUR

I saw her at Lila's funeral. She was sitting on the side, looking at me and not the casket with the red and purple flowers. The church was too small for all the people coming to say goodbye to Lila, but she was only there for me.

I was sitting in a front pew, one row behind Lila's parents, and refused to look over from the moment I realized Viola was there. I hated her with a vengeance. For days now, she had tried to get in touch with me, and I refused every single time.

Ever since the events of that night, after the moment a car stopped at the open space, I had clammed up like an oyster. The couple in the car had been efficient. They had realized in a matter of seconds what was going on. They had recognized Lila; her parents were close friends of theirs. I had stammered that we had been sitting there enjoying the view and that she had suddenly clutched her heart and fallen forward.

My story was plausible because of Lila's issues. The police commissioner, however, did not buy it. He brought me in for interrogation and put me through the wringer, trying to create holes in my story. But in the end, it was obvious to everyone that Lila and I had been good friends, that she had a medical condition, and that this could have happened at any time, any place. So I was sent home with my parents, who were shockingly caring and gentle with me. It was a relief to have them there, taking care of me for once.

I was given a sedative, but even in my deepest sleep, I still dreamed of Lila and what I had done to her. This was my fault. Mine . . . and Viola's. If anyone was more to blame than me, it was her. Viola had caused all this. If she hadn't blackmailed Lila into hooking up with me, we would not have been at that party. If we had not been at that party, Viola would not have been able to put these thoughts in my mind. We would not have been on that hill, in that open space, having that argument.

Viola had caused Lila's death, but so had I.

I looked up, caught her gaze, and realized that I hated her. I *hated* her. And in that moment, I saw that she knew it too. She got up and left the service before it was even finished. We never spoke again, until the day of my death.

It was three months after Lila's death, and my life was one big mess of self-loathing, anxiety, and misery. Even though everyone kept telling me her death was not my fault, I couldn't shake the thought that it was and forever would be. I had heard the rumors, of course, people saying I could have driven her to the hospital. I also heard rumors that we'd had a big fight at the pool party, and I had driven too fast and she started to panic. Honestly, the driving part was true.

A lot of people claimed to have seen us arguing, but that was rebuffed quickly by Georgina, who told everyone who wanted to hear that we had been sitting by the pool having a good time. Those rumors died quickly. Nobody ever mentioned Viola at the party. If they knew, they weren't saying.

I was lost. Nobody talked to me, and I didn't want to talk to anyone. I wandered school like a ghost, and at home, Marie had a lot of trouble getting food in me. My parents knew of our relationship; my grief had made it impossible to hide. There was the whole Mr. Harrison thing, and there was Viola, never showing up to talk to me. My parents put the pieces together without ever realizing how Viola's behavior had influenced everything that night, leading indirectly to Lila's death.

I was in the cafeteria, quietly sitting with Lila's friends, when someone mentioned Annie Jones's Instagram account, how they wondered whether people could actually communicate with the dead. Wouldn't it be amazing to reach out to your loved ones and actually be able to talk to them?

I rushed to the bathroom, dug out my phone, and started scrolling through Annie's account. Something told me to connect with her. I sent her a message before I could overthink it. To my surprise, she sent me a reply within the hour.

We met at her house, in her study with the tattered chair. I told her about Lila. Not everything, of course—nobody knew the details. I just talked about how I had lost my best friend so suddenly, and how I wanted to know if a connection was possible with her.

Annie was not nice at first. She was arrogant, a bit smug, asking a lot of detailed questions, probably figuring out there was more to the story than I let on, but she ultimately decided to help me. I didn't have to pay a dime for her help. She wanted to do something to help ease the pain I was so obviously suffering from.

We never succeeded in contacting Lila.

My mom didn't talk about it—not once. She listened and then she moved on, as always.

"No point dwelling on the past."

My dad didn't know what to say. He probably thought of the man he had lost and how this was connected to all of it. If Mr. Harrison had stayed or kept in touch with Viola, would she still have been so aggressive and vicious? Or would he have been able to talk some sense into her?

"I'm sorry you lost your friend," Dad said.

"I'm sorry you lost yours," I replied.

He squeezed my shoulder and left the room.

And then a full year had passed. A year in which Viola and I were still not talking but had to endure sitting in the same classes. Whenever someone tried to pair us up for assignments, I would plead to be partnered with someone else. Ultimately, our teachers stopped trying. I told the story to one of Lila's friends earlier in the year about how Viola had snapped at Lila because we were friends, and how I was still upset with Viola for it. That rumor traveled around like wildfire, and eventually, Viola didn't even *dare* talk to me again.

She was a pariah too—not of her own free will, but because I had made it happen. It felt so good to have done that, even if it was only a small revenge. I contemplated telling the world the truth about what she had done to me, but decided against it. If I did, Lila's reputation in this crazy town would be shot. I could just see the priest giving a sermon about how God would only allow the righteous ones to survive. No, thank you. No matter what had happened between us, I didn't want Lila's parents to suffer more than they already had.

And in the end, I had to admit that I would not have forgiven Lila. Despite the heartache I was feeling, I had to accept the fact that Lila and I would not have made it. She had lied for months, and when I found out, she had blown my self-worth to shreds. I would not have been able to be with her without asking myself this one question: If Viola had not done this, would Lila have chosen me for me?

I would never know.

I still felt guilty about her death, and so I kept up the lie. When her family came to school to talk about setting up a charity to support kids with SCAD, the condition that had ultimately killed her, and asked me to take up the position of cofounder, I accepted. I became vocal about a lot of things, starting with helping those in need. It gave me a new purpose in life, one I desperately needed.

Viola and I did not speak again during that last year in high school. I wanted her out of my life, out of my mind, out of everything. Little did I know that life had one last bad surprise in store for me.

What I do know is that the moment Viola and I reconnected at long last, I died.

HERE WE ARE, THEN, AT THE END OF ALL THINGS

I look at Annie, sitting on her couch with her notepad in hand. She is quiet, and we both know why.

"I'm sorry that I killed your cousin," I say. "I really am. I'm sorry that I contacted you nine months ago, knowing that you were related. I wanted more from you than just your psychic help."

"I know." Annie smiles. "You were also trying to find out how her parents and family felt about you."

"I'm sorry that I tried to use you, but I knew how close you were—she told me during our conversations. She always spoke so fondly of you."

"Thank you," Annie says. "That means a lot. And I don't blame you. I probably would have done the same."

"Will you tell her parents the truth for me? About her death, I mean. They have a right to know. Just them, nobody else. So if you are going to talk to people about our conversation, please leave that part out."

"Of course." Annie rose from her seat and glanced at the clock. "You still haven't told me about the actual accident. Do you even want to?"

"You can guess what happened, can't you? Viola came to me with tons of excuses and accusations. We fought, she crashed the car, and I died. End of the road. I'm pretty sure she will find a lot of excuses for her behavior."

"Is that all?"

"Oh yeah. The most important thing to know is that there is no happy ending for us," I say. "No eagles who come to take us, no returning home after the ring fell into the fires of Mordor."

"I know," Annie says, but I can tell she doesn't believe me. "I'm sorry for what has happened to you, Syl. I really am. I pray, with all of my heart, that you will be reunited with Lila again. If that's what you want."

"I don't know. I want to get the opportunity to tell her how sorry I am, but I have no idea what awaits me after that. I will find out soon, won't I? My time here is almost up."

"Sadly, yes," Annie says. "It's getting harder now to see you, but you have managed to tell your story. Her parents will know Viola's part in Lila's passing, and yours. I hope you trust me to do the right thing."

"I do."

I look at the room, place my hand on the seat, and still don't feel anything. Nothing has changed in the past few hours, except a weight has been lifted from me. It was a good decision to do this, to tell Annie everything. The one thing that still remains is the actual details of the argument that led to my death. That's the one thing I won't tell her. I can't. I won't.

"So this is it, then?" she asks.

"I think so."

"It's going to be strange without you."

"You know," I say, "when something bad happens, the world seems to stand still for a second to catch its breath.

Depending on the seriousness of the situation, that release of breath will take longer. It could even last a lifetime, at least for those who were impacted by it. It happened when Lila passed away, I can vouch for that. But my mom always claimed that people move on easily from tragedy."

"I don't believe that's true," Annie tells me. "Yeah, people do move on and they continue living their lives, but it will forever be marked by their suffocating loss. Lila's loss and the grieving of her parents and family showed me for the first time, as her cousin, that Love Hill wasn't all bad."

I smile softly. "It has its moments."

"I read this theory once about how we as humans are programmed to continue existing, no matter what they throw at us," Annie continues. "That loss will be compensated by love."

"That's the whole thing, isn't it?" I say. "I have failed miserably when it came to the love part. I couldn't see past her betrayal. The worst thing about Lila's death is that after it happened, everyone thought I was grieving because of our friendship, but in truth, I was mourning knowing the truth. I would rather have seen her die without knowing any of this so I could mourn her properly."

"I can understand that. You've been beating yourself over the head for the past year, while Lila died from natural causes. Even if you and Viola had your fair share in this, Lila, in the end, still passed away because of her medical issues."

"I shouldn't have allowed Viola to manipulate me. If I hadn't reacted like that, we wouldn't have had that argument."

"That is true. But nobody can say if Lila would not have died in her sleep at some point. Her parents told me once that she was getting worse, but she was putting on a brave face. The doctors said that surgery would have only prolonged her life; she would have died at a young age nonetheless. I can vouch for the fact that she was very happy in those final months. If it's any consolation, that was because of you."

It actually makes it even worse, I want to say, but I don't get the chance. A sudden loud chime rings through the house. Annie shoots up from her seat, and even I, who cannot feel anything, am startled by the sound her doorbell makes. She glances at her watch—5:00 a.m.—and at me, and stands up, not knowing what to do.

Another chime. A knock on the door. To my surprise and shock, I hear Steve's voice. He's standing in front of her door, waiting for Annie to open it.

"Annie, please open the door. I know you're in there. Can we talk about Viola?"

Annie is not surprised at all, not for a second. I remember her picking up her phone just before she walked into the kitchen to get some water. I've seen her looking at it, typing stuff on it. I thought she was checking her recorder or making notes.

"You sent him a message," I say.

"I did," she confesses easily. "I wanted to find out if Viola was okay and figured she could be with him, especially after what you said about him."

"Why did you do that, Annie? Do you care about her?"

"She screwed up big-time, but she's just a person, too, Syl. Someone should care."

I couldn't argue with her there. I still cared too.

"What do I do? Let him in or keep him out? It's your decision."

"Open the door," I say. "I've told you my story. He came because you lured him here, so I'm curious to find out what he's going to say about Viola. I'm sure she's been sobbing on his shoulder. She's good at that. But she might have told him the truth, and I'm interested to hear it."

"Okay, then. Wait here."

Annie switches off the light that allowed her to see me throughout our conversation, and leaves the door wide open while she walks over to the front door, which is right next to her study. I can hear her surprised gasp.

"What are *you* doing here?" she asks.

"I came to talk to you." I recognize Viola's voice. She sounds clearheaded and sober. Steve is with her; I can tell he's feeling protective over her. She must have gone to him after the accident, and now he's doing what he had done during those months they were together and I was with Lila.

Annie steers them into her study, straight toward her phone, which is still recording—or so she probably hopes. I hold my breath. I don't know what they can see, if they are even aware of the fact that I am here in this very room. Of course they're not.

"Sit down," she offers, waving to the couch.

Viola looks exhausted and sad, while Steve is extremely gentle with her. They don't even look at the chair, and although Steve seems to be wondering what Annie was doing, he doesn't ask any questions.

"Are you okay?" Viola asks her.

"Yes, why wouldn't I be?"

"You saw the car. You were there."

"I'm okay. I slept a few hours and woke up early." She waves at her notepad. "I'm trying to remember all that's happened. I need to go to the police station this morning for a statement. Why are you here?"

"We came to talk to you," Steve says. "We're looking for proof that Viola didn't do what people are accusing her of. She did not crash that car on purpose."

"Oh? Then who was responsible?"

"I was there," Viola begins. "But it wasn't like it's being told all over town. I'm being accused of murder, but I did not kill Syl—"

"I don't know what people are saying," Annie interrupts her. "I've been here the whole time, not talking to anyone."

"So you don't know anything? About how they are accusing her of cold-blooded murder?" Steve says.

"No." Annie pointedly looks at Viola. "Were you driving your car?"

"Yes, I was."

"Did you move her body?"

"Yes, I did."

"Why?"

"I was in a panic. I figured that nobody would be the wiser if I put her behind the wheel. She was dead already, so what would it change? I would have come clean sooner or later; I just needed time to think."

"Well, it sounds to me like you did something worse than just leave her there, then," Annie says. "You pinned the blame on her. Have you ever thought about that?"

Viola sighs. "The thing is, Syl *did* cause the accident herself. I swear on my mother's life that she did. I just need someone to believe me." She starts crying.

I know Annie can't see me right now, but she can sure as hell still hear me. She's stunned into silence, but I'm not.

"That lying bitch," I mutter.

WHAT DO YOU THINK HAPPENED THAT NIGHT?

To find out the whole story, you have to read Viola's version of events too. If you haven't read it yet, turn to page 169.
    And if you're ready for the ending, then move on to page 345.

DEAD GIRLS DON'T TALK

...LUCKY FOR ME

PROLOGUE

What a mess. What a terrible, terrible mess.
My car rests crumpled against the tree. It's century-old wood that is now split in half. Half the tree's branches lean forward over the edge of the slightly elevated road, while the other half dangles broken over the vehicle, threatening to fall on top of it. In between that mess lies the body of the one I used to call my best friend.

Syl is dead. She is really, really dead.

There's no point in trying to help her. Her skull is split open; brain matter and blood ooze together through her hair.

I look numbly at the disaster area I have created. I was driving the vehicle. I sat behind the steering wheel. I parked this car against that tree, crashing half of the front and right side as I lost control.

My mind goes blank. Panic takes over.

I crawl back into the car and pull at Syl's body while trying not to vomit, and shove her behind the steering wheel.

Then I leave.

THE GIRL ON THE RUN AND THE BOY SHE USED TO LOVE

"Why are you here, Viola?"
Steve Andrews. Nice, decent Steve Andrews. That's how I think of him whenever he comes to mind. Nice, decent, trustworthy, boring old Steve Andrews. Nice, decent, trustworthy, boring old Steve, who dumped me as soon as things got tough. But he never really argued with me, never told me I wasn't welcome anymore. And I am counting on his emotional intelligence to help me get through this situation.
"I need your help," I say. "Something's happened."
"Oh? What is it now?"
I'm startled by his sharp tone and the way he won't let me inside his house. He lives with his dad; his mom died ten years ago. His father never remarried but is seeing someone who lives on the outskirts of Love Hill. He owns a supermarket and works a lot, but Steve insists that he should have a personal life, too, and is very supportive of that relationship.
This is precisely what Steve Andrews is made of: love, compassion, and decency. He's one of the good guys. When we were dating, he became the most reliable person in my life, even more so than my mom used to be when we

were still on speaking terms. He would listen and give the answers normal people give, not the replies that come from freaks like me, who thrive on thinking differently.

I never really understood why he put up with me for so long. I'm not so sure that if things had been the other way around, I would have been able to do the same. Steve's dad is very supportive of him, and he doesn't expect him to take over the supermarket, now that he has a college scholarship to NYU in his back pocket that will take him far away from here. He's planning big, at one of the largest universities, to pursue a swimming career. He's good enough to train for the Olympics, the ultimate goal. He has the right build for it: large hands; a fit and well-shaped, lean body with just enough muscle. He also has the stamina to put in the hours.

For a while, when we were dating, I thought we could last until the end of our high school years, but that didn't turn out to be the case. Last June, right before the end of the school year, Steve broke up with me. I still believe he did it under pressure from his dad and his friends, and not because he no longer cared. They all thought I wasn't good for him, and truth be told, they were absolutely right. I have a tendency to hurt the people in my life.

I enjoyed our relationship while it lasted. It was fun for a while, and then reality returned with a vengeance. Ah, well, those were things that happened. He was the perfect guy for me to hang out with for a bit. To pull me back up whenever I was down and support me when I needed it. But he wasn't the one who kept me straight on my feet, and we both knew that.

"Viola? Are you listening to me? Are you high again? I swear I will close the door in your face right now if you are," he says, and that brings me back to my senses.

"Don't be so rude," I say. "I'm not high. I never was when I was with you."

He snorts. *Yeah, right.*

"Why did you come? Do you need something? What's going on? What's happened?" He's friendlier now.

"Can I please come in?"

Again, that hesitation.

"It's late; I have practice at six. Do we really have to do this now?"

He's obviously looking for ways to get rid of me, and I am as determined not to let him kick me out.

"I need your help."

"What for?"

"It's— You haven't heard yet?"

"Heard what?"

I calculate in my mind how long it took me to get from the crash site to here. At least an hour. The first part of the way, I had to be careful not to get caught. The second part, when I was already in downtown Love Hill, I wanted to make sure that nobody saw me walking on the streets. So again, cautious.

Until I reached his dad's town house, adjacent to the supermarket. I rang the doorbell quickly, praying nobody would see me here either. I would have to explain why I was up this late.

"There's been an accident," I say. "On the outskirts, on the open space. You know where."

He looks at me, startled.

"Where she—"

"Yeah, exactly there."

"You were there?"

I swallow my anxiety.

"Yeah, I was."

"Oh my God, are you okay?"

"I'm fine," I say quickly. "I'm sorry, I didn't mean to frighten you. I'm okay. I was— Look, I really don't want to talk about this standing in the street. Can I please come in?"

"That depends on what you want me to do."

Steve's brutal honesty surprises me. When we were together, he never really showed me what he was feeling or thinking. He was there all the time, helped and supported me through my issues. But he always hid what he was really feeling. This is refreshingly new, and I like it.

"I was driving the car," I blurt out. "And after we crashed, I ran away."

"'We'?"

He looks at me as if I'm from another planet. His mouth opens and closes; he gapes like a fish. Then he pulls me inside and shuts the door. "Viola, what are you talking about? Who is *we*?"

"Syl."

"Where is she? Do we need to call 911? What happened? Viola, where is she now?!"

"Don't bother," I whisper. "She's dead."

"Oh my God."

He runs his hands through his hair and looks so pale and startled that I feel sorry for him and force myself to reconsider my choice to come here and drop this on him. He's one of the good guys, and I threw this in his lap as my accomplice. Which he's not. Or at least, not yet.

"Like I said, I need your help."

"You're crazy. I'm calling 911," Steve says, and reaches for his phone. I place my hand on his wrist.

"Don't. Please. I really need your help. You need to hear me out."

He doesn't seem to know what to do, and that's no wonder. I'm dropping this disaster on his plate without any explanation. If I were a normal person, thinking in a sane way, I would probably be as frightened as he is right now. But the thing is, I know I am not like most people. I don't feel what they feel. Never have, probably never will. Whatever empathy is, I don't have it in me.

I was diagnosed last year. Something to do with my brain being wired differently. And no, that is not an excuse for my behavior, but it is a fact that thinking the way I do does not help to make me look like a regular person. Steve doesn't know about this. I'm not sure if I'm going to tell him.

"It was an accident," I say. "We got into a fight. She tried to get out, we struggled while I was going fast. She unbuckled herself, and when I tried to stop her, I lost control of the steering wheel and crashed the car into a tree."

He is speechless.

"I lost consciousness for a few moments; I'm guessing it couldn't have been longer than seconds. When I came to, she was already dead. Her body took the brunt; her skull was fractured and she had all these injuries. I— It was horrible, but I knew there was nothing I could do for her. This looks really bad for me, I know that. I didn't want to be there when they came, the cops and all. I panicked, couldn't think straight, and started walking."

"Wait. Hold on. You're going too fast," Steve says, running his hand through his hair again. He looks devastated, shocked, and confused. "What were you thinking, Vi? People just don't walk off like that. You don't abandon your best friend!"

"We haven't been friends for a long time."

"That's— My God. I don't think I want to hear anything else. You come here, telling me that your best friend—excuse me, *former* best friend—died in a car crash that you caused, asking me for help, without having the decency to call 911? Why are you here? Please don't tell me you're looking for an alibi?"

He speaks so loudly now that his voice echoes through the large hallway with the double stairs leading up to the second and third levels.

"Is your dad home?" I ask.

"No, and a good thing too. He would have your hide in a second. What are you even thinking? Your brain is affected if you believe this is normal behavior."

"It isn't, and I'm well aware of that," I say, walking past him into the kitchen.

It smells like freshly baked bread, and I smile softly because this was the scent that always used to remind me of the happy times with my parents. When my dad was still around, my mom used to bake bread all the time, as well as cookies and cakes. She was the walking cliché of a happy housewife. After my dad left us, all that disappeared. She no longer bothers to do anything around the house. All she does is wither away.

"Viola, please go."

He's standing behind me, probably with his arms folded over his chest like he used to do when he got upset about something.

"No," I say. "I can't."

"Go home to your mom. If you've done something bad, you need to go talk to her about it. I can't help you. We broke up almost a year ago, remember? Or have you been living on another planet all that time?"

"No," I tell him. "But you are the only person in this town that I still call a friend. You told me yourself that I could always come to you when I needed you. Now is that time."

"Out of pity and respect. I didn't mean it. I have a new life now, a girlfriend that isn't—"

He stops.

I smile. "A control freak?"

"Yes."

"Well, I'm happy for you. But I still need you."

"You need to get your head straight. You shouldn't be here. You should be out there, at the crash site, talking to the police. Do they even know that you have something to do with the accident? You need to go to the hospital to get checked over too."

"I'm fine," I say impatiently.

"You're bleeding."

I look at my wrist and see a gash there. My face feels bruised, too, as well as the right side of my body. But it's all just bruising and nothing major or life threatening. It doesn't matter at all.

"What do you want from me?" he asks as I sit down on a kitchen stool and push a towel he's handed me against my wrist.

"I need an alibi."

"You . . . *what*?"

"You heard me."

Steve starts laughing. It's not a triumphant or happy laugh, more of a nervous, *Are you bleeping kidding me?* sort of laugh. Can't blame him for that. I would have laughed too. "You are absolutely crazy throwing this on me, Viola. You haven't changed a bit, have you? You ruined my life for nearly a year. You tried to push me away from my friends, have eagerly pursued a rather sickening relationship between us, and threatened me after we broke up. I have gotten over you with the help of a shrink, my dad, and my friends—which, by the way, has cost me nearly six months.

I was so glad to have you out of my life. And now you just show up here to drop this into my lap? No way in hell I'm going to help you."

I remain calm. I haven't been living on another planet for the past year. I've heard the rumors of what people were saying about me, and I couldn't counter them because most were true. Yes, we had an unhealthy relationship, and all his anxiety, sorrow, and mental health issues were my fault. I had put him through the wringer. I'm not an idiot. I have this destructive thing in me that is hard to keep under control.

I didn't love Steve. Never have. To be honest, I've never really loved anyone—or at least, not in the sense that people think of when they talk about love. I used to care for people, though. My dad, my mom, Syl. Nice, decent, trustworthy, boring old Syl Jameson. But I threw her under the bus a long time ago, and now I've killed her.

No, I didn't love Steve, and that is exactly why he's the one I need to tell my story to. He will listen to it, hate me for it, and then decide whether or not to help me. If he does, I'm in luck. If he doesn't, then at least he'll know why I did what I did.

"Steve, I don't have much time," I say. "They're going to start looking for me soon, with the understanding that Syl died in *my* car and I am not in it. Nobody saw us together, but they are going to put two and two together and figure out that there was no way that Syl was driving that car after what happened to her last year. Everyone in town knows that she hates to drive, so why would she even decide to get behind the steering wheel of someone else's vehicle and crash it?"

"You're right," he says. "And that is exactly why you should come to your senses now and talk to the cops. If this really was an accident, the evidence will show it. You're making things a lot harder on yourself now."

"I am, I know that. But I have no choice."

"There are always choices and consequences."

"And what if I said that the choices I've made over the past few years have led to this moment, and I am ashamed of that?"

He laughs. "Well, I never thought I would hear Viola Harrison use the word *shame*. Could have fooled me."

"I know you hate me," I say softly. "I deserve to be hated."

"I don't hate you. I despise what you did to me and to others. You have mistreated Syl, too, haven't you?"

"Yes, I have. But before you judge me on that account, you should know there are things about Syl that nobody knows. She's not the saint everyone takes her for."

"Isn't that what you told the world about me too? You put the blame of our breakup on me, but in reality, you brought everything on yourself, Viola. You don't know what empathy is; you don't know what it's like to have normal conversations with friends. It took me a while to see how toxic our relationship was. Now I know that what happened between us was not my fault."

"I never said it was," I say. "Think of me how you want, Steve, but I did not bad-mouth you after our breakup. Ask anyone that I know, check with your friends. I'm not the one who spoke about you that way. You know I'm not a liar. I'm many things, but I have never told you anything that wasn't true."

He hesitates now, because he knows I am not a liar. I'm not exactly an easy person to talk to, but I will always tell the truth.

"Okay, so if you are not a liar, tell me what happened tonight."

"I can't."

He laughs again. "Well, there goes that confession. That didn't take too long."

"I'm sorry, but some things have to stay with me."

"Not if you want me to help you."

"That's not exactly fair," I argue.

"Your choice, Vi. If you want my help, you're going to have to start by telling me the whole truth. If you hold anything back, I will know. I've known you long enough to figure out when you are withholding information. You may not call it *lying*, but you're a master in circumventing situations."

I don't reply, because what he says is true.

He sits down on a stool across the table and folds his hands over his arms again. "I'm waiting."

"Okay," I say. "I'll tell you what happened at the crash site, but then I want your word that you'll consider providing me with an alibi."

"And how exactly am I going to do that without lying?"

"You don't really have to lie. I'm not asking that of you. Trust me, I know all too well that you wouldn't stoop that low." I take a deep breath. "I need to bend the truth a little bit."

"In what way?"

"I've thought about this. Nobody is going to believe me when I say that it was an accident, because of our shared past. A lot of people know that Syl and I didn't see eye to eye anymore, so it will be hard to defend myself."

"So?"

"So, the only thing that might work is if I convince everyone she killed herself. That she came over to my house, had an argument with me, stole the keys to my car, and crashed it into a tree out of vengeance."

"You're crazy. You're going to try to tell the world she was suicidal? That's nasty, Viola, even for you."

"It's that, or be punished for something I didn't do."

"And you need me, then, for what exactly?"

"I need you to say that you saw me tonight. Which is, technically speaking, not a lie. You just need to avoid talking about the exact time that you saw me."

"You are a piece of work, Viola. You really are," Steve says, looking at me with such disgust that my stomach churns. I know I am.

PART ONE: THE BALLAD OF THE GIRL WHO RAN

CHAPTER ONE

My car lies crumpled against the tree. Sitting next to me is the body of the one I used to call my best friend. We haven't been friends in two years, even though, for some reason or other, a lot of people still believe that we are.

Syl is dead. She is really, really dead.

My heart aches, my body trembles, and it takes me a few seconds, after waking up with a splitting headache, to realize what has transpired. There's no point in trying to help her. I don't need a medical degree to realize nobody will ever be able to save her.

She looks at me, even though the light in her eyes is broken. It's an accusing gaze, one that I will never forget. I agreed to have her in this car; I *invited* her in it, almost *forced* her. *Blackmailed* her into doing what I wanted, as I have done so many times before. She used to do what I said, but that was a long time ago.

This version of Syl, the one she became over the past few years, was one I couldn't communicate with. She had distanced herself in many ways. Tonight was my flailing attempt to resurrect our friendship, after a lot of consideration and lonely times, with no one close to me. Of course it backfired.

I honestly thought I could restore what we'd had in the blink of an eye, but things did not turn out that way. Her death is the direct result of my arrogant ambition. I should have listened to my common sense instead of trying to breach hers.

It hits me then, the anxiety and panic that was pushing beneath the surface of my consciousness. I was driving the vehicle. I sat behind the steering wheel. I smashed this car against that tree, crashing half of the front and right side as I lost control. I killed her—there is no other way of putting it.

My hands start to shake, my knees tremble, my head pounds, and my heart beats too many miles per hour. This is a goddamn nightmare. This cannot be happening. I didn't want it to end this way, never meant for her to get hurt in *my* process of finding salvation.

For a year now, she has shunned me, cut me out of her life, avoided me, bashed me with her silence. She has ignored me in front of the world, has told me off without using a single word, has created a living hell for me to exist in. I couldn't stand it anymore, and so I came over to her place tonight, on the anniversary of what she herself called "The Loss of Everything," to talk things through. It was my last chance to reconcile with her before we would both go our own separate ways in life.

She would never return to Love Hill, even though I was planning to. She didn't have to tell me or anyone else, but I could just *feel* her getting more distant from this town with every waking moment. She had no one to come back to. Her parents were cold people who had no space for her in their lives. She hardly had any friends, and there were too many bad memories here that would push her to stay away. She hated Love Hill with a vengeance. Always had. This town is terrible—that's a fact. But it's our town.

People don't really care about each other here; all they care about is money and prestige, and how to get more of both. There are people living here who own seven cars, one for each day of the week. There are people who mock others in public and get away with it. There are heartless people who couldn't care less about what was going on, as long as whatever was going on would happen to others.

There are people in this town who will have a field day about what has just happened. And that, in the end, gets me panicked even more. My mom will never live to see another day if she finds out what I've done. I can't allow that to happen. It will break her heart if I get arrested and sent to jail for driving this car at high speed and killing my friend.

I need to avoid all this.

I crawl out of the car and stand beside it on trembling legs. The whole area feels like a battlefield, the only difference being that this car hasn't been shot at. There are no bullet holes, yet there is nothing but shrapnel and blood nonetheless.

Panic takes over. I need to do something, and all I can think about is pinning the blame on Syl. That's the only way to get out of this mess. I crawl back into the car and pull at Syl's body while trying not to vomit, in order to move her behind the steering wheel. Her feet get stuck; I hear the snapping of a bone. Blood pours from her face, and I can see the crack in her skull. She still feels warm to the touch, and that sickens me even more. It takes a few moments of pulling and shoving, and then she's in the driver's seat of my car, her face resting sideways on the steering wheel. She continues to gaze at me with that accusing, curious stare. Her eyes see nothing anymore.

I don't believe in ghosts or spirits or whatever you may call them. There's this woman in town who does; her name is Annie Jones. She's nice but completely insane. For a long moment, I contemplate the thought of Syl being able to speak to someone like that to say goodbye to this world. I push it away quickly.

No sense in trying to hope for something that is utterly impossible.

"I'm sorry, Syl," I say. "For everything."

And leave.

CHAPTER TWO

I start walking into the dark night, over the slippery road. It's only August, but we've had our fair share of thunderstorms lately, causing the area to suffer from an amazing amount of water. I never thought there could be so much rain this time of year, when it's usually still quite warm here. All that climate talk has made people itchy, and whenever things seem abnormal, they start arguing about it.

The other day I read this interview with the activist Greta Thunberg about how she's eager to get some sense into people. Syl went protesting a couple of times, too, but I have never stood up for anything in my life. To be honest, I've been too busy for that, too focused on keeping my head straight. That was hard enough as it was. The fact that I went out of my way to talk to Syl tonight on this special date was a miracle of its own. I was so convinced she wouldn't see me that I hesitated up until the last minute to even bother getting in my car. I should have saved myself the trouble. It would have kept her alive too. Syl is dead because I had it in my head to go over to her place, convince her to have a chat about things that bothered us both, and drive around in my car, which indirectly led us to this point. Trust me when I say I had no clue myself that this was the area I was headed toward, until we'd already reached it.

The argument between us was fierce and harsh, and at one point she started unbuckling herself, threatening to jump out of the car.

"Don't be such an idiot," was my snappy remark. "Are you insane? Put your belt back on!" But she wouldn't. She unstrapped herself, and then she made a move toward the door. And me? Instead of slowing down, my foot hit the wrong pedal and started the acceleration.

Syl grabbed my arm and screamed. "Slow down! Let me out!"

She was panicking in the way a victim would when being abducted by a serial killer.

"Are you crazy?" I yelled back. "Put your seat belt back on, you idiot."

And then we hit a slippery spot, and the next thing I knew, we'd reached the open spot, where Syl's personal tragedy happened last year, and the car crashed against the tree. I passed out in a flash.

I walk and I walk, and then I stop a couple of yards away from the crash site. What is this? What the hell am I doing? What is this nightmare I've found myself in? I can't do this! I can't just leave Syl to her own devices in that car. Not like this. I have to do *something*. Maybe she's not dead yet. I could still save her. I could— Oh God, I *need* to save her!

I run back to the car, despite the growing soreness in my limbs and the feeling that I'm out of my body, watching the whole situation. I'm out of breath by the time I reach the vehicle and look in. She's still in the exact same position with her eyes wide open. I want to touch her, to shake her back to life. But I can't. I *can't*. She's dead. She's really gone.

I'm suddenly fascinated by the sight of her. I've never seen a dead person before. I could have if I wanted to, but the last time someone dear to me passed away, I refused to greet the body. The casket was closed due to the gruesome circumstances. That had been a car accident too. Strange and ironic that Syl would die in a similar fashion. Perhaps the past really returns to catch up in the present.

I move away from the vehicle and start walking again. A car's engine is heard in the distance, coming from the bottom of the small inclining area. I need to get away *now* and find a solution. If the people in that car find Syl, they will help her. I can't. Not anymore.

What I'm doing is terribly wrong, but it's the only thing I can do. I start running in the other direction while a thousand thoughts of guilt overwhelm me. I should have called 911 straightaway, have them come over, have them find her, have them take away her body. I should have told them the truth, and I still can. I can return and make this right.

But I keep on running, and then I'm off the road and into the bushes, blindly searching for the walking path so many people use here. I can't stay; it won't do any good. I can't help her anymore.

But maybe someone else can. Someone who cares about her.

CHAPTER THREE

I feel the fatigue in my legs as I walk down the path to Love Hill while I try not to think of my deeds. This is terrible, all of it. I can't look myself in the eye ever again.

Not so far away from me, I can hear several sirens. People are approaching the scene. Cops, paramedics, perhaps the press, too, and curious townsfolk. Everyone who has anything to do with this town will soon find out what has happened. They will find Syl alone in that car, and they will wonder if I had been with her, and then they will come looking for me.

I need to talk to someone. My mom? No, she can't handle this. She's the main reason why I took off in the first place.

Who else?

I come to the alarming conclusion that there are only a few options, and none of them seem appealing enough to try. What would I even say or do? Perhaps I should just run away, travel on foot or by bus to the next town, and live from day to day. I won't need much money or food; I'm not a big eater or spender. I could find a job somewhere far away from here. I could travel to California, like my dad did, and start there. Everyone needs to start somewhere, so why not me too? I'm not unattractive; I could find a job if I use my looks right. I could work at a bar or in a diner. The latter sounds the most interesting because I'm not eighteen yet and don't want people to ask questions.

And then what?

I have these AMBER Alert thoughts popping in my mind. People will start looking for me. They will be curious as to what could have happened to a seventeen-year-old. They will know something's not right with this whole scenario, and will probably believe that I ran off after killing my best friend. My face will be all over the news.

No, I can't run away. I need to stay and pretend that nothing's wrong. And the only person I can think to turn to is Steve. Good old decent, trustworthy Steve. If I can talk to anyone, it's him.

I'm supposed to leave for NYU soon, just like he is. I won a scholarship for my academic skills. I'm planning to become a reporter one day. I could always picture myself chasing the next big news story, rising in the ranks until I got offered an anchor position for a daytime news show or something like that.

I haven't told Steve about NYU yet. He thinks I'm heading to UCLA. I told him once that sunny California really appealed to me, and after we broke up, I never bothered telling him that my heart truly lies with NYU. That was my dad's alma mater, and as an homage to him, I felt it was really important to apply to the same college. If Steve knew, he would have freaked out. We haven't spoken in a while.

Steve.

I loved having him around, and since he dumped me last year, I have been the loneliest I've ever been. I think of him now, of how he would comfort me after finding out that Syl passed away. Nah. I shake off the thought. He would not believe that I missed him. He thinks I'm the most selfish person in the world. Which is probably true. If I weren't, I would not have left Syl behind like that.

While the area seems to fill with sounds of ambulances, police vehicles, and other cars, all heading toward the accident, I reach the bottom of the walking path and the edge of town. Steve's house is four blocks from here, but I stop, not wanting to go there straightaway.

This is also the area where Syl lives. Her parents' house is only two blocks away, in the same nice cul-de-sac where I used to live until last year. Now my mom and I live on the other side of town, too far for me to go to on foot, which I'm unwilling to do. It would be a stupid plan to even consider.

If I go home now, sneak into the house, and pretend I'm asleep, no one in their right mind would believe my mom if she were to vouch for me. She knows I wasn't at home. I told her I was going to be with friends, without telling her exactly who those friends were. She will tell the cops she saw me taking off. She will not lie for me. My mom is many things, but not a liar.

I also can't rely on her being too drunk to remember what happened tonight. She gets drunk, yes, but never so much that she has blackouts. For once, I wish she would. Even though I have major problems with her drinking—mostly because I'm prone to addiction too—she never goes so far as drinking to the point of oblivion.

No, the plan has to be simple and easy, and I have to stick to one person, and one alone: Steve. If I can convince him to bend the truth for me, if I can tell the cops that I picked up Syl, that we had been at Steve's, and that she took off when we had a fight, grabbing my car keys because she had no means of transportation, that could do the trick.

But first, I need to convince him.

I push away all thoughts of going to Syl's house first to say my goodbyes, and start walking in the direction of Steve's, when a loud sound shakes the ground beneath my feet. I am standing on shaking legs again, but this time not because of stress from the crash.

Not so far above me, at the scene of the accident, a roaring, hissing sound is followed by an explosion so loud that it seems to shake the houses around me. I fall to the ground and sit down between the bushes, invisible but shaken to the core of my very being.

Around me, people start coming out of their houses. Lights are turning on; the Love Hill townsfolk are confused and scared. Door after door is being opened, and several people walk outside.

I crawl farther into the bushes, hidden from the outside world, and try to make sense of what just happened, only to realize that this was the sound of my car exploding.

Oh my God. Oh my God. I stand up again and hope and pray that nobody else has gotten hurt. I push my knuckles against my mouth and send up a silent prayer to a god I hardly believe in—even though it is expected from everyone in this town to do so—and try to ignore the fact that I may have caused more deaths because I ran away.

No, *no*! If other people got hurt, it wasn't because of me. I can't put the blame on myself for that. I just *can't*! If I had stayed at the scene, I could be dead right now too. I could have been killed by the explosion. This only proves I did the right thing by escaping.

Syl will not have suffered more; she was already dead.

But what if she wasn't?

I can't shake off the thought that I have made a big mistake. Maybe I could have saved her if I had pulled her out of the vehicle.

No.

She was dead. She. Was. Dead.

I have to accept that. I saw it for myself. I did not leave behind a living person. Nobody survives a crash like that with their skull split open.

She's dead only because she didn't wear that seat belt. Because she panicked and started screeching. God, why did I even leave the scene? I should have told the cops she wasn't wearing her seat belt, that it was her own fault. She wasn't killed because we were in an argument. I hadn't been drinking, I hadn't taken any sort of drugs. I was driving sensibly, albeit maybe a bit too fast. We were talking, not arguing. She had forgotten to buckle up, and I didn't notice until it was too late.

I should not have left her in the car like that. I should not have panicked. I should have—

But this town isn't like other towns. People here don't believe a word you say until they see the proof for themselves. *Nobody* would have believed me. Not a soul who lives here. They would have started asking questions, and I would have buckled and told the truth.

And then they would find out about what happened last year, and I would become a pariah. Living in this town would be impossible. They would hurt my mom too. No, I did the right thing, made the right decision. I have to stick by that.

Cars start leaving Love Hill. Everyone—or at least, those living on the outskirts near the path—is headed up the slight hill to find out what is going on. I push myself up again, try to ignore the headache that is now so fierce I can feel it pounding beneath my skull, and move on.

My legs don't carry me straight to Steve's house. They start walking up to Syl's instead. Of course they do, because my legs won't listen to me anymore. They seem determined to show me what I have done and lost.

It starts to rain. The streets are shadowy like they would be in the late fall. There are barely any streetlights on, and the rain makes the concrete shine in the dark.

A car passes me by as I stumble down the road with the hood of my dark raincoat over me. The only thing that seems to reflect in the car's headlights are my shoes. I look away against the brightness of the lights, but not before I recognize Syl's parents.

They, too, are on their way to the crash site. My heart plummets again.

CHAPTER FOUR

I wind up not going to Syl's house. It's too hard. Tears stream down my face, mixed with the rain that is now soaking the area. It started with a couple of raindrops, but now it's falling as if there is no tomorrow.

They predicted a summer storm, but this no longer seems like one—more like a prediction of an autumn season that will often be hard to bear. Living in this area means we hardly have any seasons; we always seem to go from summer to winter in a heartbeat. It could be sunny and hot one day, then icy cold the next.

I'm wearing jeans and a thin T-shirt, and fortunately had the good sense at the last minute to take my raincoat with me, which now also feels soaked and cold to the touch. It suits the situation; I don't deserve any better than this.

The rain gives me one big advantage, though: Except for the curious ones racing to the crash site, most people will stay indoors. The streets are empty; there are hardly any cars around. And no one will be as crazy as I am to walk through Love Hill. Not when you have expensive cars to show off.

Nobody walks these streets. I usually don't either.

I can't help but wonder what people at the crash site are saying about all this. I have this idea in my mind about how the conversations and investigation will go, but to be honest, I'd be lying to myself if I didn't accept the fact that I messed up big-time.

I've seen enough cop shows to know they will figure out all too quickly that Syl was not driving my car, that I was the one behind the wheel. People know she was too scared to drive these days—she was even seeing a psychologist to get over her issues. And that whole scenario about me picking her up and going to Steve's house, where she would steal my keys and drive away, was flimsy, and stood or fell with Steve's cooperation in all this.

The fact that the vehicle exploded might help in the sense that it would destroy a lot of the evidence. But even though Love Hill isn't exactly a major crime city with top-notch detectives, I would still have to explain how we got from point A to point B, considering people *did* see me picking up Syl.

Their housekeeper, Marie, would be a major witness to that account. Not her parents, who weren't even home yet, as usual. Marie loved Syl, who was like a surrogate daughter to her. I heard through the grapevine that she always regretted the fact that we were no longer friends. Perhaps I could reel her in, even if we had barely spoken over the years.

I contemplate going home instead of seeking Steve's help, but that would turn into a disappointment and an argument for sure. I can't talk to Mom about this.

I love my mom, I really do, but the way she will sometimes go over-the-top about things that seem so irrelevant, or about decisions I've made that weren't always the wisest, makes me realize already that she would never protect me or defend me when it comes down to it.

When she was sober, she was overbearing and suffocating, so I actually prefer her like this. And it isn't as if I can say anything about the drinking, because I do it too. Or I used to, at least. Last year, I was forced to face my reality and fate if I continued on like this. That was probably the best thing that could happen, even if it meant that the pain isn't numb right now.

If I went home and told her, I would end up disappointed by her reaction. We would wind up at an impasse. And she would feel more sorry for Syl than she would for me. She always has. Sometimes I believe she would have been better off with Holy Syl as her daughter. It would have made her life a lot easier.

God, I need a drink. No matter what they say about it getting better, the urge has always stayed. It will never go away, and I have to live with that. But at least I realize this, unlike my mom.

Going home is not an option.

CHAPTER FIVE

Holy Syl.

That's what I used to call her whenever we went out to do things together. She had this way about her that made people look twice and listen to every word she had to say. She couldn't help it, of course; she didn't think about it. She never considered the fact that the two of us were so unalike that everything she did would always end up reflecting on me. That's why I loved her but detested her too. I loved her for her good manners and her quiet support, but I hated her for being such a good person too. It made me look very bad. Which, looking back on a lot of things I've done, I probably was.

I never said I was good, did I? I know who I am, I know what I'm capable of. But I would never, ever murder Syl in cold blood. That's not what I've done, but it's what the people in this lousy town would think I did.

I really, desperately, urgently need Steve. I need him to see eye to eye with me, to understand what I've done and why I did it, and I hope and pray he will support me.

I need to avoid talking to the cops before seeing him first. I need to make sure nobody sees me skulking around before I can reach out to him.

The rain is finally slowing down, which makes it a lot easier now to walk the dark streets of Love Hill. I hate the name of this town, hate the way that people use it; it doesn't make any sense at all.

"This town is called Lovell," I would sometimes say when even schoolteachers used it during their history classes. "It's ridiculous to call it by any other name."

"Ah, well, this isn't the only town with a nickname, now, is it?" they would say. "Look at New York City—*the Big Apple.*"

"Yeah, but it's still officially called New York City. No one calls it the Big Apple when they talk about the city. We use Love Hill every day, as if that's the original name. Like I said, ridiculous. We're not some commune, you know."

I'm the type of person who never really accepts anything as normal when it isn't. I will rebuff and come up with good explanations as to why I will not agree with whatever is being said. I'm the type of student teachers hate having in class because my behavior makes them rethink things in ways they don't want to.

School is a joke, really. The teachers are idiots who got stuck in their routine. They aren't ready or eager to discuss or argue about anything of value. They just want to get it over and done with so they can move on to the next year, hoping things will get better.

Some of us are vocal and start debates, while others sit in their corners pretending the information the teachers hand us on a plate is indisputable. Syl was one of those people. She would never object to anything, but hover over her books instead, pretending that everything was well with the world.

It worked for her, but not for me. I felt so much annoyance toward her in the last year that we were friends, and it became a living, breathing thing between us that ultimately killed our relationship.

Do I want to take back some of the things I said and did to her? Sure. But in the end, not having her around makes life a whole lot easier for the both of us. Especially in the last year, when things became unbearable, it would have been madness to reconnect with her.

A sudden tiredness overwhelms me. It's dark, it's still wet outside, and behind me the sirens are audible again, as if someone has set up a huge loudspeaker to clue the town in on the tragedy.

I can't shake the thought, though, that they are now looking for me. It feels as if someone has put a marker on me and several people are tracking it down.

If this really were the Big Apple, I would be on a wanted list by now. Cops would be searching for me, perhaps even setting up an AMBER Alert. But this being Love Hill, they probably haven't even approached my mom's house yet.

My phone rings, startling me. I gasp, then realize I've had it in my pocket all this time. The sound chimes so loudly in the darkness that I struggle to get it out of my pocket and lower the volume.

My mom.

God, it's my mom on the phone.

My hand trembles as I stare at the screen. What am I supposed to do? I can't—just *can't*.

It stops, and then she calls me again. And again. Five times in a row.

Oh God, they've reached out to her. They're searching for me. I can feel it. They've moved a lot faster than I thought they would. They're making haste with the search party, probably because they believe I'm confused and hurt, wandering around somewhere on my own.

Which is technically true.

Then the text messages start.

Hon, where are you?

Hon, answer me.

Hon, there are policemen here. They say there's been an accident. They want to know if you're all right. I'm worried. Please, hon, call me back. WHERE ARE YOU?!

A long time ago I set up WhatsApp in such a way that no one could see when I was online. I hate the pressure being on socials brings with it. Sometimes it really feels as if we are all forced to be reachable all the time, and I decided to stop feeling guilty for not responding immediately. I'm grateful now that my mother can't see that I've read the messages.

A second plan is brewing in my head. If the whole thing with Steve does not work out, I can pretend to be hurt, confused, and suffering from amnesia. That seems to work in the movies, so why not with me? It would certainly explain the whole "running off" thing.

I could pretend to pass out somewhere where people would find me. They would bring me to the hospital, where a doctor would confirm that accidents like this can cause amnesia. But it still won't take away the guilt. I would remain the girl who had taken her former best friend and her car and destroyed them both. That would always stay.

Even if people believe me, they will still blame me for Syl's death. In the end, my mom will also still be blamed for being connected and so close to me.

No, Steve it is. Steve it remains.

Another phone call. A number I don't know.

I wait for it to stop, but it doesn't.

Another call. Another number. Another one. And another one.

Then I start getting calls from people I know. Friends from school, acquaintances. My mom again. Syl's mother, whose number I stored many years ago at her own request. Is she looking for me too?

I run up to the wet bench beneath the tree in the small park with the kids' playground in the cul-de-sac, one block from Steve's house, and hide in the darkness as I sit. On a whim, and with a sense of foreboding, I open the browser of my phone and head to the local news. And yes, there it is: the live report of the crash, with Syl's and my picture next to it.

CHAPTER SIX

"We're here again for this live report coming from the crash site where the unspeakable has happened. Again, the streets of Love Hill are witness to another tragic incident that has cost the life of a young woman.

"An eyewitness statement from Ms. Annie Jones, who was the first person to reach the scene, has confirmed the tragic passing of seventeen-year-old Syl Jameson. She was pronounced dead at the scene.

"Ms. Jones has confirmed that Syl was the only one in the vehicle. However, the car was registered to seventeen-year-old Viola Harrison. The two were lifelong best friends."

Yeah, right. Don't they have any clue that we haven't been on speaking terms in a long time? The first time Syl and I communicated again was tonight, after a radio silence that lasted forever. I should not have broken my vow not to talk to her again.

Regret shoots through me, but I push it away. Things happened and I can't undo them. What's the point in feeling sorry for myself? Here I am, stuck in the darkness that I created and will probably remain in for a long time to come. But it's one of my own making, and I have to deal with that.

"Even though it is uncertain at this moment that Ms. Harrison was in the vehicle at the time of the crash, there is a possibility that she was. The police and medical staff believe that Viola Harrison took off, confused and hurt. She may have been under the influence of alcohol or illegal substances, but that cannot be confirmed at this point. As long as the official

reports cannot clear her presence or absence at the scene, we have to assume the worst.

"The police have asked us to share this information with the public. We therefore request the people of Love Hill to look for Ms. Harrison. She could be hurt and lying somewhere in the streets, but she could also have found her way to a garden shed or pool house. We ask you to check your backyards.

"A search party is already on the way to scan the area around the crash site. The police commissioner requests volunteers to help. We hope to locate Ms. Harrison before dawn. If you are willing to help tonight, please let us know by calling the following number: 555-5242. If you have any idea of where Viola Harrison might be, or if you are connected to her in some capacity, please reach out to us.

"In the meantime, we share our sympathy and condolences with the Jameson family, who have lost their only daughter tonight. Please burn a candle and keep Syl in your prayers. An early-morning remembrance mass will be organized."

The reporter standing in front of the camera looks so smug that I just want to smack her. I know this woman; she's a real vulture. Last year, she reported on another tragedy that happened at the same location, using words that made us all cringe.

I had no relationship with Syl at the time of that incident—we had been avoiding each other—but I felt so sorry for her, knowing that what happened was not her fault even though she was being blamed. That is probably the most important reason why I'm here right now. If they could do it to her, they will definitely do it to me.

I don't care about me, but I do care about my mom.

Who is calling me again, and sending me messages. I realize that my phone can be tracked, but they will probably need a court order for that. We learned about those things during one of our classes this year.

An AMBER Alert, however, could be set up in a couple of hours. I'm seventeen, which makes me a minor. Which means they could speed things up. God, my head is killing me. I need to *think*!

I start moving again, away from the park and the cul-de-sac, horrified that people might start leaving their houses to start this ridiculous search for me. Of course, they don't; the streets stay quiet and dark. Those who are in their homes are probably going to bed, or they simply don't consider putting on clothes to help with the search.

"Others will do it." That's what they usually say, unbothered by feelings of guilt or compassion. They might not even take it that seriously.

I start walking again. Just one more block to Steve's house, and suddenly I get cold feet. If Steve learns about this on the news, too, he will be mentally prepared if I show up on his doorstep asking for help. What do I do?

There's an urgency now that I've not foreseen. How could I have underestimated this town? I know the police commissioner vaguely, mostly from things that others have told me about him. He came to our house a couple of times, and he spoke to my mom in a friendly and supportive manner.

I remember her saying things about him later on, mocking him. She wasn't that kind at times, and I can't blame her for that either. I came to realize on my sixteenth birthday that she wasn't the woman everyone took her for. To the outside world, she seemed to be a rather gentle person who took things as they came, but in truth, she was wildfire waiting to spread.

Over the past few years, I have often wondered if she would explode and take half the town with her in her vengeance. The police commissioner would be one of the first to get burned.

"Yeah, right, as if he's going to do anything to help me. He's friends with *them*; he'll never stand up for me and stick it to them. Nobody in this town will. We are the pariahs here, not them," Mom told me once.

"Then why don't we leave?" I asked. "If you hate it here that much, why stay?"

"Because I won't give them the pleasure of us leaving and taking all the bad memories with us. Nope, as long as we are around, they will be reminded every single day about what they've done, and that's going to be their hardest punishment."

"What are you going to do, Mom?"

"I don't know yet. I'm biding my time. They'll find out soon enough."

Despite my mom's harsh words, there isn't that much punishment going around. She seems to have given up fairly quickly, and that seriously pisses me off. I'm angry, but what can I do? I'm not exactly in a position to go out there and punish people myself. Truth be told, it seems as if everyone went their own way again very quickly and forgot about the misery and stress that was inflicted upon us.

Everyone but Steve.

Steve has always been the nice and supportive one. Syl? Not so much. But that could have to do with the fact that I pushed her away myself. I didn't want to face her, knowing what her parents had done to us.

I walk around the corner of the last street and see a police car approaching. I push myself into the shadows of the darkness, hoping its lights won't catch me. It will become clear in a matter of seconds who I am and why I'm here.

They don't see me. Nobody ever really does. Right now, that's a major advantage. I walk down the road and come upon the supermarket, which is open twenty-four seven. I glance inside as I pass the huge windows. An older man is filling brown bags for a young woman who is more interested in her phone than she is in her own groceries. Two teenagers head toward the door with a bag in their hands. I rush away, then stop in front of the town house where Steve lives with his dad.

The lights are on; I can see Steve in the living room as I peek through the half-open curtains. He's on his laptop, sitting in front of the television. A strange calm takes over when I see him.

It's as if something is telling me that this is going to be okay. All of it. Steve's here, and he will listen. If anyone is willing to hear my side of the story, it's him. I just know it.

THE GIRL ON THE RUN AND THE PARENTS WHO LOVED HER TOO MUCH

"Are you okay?" Steve asks after a long silence that follows my story of what happened at the crash site and my walk here. Of course, I shared only some of my feelings with him.

He doesn't comment on the fact that I have put all my trust in him, and I'm not as sure as I was before that he will listen to the rest of the story. He's not a psychoanalyst. He's my age, and we used to be friends—and more than that. But things have changed in the meantime, and I know that I'm quite dependent on him right now.

If I made a mistake and he truly hates me, I have offered my life to him on a silver platter. He can do whatever he wants because he's the only one right now who knows the full story.

Then why does he ask if I'm okay? "I'm fine," I say.

"You're crying."

"Am I?"

I didn't even realize that tears were streaming down my cheeks. So strange. I wipe the back of my hand across my face and notice the glistening of moisture that wasn't there before.

My raincoat is dry by now, as are my jeans and shoes, which were soaked before. My socks are still wet, but I don't bother removing them. It doesn't matter.

"So tell me," he says, standing up to fill the kettle with water. "Why am I the one who is supposed to lie for you?"

"To *omit the truth*," I correct him.

He snorts. "You can call it that all you want, Vi, but it's a lie. It's called cheating people from the truth. Are you really serious about this, when you still haven't told me anything about why this is happening?"

"Reasons aren't important," I say.

"They are to me. If you want me to tell people a truth that you concocted, I want to know why I would do that for you when we aren't even friends anymore."

"You told me once I could always count on you."

"Did I?" he says, setting the kettle on the stove. "Was that before or after you cheated on me?"

"I didn't—"

"Stop it, Vi. Just stop it already. We both know that you did."

"I swear I never touched anyone else."

"But you were in love with someone else. You acted on it."

I look down at the floor. "Yes, I did."

He moves to stand in front of the stove while the water slowly starts to heat up. "Tell me this, then. Did you ever love me?"

I look up. "No."

He smiles. "Well, that's one of the first honest things I've ever heard coming from you. Thank you."

"For telling you that I never loved you?" I say, surprised.

"Yes. You finally admitted that you were never with me because of love. So then why were you?"

"You were nice. And convenient."

He looks at me, startled. "Convenient?"

"Yes."

"I don't understand."

I shrug. "I don't either. It's complex. I'm a complex person who makes a lot of decisions that other people never would. I've always been like that, and it has gotten me into trouble many times. But I do know that I never meant to hurt you. I was with you because I liked you, and we had good times together. But did I ever love you? No, I don't think so."

"Because you loved someone else."

"Yes, I believe I did."

"But you're not sure?"

"No. How can you ever be?"

"I am." He moves away from the stove and sits down.

"You mean that you love your new girlfriend?"

"Yes, I love Alicia. She's amazing. We love each other."

"But love is such a ridiculous thing, isn't it?" I say. "I mean, you're barely eighteen! How can you be so sure that you will stay with her forever?"

"I can't be, and I'm not so sure that we will be together forever. It sounds too weird to even say that," Steve says. "However, we both believe in living in the moment, enjoying the small things that we care about so much. That's what drives us, what makes us happy."

"I see," I say. "So you're basically telling me now that I shouldn't overthink whatever is happening in my life, and enjoy the things as they come?"

"Yes, I guess that's what I'm saying."

"Did you ever love me?" I ask.

He smiles. "I thought I did. But I'm not so sure about that anymore. I do believe that I had a lot of affection for you. Otherwise, I wouldn't have put up with you the way I did."

"You mean, with all my antics?"

"Yes. You were not an easy person to be with, Vi. It's not a secret that a lot of people don't like you. You have this habit of rubbing people the wrong way. You always seem to be looking for the more difficult path instead of the easier one. Look at this situation. You could have easily called 911 and stayed at the scene. I can't for the life of me imagine that anyone would accuse you of murdering your best friend in cold blood."

"Then what do you think happened?"

"You went for a drive, got into a fight, she unbuckled her seat belt, you tried to stop her, and, by doing so, you crashed the car into a tree."

"That sounds about right," I say.

Hope fills my thoughts. If he believes my story, then he is willing to help. Right?

"Oh no," Steve says. "I'm not going to let you off the hook just yet. I still don't know what the fight was about. You've been conveniently withholding that information."

"Because it's not relevant," I repeat.

"It is to me. I liked Syl. I respected her."

"You barely even knew her."

"Enough to know that she was a good kid."

"And I'm not?"

"Not always, no. So if you want me to help you get out of this mess, I want to know exactly what happened before the accident and why you two had that fight."

"I can't," I say, looking down again. "It's too private."

The kettle starts whistling, which almost makes me jump out of my skin. Steve stands, takes it off the stove, and fills two cups with hot water. He takes a box of tea bags and puts it on the table. Then he grabs a bowl of sugar and a spoon.

"You need to get some sugar in you. That works wonders against shock."

"I'm not in shock."

"Please. You're shaking and look as pale as a ghost. And I need to take a look at that wound too. It might get infected. How come you're hardly scathed, while she died?"

"Her side of the car took the brunt of the impact," I say.

"How?"

"I turned the wheel at the last second. If I hadn't, we'd have gone full force and straight forward into that tree."

My words come out so wrong. I realize that the moment I start saying them, but by then it's too late. Steve looks at me with renewed interest and a certain surprise. "Hm," he says, but he doesn't ask any more questions.

I add extra sugar to my tea and hold the cup while I try to get warm. This is going the wrong way; I can feel it. He no longer believes me. He's starting to wonder how Syl died so gruesomely, while I'm sitting here with a cup of tea and hardly any bruises or cuts on me.

"Listen," I say weakly, "it's not the first time one person was killed in an accident and the other one wasn't. I swear I didn't intentionally pull at the wheel. It just happened, okay? I acted on a reflex but didn't realize that it would cost Syl her life. If I could, I would swap places."

No, I wouldn't. But isn't that what people usually say in situations like this? God, I'm only making things worse, and we both know it.

"Okay, then," Steve says, sitting down again. "Let's start at the beginning and go from there. You had an accident. I believe that. I can't for the life of me even imagine you doing this on purpose. When you came to, Syl was dead and you were sitting unscathed behind the steering wheel and started thinking the whole thing through."

"Yes."

"So you started thinking: What will the people in this town say? How am I going to survive?"

"Yes, but it wasn't about me. It was about my mom."

"Why? What does she have to do with this?"

"My mom and I are very close; I'm protective over her. She's been through a lot, as you know. She's still recovering, and she's—well, she's prone to addiction."

"Like you."

"Yes," I say, not denying it, because he lived through it when he saw me reaching for booze and drugs when we were together.

"So you wanted to protect her? By running away?"

"I started figuring that people would believe that I did this on purpose, and then my reputation would be shot and she would be directly impacted too. You know what Love Hill is like. People will start making up stories, and her life here will become unbearable. I couldn't have that. She wouldn't survive."

"That's a bit dramatic, isn't it? Why not believe that she would stand by your side and come out stronger because of this?"

"Because she won't. She's not like that. My mom is too soft, too vulnerable. She won't get over it."

Steve has met my mom multiple times, but he's only seen her on her good days. On bad days, I would come up with excuses not to see her. I was getting good at it too. Protecting her meant I had to make sure not too many people knew about the drinking.

I had managed to do so successfully. Look at Steve's reaction. He's not buying it. He has never seen her drunk, so why would he?

"Look, if you'd come with me to my house tonight, you would get to see the real version of my mom that she keeps hidden. She orders her liquor and wine online so that she doesn't have to go to your dad's supermarket and be scrutinized. She's good at hiding the truth, takes away the bottles late at night. Or she makes me do it—"

"Vi," Steve says.

I stop my rant and look up.

"I need to know one thing: Were you drunk tonight?"

"No!"

"Are you sure? Or are you in denial? Because if what you're telling me is true, then there is more reason to believe that you were drinking than that you were sober. How can you reassure me that you were sober when you're living in a house with a drunk?"

"Because I know what's at stake," I say.

"Which is?"

"My whole future, my life, my career. My life away from this place."

"I thought you would never leave Love Hill because of all the memories."

"I was convinced of that too," I say. "But I haven't been sure about anything since I applied to college and got accepted. That changed everything for me."

"How so?"

"A long time ago, I was planning on going to college in California to be with my dad, and honestly, I had planned on sticking to that plan to be close to him somehow, even long after he was gone. But when I started filling out the applications, I realized there was another place I needed to go to. So I applied there and got in."

Steve looks at me with a frown on his face, and then he suddenly realizes what I'm talking about.

"NYU."

"Yes," I say.

"Why didn't you tell me?"

"I knew how you would feel about it. You're going to NYU too. I wasn't planning on looking you up there. It's a huge school; we can go our separate ways, even on the same campus."

Steve sips from his cup of tea, obviously not sure what to do with this information. "Look, Vi, it's not that I hate you or anything, but going to the same college? That would be pretty rough."

"You'll be occupied with combining swim practice with your studies," I say. "I'll be combining journalism with a major in English. So basically, we can coexist without bothering each other."

"Alicia is going to NYU too."

"I know. We used to hang out in the same circles, remember? I know these things."

"And you wouldn't be bothered with her being there? Being with me?"

"No." I laugh, and the sound is odd on this unusual night. "I'm not in love with you, remember? And you're not with me. So we're practically strangers. Nobody there needs to know."

"You don't love me, you don't mind going to the same college as me, yet you're asking me to lie for you."

"Yes, but my request is perfectly logical."

"Because the outside world needs to have a believable person that has nothing to do with you anymore but still had a bond in the past that would make it acceptable. You want me to lie, because if I do, people will believe it. They will think I have no reason to protect you."

"Exactly."

I drain the cup of tea, stand, and stretch my body. I'm so exhausted that I just want to catch some sleep and rest my aching limbs, but that's not going to happen just yet. Steve's a tough cookie; I will need all my persuasion skills to get him to do what I'm asking.

"Okay," I say. "Tell me what you want in exchange."

"Excuse me?"

"You obviously don't want to help me willingly, so you might as well tell me what you need or want."

"Are you bribing me now, Vi?" he says, and I'm not sure if he's smiling or looking upset at the prospect of being offered something.

"Not bribing. Just asking if you need anything."

"You really are good at omitting truths, aren't you?"

"I'm used to getting what I want."

"I know that. Your mother loves you too much; she always has. If she had been tougher on you, we would not be having this conversation."

"You're a good one to talk. Your dad is overprotective too," I blurt out.

"My old man is a good guy. Leave him out of this," Steve responds sharply.

"Sorry," I say, instantly regretting my words. "I overstepped."

"Yes, you did, but that's not new, either, is it? My dad always warned me about you, did you know that? He said that you were the type of person that would cross whatever line or break whatever law to get what she wanted."

"Well, I guess he was right," I say softly.

"He also said that you are a child, deep down. Someone who doesn't have empathy towards others because she never learned how to feel anything. Is that true, Vi? Is that the real reason why you left Syl alone in that car tonight? Do you even feel anything for her? Remorse? Sadness? Grief?"

"I feel it all," I say, hurt. "What makes you think I wouldn't?"

"Because you sure as hell aren't showing it. You're acting as if she's nonexistent. You should be bawling your eyes out right now about losing her, but to me, it comes across as if she's a simple inconvenience you have to deal with."

"That's not true," I say, again hurt by his words. "Is this really how you see me?"

"Yes. Some of us do."

"I'm sorry," I say. "I'm really sorry that I come across as this coldhearted bitch that doesn't give a damn about the people in her life. I do care. I loved Syl. I thought she was amazing. But thinking back on her now makes me want to scratch my eyes out, and I can't afford to do that. My mom is the most important person in my life, and I need to protect her."

"Like she always protected you."

"Yes!"

"What about your dad?"

"What about him?" I ask sharply.

"How would he react to all of this, knowing that you've abandoned Syl? You were best friends once, weren't you? What would he say?"

"He would be devastated," I admit. "He loved Syl. He respected her, cared about her. He saw her as his second daughter. We were born on the same day, after all, and we've always been connected. But it was exactly that which made this whole mess so much harder."

Steve sits in silence for a while, and then he looks at his cup of tea, which is still half full.

"You're no longer talking about the accident, are you?"

"No."

"You're talking about Syl's parents and yours. That whole thing with your dad."

"Yes. I'm so mad about it, even now."

He doesn't look at me while he tries to find the correct words to say in the least hurtful way. But in the end, we both know that whatever he's going to say will still end up destroying me.

"Vi, have you considered that you might have deliberately crashed that car into that tree, swerving at the last second so that it would hurt Syl the most?"

"No!"

"That you did it to punish her for the misdeeds of your parents?"

"No! How can you say that? I loved her!"

I stand up angrily. The chair flies backward. My cup crashes to the floor, shattering into several pieces. I can feel them hit the legs of my pants.

"Go to hell," I snap.

He's by my side before I can even reach the door and grabs me by the arm. "Vi, don't go. I'm sorry."

His arms find their way around me, and he pulls me against him. I can feel his heartbeat as he cups me in his grip and holds me so tight I can hardly breathe. But it feels good to be held again. I wrap my arms around him and burst into tears.

"It's okay," he soothes me. "I'm sorry, I just needed to make sure that you were telling the truth. I'll help you, okay? I'll help you."

He settles me back on the chair, cleans up the mess, and gives me a new cup of tea.

"I'll tell you everything," I say.

This time, he doesn't react. He sits down and listens as I tell him the story of me and Syl.

PART TWO: THE GIRL WHO WAS BORN FIRST

CHAPTER SEVEN

"Are you coming with me?" I asked.

Syl looked up from tying her shoes and gazed at the clock above the door. We'd just had practice and she was obviously tired, but I needed her to do this one thing for me or I would fail class.

I pulled my typical *Please feel sorry for me* face and watched her fold. She always did.

"Sure."

"I need some input," I clarified. "Math isn't going well right now, and you're so much smarter than I am. Which is why you're going to be a scientist one day and I will stick to languages and literature."

"Don't be silly," she said. "You're smart. Don't act as if you don't know how to do math. It's not that hard; you just need to figure things out."

"That's why I have you."

She went quiet after my remark, and I realized she didn't like it when I openly stated that I needed her to do things for me. Lately, she had been awkward about that, like it wasn't normal for friends to help each other out. But hey, it had always been like that, so what difference did it make?

We walked silently side by side to my mom's car, sitting in the same old spot, waiting for us like she did every day. Even though it was only a five-minute car ride and we could easily take our bikes, I never minded that my mom insisted on dropping us off and picking us up. In a couple of months I would get my license and, hopefully, a car of my own. In this town, everyone needed wheels. "Hey," I said, in order to break the silence. "My mom is making roast chicken for dinner. Your favorite, right? Knowing her, she'll invite you to stay. How does that sound in return for a bit of math tutoring?"

That made her face shine brightly, as if I had just given her a lollipop like when we were kids. Lollipops were the only thing back then that could cheer her up. These days, it was home-cooked meals at our place.

Things had been rough at her house recently, which made me invite her over more often than not, even though I was getting a bit fed up with always hanging around her. Syl was important to me, but I had other things going on too—like Steve, the guy in our class I had a massive crush on. He was charming, cool, friendly, and, above all else, quite smart and attractive. Every girl in school wanted him, and I felt the same.

But the competition was huge. Alicia had her eyes set on him, as well as Laura and Danielle, all potential threats who would make it hard for me to conquer him. I had been giving that a lot of thought lately, and was trying to come up with a plan.

My mom stepped out of the car and hugged me and then Syl, like she always did. She was genuinely happy to see Syl. Of course she was. Syl was the easygoing second daughter Mom had never managed to have. After my birth, there had been some medical issues, so she had to bury her dream of having more kids. She had told me a couple of years ago, once I started asking why I didn't have any siblings, that she and Dad had contemplated adoption or foster care but decided against it because they didn't want to tempt fate.

"Besides, we have Syl, right?" she had said. "She's practically another daughter."

Somehow, those words had irked me. Even though I liked Syl, I was often annoyed by her goody-two-shoes behavior. I wasn't the perfect daughter, I knew that, but it wasn't as if I was evil incarnate either. I just had a way with words and getting things done my way, which didn't always work with the people around me. Even Syl, the most patient person I knew, would sometimes groan, roll her eyes, and tell me bluntly that she would go home so I could cool off.

"Are you staying for dinner?" my mom asked faithfully.

"Sure. Thanks," Syl replied faithfully too. As if there was any discussion about that.

"So, how are your parents?" Yep, another daily routine question from my mom.

"Good, thanks."

"Have you seen them lately?" Like it's normal for a teenager not to see their parents every single day.

"Not today. I'm sure they'll be home tonight."

My mom had this thing with her face. She could shift her expression from gentle caring to pity and distress in a split second. Sometimes I believed she suffered from dissociative personality disorder and could just pull the switch to show another version of herself. I sat next to her in the front, while Syl took her usual spot in the back seat, and decided that I wanted to talk about anything other than the sadness of Syl's home.

"So, Mom, remember Steve, that guy I was talking about?"

"Yeah?" Mom said.

"Well, he did this crazy thing today. He went to football practice *and* played in an unexpected game because someone got sick and they needed another player. They won thanks to his touchdown. How crazy is that?"

"Crazy," Mom said, even though she obviously didn't know anything about football and the difficulties of scoring a touchdown at Steve's age. He had been filling in for a guy who was almost two years older than he was, which was nuts all on its own.

"He also did it while remaining cool and sexy. I'm pretty sure he doesn't suffer from helmet hair, believe me. And those eyes, Mom—they shone when he scored. That is just amazing, isn't it?"

My mom smiled, but before she could say anything, Syl rolled her eyes—which I could see in the rearview mirror—and sighed as if she was not feeling well.

"Seriously?" she said. "You're fifteen and in love? Come on, Viola. That's a load of crap. You can't be in love at our age."

"Why not?" I asked, shocked that Syl would actually go against me. She never did. Well, to be honest, she'd been doing that more lately.

And truth be told, that had really started to bug me.

CHAPTER EIGHT

We walked into our kitchen, where the smells of cinnamon and chicken seemed to mingle. It was an odd scent, and I wasn't so sure I liked it, but it was typical for our house, where my mom was constantly cooking. She was bored, even though she would never state that out loud. Cooking and baking occupied her thoughts and gave her peace of mind. Going out with friends did the same, but since she hardly had any, there was no point mentioning that.

"I've been doing a lot of baking," Mom said when we saw the mess she had made and hadn't been able to clean up yet. She looked like a disheveled housewife who didn't really like the part but played it anyhow. "Hope you guys are hungry. I've got cinnamon cookies."

"Really? Thought it was a chocolate cake," I said while reaching for the basket with the still-warm cookies. Well, at least they were good. She did have a knack for baking. In a different life, she could have opened her own bakery.

"Why don't you guys sit down, and I'll make you some hot chocolate."

"It's warm outside, Mom," I said.

"So? There's always time for hot cocoa."

Syl looked quite happy as she sat down at the kitchen table, clearly forgetting all about the main reason why I had invited her over. Math, remember?

My mom started melting chocolate and engaged Syl in a conversation about this idiotic TV show they'd seen on HBO, and before long, I was shut out, as usual. My favorite kind of shows were fantasy and horror—the more mature, the better. The classics, of course (*Game of Thrones*, *The Walking Dead*), but I liked old series, too, and thought it was fascinating how they would incorporate self-invented languages into those shows based on old European languages, like Tolkien had done. The *Lord of the Rings* was actually the only trilogy Syl and I shared a passion for.

While I listened to my mom and Syl chat, I felt frustrated and unsure of what to do. Steve had texted me back saying he wanted to meet for a movie tonight, but with the speed that things were progressing here, it would take us ages to get through my math. I contemplated throwing the whole thing out the window, leaving Syl with my mom, and just going out to meet Steve, who had, surprisingly enough, responded within five minutes after I had texted him. I couldn't ignore his message.

But could I do that? It would be the first time I'd dropped Syl like that, and it felt impolite. Then again, why not? She loved it here; she didn't need me when she had my mom.

I sighed and ignored the cup of hot chocolate while I took my backpack and walked over to the stairs. They didn't even comment on it. Why was I even here? Why was I a Harrison and she a Jameson? We should have swapped places. Our respective characters fit better with the other's parents. I could have easily lived in a house where there were no parents bugging me all the time. Syl had no idea how good that would feel to be left alone without someone hovering over me.

She obviously needed the warmth and care of a parent, and almost clung to my mom as if she were her lifeguard. She hadn't come here to be with me—no, she'd come to be with my mom. It was so obvious.

Perhaps we were switched at birth or something. There simply was no other explanation for the way that she stuck so close to my mom and saw things the exact same way, while I hated every second of these days that I had to spend with my overbearing parents.

This used to be my favorite time of the day when Syl and I were younger. I used to love hanging around in the kitchen, watching my mom prepare whatever meal it was she had in mind or making cake or pie without using a recipe. But that was when I was a kid—when I was immature, when I didn't know any better. Now I did, and it felt quite embarrassing to have a parent who didn't have the ambition this town expected.

Mom was an exception in Love Hill, where most women had jobs and a lot of drive. This was a very Christian town, founded by white supremacists who used to think that women did not belong in the workplace. Some—mostly old-schoolers—still believed that, but now most supported women having goals for themselves. Now it was seen as something special, and it was supported in many ways. There were even local awards for female entrepreneurs.

Syl's mom was like that too. She was co-CEO of a company Syl's grandfather had founded a long time ago, which meant she was hardly at home. Syl's parents had their lives, and she obviously didn't fit in them. Perhaps they'd never wanted to be parents. Her mom alluded to that some years ago, or so Syl had said.

We were very good friends, always together, always inventing fun things to do. Mostly childish stuff, to be honest, often annoying, too, but I didn't really consider that back then. Nobody really thought of how annoying their best friends were when they were little, right? Neither did we, even though it had already started nagging at me that the things we did weren't exactly mature. Like I said: Little did we know . . .

For years, Syl and I both felt as if our lives were cosmically connected. As if somehow the fact that we were born on the same day, with only five hours of difference—me being the oldest—made us sisters and besties for life.

Still, as we grew older, the differences between us became all too apparent to me, but not to her. If she had things her way, we would be stuck together forever, even sharing colleges, friends, and lives. She was getting lonelier by the year, and had started retreating into this shell of herself, a shadow of the cheerful girl she used to be when she hadn't yet realized her family situation wasn't exactly normal. Now that she did, she wanted someone like my mom.

And that was exactly the problem.

She wanted my life, my house, and my bedroom with the colorful walls and all the posters my mom had allowed me to hang up. Her own bedroom felt stark and impersonal.

A knock on the door startled me. I'd sat down at my desk with my laptop open and books on the floor without even realizing I had done so. Syl walked in without waiting for an answer.

"Sorry about that," she said. "I got distracted. Your mom was telling me all these stories, and I forgot the time. Shall we take a look at your math—"

"Don't bother," I interrupted her. "Just go away."

"Viola, what?"

"I have it figured out. I don't need you anymore. I'm fine. You can hang out with my mom since that's what you prefer to do, isn't it?"

She closed the door behind her and sat down on the bed, seemingly shocked by my words. I had hurt her, and it felt oh so good for one long moment. What was it with me and Syl these days? I just couldn't stop hurting her, like she was this mental punching bag I couldn't get enough of.

"Viola, what's going on?" she said softly—not wanting to leave, apparently. "Why are you acting like this?"

"It's nothing."

"Come on, it's me you're talking to. What's going on?"

I refused to look at her but focused on my laptop screen instead, trying to figure out how to get her out of my room without this ending in a fight.

"I'm just tired. Nothing's wrong. I can't figure out this whole math thing, and you're not helping."

"I'm sorry. I'm here for you now."

"Then grab a chair. You're here, you might as well help."

I knew my words were hurting her, that I was putting the blame for my negative thoughts on her, but I couldn't help myself. Looking at her, even now, I was so fed up with her soft, too-gentle behavior. I needed people I could really communicate and connect with, people who were like minded. Who didn't sit at parties with a goddamn book in their hands while others had fun dancing. I wanted to have fun, and she obviously had different priorities.

I cleared my throat, realizing that I needed to tell her this, that I wanted some distance between us and more room to explore other people. Like Steve, who would be meeting me in two hours at the movies. Who I wanted to kiss in the darkness of the theater. He was fun *and* he had interesting things to say. He loved to debate and question everything, while Syl just sat back and took it all in. I needed time away from her, and I would get it, because in a couple of weeks summer break would start and allow me some breathing room.

"I have to ask you something," she said as she sat down on the chair, plucking at her fingernails. "I wanted to run it by you because I'm happy but also a bit worried that you won't let me do it."

"What is it?"

"Your dad just walked in, and when we were talking about the summer, he and your mom invited me for a week away with you guys. He said it was a shame my family never went on vacation, so he invited me to go with you. I said I wanted to run it by you first, but they insisted you wouldn't have a problem with this. It still felt uncomfortable to me, though, so I thought I'd ask."

The annoyance on my face must have been apparent, because she flinched and sighed.

"I knew this was a bad idea. Of course you don't want me to go. You need time alone with your parents. Forget I ever said anything. Let's focus on your math."

I was stuck between a rock and a hard place. What to do? I *hated* our summer vacations together. My mom and dad went to this place called Westport every year at my dad's insistence. They called it their second home, and honestly it was probably the most relaxed time I had all year. But it was so boring, and always the same, even with the interesting people who lived there. It wasn't as if we were spending our time going to bohemian parties or anything like that. It was still a family vacation spent with people who treated me like a child. Every year was the same. The same places to eat, the same hotel, the same people, the same shops, the same beach walks. If anything, Syl could brighten it up by being there. At least then I would have someone to talk to.

"You know what? We're going to have an amazing time," I said. "You'll love it! We go to the same place every year, and it's like a second home to us."

And maybe, for once, I was going to have fun. I could at least share my boredom with someone else.

CHAPTER NINE

According to that woman with the YouTube channel, Annie Jones—one of the town's most (in)famous women—there were people out there who experienced predictions of things to come. She claimed we all had a sixth sense, we just didn't know how to use it.

I wasn't one of them.

If I had been, I would not have allowed Syl to come with us during that week in Westport. I would have used all my emotional resources on my dad to persuade him not to take her with us. But here we were, in July, driving out to Westport. Every single year I prayed this would be the last time we'd go to that place, because I wasn't a kid anymore and there was hardly anything for nearly sixteen-year-old girls to do. *At least I have someone to occupy myself with now,* I thought as I watched Syl's excitement grow with every waking moment. She was still such a kid.

We arrived at the four-star hotel, the Beach House, where my dad had booked our usual suite overlooking the ocean. The hotel had a private beach, which was never overcrowded. From there, it was a five-minute walk into town and the shops, which were a variation of colorful tourist places and luxury boutiques. A lot of rich people had their second pad here, and the shop owners knew that all too well.

You could distinguish the locals, the rich, and the tourists easily by the way they dressed and behaved. I hated the last group with a vengeance, mostly the ones who came packed and stacked with a dozen loud kids, as if they were the family von Trapp incarnate. The only thing missing was the whistle and the governess. Most families could do with a firm hand.

My parents knew everyone by now, and thus, so did I. As soon as we started seeing people we knew, I was treated like the child I used to be.

"Wow, Viola, you've grown! Where is that cute little girl with the ponytail? You're beautiful, just like your mom. The boys will be chasing you in droves."

Yeah, yeah. As if I would be interested in any of the guys here after being with Steve. We were on the brink of becoming an item. He was sending me text messages at the rate of a high-speed train, and I was constantly texting him back, no matter where we were or what we were doing. Syl often frowned at the way my phone was glued to my hand, but she didn't comment on it.

Of course, Syl caught some attention too.

"So good to see you again!" the owner of the boutique my mom loved to frequent said. "Oh, a new girl in town? Who is this beauty? Did you adopt her?"

Mom laughed, which annoyed me. "It almost feels like that. This is Syl, she's Viola's best friend."

"Pleased to meet you. Wow, you are beautiful. Viola has strong competition here."

That annoyed me even more.

"Thank you," Syl said. "Nice to meet you."

"And she has manners, too, that's nice. These days, young kids don't have any respect at all anymore, don't you think?"

My mom engaged in conversation with the boutique owner as she started going through the racks of clothes. My dad winked at us and whispered, "I need ice cream. Come on, let's go. She only needs me to pay the bill, anyhow."

Syl laughed, I rolled my eyes. We walked outside to the gelateria across the street, which had the best ice cream in town.

Syl seemed preoccupied; she had been since the moment we arrived. Sometimes it felt like she wasn't here at all. I caught her looking around quite a lot, as if she was looking for someone or something. She would ask to go for a walk on her own, and she didn't bother telling us where she went. She would often head for the bathroom. At the hotel, she would sometimes go to the lobby or the restaurant to have a drink on her own. I didn't get that.

"She likes to spend time alone," my mom said. "You don't have to take it so personally."

"She's here with us, isn't she?"

"Yeah, but that doesn't mean she has to be with us twenty-four seven."

My dad had this habit of taking photos. He did that a lot. He would use an actual camera and ask us to pose wherever we went. Later, he would have photos developed old-school and keep them as mementos.

At first, Syl didn't like that. She wasn't used to posing and felt awkward. "I don't like myself in pictures," she said.

"Why not? It's the perfect memento of good times."

"I never have good times with my parents," she said.

And that reminded me again why she had come with us on this trip. I felt embarrassment for questioning her behavior sometimes.

That day, at the ice-cream parlor, after my dad had once again taken pictures of us—this time without my mom around—she was all attention. I chose two scoops, Syl one, my dad four. We sat down on a bench to eat our ice cream. Syl sat next to my dad, and they started talking about superhero movies and comic books. I immediately lost my appetite.

Syl talking superheroes and comics? What the . . . ?

"I thought you hated anything supernatural," I muttered, which earned me a surprised glance from Syl.

"What made you think that?"

"You're always talking about these bullshit romantic crappy flicks with my mom."

"I have broad interests."

"Don't pick on her, Vi," my dad said. "It's fun to talk about interesting stuff."

"I'm not picking on her."

"Yes, you are. You often do."

I felt blood rushing to my cheeks, stood, and threw away the rest of my ice cream. "Well, thanks for that, Dad. Always fun to talk with you."

I walked away, thinking that he would come after me to make amends like he always did. But he stayed put and continued chatting with Syl, who hardly looked at me, eating her ice cream as if it was the best thing in the world. I stomped off, feeling ignored and upset. Why was it that whenever Syl hung around, my parents barely knew I existed? Why did they ignore me and adore her?

I hated them. I hated *her*. I missed Steve.

I sat down on a bench and called him. He didn't pick up the phone, and I remembered he had been talking about this football camp he wanted to check out today.

Feeling sad and lonely, I walked farther down the street, unsure of what to do with myself. In the end, I walked back to the same bench, where Syl was sitting alone this time. My dad was in the boutique, paying the bill my mom had racked up.

"Are you okay?" Syl asked. "You took off in a hurry."

"Yeah, well, that happens when your dad starts mocking and ignoring you."

"He wasn't doing that. He just wanted to make a point of you picking on me."

"I never pick on you."

Syl took a deep breath and looked at me with her typical puppy eyes that I had come to hate. She was getting really good at playing the victim, that much was obvious. How had we gotten to this point? My mom had always said that I should stop picking her brain to get better grades, that I should appreciate her more for who she was. But she didn't see the Syl I saw. She didn't notice the small things that were becoming more apparent these days. Syl was a manipulator; what she wanted, she got. And I'd had enough of it.

But if I told her that, if I confronted her with *my* reality, all hell would break loose. We had five more excruciating days to go. I couldn't bear a cold-shoulder situation for that long.

Syl obviously couldn't either. The moment had passed, and she didn't say anything about her true feelings. I sat down on the bench and looked straight ahead, ignoring her for a long time. It felt like the best thing to do.

When my mom and dad walked out of the boutique, they didn't say anything either. My dad reached for my hand and squeezed my fingers, and I knew this was his way of apologizing. For now, the storm had blown over, but I knew there were more to come.

In the days that followed, I spent more time with my parents and tried not to be bothered whenever Syl said or did something that got on my nerves. I even managed to survive without another sharp word or argument. And then the week was almost over, with only a few days to go. It hadn't been that bad.

Except this. There was this thing about Syl that really bothered me: She openly stared at all the people walking around town. There were same-sex couples holding hands, who would have been considered eccentric in our town but fit right in here. I could see her confusion, and that night, when we sat down for dinner, she started asking questions about it.

"Most of the people in our town simply don't get it," my dad said. "They don't want to know about how the people live here. They would call it evil—blasphemy, even."

"But why is it so difficult in Love Hill? We're in the twenty-first century, but it seems like our town is stuck in the past."

"Because sometimes people don't like to see other people being happy with who they are. It's that simple."

My dad was very vocal about his feelings toward this community, and his passion shone through his voice. In his line of work, he often had to travel to major cities, where people had accepted that the concept of a marriage between a man and a woman wasn't the norm anymore, that in today's society, a lot of people proudly showed who they were. To me, it felt normal too. To Syl, it was as if a whole new world had opened up.

"I hate our town's narrow-mindedness," I said. "I really do."

My dad seemed surprised. "Do you really feel that way about it?"

"Oh yeah."

"I didn't know."

"There are a lot of things you don't know about me, Dad," I said. "I'm not a child anymore, you know. You should start treating me like an adult."

My dad smiled and reached for my hand. "Perhaps I should," he said.

"Love you, Dad."

"Love you, hon. Let's do something together tomorrow, just the two of us."

"That sounds great."

I ignored Syl's reaction, not wanting to see the hurt in her eyes. But at least now she knew that she shouldn't even try to steal my father away from me.

The next morning, Syl was extremely quiet and looked as if she had barely slept a wink. I, on the other hand, had slept like a baby.

CHAPTER TEN

My dad and I took the afternoon to ourselves. Syl said she would go out and buy some gifts for her parents. My mom was going to stay back at the hotel for a lazy afternoon and a massage. We walked down the beach, enjoyed an amazing brunch, went to the arcade, caught a movie, and had a late-night dinner together. It was the best day ever.

We had always been very close, despite the fact that my dad worked so many long hours. I was always still awake when he came home at night, and every morning, unless he was traveling, we had breakfast together. On Sundays we would have a chat about our week, and he would give advice on whatever was bothering me.

Of all the people in my life, my dad knew me best. He was one of the good guys, never had a sharp word to say, even though he could state the truth rather bluntly now and then. Of course, I knew that the conversation would turn to the subject of Syl sooner or later, so during our brunch, I brought it up myself.

"Spill the beans, Dad. Come on, you have questions about me and Syl."

"I do, actually," he said. "And again, I can see how you and I are so similar. Your mom would rather ignore the sensitive topics, but you just blurt them out, don't you?"

"Of course. No point in beating around the bush."

"Okay, then," Dad said, putting his fork and knife aside in the middle of eating a piece of cake. "What's going on between the two of you?"

"Nothing much," I said. "And that's exactly the problem."

"Meaning?"

"Meaning that I'm growing bored with her, and I have no idea how to deal with that."

"You mean that you're finally starting to realize that you two are totally different people and you want to go in a different direction when it comes to your friendship?"

"Yeah."

He smiled, apparently not upset. "I've been waiting for you to come to that insight, Vi. It's been pretty clear to me that you guys have hardly anything in common. You're like two people in a marriage that's been going on for far too long, where the partners start realizing that the things that brought them together no longer exist."

I was surprised. "Dad, are you talking about you and Mom?"

"Oh no, not at all. We still love each other, and I don't think that will ever change, but we did have to come to terms with the fact that we're different people now. Our relationship has evolved, which is normal. It would be unusual to be exactly the same as we were when we were teenagers."

"So you're saying, basically, that I need to find a way to deal with my changed feelings towards Syl if I want to keep her in my life?"

"Yes, that's exactly what I'm saying. Have you spoken to her about it?"

"No, I don't dare."

"Why not? She'll understand."

"Which part, exactly? Have you seen how much she clings to me and you guys? She's like this leech trying to get the best hold possible. I hate when she sucks up to you because she's afraid to hurt you or get you upset. She's constantly trying to figure out ways to please people. Not just here, but in school too. She's a pleaser."

Dad started laughing as he picked up his cutlery again. "She's not as bad as you make her out to be, Viola. She's nice and appreciative. She has it rough, and she needs all the friends and support she can get. What her mom is doing to her is terrible."

"Not just her mom—her dad too."

"Nah, he's not that bad. He's just very submissive to his wife."

I was surprised that my dad would defend Mr. Jameson like that, but of course they were friends. They went golfing together, and sometimes Mr. Jameson took Dad to the shooting range to show off his handgun. He probably saw a different man than I did. Honestly, I barely knew Mr. Jameson, so what did I know?

"Listen, Vi. Syl is not a leech. She's a very lonely person who tries to hold on to everything she can because she's used to people abandoning her. She's had so many nannies and caretakers, but never a parent to guide her through life. I feel sorry for her, and I don't blame her for being so clingy. She needs you, and if you can't be there for her, you need to ask yourself why that is. You're not an easygoing person, let's be honest. You come with a manual."

"I know, Dad," I said impatiently. "But you would think that after all these years, she knows what that manual is."

"She does, but you've changed some of the pages. She doesn't know that. Tell her that you need some time to yourself. Tell her that you like to hang out with boys, too, and that you can't do that with her around all the time. Perhaps then she will come to realize that you really need that space, and that will give her some room to explore other things too."

"She won't understand."

"She will. Just give her time."

"I'll try, Dad."

"You've got this, Vi. Oh, and that manual of yours? It's not that long, trust me. You may think it is, but it's not."

I laughed. "Well, at least that's something, I guess."

———

We didn't talk about Syl again that day, and when we walked back to the hotel, we found her and Mom in the swimming pool together. Her bag was sitting by the pool, and I spotted a few wrapped gifts in them. She seemed elated and happy, more so than usual.

"Hey," my mom said. "How did you guys enjoy your time?"

"It was great," I said, turning to Syl. "Thank you for your understanding."

She looked surprised and then smiled broadly. "You're welcome. Everyone needs some time alone, right?"

"Sure do. How was your day?"

"Amazing," she gushed, but she didn't say anything else. Her behavior was odd. I brushed it off.

"Why don't you guys do some fun stuff together tomorrow?" Dad suggested. "I can chauffeur you around. I have some work to do and can take my laptop with me while you are out having fun. I'll be out of your hair, of course, but it will be nice for the two of you to spend some time together. What do you think?"

I stared at him. "Are you kidding, Dad?"

"Nope. By the way, once you get your learner's permit in November, we should start looking for a car. What do you think?"

I flung my arms around him, then turned and looked at Syl.

"Where do you want to go?" Dad asked. "I'll drive you anywhere you want."

"Just cruising sounds good," she said. "Thanks, Mr. Harrison!"

For the second time that week, I felt elated. First with my dad, and now with Syl, which I had not expected. She was as excited as I was. I remembered everything Dad had said about her and vowed to see her differently from now on. If I could get past the sense of her taking advantage of the situation with my parents, we could be those old friends again. Yeah, this could work.

The next morning, we set out to leave early. It was going to be a hot summer day, which meant sandals, a dress, a lot of water, my bathing suit, a towel, and sunscreen. My dad had given me a credit card I could use freely.

The valet brought the car in front of the hotel, and off we went. Dad behind the wheel, me beside him, and Syl behind us, dressed in almost the same outfit as I was, except she had on a bikini and wore big sunglasses, which made her look a bit like a fashion model from the seventies. I liked big sunglasses; they were elegant and they suited her. I wore my own set of designer glasses that I had gotten for my fifteenth birthday.

Syl didn't speak for at least an hour, but she didn't have to. Dad and I were chatting about everything and nothing, having a good time, happy to just cruise on the beach route while looking at houses and people. It was busy in this area, as it always was.

"I've googled this beautiful lookout where you can also have lunch," Dad said. "Want to head there? Syl? What do you think?"

"Sure," she said. "Whatever works for you is fine for me."

Her words immediately annoyed me.

"You can pick some options, too, you know."

"Oh, that's okay," she said. "I'm fine with your choices."

Yep, irritation. My dad didn't notice. He was humming away to some song he loved.

"Syl, you are entitled to your own opinion, you know," I blurted out. "Why do you always agree with me without putting up a fight?"

She smiled. "You really don't know?"

"No, I don't."

"Because it's so much easier to agree than to start an argument. You do tend to do that."

My dad snorted, and I got annoyed even more.

"I don't—" I started, but then I stopped. Yeah I did. I argued about everything, just like my dad had pointed out several times. "Fine. Sorry."

She started laughing; so did my dad. "It's okay. This is who you are, and I love you for it."

Maybe you love me a bit too much, I thought, but I didn't say it.

CHAPTER ELEVEN

Our day went really well—until it all got shot to hell, and I had Syl to thank for that. I tried to ignore my dad's part in it.

We had an amazing seafood lunch at the lookout. Dad made sure we were being treated like two princesses, probably because we looked and acted the part. Syl was having the best time, laughing, joking, and making it one of the best days we'd had in a while. I finally saw a version of her I would really enjoy having as a friend, and a nagging feeling that maybe I had been overreacting lately started in my mind.

"Things will work out fine," my dad whispered in my ear after lunch, having obviously noticed the change in the air.

"I hope so," I said.

He squeezed my fingers and smiled reassuringly.

After lunch we took a walk on the beach and enjoyed the view before getting back into the car. Syl had chosen a Spotify playlist with R & B and hip-hop, talking about how she loved to listen to Travis Scott, giving insights on his music and lyrics. R & B wasn't my cup of tea, but hey, she was enjoying herself, so who was I to complain. We drove to another beach that was quieter than the previous one. We had come to a rougher patch of land where there was more wind, but I liked it that way. I liked feeling nature around me, tugging at my clothes. It made me feel alive.

"I'm going to head into that beach restaurant and get some coffee while I make some calls, okay?" Dad said. "Why don't you girls enjoy yourselves here. Take all the time you need; I have plenty of things to do."

"Sure, Dad," I said. "Thanks."

He walked over to the restaurant while we took our bags and walked over to a nice area and laid out our towels.

We took off our sundresses and settled down in our bathing suits: me in the colorful one with the deep V cut and sarong I had bought a few weeks ago to woo Steve—even though my mom didn't find it appropriate for someone my age—and Syl in her black bikini that didn't really bring out her curves or figure. She wasn't as pronounced yet as I was when it came to physical appearances, still growing into the body she would have as an adult. I could see the beauty she would become someday, and thought it was a shame that she didn't pay more attention to her clothes. At home, she didn't care about designer outfits at all, always went for baggy jeans and large T-shirts.

"Don't laugh at my outfits," she would say. "Baggy jeans are the new trend."

I had to agree there, even though I hated them myself. They made me look like a sack of potatoes.

When we settled down, I tried to enjoy the sun on my skin, but something was up, even though I had no idea what. Syl had grown very quiet; I could hardly feel her presence by my side. If I had to make a guess, I would say it had to do with the fact that we would be going home tomorrow, but maybe it also had to do with the fact that my dad wasn't here.

I'd always had this sense that she liked to hang out with him more because he constantly tried to make her feel at ease. She wasn't comfortable with me anymore, hadn't been for quite some time. I knew why, didn't need a manual to explain it. She knew all too well that we were growing apart.

My phone chimed. A text message from Steve. I reached for it and smiled when I saw what he had sent me.

Sandra J. Paul

Can't wait to see you again tomorrow. Let's catch up soon.

Looking forward to it, I sent back.

When? How about dinner?

Sounds great, I think we'll be back around three.

Early dinner, then. Deal.

Hey and . . . ?

Yeah?

I got you a present.

Oh? What is it?

If I tell you, it won't be a surprise anymore.

I hate surprises.

Don't be such a baby. You'll find out tomorrow.

You can't convince your folks to leave tonight already?

No chance in hell.

Sigh. Okay, early dinner it is.

See you.

Are you seriously NOT going to text me before tomorrow?

Of course not. I just want you eager to see me tomorrow.

You are Sly Vi.

You're Evil Steve. Later.

Later.

I tucked away my phone and looked up at Syl, who had moved away quite a bit and was gazing the other way. I had neglected her without even realizing it. Why didn't she just pick up her phone and start texting her own friends? Oh wait, she had no one except for me.

"Are you okay?" I asked cautiously.

"Yeah," she said, barely looking at me. "Just a bit sad."

"I can imagine," I said, because what else was I supposed to say? "It will be fine. When we get back, your parents will have missed you and they will realize they do love you."

"Yeah, right."

"Come on, Syl, let's not waste our last afternoon feeling gloomy. You had a good time, right?"

"I had an amazing time."

She moved closer to me and looked me in the eye. And then she came to sit even closer, which made me feel uncomfortable. "I wish this would last forever," she said.

She leaned into me and placed her head on my shoulder. I startled. We hadn't been this close to each other for ages; we weren't huggers or anything like that. And here she was, so close to me that I could feel her warmth. I wrapped my arm around her because it was obvious she needed that right now.

"I know," I said.

"I don't want to go home," she continued, her voice breaking as if she was on the verge of crying. "Not ever. I want to stay here forever."

I was surprised by her words, and immediately thought of Steve and how different he was. He made jokes and liked to have fun, and he showed his feelings in a way that didn't come across as pushy or clingy. God, I needed breathing space. I really did. This was too close for me.

"Why?" I said, probably harder than intended, but she didn't seem to hear it. "This isn't real life, you know."

"I know." She sighed. "And that's the hardest part. Even going back to the hotel, to your parents, is hard when I want to spend my time with you."

Oh God. What the hell was this? I felt uncomfortable and suffocated, almost scared to move.

"I don't get it," I said.

I wanted to add that I had no clue what was going on, and then Syl ruined it by saying what I was afraid of hearing. What I felt she would say and wouldn't sit right with me. I was *not gay*. I was straight; I was in love with Steve, and Syl knew that. She *knew* and she pushed on anyhow.

"I don't want to ever *not* see you," she said. "I want to be with you forever. In every way." Her hand moved to my chest, and I shot up and let go of her. My arm slipped away and I crawled backward, and I was on my feet in a flash. I pulled the sarong over my chest, reached for my shoes, and walked away. I was stunned into silence. What was I supposed to do about this?

I was not in love with her, nor with any other girl! This had nothing to do with Syl, I just did not love her the way she needed to be loved.

I had misread all the signs, all the efforts she'd made to be close to me, all the ways that she spoke about things that should not be discussed between two girls who didn't love each other in that way. I felt sorry for her. My heart sank, and I was ashamed. Not for what she had attempted to do, but for the way I had to brush her off to keep the distance between us. This could never happen, not even once.

I thought about that Katy Perry song. I couldn't even let it come to that. It would give her hope I couldn't afford her to have. I was going home to Steve in the morning, and she would have to accept that.

I called my dad while walking back to the car. He came out of the restaurant pretty quickly.

"Hey, what's wrong?"

"Nothing."

He unlocked the car and I got in, without waiting to see if Syl was coming too. She got in, ignoring my dad's failed attempts to get her talking. We didn't speak another word the whole drive home, the fun day completely forgotten. We made it back to the hotel right before dinnertime, but instead of going inside with my dad and Syl, I turned around and walked away, leaving them standing at the hotel entrance.

"What's going on, Vi?" Dad called out. I ignored him, angry at him, too, for suggesting this day in the first place.

I walked down the streets of Westport, sat down for a bagel, and tried to gather all my senses. It was over. I could no longer stay friends with Syl, not even from the distance I had planned to create. We would no longer be able to communicate, to talk about whatever things we needed to discuss, without thinking of her ulterior motives. How could we ever be friends again if I would believe that everything she said was meant differently than she intended it to be?

I didn't have gay friends. In Love Hill, being different was not acceptable. I didn't know how they felt, how they acted, what they did, how they saw things, how they identified other gay people. Syl obviously sucked at it, or she wouldn't have come on to me like that. She should have known that I wasn't like her, that I really did like Steve. How could she think otherwise? Had I ever given her the impression that I felt this way about her?

I felt guilt more than anything. Also anger and distress, disgust at my own reaction. I had to find a way to show her that I wasn't upset with her while trying to come to terms with it myself. And find a way of brushing her off gently in order to protect her against herself.

My dad called while I was sitting on the terrace of the bagel shop, nursing a cup of coffee.

"Are you okay?" he asked.

"No, I'm not."

"Where are you?"

"The Bagels R Us place."

"I'm coming over."

"Just you, Dad. No one else, okay?"

"Okay."

He got there in ten minutes' time, ordered coffee and two desserts—even though I didn't ask for one—and faced me.

"What's going on, Vi? Syl wouldn't say anything. She went to the suite without a single word. Did you guys have a fight?"

"She tried to kiss me, Dad."

"Oh."

That's all he said. Enough for me to realize that he knew about her feelings for me. "Why aren't you surprised?"

"I had suspected for a while that she felt more for you than she probably should."

"You're saying that you knew she's gay?"

"The fact that she tried to kiss you doesn't necessarily mean she's gay. She could be experimenting. Lots of teenagers do that—adults as well, even though we don't really talk about it at a certain age."

I narrowed my eyes, surprised to the core by his words. "Dad, what are you saying exactly?"

"Just that you should give her a chance to figure things out for herself. Everyone is entitled to that."

I looked at the dessert in front of me that suddenly looked quite appealing and dug in.

Chocolate, the perfect comfort food.

"I know you're upset, Vi, but please don't take this out on your best friend. Syl needs a friend, not someone to judge her."

"I'm not judging her, Dad, I'm just . . . you know."

"Surprised? Embarrassed?"

"Yeah, something like that."

Dad smiled and drank his coffee before fixing his gaze on me. He was stern and not as sympathetic as I would have expected him to be. What did Syl have that made him always seem to feel the need to protect her?

"Listen, Vi, this is important for you to realize. There will come a time—and it will be here sooner than you think—that you'll become friends with people who will be a whole lot better for you than the hypocrites that live in Love Hill. We both know this town is poison; it always has been. It was founded by people who may have represented the world as it was way back when it was normal to treat women like garbage. Unfortunately, a lot of their descendants still feel the same. If you think of the way the world is evolving today and then compare it to the narrow-mindedness of our town and the way people who are different are being treated there, I regret ever having moved there. I love a lot about Love Hill. I love its location, the nature, the tranquility. But more often than not, I consider leaving it. Our town is not a representation of reality, and if there is one thing I really regret, it's that you're growing up surrounded by people who think it's okay to look down on everyone who is different."

"Dad, I don't look down on people who are different," I said. "And I'm not blind or stupid, you know. I know what's out there, and I'm actually looking forward to exploring a whole new world. This is not about that. It's about the fact that I didn't even realize that my best friend had a crush on me. It's silly that she does, simply because we are too different to even match. I couldn't for the life of me imagine building a relationship with her, when I find certain parts about her annoying and . . ." *Dull.* "Anyhow, I was just shocked, not upset. I'm not angry at her, I'm just wondering why she would even think of me that way."

"You really don't know, do you?" Dad said.

"I really don't."

"You're her hero, Vi, you always have been. All the things she does and says are all about you. She has no one and nowhere else to go. She needs you, but you are blind to her needs. You need to discuss this with her, or your friendship will not survive."

He placed his credit card on the table and gave the waitress a large tip. That was his signal to end the conversation. We walked back to the hotel, where I found Syl sitting on the couch next to my mom.

"Hey, hon," Mom said. "How was your evening?"

"Good. I'm going to bed. Good night, everyone."

I purposely didn't look at Syl, not wanting to be persuaded by her big eyes and fearful gaze. She was scared, not just because this could mean losing me, but also because this could mean the end of her relationship with my parents as well. Why would she come to our house if we weren't friends anymore?

I lay awake in bed and listened to the sound of the television. It didn't take long for my parents to go to bed, but Syl didn't follow suit. About an hour later, she finally came in. I was on my side, facing away from her. She knew, of course, that I was awake.

"I'm sorry," she said. "I really am. Please forget what I said."

I sat up, switched on the light, and looked at her with unconcealed concern and pity.

This had to stop, or our days at school would be hell.

She stood in the middle of the room with her arms folded over her chest. Normally, she would undress casually to her underwear, but this time she didn't. Stress lingered in the room. She started gathering her things, obviously planning on changing in the bathroom. Oh yes, this was not going to end well.

"I'm not what you're looking for," I said while she had her back turned toward me.

"I know," she whispered.

I got out of bed and placed my hand on her arm.

"I'm sorry. I didn't mean to be so insensitive and rude. I was caught off guard, I guess."

She turned around with tears in her eyes.

"It's okay. Just . . . please stay my friend. I will never say things like that again," she said. I felt guilty as hell. All our shared memories came back. What had I done? I had almost thrown away the best thing I had. I had to put an end to this situation.

"But it's okay to say them," I said gently. "You just need to know that I don't feel that way about you."

"I know," she said, rolling her eyes. "Steve."

I smiled. Oh yes, Steve. Even now, I couldn't wait to see him again. But he didn't have to know what had happened. I would not tell anyone.

She walked into the bathroom and closed the door behind her. I sat on the bed, feeling better, even though I realized all too well there was now a rift between us that could expand easily. I wanted to be careful, to think of myself first and her second. I couldn't risk her flirting with me openly, her thinking that I was open for possibilities because I was being nice to her.

I had to find a way out of this, had to get her to talk to others who were like her, who really were interested in girls.

I needed to get her into the arms of someone who would take the stress off me. Someone at school. In our class, maybe? But who? I didn't have a sense of who liked other girls; we didn't talk about this at all. I sure as hell didn't have a radar or sixth sense for this. But others might know. There were kids at school other people were gossiping about. If I could figure out who, I could get Syl off my hands and the problem would be solved.

"Good night, Syl," I said when she walked to her bed and crawled in.

"Night, Vi. And thanks."

"For what?"

"For not throwing me away."

Her words lingered for a long time. I barely slept that night. I could hear soft breathing.

Early the next morning, when we walked on the beach for the last time before leaving, I used the opportunity to get to know more about her. I poked her and pointed at a girl who seemed attractive enough to draw anyone's attention.

"Isn't she your type?"

Syl looked at me, stunned, then smiled lightly.

"No. I like a different type."

"Like who?"

"Some girls at school; it varies. It's hard to explain."

People like you, she obviously wanted to add, but I didn't comment or ask more details. "Well, the moment you figure it out, let me know and I'll help you find the perfect one," I said.

She was absolutely flabbergasted. I could see relief dancing in her eyes, followed by a sense of appreciation. I knew what she was thinking: I had forgiven her for her boldness, and I had accepted her coming out. I would stick by her side and help her through this. I needed to find someone who could make her happy so I could concentrate on my own happiness as well.

"Ready to go?" my dad asked when we came back.

The bags were in the trunk; he was holding the car keys. My mom was already waiting.

I looked up at the hotel and said a quiet goodbye. I didn't know what I was feeling, but something came over me. I just knew that this would be the last time we came here as a family.

We left town through its main street, to its outskirts, to the only road that would bring us out of Westport. It was just a two-hour drive, and Dad announced we wouldn't stop for lunch but head home immediately. I sent Steve a text to let him know, sat back, and listened to the radio station that played a lot of Spanish summer songs. Syl was quiet and closed her eyes. My mom slept. My dad hummed.

It felt as if we were leaving the vacation mood behind us and were returning to a reality nobody liked, even me.

"Are you looking forward to seeing your parents again, Syl?" Dad asked.

"Uh-huh," she said, which almost made me laugh. Of course not, she hated going back.

"Will you please give my regards to your parents when you see them?"

"I will, Mr. Harrison."

"I'll give your dad a call to meet up for golf."

Dad parked the car in front of our house and helped Syl with her large and small suitcase.

"Thanks for everything," Syl said, hugging my mom and dad. Then she hugged me.

"Thank you for understanding."

"Sure," I said.

"Want to meet up later today?"

"I'm seeing Steve tonight, but I'll give you a call tomorrow. We can meet up with some of the others?"

"Okay," she said. "I'll wait for your call, then."

"Great. See ya."

I walked into our house with my suitcases in hand while she made her way across the street. I didn't look back once. Steve was already on my mind.

CHAPTER TWELVE

Steve came to our house to pick me up for dinner and a movie. He already had a car, a secondhand Ford he had partially paid for himself by doing all kinds of jobs at his dad's supermarket. His dad said it was really important for him to learn the value of money, and so he made him work. Not that Steve seemed to mind. He actually liked working there.

"How was your trip?" he asked after kissing me on the cheek. I closed the door behind me. My parents were upstairs talking, but I didn't know what about.

Something was up between them. I could feel it. They'd had an argument earlier that morning while Syl and I were walking on the beach. Right now, the atmosphere still hadn't cleared, but that didn't concern me. My mom could have these dramatic moods at times, and they always passed.

"Fine," I said. "Boring at times, fun at others."

"Be glad you get to go on vacation. My dad never wants to; he's always working."

"I know, and I appreciate what my parents are doing for me, but sometimes it really does feel as if I'm still a little girl going on vacation with her folks."

"Maybe you and I can go away together for a weekend or something."

I was startled by his suggestion, and then smiled while I reached for his hand. "Are you coming on to me?"

"Shouldn't I do that?"

"You should—the more, the better."

"Good," he said, leaning over to embrace me. We shared a small kiss, which was lovely and felt absolutely amazing. He sighed happily as he released me.

"God, that feels good. You're amazing, Vi. You smell so nice, you look fantastic. Why and when did I get this lucky to get to be with you?"

"I'm the lucky one," I said, running my hands through his hair. "You are perfect."

He laughed. "No, I'm not. I have a lot of flaws."

"Then don't tell me about them now; I don't want to know. I just want to enjoy the fact that I have a perfect boyfriend and he will do everything he can to make me happy."

"Am I your boyfriend, then?"

"Oh yes, you are. Unless you're with another girl I don't know of?"

"Oh no," he said, "I wouldn't dare."

"Good. I want to keep you all to myself."

He laughed and we kissed again before getting into his car. It was only then that I realized the entire street could have seen us making out in my dad's driveway. Not that I cared.

He took me to a place that was known for their broad range of vegan and veggie options. He wasn't a vegetarian himself, but he knew I had decided to go full-blown vegetarian at the beginning of this summer, and he was obviously willing to do this for me. My mom called it a fashion statement and continued to put roast chicken on the menu, which I continued to refuse to eat.

"This is really cool, but you don't have to do this for me," I said. "Regular burger places have a lot of veggie food, too, these days."

"I actually have three veggie days per week," he said. "Didn't you know?"

"You're becoming more perfect by the day, Steve. Are you sure you're human? I truly believe that you aren't."

He laughed. "I am. But if you doubt my existence, I can show you my birth certificate."

"That's okay, I believe you," I said. "You could still be swapped or something, but for now, I'll just take advantage of the fact that you are here with me and that you are willing to eat vegetarian food."

"Good."

We sat down and chose different dishes, which we ended up sharing. I told him about Westport and the things we had done, without going into too much detail. I hardly mentioned Syl, and he didn't ask about her.

"Sounds like it was amazing."

I shrugged. "It was okay. To be honest, I'm dying to go to New York, but my mom doesn't like big cities. She has this thing with crowds. I guess that's what happens when you grow up in a small town."

"And you don't mind going to large cities, then?"

"No. Well, I've never been there, but I have this idea of what it would be like."

"Then I think we should go."

"What, you and me?"

"Yeah, why not?"

"New York, just the two of us, while I'm still fifteen? That's never going to happen."

"So? New York won't go away. We can start making plans for spring break or something."

We had a fantastic time at the movies, where we settled into the back and held hands. I knew all this still didn't mean anything, that we were just kids flirting and having a good time, but for the first time, it felt to me as if there was someone in my life who actually felt the same way I did. We were connecting in a good way. When we walked back to his car, he reached for my hand.

"Is everything okay with you and Syl?"

"Everything's fine," I said. "Why?"

"I don't know. Just a feeling."

"Don't worry about her. Just worry about me."

He laughed. "Should I be worrying?"

"Nah. Well, except for the fact that you should find ways of paying attention to me and getting to know me."

"Looking forward to it too," he said.

This was going to be the best summer ever.

THE GIRL ON THE RUN AND THE DAD SHE LOST

I try not to look too much at Steve, who is sitting quietly on his kitchen stool, taking in everything I have just told him about that summer vacation in Westport and what Syl did.

"Damn," he says. "Yeah, there were rumors about her falling for girls, but I never realized they were true. Not that it matters to me; I don't care who people fall in love with."

"Unfortunately, most people in this town do, and they would not have liked it if it had come out."

"But it never did."

"I told my dad, and you saw how that turned out."

"He was very open-minded about these things, which I can appreciate."

"Well, that's the thing, isn't it?" I say. "I know why he was, and I know why he hated this town so much, but I'm really angry about it too."

"I don't understand."

I sigh. "You really never knew my dad, did you?"

"Not really. We spoke a couple of times, but usually about the typical stuff. Football and that sort of thing. He was nice, though; I would have loved to know him better."

"I wished you would have known him better too," I say sadly. "Now it feels as if I can't talk about him with anyone."

"Your mom?"

"She still won't talk about him, and she gets upset when I do."

"I'm really sorry to hear that. I hope things will change someday, Vi. He doesn't deserve that."

"Doesn't he, though?" I say, sounding bitter, I know. I can hear it myself.

"What do you mean by that? Vi, you are not making sense at all. What are you hiding? What aren't you telling me?"

"There were more things happening during that vacation that I honestly had no idea about until it all started making sense. My mom's behavior, the conversations between my parents, the way they were acting. Something was amiss, but I only started realizing that much later. I was blind to it, I think, caught in a tunnel vision that had to do with you."

"Me?"

"Yeah, we were just falling for each other, remember? That is usually the fun part about a new relationship, and since you were my first real boyfriend, I was falling head over heels for you and ignoring everything else."

"I do remember that we were together all the time that summer," Steve says.

"Do you regret that, looking back on it now?"

"Oh no, not at all. I was happy to be with you, and despite our breakup, I don't regret having spent that time with you. I do regret the way things went after summer, but I've forgiven you for everything."

"Forgiven me?"

"Yeah, Vi, forgiven you. You did awful things to me, and you know that I'm telling you the truth. You were not an easy person to be with; I've told you that before. And you've been putting me through the wringer in many different ways. So yeah, I had a hard time getting to know you, then went through a lot of difficulties trying to understand you, to having all these mixed feelings inside about wanting to help you but being unable to, to having to decide what to do with you while realizing that could be the final nail in your coffin."

I'm startled by his words. "Was I that bad?"

"Not always, but yes, in many ways you were. You have done things I would not have forgiven other people for, but I knew where they were coming from and I understood."

I swallow the sadness that lingers inside my mind, thinking about that summer and the best time of my life. After coming back from Westport, I spent so much time with Steve doing all these amazing things, and when school started again and all hell broke loose, we never really captured that sense of belonging anymore.

"I wish I could go back and keep that momentum," I say sadly.

"I know," Steve says. "If you had stayed the person you were then, during those six weeks we spent together, I would be with you today. But that didn't happen, and I do get why."

"My dad."

"Yeah, your dad. And all the secrets and details you've kept from me. Your dad left, and you took it hard, and I get all that. I *know* something terrible happened to him, Vi, but you never told me what, or why you felt like you did. I have tried to ask you over and over again, and you just shunned me. You used me when you needed me, but you did everything in our relationship on your terms and conditions, and

I just couldn't stand for that anymore. It became too much to bear, especially when you started to drink."

"I know," I say. "And again, I am sorry."

"Now that we are here, talking openly, I need to ask you this: Are you willing to tell me the truth now?"

"I might as well," I say. "I mean, there are no more secrets to be kept from you if I want your help. I need you to understand everything, so yeah, I need to tell you about my dad and how I lost him."

Steve gets up and starts busying himself with food and coffee. I already feel like I'm agitated, sitting on the edge of my seat, pumped up with a lot of adrenaline. My nerves feel shattered, and my body is strained, and there is still this whole sense that I'm living on borrowed time.

That Steve will lie for me is almost a certainty by now. He could have thrown me out an hour ago, but he didn't. He is calm and gentle with me, and it's obvious he cares. I don't know if he has forgiven me for leaving Syl behind, though. I haven't forgiven myself yet either.

Syl.

I try not to think about her as being dead. In my mind, while telling this story, she is still very much alive, and I want to keep it that way.

I don't want to think about her in that car, dead, her broken eyes staring at me accusingly. I see her as the girl she was on that beach, in her black bikini, sitting next to me.

That final day, when we were walking on the beach, was the last real fun moment I had with her. We were talking about girls, and I had made this whole plan for her. She looked happy that I understood where she was coming from. That I didn't judge her for choosing a different path.

In the end, though, I still failed in every single way. No, hang on—I didn't. I did get what she needed. "Vi?"

I look up.

A plate of cookies and a cup of coffee are sitting in front of me.

"You're fading out. What's going on?"

"Nothing." I blink and rub my eyes. "Just tired."

"Do you want to get some rest?"

"No. I'm fine."

He sits down again, takes his coffee, and sips it. I do the same. The coffee reinvigorates me.

"Ready when you are," Steve says. "Do you want to continue?"

"Yeah, I guess."

This is going to be the hard part. I need to get myself through this; there is no choice. But the next part is the most difficult because it will bring me back to memories I prefer to push away but cannot ignore.

I take a deep breath and look at my hands, bringing me back to that time in Westport, the final vacation we had as a family. The only regret I have about that week is that we weren't there alone.

If Syl hadn't been there with us, I would have seen all the issues and trouble my parents were going through, but because she was there, I actually ignored all the signs that my parents' marriage was in deep trouble.

"I said that I had ignored all the telltale signs that something was up," I begin, "but there was a lot more to it that you have to know. I just don't know where to begin."

"From the beginning."

"Which is?"

"You choose," he says. "But perhaps you should start with the easiest factor: Syl."

"Yeah, Syl," I say, flashing back to that girl on the beach who'd seemed so happy for once. "Every time I hear Travis Scott on the radio, I turn it off. Can't stand to hear his songs anymore; they remind me too much of her."

"Because you feel guilty thinking of her."

"Yeah, I do."

"What was her part in this? She was with you guys on vacation, but did she know anything about what you're going to tell me?" Steve prods.

"No. She was just there, part of the whole scene, but she never realized what was going on. You have to consider the fact that she only saw my mom in her role as caretaker. The woman who baked cookies and made delicious roast chicken. She never really saw the other side of her."

"But you did, of course, because you live with her."

"Yeah, which wasn't always easy, either, and it had only gotten worse as the years went by."

I nurse my coffee, remembering all the times that my dad and mom had casual conversations about anything and nothing, always avoiding intense subjects or topics.

"My parents never really talked. Not here in Love Hill, and certainly not there, in Westport."

"What do you mean by that?"

"I've never known them to have an in-depth conversation about politics or current events. My mom simply did not care about those things. If she had been born thirty years earlier, she would have been the happiest housewife in the world. My dad would have gone to work every day and come home to a house smelling delicious. They would have been content. But now they weren't, and the cracks in their marriage started to appear swiftly."

"Your dad no longer felt happy?"

"No. And I got where he was coming from. My dad had always accepted her for who she was, but two years ago, that summer in Westport, it all came to an end."

"Your dad left."

I look up. "He didn't just leave, Steve. He ruined everything."

PART THREE: THE FATHER WHO LEFT AND BROKE THEIR HEARTS

CHAPTER THIRTEEN

Westport, July

Too occupied with Syl and getting annoyed by her meek behavior, I only realized many months later that I had missed a lot of the telltale signs that my parents' marriage was in deep trouble. If I had not been so busy being irritated by her, we might not have wound up in the situation we are in today. My dad might still be here. I blame myself for that.

That morning, I think it was the fourth day that we were there, my dad was sitting at the breakfast table with a local newspaper and his phone by his side. He had the sound on and was receiving tons of text messages.

My mom, trying to enjoy her breakfast, was getting visibly annoyed. I was on my phone, scrolling through Instagram, while Syl was at the breakfast buffet, deciding between eggs and sausages. I always went for the healthy stuff, having turned vegetarian at the beginning of summer, a fact my mom was still ignoring. She would fill up her plate with sausages and show them to me as if that would change my mind about my dietary choices.

"Who is constantly texting you?" my mom grunted and reached for my dad's phone.

He shot up and pulled the thing away from her before her fingers even touched it, switched off the sound, and put it away.

"People at work," he said. "They're having issues on this deal and wanted my advice. I will probably need to get some work done later today."

"Of course," Mom said. "The business will fall apart because you're not there, right?"

"Don't be like that; you know it's just a few calls. Won't take me longer than an hour or so."

"Then why are you still here having your breakfast so calmly?" she commented. "Because it's not *that* important."

"They're dropping the information in my inbox, so I just have to read through it when I have the time. Why are you so inquisitive?"

"You're not acting like yourself."

"I am. You aren't," my dad said sharply, obviously getting more irritated by the second. "Stop poking like that. I will take a look at it later, and when I do, I will take my time. Now, can I please have my breakfast in peace and quiet? Thank you."

"Sorry," Mom muttered.

She was obviously distressed. I didn't really care what was going on. My dad worked all the time, it didn't matter to him if we were on vacation or not. He took an hour here or there to make calls and start up his laptop, and then he flipped the switch in his head and moved on to do fun stuff with us. It had always been like that. He was good at the flipping part. He could change from being the fun-at-home dad into the professional dad in a flash.

"Mom, what are we going to do today?" I asked, trying to get her attention away from him.

To my surprise, she had tears in her eyes. I was shocked, but my dad was not fazed by her reaction at all. He folded the newspaper, got up, and left for our room.

Syl sat down with her plate. Mom didn't say anything. Instead, she got up and walked to the buffet, seemingly to fill her plate again. That gave her the opportunity to wipe her face without Syl noticing that anything was amiss.

Syl started eating, unaware of the weird conversation. Mom returned to the table with a broad smile on her face and started eating. She had stashed chocolate bread and chocolates on her plate. Emo food.

"Mom?" I repeated. "What are we going to do today? Do we have any particular plans?"

"How about a movie?" she said. "There's a drive-in tonight. We could go there."

"Sure. And what about during the day?"

"I was thinking of going away with your dad. Would that be okay?"

I thought about the long day that loomed ahead of me with nothing to do.

"Why don't you guys go shopping? I'll give you Dad's credit card," Mom suggested.

"Are you serious?" I said. That would be a first.

"Yeah, why not? You could do with some new clothes."

Syl looked up expectantly. She hated clothes and she hated shopping, but I didn't.

I loved it.

"Okay," I said. "Thanks, Mom."

"Sure, sweetie."

After breakfast, when we walked up to the suite, my dad was sitting behind his desk with his laptop open, typing away. He stood up, went to my mom, and hugged her.

"Sorry about that," he said.

"I'm sorry too," she said, clinging to him.

But I noticed that he never left his phone alone again.

―――

As I look back on the whole situation now, my parents hardly spoke to each other as the days passed by. They had gone away together, and there were things said that day that changed everything, but I hadn't noticed it until it was too late.

My mom became very quiet and cautious with her actions. She would stay at a distance, would often go for walks on her own, would sometimes even stay away from dinner, saying she had a headache. She didn't even do it subtly, but because I was too busy worrying about other things, I didn't care.

They went for a long beach walk at some point. I had nothing to do, so I decided to go to the beach too. Not with the intent of following them or being with them, but to have a long phone call with Steve.

As I was on the beach having that chat with him, I noticed my parents walking in front of me. They were obviously arguing about something, but I couldn't make out what it was and wasn't too interested in getting involved in my parents' conversation. They were adults, they had another life apart from being my parents, and I wanted to give them the privacy they needed.

My parents argued sometimes; that was nothing new. Sometimes it was about my dad's long hours or the project he was currently working on that took him away from home more than my mom liked. Sometimes it was about me. She felt that he spoiled me too much, he said she should give me more freedom. I agreed with the latter.

In the end, though, they always made up quickly.

That day, there was something different about the arguing. My mom gestured broadly; he seemed small and subdued. In the end, they walked into a restaurant, and I could see them choosing a table by the window. I hurried past so that they wouldn't see me, and concentrated on Steve again.

When we returned from vacation, I couldn't wait to see Steve, so I ignored the stuff that was going on at home. My dad immediately went into his office and let my mom deal with unpacking the suitcases. He basically locked himself up.

She started doing the laundry, and that afternoon, she went into a baking frenzy, using loads of chocolate and sugar. Emo food again. My mom wasn't overweight, but she wasn't as skinny as a lot of women in this town, either, and I knew this was because she had plenty of time to eat stuff that wasn't good for her.

I didn't know about the eating frenzy until I came home much later that night and found all these baked goods—half of them already devoured by her—in the cupboards. My dad was not home. She sat in front of the television, hardly caring about my return.

"How was your evening?" she asked without looking up from the series she was bingeing.

"Great. Where's Dad?"

"Out."

"Out? Where to?"

"Don't know, don't care."

I sat down next to her and looked at the plate of cookies and cup of hot chocolate she had in front of her. I could tell she had been eating and crying for a while.

"Mom, what's going on?" I asked.

"Nothing. Why?"

"You're not being yourself."

She looked at me with such disdain that it made me cringe. I knew she didn't like that I was very close to my dad. He and I were the same in many ways, while she was not the type of person I connected with. I never knew what to say to her; we simply did not have that much in common.

"Do you care, Viola? Do you actually care about your good old mom?"

"Of course I do," I said. "What are you talking about? What's wrong, Mom?"

"Would you care if something happened to me?"

Again, I was taken aback. "Mom, why are you talking like that?"

"Your dad doesn't give a shit about me, so why should you? You are two of a kind, aren't you? You really don't care about anything except yourselves."

"You know that isn't true."

"Isn't it? Then why do you treat Syl like dirt all the time?"

"I don't," I said, hurt by her accusation.

"You do and you know it. Your dad knows it too; that's why he came to talk to you. But then again, he knows all about putting people through the wringer, doesn't he? He's doing exactly the same."

"Mom, I really don't get it," I said.

"Of course you don't," she said, with such hatred in her voice that it made me cringe again. "You really have no clue."

In the end, I got up and left the room. What was I supposed to do? She was making no sense at all.

CHAPTER FOURTEEN

Those last weeks of summer passed too quickly. Steve and I were getting closer by the day. We were together whenever we could be, enjoying the days as they came.

Looking back on those whirlwind weeks with Steve now, being so stupidly in love, I knew that I was ignoring so much else—Syl being the most important part. After Westport, I was just so eager not to have her by my side all the time that I wound up canceling plans we had tentatively set up. They weren't really that definite, so what did it matter that we didn't go through with them? Besides, she had other friends; she could easily hook up with other people.

Steve and I did a lot of fun stuff together. We went to the movies a lot, hung out with friends, went to parties, spent time with his dad, and just had fun. Fun. Fun. So much fun.

It became quite clear by the end of the summer that we were an official item, and the entire school was aware of it by the time we started again in September. It was all over the group WhatsApp chat we had with our classmates. I enjoyed them teasing us, and Steve obviously didn't seem to mind.

A couple of days before school started, Steve and I made out in my bedroom. It was absolutely amazing. It was incredible. When he went home after telling me over and over again how great I was, I lay awake in bed for hours thinking about him.

The next day, out of the blue, Syl sent me a text message.

Leave me alone from now on. We're through.

Funny, I thought I had made it clear a while ago that she wasn't the only friend I had, but it still hurt that she would make it so official now. I was upset, ridiculously so, as if she had dumped me for someone else.

I shouldn't be angry. After all, *I* had been ignoring *her* for quite a while now, happy that there were other more exciting things in my life, but it still hurt. Which was really, really stupid.

I walked downstairs and found my parents sitting at the breakfast table, not speaking to each other like they had been doing for some time now. I made a bowl of oatmeal and started eating while I reread that message.

Leave me alone from now on. We're through.

I decided to send her one back.

What's going on?

It bounced.
Bounced?!
I couldn't find her in my WhatsApp box anymore. She had blocked me. She had actually *blocked* me! I became more upset by the minute, and my mom noticed suddenly.
"What's going on?"
"Syl blocked me."
Mom smiled. "At last, I would say."
"Excuse me?"
"Come on, Viola, you've been ignoring that poor girl for six weeks. Did you really think she would sit back and take that? She's not stupid, you know."
"I never said she was."
"But you did treat her like she is," Mom remarked. "I would say she's in her right mind, blocking you now. You had it coming."

Dead Girls Don't Talk

My dad looked up and banged his hand on the table.

"Enough!" he yelled. "Stop putting your daughter down like that."

"Like you're doing to me?" Mom remarked coolly.

"Like *you* have been doing to *me*, you mean," he said sharply. "And then you are surprised that I don't like you anymore?"

He walked out of the room and we remained behind, taken aback. I looked at Mom, who was trembling. Tears fell onto her uneaten slice of toast. She shoved her chair back and fled the room.

I didn't know what to say, what to do. So I tried to call Syl but did not get through. She really had blocked me.

I sent Steve a message to tell him I had some things to do before school, then left the house. I crossed the street to Syl's and rang the bell. Her housekeeper opened the door after a while and looked me up and down, as if she were the owner of this mansion and I was just a servant.

"Yes?"

"I came to see if Syl is home," I said.

"She isn't."

"When will she be back?"

"I don't know."

"Can you please leave a message for her?"

"No."

"No?"

"No. I don't take messages. If you want to talk to her, you will need to come back when she's home."

"And when will that be?"

"I don't know."

"You're quite helpful," I said, laughing nervously. "Is she really not here?"

"She isn't. And if she was, she would not want to talk to you."

"So she is."

"No, she isn't. Is there anything else? I would like to finish my tasks."

"No," I said. "Apparently, there is nothing else. Thank you."

She shut the door in my face and I stood there, stunned and upset. Who the hell did she think she was?

I didn't give up, of course. Syl shouldn't think she could just get away from me like that. Yes, I had been ignoring her, but I didn't do it because I didn't want to be friends anymore. I'd just felt I needed time away from her.

Before that message this morning, I had believed things would be like they had always been at school. There hadn't been a single reason to assume anything had changed. Well, apart from me taking time for myself and sending her messages whenever I couldn't make it. But hey, we weren't joined at the hip, were we?

Later that day, when looking out the window, I saw her walking down the street, so I rushed out and tried to catch up, but she was gone before I could reach her. She had fled back into the house, as if that would help.

That night, I rang the doorbell. This time, I was counting on her housekeeper not being there and her parents being at home, so she would have to talk to me. I was right. Syl looked at me coolly, but she could not hide the anxiety and eagerness to reconnect. I knew her all too well. It wouldn't be that hard to reel her back in. I just need to connect with her on her level.

"What do you want?" she demanded.

"I need to talk to you," I said as gently as I could. "I'm sorry. I'm sorry that I ghosted you, that I ignored you, that I treated you like I did. I was— I needed time to think about everything."

"Oh?"

"Yeah, and I—well, I realized I didn't want to lose you. You're my best friend and I screwed up, and I'm sorry."

She was clearly caught off guard by my words, not expecting me to apologize like this. She had obviously expected a whole array of accusations or excuses, but I didn't have them. The only one I had was that I had been selfish for taking time for myself and Steve.

"Okay," she said. "I forgive you."

Now I was surprised, after expecting a whole litany about why she had dumped me.

"Just like that?"

"Yeah, why not?"

We didn't hug. Just smiled. And it felt okay, I guess, even though I was frustrated over the time that had been wasted in sorting this out. She could have just called me without all the dramatic antics.

Ah, well. Sorted out. Now I had to sort out my parents.

CHAPTER FIFTEEN

I did my best to be normal to everyone around me. I was kind and supportive to my mom, cut back on the sassy comments, and made sure she felt that I did care about her, even though she would sometimes still remark that I always picked my dad's side, despite me hardly saying anything. I was kind to my dad, who kept away from home more often than usual, hinting that things really weren't good between him and Mom.

I spent a lot of time with Steve as school started again, but I also spent a lot of time with Syl. We went to the bleachers behind the football field like we used to last year, and we talked about school and classmates, pretended that nothing was wrong between us, but of course there was. I felt like I needed to be careful in choosing the right words and had to watch what I said all the time. It was frustrating to see her eyes light up whenever I said something nice, and get dark and moody when I mentioned something she didn't like. Mostly, that last part became more apparent by the day.

Syl was emotionally blackmailing me. I could tell in everything she did and said. She was clinging to me, and honestly, I regretted having gone to her house to apologize. I did so because I didn't feel it was her right to break off things between us the way she had done, but now I had to accept that that had cost me dearly. She was using me against myself.

When I went to Steve, she would say things like, "Oh, leaving already? Can I come? I won't bother you guys."

"You really can't. Sorry, Syl. I'll see you later."

She helped me with my assignments again, at her own request. She went back to my house and would stay with us, but not as long as she used to. Probably because she also sensed my mom's change in behavior. And she obviously also noticed the very embarrassing fact that my mom had started to drink during the day.

At first, I barely noticed it myself, but then it became so obvious that it couldn't be ignored any longer. There were empty bottles of wine everywhere. Mom's eyes were bleary and bloodshot. She stopped taking us to school. She no longer cared about her appearance, and she rarely did any shopping. She ate for ten people, bingeing everything she could, and she kept on drinking while my dad stayed away from the house more often.

Then it all went to hell, and I forgot all about Syl. Or at least, I stopped pretending to care. That morning in September, as I entered the school grounds after a short walk with Syl, Alicia, a girl who was a member of Steve's friend group and who I had befriended, came up to me.

"Hey, Viola, are you okay?"

"Sure, why wouldn't I be?" I asked hesitantly, already worrying about what would come next. In this school, gossip was never far away, and people loved to see someone else fall flat on their face.

"I heard a rumor. I hope it isn't true! But if it is, know that I'm here for you. We don't really know each other that well, but please know that I care—so if you need someone to talk to, I'll be there for you."

I had no idea what she was going on about, so I walked faster into the school's main building and was on my way to my locker when I spotted other kids staring at me. They were talking about me, which gave me cold shivers that ran up and down my spine.

"What's going on?" I muttered as I opened my locker and suddenly saw Steve heading toward me.

"Are you okay?" he asked worriedly, and hugged me close to him.

"Why shouldn't I be? Steve, what's going on? Why is everyone acting so weird?"

He let go of me. "You mean you don't know?"

"I have no idea."

"Okay, come with me."

He took me outside the building, into the park, and settled me down on a bench. The bell would ring in five minutes, but he didn't seem to care. He took my hands as if I had just lost a loved one.

"There's a rumor going around town about your dad. It's pretty vicious, and people are talking about it everywhere."

"A rumor?"

"Yeah."

"What rumor?"

"I'm not sure if you need to hear this from me."

"You might as well tell me now, because I'm going to find out anyway," I said.

"Your dad is having an affair."

I stared at him. And then I started laughing. "My dad? You're kidding me, right?"

He didn't say anything, making it clear that he was not joking around. I thought about my parents and their weird behavior lately. The coldness, my mom blurting out all those things, her emo-bingeing sessions. It all made sense now. Of course Dad would hardly be at home; he was busy screwing someone else.

"It's not true," I said, but at the same time I knew that it was. It made sense. It made perfect sense.

"I'm sorry, Vi. I wish it weren't. But you know what this town is like. If the rumor is out there, it means that it's happening as we speak. They all tend to keep their secrets to themselves, so when something like this spreads like wildfire, it's almost always true."

It was true, and we both knew it.

"I've got to go," I said, reaching for my backpack. "I need to go talk to him and debunk this."

"I'll go with you."

I could kiss him right there and then, but I knew I couldn't risk getting him involved in this. It would mean his reputation, too, if this were true. He was already linked to me, and people would not hesitate to also drag his name through the mud.

"You're so sweet, Steve. I really appreciate what you want to do, but you need to stay here for now. I need to do this alone. It looks like I've been ignoring a lot of things in my life, and I need to get this sorted out."

"Are you sure?"

"Yeah."

The bell rang. I kissed Steve and left the school premises, ignoring the looks from some of the kids still on the lawn. I ran home, where I spotted my father's car still in the driveway. He usually left right after I did, but he was home—and that was not a good sign.

The moment I opened the front door, I heard my mom's screams. She was mad as hell.

"How could you?" she screeched. "How dare you humiliate me like that?"

"I didn't want any of this," he said softly, trying to keep his cool.

I walked into the living room and dropped my bag on the floor.

"Vi? What are you doing here?" my dad asked.

"I had to come back after finding out from Steve that you're supposedly having an affair with someone in town. Is it true, Dad? Everyone at school looked at me as if I was a pariah."

He sighed and rubbed his hand over his face. "I can't . . . not like this."

"Tell me!" I yelled, taking over my mom's behavior, who had slumped down on the couch. For the first time in a long while, I sympathized with my mom and felt angry for not having noticed this before.

"Is it true?" I repeated.

"It is. I'm having an affair," Dad said quietly.

"How could you do that, Dad? Who is it?"

"That's not important."

"Isn't it? You know what this place is like. How could you do this to us?"

"I didn't mean for any of this to happen, okay?" he yelled. "I fell in love. It's— You really don't get what this is about, Vi. You only know half of the story—"

"And she doesn't need to hear anything more," my mom interrupted. "I want you out of this house right now, Felix. Go to a hotel for the night and figure things out. Then come back in the morning, and we'll talk about this when you've come to your senses."

My dad looked at both of us and stood defeated in the living room. I loved my dad. He was my god, my hero, my everything. I used to go to him with everything that I ever felt, my emotions and my fears. We always used to see eye to eye. But now he was a total stranger to me.

"No," he said. "I won't come back. I can't."

I was stunned. My mom looked at him with sudden fear in her eyes. There was more to this than met the eye, things they were hiding from me. Secrets of their own.

"What is going on?" I asked.

"I'm leaving Love Hill," Dad said. "I've packed up my things. I'm moving to California. I broke off the relationship, but it made me realize that I don't belong with you either. I can't stay here anymore and fool us all. I'm going to start all over."

"Y-you . . . what?!" I stuttered.

Suddenly I saw the suitcases sitting next to the couch, and I put two and two together.

"You were going to leave without even saying goodbye," I said.

"Vi—"

"You were going to abandon me just like that?"

"I can't stay here. You don't get what's going on."

"Yeah, I do. Why are you doing this, Dad?"

"I can't explain. I have to go. You have to let me go, Vi."

He walked over to his suitcases, picked them both up, and walked to the front door without so much as a goodbye. Something didn't add up. This was not my dad talking, but I couldn't figure out why. I was completely lost.

Before he opened the door, he looked at us sadly. "I really am sorry about all the pain I've caused you both. If I could, I would have done things differently. Please forgive me."

I didn't run after him, didn't plead with him, didn't beg him to stay. Anger surged through me, and I couldn't stop it anymore. If this was what he wanted, he could have it.

"You know what? Go, then!" I screamed. "Don't bother ever coming back. Go to hell, Dad. I hope you crash your car on the way and be done with it."

He looked at me with sadness in his eyes.

"Maybe I should," he said softly before closing the door.

I stood there shaking like a leaf, too angry and upset to go after him. Little did I know that this was the last time I'd ever see or speak to him. I've regretted my words ever since.

CHAPTER SIXTEEN

From the moment the door shut behind Dad, I started living in a freaking nightmare, where my mom had turned into a monstrous version of herself and my father was no longer part of my life. He had taken all the good things with him, leaving nothing but a void in our home. Everything that had ever been good in our lives was gone forever.

Mom and I sat quietly in the living room with a million questions between us and a ton of secrets she kept to herself. I knew it would be pointless to even attempt to ask her to confide in me. She wouldn't. In her eyes, I was Daddy's little girl, and she hated me for it.

I went up to my room, closed the door, and cried for hours on the bed. My phone was flooded with messages and missed calls. Several friends had tried to get in touch. Steve sent me message after message. Even Syl had tried to get in touch with me, but I ignored her.

Then, after I had calmed down, I started to realize this wasn't her fault. She couldn't have prevented this from happening; she wasn't to blame for this. I felt sorry for her too.

I wanted to respond to the messages but was too exhausted and confused, so I ended up shutting off my phone and finally fell asleep. Later that day, when it was already getting dark, I woke up and found myself fully dressed on the bed, mind boggled that I had slept for hours and had missed lunch and whatever else was going on in the house.

My mom stood in the doorway with a tear-streaked face, but she was sober and clearheaded.

"I'm sorry," she said. "I was thinking only about myself."

"It's okay," I said. "So was I."

"What a pair we make, huh?"

"I know."

She sat on the bed and reached for my hand, rubbing it gently.

"We need to look out for ourselves from now on," she said. "Your dad is not coming back. We're on our own now. I need to start thinking about you and face the truth. It's over."

"He has to come back," I said. "He can't just stay away forever."

"He can and he will. He has made his choice."

"Without even asking us how we feel about this?"

"Listen, Vi," my mom said. "Your dad made this decision to protect us. I can't tell you more about what's going on; it would be too hard on you. But know that whatever he did and whatever mistake he made, he is trying to make up for that now by protecting us."

"He left us, Mom!"

"He did it because he has to. You will understand at some point, but not now. Please trust me. Look, I'm going to give the school a call, tell them what's going on, and ask if you can stay home for a while. They'll agree, I'm sure. You and I need some time to ourselves, and I want to get my head straight before we take the next step. Or do you want to go back tomorrow?"

I thought about the stares and the gloating, and shook my head. "No. Sounds good."

"Okay, then." She stood up to leave but turned back again by the door. "There's going to be some changes around here, Vi. I hope you can cope with them. I will talk to you later."

She left me with the feeling that the bad things were only getting started.

I showered, walked downstairs, and found her ordering pizza from our favorite place. She didn't bother to do any cooking—another indication that she wasn't doing well.

There was wine on the table, the bottle already half empty. Her eyes were bloodshot now, and it was obvious she had gone back to the habit I found so foul.

"Do you want some too?" she asked, watching me glare at the bottle.

I was disgusted. And then I thought about those kids at school mocking me silently, enjoying this whole thing, and shrugged.

"You're crazy, Mom!"

I snatched the bottle from her hand and poured the contents down the drain before she could stop me. She didn't even attempt to; she just folded one arm over the other and watched me, amused.

"I have plenty more, you know."

"Then I'll find them and get rid of them all," I said.

"No, you won't. You can't order me around like you did with your dad, Viola. From now on, there will be new rules in this house, the most important one being that you will listen to *me* for a change."

"If you really think I'm going to have you order me around, think again," I snapped. "You're my mom, but you are not the boss of me."

"Yes, I am. Your dad has spoiled you rotten, and I will have no more of your antics. You are going to do everything I say from now on."

"Or else?"

"I'll cut you off from everything that makes you believe you get to rule me. Money, new things, whatever fancy stuff you think you need to impress your friends."

"You are actually threatening me?" I said, trying to hold back laughter. "To hell with you, too, Mom. I'm out of here."

"If you walk out that door, don't bother coming back," she said. "I mean it, Viola. This is my house now, and you will obey my rules. Take it or leave it, but don't think for a second that you ever get to order me around again."

I sat on the kitchen stool staring at her, wondering what had happened to the meek mother she used to be. Was this the real version of her, the one she had been holding back as long as my dad was around? Two could play this game. She seriously had no idea how I was wired.

How could she, when the only person she had ever paid attention to was Syl?

"I bet you wanted her to be your daughter, didn't you?" I remarked.

She was the one who was stunned this time. "Excuse me?"

"You always loved her more than you did me. What went through your mind, Mom? Did you want us to be switched by accident so you could believe deep down that she's your natural daughter and I'm just a screwed-up version who was supposed to grow up at their place?"

"You're crazy."

"Am I? I've seen the way you looked at her. Syl's everything you ever wanted in a daughter, isn't she? You two can talk for hours; you can have fun just blabbing on about whatever nonsense you are interested in. While me? I was always the odd one out, even in my own house. You just wanted her to be your daughter, didn't you?"

My mom turned pale, and then red—and yep, there it was: that feeling I had always sensed but never said out loud.

"I'm right, aren't I?"

She didn't look me in the eye. She got up, started cleaning the kitchen, took another bottle of wine from the cabinet, and unscrewed it. Right in front of me, she poured another glass for herself and started drinking without any shame.

"If this is how we're going to play it, I suggest we stay out of each other's way," I said. "As far as I'm concerned, I have lost both my parents today. What type of mother gives her fifteen-year-old daughter wine, anyway?"

"Bottoms up, hon," she said, making a mocking gesture.

I left the room, unable to watch her drink herself into a stupor.

CHAPTER SEVENTEEN

It became really clear to me very quickly in the process that there was one person my mom blamed for my dad's departure. Or maybe two: the person he'd had the affair with and me, for being a daddy's girl, as she put it. If I had been a mommy's girl, we would have probably been mourning and sulking together on the couch. Now I did everything I could to avoid her while trying to find my dad.

I told Steve everything that evening. Or at least, parts of it. I couldn't stomach the idea of him knowing that my mom had offered me alcohol and called me everything under the sun while I fled up the stairs and shut the door to my room behind me with a bang.

I told him about my dad's leaving, and he promised to get to the bottom of it, meaning he would try to figure out where he could have gone to. Of course, I had my dad's number, and I called him several times, always ending up talking to his voicemail or sending him messages. He never got in touch with me and never tried to call me back. He had gone off the grid, and I started to realize there would be no way of getting in touch with him. His phone was probably disconnected, and he would already have a new device and number we couldn't trace. Whatever was going on with him, he had committed to it thoroughly.

From that day on, everything started changing quickly. I did stay at home for a while, not because I felt bad, but because I couldn't stomach facing everyone else, who were all aware by now of what had happened. I didn't want their sympathy or pity—most of all, I wanted to avoid their gloating reactions. Everyone loved drama when it was happening to someone else, and it had been a while since we'd had any real gossip. The fact that my dad had become the focal point of that drama was horrible, and I hated him for it. But I couldn't hate him for what he had done. I understood that he had fallen in love with someone else; I would have done the same thing if I had been married to someone like my mom.

Mom was drinking frequently now, and I couldn't bear to witness it. She had bottles delivered at home. I watched and avoided her, not wanting to pick up her pieces when I was sad enough as it was.

Then there was Syl. I simply couldn't face her, so I was glad to be away from her for a while too. Except for when I called her on a whim, wanting to hear her voice. At least she was predictably kind and attentive, and I'd needed that right then.

"I'm so sorry about all of this," she'd said. "I wish I could help somehow. What has gotten into your dad?"

"I want him back. I hate this mess. I hate my mom. She barely looks after herself anymore. I need my dad back home to stop the madness. I need to find out where he is so I can head over there and demand answers. I can't stand living like this. Mom is so depressed."

"I'll help you find him," she'd promised, like Steve had done.

I had snorted. "How? You can't even find your own phone in your bedroom."

That was true, and it had made us both chuckle.

Syl had ended the call by promising to get help from her dad, but we both knew that would never happen. He didn't care enough. No one did.

When I finally went back to school after two weeks, it quickly became quite clear to me that nobody knew what to say or do, but at least they left me alone. The school board sent out a serious warning, advising everyone to keep their mouths shut about the whole thing. And that, to me, was a telltale sign that they *knew* who it was he was having the affair with. It pissed me off that my father's departure, and the events leading up to it, were being swept under the rug.

My mom and I were left to our own devices, and we both knew and felt it. It made me hate this town to my core, but I still didn't want to leave. Neither did she. She seemed adamant about payback. She wanted people to feel what she was going through, even though we both knew that revenge—whatever that meant—was not on the table.

She became disgustingly overbearing, to the point that I actually wanted to throttle her.

She didn't allow me to go back to my old routine. I wasn't allowed to have hobbies anymore. "School and home," she said. "No more flirting with boys or hanging around with your friends. You're going to study and study hard to get your grades up. I'm not sure what's in store for us financially after all this, but we have to assume that you will have to work hard to get a scholarship. Your dad's funds have been partially cut off; he's only giving me enough to survive. The house is still being paid for, but if things continue like this, I'll need to find a job."

"You're kidding me, right?" I said. "You? Working? You haven't done anything for years. Who's going to hire you?"

"Steve's dad. I can set up a bakery from home."

That was the moment I started to realize that my life *was* indeed going to be totally different from now on. We would no longer be part of the standard Love Hill community; we'd become one of the outcasts who barely had enough money to afford a house.

"We'll move somewhere smaller if need be," she added for good measure. "Whatever it takes to survive."

"He's going to divorce you, isn't he?" I said.

"I don't know. I really have no clue what he's planning, but whatever it will be, it does not look good for us."

Steve was there for me in all ways possible. So was Syl. We had a long chat on the bleachers about all of this, Syl and I, where we discussed what my dad had done and who could possibly be the woman he'd had an affair with.

And then she said something I just could not shake off. She looked nervous, and like she was trying not to believe that it was true, but the moment she said it, we both realized the truth might be closer to us than we initially thought.

"I think it might be her," she said, just like that. "Powerful, someone he knows. Someone who could drive him away."

There were only a few women in this town who had that power, and her mother was one of them. Mrs. Jameson, as co-CEO and fervent, active, and valuable member of our local church, checked all the boxes. But how? She barely had time for her own daughter, let alone to sleep with a man she had absolutely nothing in common with, except for the fact that they shared the same street name and their daughters were friends.

Our parents had never connected; they didn't hang out, didn't even go to the same parties. All that there was, was us, and that seemed like not enough. But what if it was?

"It's not your mom," I said after a while.

I couldn't bear the thought of her mom and my dad in bed together. I hated her mom—she was cold and distant, didn't have an ounce of sympathy in her whole body. My dad would never fall for someone like her. Never. How low could he go?

But there it was, that nagging sense that would not go away. I watched Syl sitting on the bleachers, in all her apparent innocence, and remembered how she had clung to my dad. How she had cared about anything he'd said or did. How she had tried to get into his good graces, even at my expense.

Did she know? Had Syl actually realized, subconsciously or not, that our parents were sleeping together? Had she figured out that someday we could become stepsiblings? That she would have another father besides her own? No, that couldn't be true—could it?

But what if it was?

What if it really, really was?

CHAPTER EIGHTEEN

I needed to get rid of her. To make sure she would not get her hands on my mom ever again. I wanted her as far away from Mom as possible, contemplating the fears that were now slowly but surely taking over. I wanted to punish her so badly.

"We should start organizing our birthday party," I said, because that's what we had always done. My mom had been a great party organizer, always taking the lead. She enjoyed that tremendously.

"What?" Syl said, confused.

"Our birthday. Why not celebrate it like we always did? Life goes on, right? It's already the end of October."

"I'm not sure, Viola—"

"Come on, Syl, don't be a party pooper," I said. "My dad's gone, and I want to move on. I want to have a party, and my mom will happily organize it. It will take her mind off things. Besides, we only turn sixteen once."

She smiled nervously. "Okay," she said hesitantly. "But we could do it at my house this time? I can't imagine your mom wanting to do this now, under these circumstances."

"I'll ask her tonight," I said, getting up. Nope, that wasn't going to happen. I would not bother.

The next morning, Syl was standing at our front door like in the good old days, expecting my mom to take us to school, but I told her that we would walk so Mom could stay in bed. She had been drinking again last night.

"I'm sorry," I said as we started walking. "She wants us to spend my birthday alone at the house, without any other people there. No double party this year. I'm really sorry, Syl."

"That's okay," she said, and I saw her disappointment. "I'll do something at home, then. I'm sure my parents won't mind spending it with me. It's on a Sunday."

I saw by the way she looked at me that she was suffering, and I enjoyed every second of it. But this was only the start. From now on, I would take every opportunity to get my revenge.

In the days that followed, I started ignoring Syl. I didn't go to the bleachers with her anymore, and instead found excuses to stay in school. I didn't ask her for help with my math anymore, even though she volunteered. When she texted me, I didn't reply.

A few weeks later, she obviously got the message and stopped reaching out. It felt good to see her puppy dog eyes staring at me in class, pleading with me silently to talk again. I didn't cave.

Every single time I thought about mending our friendship again, I started thinking about her mom and my dad and how they had been meeting secretly in some motel somewhere outside of town. Oh yeah, I had put a lot of the details together, but still, no one would tell me if it really had been Mrs. Jameson he had been seeing. All signs led to it, anyhow.

I went to see our town's pastor. I wasn't a religious person, and frankly, even before my dad had left, we hadn't exactly been churchgoers. There had always been some excuse for us not to attend mass. The church was usually packed with all these Love Hill hypocrites trying to get forgiven for whatever nasty stuff they had been doing as of late, and my dad simply did not do nasty stuff. Or at least, that's what we had always assumed. As it turned out, he was the nastiest of them all.

I assumed the pastor would be the person to talk to when it came to finding out the town's secrets. If Mrs. Jameson had really crossed the line, she would have confessed her sins to him. And if he knew, he would probably have a hard time keeping it to himself.

On a Friday evening, when the church was open for anyone to come in for confession, I walked in and saw the pastor by the altar. He was rearranging candles and flowers, not dressed as a priest but wearing a black suit. He looked glum; his pale skin almost radiated against his dark clothes.

"I hope you don't mind me bothering you," I said as I folded my hands neatly together.

"Of course not, child. What can I do for you?"

"I would like to talk about my father," I said.

"Ah. I see."

The priest didn't ask for my name; he knew perfectly well who I was, as he did with everyone in this town.

"Are you aware of his situation?"

"Yes. I pray for him every day," the pastor said. "Why don't we sit down and pray together?"

"I didn't come here for prayer," I said. "I came to ask you if you know who did this to him?"

"What do you mean?"

"My father was driven away by someone in this very town, most likely the person who he had a relationship with. I want to know who that person is."

"Child, I really don't know," the priest said. "But even if someone had confessed this sin to me, I would not be empowered to tell you. Confessions are sacred, meant to forgive sins. I would not be able to share with you what was said to me."

"But you do know?"

He didn't answer.

"You know and you won't tell me?"

"I'm afraid I can't help you, child. If you want to find the truth, you need to speak to your father."

"That won't work. He refuses to talk to me. He's cut me off."

"Perhaps there are important reasons for that. I will add a prayer in my thoughts for you as well, and I hope you can find each other again."

I snorted. "Is that really all you can offer me?"

"I'm afraid it is."

"You are the worst of them all, then," I said sharply. "This town is riddled with idiots who truly believe that everything happens for a reason, while in fact, it's people who make our lives miserable. I hope you choke on it."

He didn't seem upset from me speaking to him in a way I shouldn't have, but I couldn't care less. Another dead end, another idiot stopping me from getting to the truth.

"I think you should head home now, say a few prayers, and hope for the best," the priest said. "Now, if you'll excuse me, I would like to close the church and go home. I'm sorry I can't help you, but if you can find it in your heart, come to church on Sunday. God listens. He will help."

"Nobody is helping me," I said, feeling tears stream down my face. "No one in this town."

"I am sorry about that too."

I stood and left without another glance. I could feel his eyes piercing my back. Never again would I believe that people only wanted the best for me. Nobody ever did. And least of all, Syl Jameson, the hypocrite's daughter.

On a Monday late in October, not so long before our mutual birthdays, I put the last nail in the coffin.

Syl came with me to school. Mom took us, sobering up enough to drive us. We didn't speak a word. The silence in the car was deafening. She hurried out of the car quickly once we arrived and ran off. I found her again by the lockers, walked over to her, extended my hand, and said, "Listen, I know I've been too occupied with myself lately, and I'm sorry. I really am. Please forgive me?"

She looked so uncertain and pale that I almost forgot about the whole thing. But then I remembered everything that had caused this, and hardened up again.

"I don't know," she said softly. "I'm not sure if I can do this again."

"Do what?"

"Accept your apology and hope that you'll stay in my life this time."

I laughed. "I've always been here. Don't be so silly."

"No, you haven't been. You've been distant, cold, and hard towards me, and I don't know why."

I was surprised by her reaction, but there it was at long last. She was finally showing me how hurt she was, and it felt so good.

"Listen, why don't we meet for lunch? We can sit down together and just catch up. I promise I'll be good," I said, placing my hand on her upper arm. "Please?"

"Okay, then," she said.

A few hours later, we walked into the cafeteria together. I stacked food on my plate while looking at Steve, who had already told me he would reserve a seat for me with his friends. Once I started walking, he beckoned me closer. I sat down quickly and could almost feel Syl freeze behind me like a deer caught in the headlights of a truck.

I didn't bother looking at her while she stood there, unsure of what to do. It felt so good to punish her like this in front of the whole school. I couldn't get to her mom, but I could get to her.

I leaned over to Steve and whispered in his ear, "Kiss me. Please."

He was surprised but did as I'd asked. He hugged and kissed me and claimed me publicly as his girlfriend, which caused loud whistling. Around us, others started to clap their hands. The whole cafeteria was in a frenzy.

I laughed and looked at Syl with such disdain that she actually backed away. There she was, standing behind us with her tray filled with food. She finally walked away. I turned around and watched her sit down at a table with some girls from class. The one sitting next to her turned toward her.

Lila Jenkins. Freaking Gorgeous Lila Jenkins. Well, well. This could be fun.

THE TALE OF MY POOR FATHER

Steve is shocked into silence; I can tell by the way he looks at me. He's more upset than he was before, finally figuring out that I had been using him to get what I wanted. He was part of an act of revenge I had never told him about.

"You know," he says slowly, "I never really believed my friends when they told me to be careful around you. They kept on saying that you were poisonous towards Syl and her family. I always believed you two had grown apart, never really thought about it in a different way. But in truth, you were gaslighting that girl. Bashing her behind her back. Punishing her for something she was never even part of. I feel disgusted that you used me to get what you wanted."

"I'm not proud of what I did," I say. "I know now that it was all wrong, but then, at that moment, it felt like it was the only way to get a bit of revenge for what her mom had done to my family."

"Syl was your friend! She has never done anything but support you and be there for you."

"That's not exactly true," I say.

"What do you mean by that?"

"She was trying to get into my parents' good graces the whole time. She was trying to be their perfect daughter. She wanted everything that I had, and she even told me so."

"When?"

"The day after that lunch. She came by my locker in the morning, slammed it shut in my face, and looked me up and down as if I was a worm she could crush."

"Rightfully so, I would say."

I smile lightly, because that is true. "She said, again, that we were through."

"And you reacted by saying that this was just fine?"

"I did."

"Did it feel good?"

"No, it felt horrible. All of it did. But nothing felt as crushing as finding out what happened to my dad on my birthday. That really put a spin on things. You know that, Steve. You were there—or at least you were for a part of it."

He looks at me strangely, not getting what I want to say. He's confused, obviously.

"I know that your dad died while crossing the street in LA. He was struck by a car and died on impact. That happened the night before your sixteenth birthday. You were at home in the morning when you got the call from the police giving you the bad news. I wanted to come over to your house to be with you, but you asked me to stay at home because of the chaos. That's what I remember of that day."

"And all of that really happened as you described it," I say. "But what you don't know about that day is what happened after we received that phone call."

He looks exhausted and worn down, but still isn't requesting to get some rest. Morning is coming, and we know that the police are probably going to be knocking on his door soon enough.

"That morning started off normal," I say, "even though it was my sixteenth birthday and there would be nothing sweet about it. You and I had agreed to go for a walk or something, but other than that, I had no plans, given the circumstances. So I was sitting at the breakfast table alone, eating my bagel, when our landline rang, and there was this police officer from Los Angeles calling, asking me if I was related to Felix Harrison."

"It's terrible that you have to relive this," Steve says, but I wave him off. Nothing is as terrible as what happened after that.

"The cop said that my dad was gone, so I ran to the bedroom and woke up my mom, who didn't understand at first. She kept on repeating that this had to be a mistake and I had misheard, but of course my dad was really gone."

"You mentioned that she called the cops herself?"

"Yeah, she did. As soon as she was able to, she got back in touch with the police officer who had called us, and she got the nitty-gritty of it. How my dad was out in the streets of LA while it was way past midnight. He had gone to this bar downtown, and when he walked out and was crossing the street, he got hit by a car. There were several witnesses who all said it was a terrible accident, that it wasn't the driver's fault but that my dad had crossed the street last minute."

"Did they hint that he did it on purpose?" Steve asks. "You mentioned that once, that it was classified as an accident but there always remained some dispute about it."

"We'll never know," I say. "Some people he was with tried to resuscitate him, but he was already gone. He didn't suffer."

"I'm sorry, Vi."

I nod and sigh.

"You still haven't told me anything new, though. I know all of this."

"I know," I say impatiently, "but then we come to the issue of that bar. My mom, as his registered next of kin, asked where he had been and who he had been with, and they said he had been at this place called the Meetup, with two other men. My mom instantly started putting two and two together. She sent me away to my room, but I had heard the name of the bar, and Google quickly confirmed that this was a gay bar."

Steve reacts, startled. "Wait a second. A gay bar?"

"Yep."

"Your dad was . . . ?"

"Yes, as it turns out, he was. And the worst thing is that my mom knew about it. She has known all along. I don't care that my dad was bisexual or gay, Steve. I don't care at all, as long as he was happy. But I do care that my mom lied to me all these months about the real reason he left Love Hill. He didn't go away because he was having an affair with Mrs. Jameson and she threatened him into leaving after they broke it off. No, he left because he was having a relationship with Mr. Jameson and Syl's mom emotionally blackmailed him into leaving."

"Are you telling me that Mrs. Jameson knew about this?"

"Oh yeah. And she took the fall for it. You see, as you can remember, soon after my dad's death, people were very curious about this whole thing again, and so they started prodding and poking into the finer details the Jamesons and my mom had been concealing. As it turns out, in order to avoid the truth being exposed—thus also exposing Mr. Jameson as being bisexual or gay—Mrs. Jameson took the blame. She went to church, prayed a couple of times, confessed, and got forgiven. The priest actually used her as an example of the ultimate act of forgiveness. Mr. Jameson was considered a saint because he had done the forgiving, while Mrs. Jameson got off with a couple of mea culpas and an I-promise-I-won't-ever-do-this-again. But my dad? He died because he was the scapegoat in all of this. He took the fall, and we were left with nothing."

"I am so sorry, Viola," Steve says. "You should have told me. This explains so much about your behavior and how you reacted to your father's passing. Now it's all becoming clear to me."

"I couldn't tell anyone, not even you," I say quietly. "Everyone would have started treating me differently, so it felt better not to tell the truth about him. What good would it have done? He was gone, there was no point in sharing the details with the outside world."

"Did Syl know?"

"She did, eventually. I don't believe now that she was aware of all the details, and I regret having put this on her. I shouldn't have done that. I blamed her for something our parents did, and she wasn't even aware they were doing it."

"Did you tell her?"

"No. Her mom did, even though she didn't share the details with me, because we weren't on speaking terms anymore at the time. There were a lot of other things at play, too, and I was too busy with you, my schoolwork, new friends, going out and having some fun while trying to balance my mom's increasingly erratic behavior and having a life. In the months leading up to my birthday, I actually did find that balance, but then this happened and it got all messed up. My mom didn't react so well either."

"I know. Didn't she go have a screaming fit at Syl's house?"

"Yeah. She actually walked up to their house and started bashing Mr. and Mrs. Jameson, no longer caring who knew what. She told me she went up there and started giving Mrs. Jameson an earful. She actually wanted to throw it in her face, how she would expose them for the people they really were, but then she spotted Syl standing at the top of the stairs, obviously upset by the whole thing."

"So she didn't say anything, I presume?"

"No, she backed off at the last minute, but not before giving Mrs. Jameson a piece of her mind. That woman actually came to our house the following day with her checkbook, offering money to help us out. My mom threw her out."

"I can imagine," Steve says.

"Nobody gets to bribe us emotionally," I say, proudly thinking back to the moment my mom told that woman off, even though we could have used the money.

"But you did end up financially secure, though, I remember you telling me that," Steve says. "You never asked me for anything, and I never offered because you were always so proud."

"My dad fortunately had more than enough money saved for us. He also had a life insurance policy, some assets, and then the house, of course. I think he knew that proven suicide would stop them from paying us life insurance money, and so he did it this way to secure us financially."

"So you believe he did it on purpose?"

"Yes."

"But why? He could have asked you to come live with him in LA. It didn't have to be this drastic."

"I think he was ashamed—not of his nature, but of what he had done to us. He couldn't live with himself anymore."

"I get that," Steve says. "But what did you do next, Viola? Are you willing to tell me?"

"Yeah," I say after a brief silence. "I need to tell you about Syl and Lila, and what I did."

PART FOUR: THE STORY OF THE OTHER GIRL AND THE BOY WHO DIDN'T LAST

CHAPTER NINETEEN

Weeks after my father's funeral, I was still living in a state of shock and despair. Most of all, though, I was angry as hell. I had accepted the fact that he would stay in LA forever, but I had also kept my hopes up that we would see each other again soon. I had even been doing research about going to UCLA in two years so I could be close to him again. I had made plans to tell him about this. I had talked to Steve about going to LA to find him.

But all those plans were shattered when he passed away, and I couldn't stop thinking about the very last words I had said to him on the day he left us—how I had wished for him to crash his car. Those had been words said in anger, but it still felt as if I had condemned him to this death.

Steve was there for me all the time, but I started treating him badly. I was angry at him, too, for not acting quickly, for not pushing the idea of heading to Los Angeles sooner. Steve had his own life, which I barely fit into. There were days we hardly saw each other, when he had practice or games, or when we had so much homework to do that we could hardly breathe. I felt a distance growing between us, and I couldn't help but wonder if I had been born for bad luck. Of course, I had myself to blame for us growing apart too. He hated my drinking.

Yeah, there it was: me becoming my mom. More than the drinking, there was the smoking. The soft drugs. The kids at school offering me substances that took away the edge, the sorrow. I no longer said no when Mom offered to share a bottle of wine together to drown our sorrows. I barely thought about how wrong it was.

I was sixteen years old and drinking and smoking—turning, in a few weeks' time, from being a sensible person in control into someone I loathed for her weaknesses. I just couldn't stop myself. The more I drank, the madder I got at the world. The madder I got at the world, the more I lashed out. Those weren't my finest days. I took Steve away from his friends, demanded his attention. He started neglecting his homework and his practices. He had already been doing less before my dad died, but now he was totally occupied with me. He hated it, I could tell, but every time I called him, I reeled him in. He showed up in no time, no matter where he was, too scared I would hurt myself. I used his emotions against him and won every single time.

And then there was Lila Jenkins. Freaking Gorgeous Lila Jenkins, obviously the type of girl Syl would fall for.

After I stood her up at school in front of everyone the week before my father passed away, I felt a momentary sense of contentment with the level of vengeance. It was over between us and I was okay with that, even if I couldn't brush it off.

I sat at the lunch table with Steve and his friends and observed Syl, who had sat down at the next table beside Lila Jenkins. She was pretty and had a lot going for her, but she was also a person with a lot of issues. Apparently, according to what I knew about her, she had a heart condition, which made it difficult for her to participate in physical activities. She was often sitting alone on the bench while the rest of us played sports. She wasn't allowed to take long walks or even ride a bike for more than a few miles. She couldn't get excited or angry about things. Lila Jenkins was so sick that she needed weekly heart monitoring at the hospital.

And she connected with Syl. Just like that, while they were sitting at the lunch table and everyone else at their table had already gone. I was angry at this course of events, even though I had gotten everything I had wanted. I brushed away the guilt, feeling upset now that Syl would replace me so easily, ignoring the fact that I had done the exact same by happily hanging around with Steve and his friends, basking in the attention they gave me. Typical for jocks, that they have no clue what us girls go through mentally or how we brood over things they find irrelevant.

I was brooding.

Syl ignored me for the rest of that lunch, and I got angrier by the minute. She did not react the way I had expected. She also didn't do what I'd wanted. I had wished for her to be drowning in loneliness and darkness. I had wanted her to hurt like I was hurting. I did not want happiness for her. I wanted her to suffer.

After lunch, I watched Syl happily go one way, while Lila went the other. Both seemed elated after their long conversation, and I could *feel* something hanging in the air. This was going in the wrong direction.

I was supposed to go to English class next, but I decided instead to catch up with Lila before she reached the entrance of the C building.

"Hey," I said.

She turned around; then a small smile broke out. "Well, well, if it isn't Queen Viola. That didn't take you long."

"I have no idea what you're talking about," I replied.

"Really? Don't think I didn't notice your eyes shooting daggers in our direction all through lunch. What's wrong? Are you upset because Syl has finally freed herself from you? I'm happy for her that she did. It was about time she started to realize that you do not have her best interests at heart."

"I still have no idea what you're talking about," I said, hurt by the (true) accusation. "We're still friends."

"Sure."

"Did I do anything to hurt you or something? Why are you being so cold?" I asked.

"Maybe because you haven't given me the time of day in the past twelve years or so, and now, all of a sudden, when I'm having a nice and friendly chat with your former bestie, you suddenly want to have a conversation? That's not going to happen. I'm not like Syl; you can't influence or bash me."

"I never bash Syl."

This time she laughed.

"You keep on telling yourself that," Lila said calmly. "Now, then, I need to get to class, so if you don't mind . . ."

"Can we sit down and have a quick chat? I want to talk about Syl, but not in the way that you think," I said. "Listen, I'm really happy that she's connecting with you, but there are some things you need to know. I'm worried about her."

Now I'd caught her attention.

"This should be good. Okay, then."

We sat down on the bench in front of the school building, both ignoring the fact that the bell had rung and we were supposed to go inside. She picked at her fingernails while I looked in front of me.

"Look, Syl and I are going through a rough patch," I said. "That's true. There are a lot of reasons for that, but most of all, I guess it has to do with my dad leaving. I'm not in a place to give her the attention she needs as a friend. She can be a bit overwhelming, and I just can't cope with that right now."

"You mean that she needs attention you can't offer her?"

"Yeah, I guess. I don't have a lot of spare time, my mom is in a bad state, and Steve also needs me—and I'm trying to find a way of coping with this situation with my dad too."

Lila seemed to soften when I told her all this. She appeared friendlier, started to listen properly.

"I get that," she said. "You're in a bad place and you want to protect Syl. But you're going about it the wrong way, you know. You're pushing her away, while you should keep her closer to you instead. Do you know how rare a friendship like yours is?"

"It is rare," I said, grabbing the opportunity when I had Lila's attention. "But sometimes it can feel suffocating too. I want her to be happy—I really do. I'm just not in a position that I can afford to spend the time with her that she needs."

"So instead of telling her that, you're pushing her away. Is that it?"

"That's it."

Lila started laughing. "Come on, Viola. Everyone can see this is bullshit. You're treating her like dirt; you always have. Even if she is as overbearing as you claim, she doesn't deserve to be treated this way. You've used her for years, and everyone at school knows she was your little worker bee whenever you needed her. You guys were forced together by a fluke of nature, but in truth, she needs a lot better friends than you. Stop acting like you're holier than thou. You're nothing but a bully."

I was taken aback. How dare she speak to me like that when she'd barely had any conversations with Syl before today? But she was right about everything. Every detail. She placed her hand on my arm.

"Let her go, Viola. If you love her, let her go."

I took a deep breath and knew exactly what I had to say. Every word. "You're in love with her."

CHAPTER TWENTY

Lila Jenkins. Freaking Gorgeous Lila Jenkins was in love with Syl.

"We both know that you are gay too," I stated matter-of-factly while placing my hand on her arm. "And that's perfectly fine, Lila. It's great, actually, that Syl has found a kindred spirit, thanks to me. But now you also know why I'm really pushing her away. She's in love with me, but I can't be that person for her. She needs someone else in her life—someone like you. Someone who can fill that gap that I left."

"I-is this a joke?" she asked suspiciously, not seeming to understand at first what I was trying to say.

"I'll save you the trouble of pretending. It's pretty obvious."

Lila turned pale. "What do you want?"

"I'm thinking that you and Syl would fit together perfectly. Ellie moved on to boys, didn't she? She was probably experimenting with you, but Syl would never do that. So I'm thinking that maybe you could take her off my hands and become that person she needs?"

"I can't do that. We don't have much in common," Lila said to my great surprise. "I don't feel anything for her. I just like her; she's fun."

"Hmm. Whatever. You're going to be her friend, Lila, whether you like it or not. Put some effort into it, get to know her. I can tell you everything you need to make it look real. You can do this."

"Why?" Lila said. "I don't understand what's in it for you. Why would you have me build a relationship with her?"

"Because you're going to tear it apart at some point. I don't care when or how you do it, but ultimately, you are going to break her heart."

Lila sat quietly, still plucking at her fingernails. "And if I don't?"

"Then the whole school will know about you and Ellie kissing. It might not ruin your reputation, but it will certainly ruin hers. And Ellie, as the mayor's daughter, has a lot more to lose than you do. I know you still care about her; it's quite obvious. So what do you say? Do we have an agreement?"

"You're a monster," she whispered.

"Maybe I am, but you have no idea what Syl and her family have done to me. If you knew, you wouldn't be so surprised right now."

She looked me in the eye, putting the pieces of the puzzle together. That slyness came back in her expression, the one I had been waiting for. Lila Jenkins always got what she wanted, and she didn't hesitate to use her health issues in her favor. She received a lot of pity-attention, the sort people only got when they were sick. She was used to getting things her way. And she was very, very smart.

"Your dad and her mom. Is that why he left?"

"Yeah," I said, not bothering to deny it.

"Ah. Taking out your anger on the daughter of the woman who ruined your life. You are a nasty piece of work, Viola Harrison."

"I know," I said. "But I don't care. They have hurt me too much and too often. Now it's my turn."

"I need to think about this. I'm not sure if I can do this to someone innocent like her. And she *is* cool."

"You have until tomorrow morning," I said. "Oh, and don't see this as a job or a difficult task. Syl really can be fun to be with, so it won't be that terrible."

"You don't call lying to her 'terrible'?"

"Depends on how you sell the lie."

"Like I said: You're nasty."

"It takes one to know one. And I know exactly who you are and what makes you tick, Lila. Bye, now."

I got up and left her sitting on that bench. Adrenaline rushed through me. I had taken a leap of faith with Lila, and we both knew it. If she told the rest of the world about my proposal, it would backfire immediately. I knew she wouldn't, though. She was hung up on her *poor little sick girl* reputation, and she would do anything to protect it, even if it meant having to lie to Syl at all times. The fact that she would have to do just that made me happier than I had been in a long time.

The next morning, I saw Syl and Lila walking to class together, chatting away. I walked in behind them and saw Lila quickly brushing past Syl's hand. When they sat down, Lila gazed over her shoulder toward me and nodded quickly. I smiled and opened my books.

In the weeks that followed, Lila and Syl were growing closer by the day, which was obvious to a lot of people in school. Some even cracked jokes about how close they really were, but no one dared to comment on their relationship out loud. By that time, my dad had died and I had other issues in my life.

On our birthdays, after she had learned that my father had passed away, she sent me a text message, trying to sympathize.

> I'm so sorry. Please tell me what I can do to help you. I want to be there for you.

I sent her one back in a matter of seconds.

> Nothing. Have a great birthday.

Bitch. Like I would need her now after all she and her family had done to us? Now that I knew the whole story about her dad's affair with mine, and her mom blackmailing my father, I couldn't stand the sight of her. (I conveniently ignored the fact that I had blackmailed Lila too.)

From then on, my life, as I mentioned, went down the drain. Syl's, however, didn't. In fact, it seemed to get better by the day. Lila seemed to rejoice in her role as "girlfriend," and to my great frustration, they started to like hanging out together. In the months that passed, I could see them connecting, so I often reminded Lila of our little arrangement. "Don't get too close to her," I would say. "Remember the deal."

Sometime in February, right before Valentine's Day, I bumped into Lila at the lockers and cornered her there.

"Steve's planning something special for me. What are you going to give Syl?"

"Just a card," she said.

"No ring?"

"No."

"You should give her something. A necklace or a ring. She'd like that. It'll make things so much more special for her."

"I don't want to," Lila said.

"Why not? You like her, don't you? I see the way you look at her. You can see yourself having a future with her."

She didn't deny it.

"I'm not a monster, Lila. Just buy her something."

"You blackmailed me into wooing her just to dump her," she stated sharply. "Of course you're a monster. Leave me the hell alone."

She pushed me away and walked quickly into class without her books. When I turned around, I saw Steve looking at me curiously. I walked over to him and kissed him.

"You smell like pot," he remarked, scrunching up his nose in disgust.

I laughed. "Yeah, well, live with it."

"I'm not so sure I can," he muttered, turning around and leaving me standing at the lockers.

On Valentine's Day, he gave me a necklace. The next day, I saw Syl wearing a new one around her neck too.

Life had this tendency of backfiring against anything and everything we pulled on it, which was exactly what happened to me during the school year that my father passed away.

For months, my life had been going down the drain, and the future wasn't looking any better. Syl was cut out of my life—I hadn't spoken to her in months, despite the fact that we often sat in the same classroom and just had to look at each other to reconnect. I didn't want to.

I didn't bother with Lila either. If I wanted to talk to her and threaten her again, I had to make a lot of effort to be with her alone, effort I didn't want to put in. I had other fish to fry, so I let her be. I hadn't really said when I'd expected her to break up with Syl, nor had I followed through with my earlier threats of telling Syl the truth. It didn't matter anymore, not when everything else had been shot to hell.

I had trouble focusing on my schoolwork, difficulties keeping up with Steve and finding enough quality time with him, and problems with my mom, who had decided we would sell our house and move to a smaller one on the other side of town, where we wouldn't have to bump into Syl's parents all the time.

I didn't really want to move. I wanted to stay here so that the Jamesons would be confronted with us on a daily basis. Of course, that wasn't exactly a good idea. Our mental health, mine and my mom's, was at stake. Even if she didn't feel it, I surely did. So I agreed to take a look at some houses in the brand-new cul-de-sac at the other end of town. My mom made genuine efforts to cut down on her drinking, but I was doing it in secret now, buying my own liquor using others and, of course, adding the drugs that still gave me that edge I so needed.

In June, right in the middle of my finals, she made an appointment with a real estate agent, and we went over to her office to take a look at her options. The agent took us to one of the smaller ones, which still had four bedrooms, three bathrooms, and a huge open-plan living area. There were two offices, a gigantic basement, and an attic we would use for storage while also using part of it as a gym. We could move in within six months.

I wouldn't be there for long, and it felt ridiculous having so much space for just one person after I left for college, so I wanted to vote against it, but didn't get the chance.

"It's gorgeous. We'll take it," my mom said.

We went back to her office, where my mom signed the necessary paperwork without hesitation. She could afford it, I knew. Our current house was quite valuable and would be sold within a week.

The real estate agent signed the papers that gave her the authority to sell our house for us. We said goodbye and walked back to the car. Once we got in, my mom reached for my hand and squeezed my fingers.

"We need to talk," she said.

CHAPTER TWENTY-ONE

So there we were, Mom and me, sitting in her car on our way back from buying a house that would mean a new start for us, and suddenly she'd become this responsible parent again whom I hadn't seen for nearly a year. Like that would solve everything. She drove to a restaurant, where we settled down for lunch, even though I was supposed to study for the French test I had tomorrow morning.

"I know that things have been rough on you lately," she said after ordering Diet Coke for me and water for her, "but that's all going to change. I'm going to throw away all the wine and bottles of liquor, and I'm going to completely stop the drinking. I have my first AA meeting in two days, and you are going with me."

"I don't have a problem," I said without looking at her. What the hell was this? Was she suddenly going to become Mom of the Year? Fat chance of that happening, and too little, too late.

"Yes, you do, hon. You've had one for months. Don't think I don't know about your hidden stash or the drugs you've been getting at school. I've called the principal, and he is aware of the problem. I want you to start living a normal life again. You're sixteen, and you have your whole life ahead of you. Please stop damaging yourself like you're doing right now."

I was furious that Mom was interfering with my life. So angry that I wanted to hit something.

"I've talked to Steve about it too," she said. "He knows I'm having this conversation with you. He supports it."

"What? You've been talking to my boyfriend behind my back?"

"Yes."

Mom looked up when the restaurant door opened and a small bell chimed, and I knew exactly who was entering and heading toward us. Steve sat down next to my mom after giving her a hug. When his hand reached out for me, I pulled mine back.

"Are you seriously doing an intervention?" I said. "You guys are nuts. Why don't you start looking out for yourselves first instead of trying to save my soul?"

"That's exactly what I'm doing, Viola," Steve said, his voice trembling. "I came to tell you I can't do this anymore. I just can't. It's over."

"What's over?"

"We can't be together anymore. You're wearing me down, and you're ruining both our lives. This needs to stop."

I stared at Steve, then at my mom, and then back at him. "Are you breaking up with me?"

"Yes."

"You're crazy! What have I done to you that you would do this to me?"

"Enough to make my life a living hell right now," he said, and his voice grew in certainty as he spoke. "I'm really sorry, but it's the truth. You had been so good to me at first, but then things started to change. *You've* changed. You just refuse to see it, Vi. You're no longer the fun person I connected with a year ago, and I get why this is happening, but enough is enough. Your dad's been gone for ten months now; you have to stop grieving and get on with your life."

"Which is why we're here," my mom said. "I have spoken to some people about your situation, and we came to an agreement that you will be spending the summer there. It's not a rehab center—more of a life-coaching center for teenagers. You will get all the help you need in a beautiful, relaxing environment."

I laughed. "You're not serious about this, are you?"

"I am. Viola, honey, I am the one to blame here, not you. You need help, and I am willing to give you all you need, but you'll have to do it away from home. As long as we're here together, I am poison for you. I need my rehabilitation, and in order to do so, I need time away from you and Love Hill too. So I'm going to AA meetings now, and when summertime comes, you are going to head to the coast, and I am going to head to another center. By the end of the summer, we will be ourselves again, I promise."

I saw myself being dragged away kicking and screaming like the teenagers on the *Dr. Phil* show, and I'd be damned if I would not keep my pride. I took a deep breath, thinking of all the black periods in my life over the past year. Perhaps this was a good idea. Maybe this was what I needed. Staying in Love Hill like this would not help me. Going away might.

"Okay," I said. "Okay, I get it. I'll do it."

My mom and Steve reacted so surprised that their mouths almost fell open. I smiled sadly.

"I don't want to be this person anymore, Mom. I'm fed up with everything."

She reached for my hand.

"I'm so glad to hear that."

Of course, agreeing with the whole thing didn't mean I couldn't get one last night of fun. Steve and I had broken up in a bizarrely gentle and friendly way, and he stayed supportive toward me in the days that followed. I actually managed to get decent grades on my finals, and, in the weeks that followed, everyone at school started talking about the summer dance that would celebrate the end of yet another year.

Dead Girls Don't Talk

My mom asked me not to go, but I was adamant about attending, not wanting people to know about the whole rehab thing, even though we all knew it would leak out anyhow. So I went, and she didn't stop me.

Once I got there—alone—I saw all these groups of people hanging out together. Steve was with his friends, and they all knew we had broken up, so I couldn't mingle with them. My friends, whom I had neglected so much lately, were sitting together. I didn't want to go over there either.

One of the kids who had helped me get my hands on drugs and liquor walked over to me casually. "Hey, want a Coke?"

We both knew that it wasn't just Coke. I looked at it and at him, and took it. It felt like gold in my hands. I hadn't touched a drop in three weeks, forcing myself to focus on finals—but hey, I was leaving for the summer soon, so what did it matter? I drank one. And then another. And another. And soon enough, the buzzing feeling in my head started. It felt so damn good.

I spotted them, Lila and Syl, sitting at a small table for four, with two empty chairs left. They weren't holding hands, but I could see how infatuated they were with each other. God, I hated them. I walked over to them and sat down in the chair next to Syl. She sniffed—of course she did. And I didn't care.

"What are you doing?" Syl said. "Are you drinking?"

"Drinking? Only a Coke," I said, raising my glass. "Cheers, ladies." I drank.

"She's smoking too," Lila mentioned, looking at me with disdain. "And I don't mean cigarettes. Don't you smell it?"

Poor, innocent Syl was appalled.

"My God," she whispered. "Are you crazy?"

"Nope. Just sad," I blurted out.

"Why are you sad?"

"I'm sad because everyone dumps me all the time," I said. "You. My dad. Steve. Not even my mom likes me these days."

I saw the wheels in Syl's head turn. Her fear turned into sympathy. "How long have you been drinking?" she asked.

Oh yeah, she was still that Syl, who was so easily influenced by other people's emotions. I just needed to pull the strings, and she would be back in my life. I reached for her hand, but she shot up and stumbled backward. Her chair fell to the ground. Lila pulled her away from me.

"I want us to be friends again," I said. "Please, Syl. I love you. I can't go on without you."

She didn't reply.

"Stop ignoring me, Syl! I exist!"

Around us, people were watching, but I didn't care. So what if they all knew?

Something changed in the air. Syl changed when Lila squeezed her hand for support. So there it was—the two of them against me. God, I hated Lila, the backstabbing liar.

"Go to hell," Syl said, and she left the dance.

You first.

CHAPTER TWENTY-TWO

That summer at the coast was probably the best thing that could have ever happened to me, even though it didn't feel like it at the time. I felt like I was being punished for events that weren't my fault, and for at least two weeks, I struggled against everything that people told me I should or should not do. Ultimately, though, I came back a different person.

I know it's ridiculous to say that about myself. And yes, one might argue that people don't change overnight and too much water under the bridge had passed to just forget about everything I had ever said or done, but I did change. I could feel it in my bones.

Therapy, both individual and in group sessions, taught me that I had never dealt with my issues and losses, and once I started to realize that these conversations had value, I started embracing them. I got my head sorted out and started to feel like myself again.

I could go home after a month—or at least, that was the plan. But I requested to stay for another two weeks, and my mom agreed. She was back home already, and she told me she was going to daily AA meetings. I agreed to go with her once I returned home.

"I'm sorry about everything, hon," she said. "I handled this the wrong way, and it has cost us dearly."

"Stop, Mom. It's not your fault. We were both in a bad place," I said. "We are starting a new life together in our new house. Whatever's happened is in the past."

"I'm glad you feel that way," she said, "because I've got a surprise for you. I've arranged for us to move into our new home immediately. Your room is all packed up and ready to go, so I hope to be able to show you your new rooms—both bedroom and study—by the time you get back."

I felt a slight sense of irritation that she hadn't waited for me, but was proud at the same time that she had taken the reins of life again. One week later, she picked me up and we drove straight to our new house. I never set foot in the other one again. It had already been sold, and the new owners had the keys to it. I think my mom did it on purpose so I could concentrate on a fresh start.

Those first days in our new house were amazing. We had a small pool and a beautiful deck and garden. There was a gardener who took care of the backyard, and we had a housekeeper who came in three times per week to help us out.

"I'm going to do some charity work," Mom said while we lingered by the pool with nonalcoholic cocktails. "I want to do something useful with my life."

"That would be great, Mom."

"Yeah, the beginning of the second phase of my life," she said, readjusting her sunglasses. "I'm young; I have a whole life ahead of me. I can't just waste it away. But what about you?"

"Me? Eh, going back to school will be hard, but I can handle it. And then study hard to get into NYU."

She smiled because we both knew why NYU was the only university I wanted to go to.

"And I'm ready to pick up my life again too," I said.

"You should go to that summer party."

"The one Georgina is organizing? Nah."

"Why not?"

"There will be drinks, and I don't want to be tempted."

Mom sat up and took off her sunglasses to look at me. "Hon, you'll need to get past that. When you go to college, there will be a lot of temptations too. You will have to learn to deal with that."

"I know," I said. "But I'm not so sure if this is the way to do it."
"Of course it is. Georgina's a friend; she's missed you. They all did."
"Not everyone," I said.
"You mean Syl."
"Yeah."
"That's on you, I'm afraid. You can't blame Syl for not wanting to talk to you, but you could try to apologize. Look, you'll have to face her in school too. You can't avoid her, even if she has a new best friend now."

I thought about Lila and what I had asked her to do, and what I had never shared with anyone else. Mom sure as hell was not going to find out. It was shameful. The thing was, I didn't trust Lila as far as I could throw her, and that feeling had only grown over the past two months. I had given the situation a lot of thought; it had been part of my therapy to look at the bad things.

I had driven Syl into Lila's arms, and she still had absolutely no clue what was going on. I had heard rumors about Lila, about a fight between the two of them after the summer dance, where I had made my dramatic entrance. I had heard from Georgina and others that Lila was super controlling over Syl now, that they had spent their entire summer together. How they had gone to *our* Westport. That probably hurt the most. But I couldn't be angry anymore. I was tired of being mad at people. I wanted Syl back in my life, and in order to do so, I needed to tell her the truth about Lila.

"Okay," I said. "I'll go."
"Then you'd best get ready."

A few hours later, I drove to Georgina's house and was greeted like an old friend by almost everyone. A DJ was playing amazing tunes, people were dancing on the huge lawn. This was one of the biggest houses in town, and everyone wanted to be at this party. Steve was there too. I walked over and hugged him.

"You look amazing," he said.

"I know, I feel amazing too."

"That vacation has done you a world of good," he said, glancing at the others around us who were listening in on the conversation.

I laughed. "You can call it a health or rehab center because that's what it was, and I'm not ashamed of it. Thank you for convincing me to go."

"You're welcome, Vi. Look, I know we're never going to be together again like that—too much has happened. But know that I'm always here for you. Don't hesitate to call."

"Thank you. I really appreciate it," I said. "Listen, do you know if Syl is here? I want to apologize to her too."

"Yeah, they're outside somewhere."

They. So she was still together with Lila. I hadn't been sure because I had been too busy settling into the new house and getting readjusted to Love Hill. That answered one of my questions.

"Thanks."

I took a Diet Coke and walked outside to the pool area and found them relatively quickly at a table stacked with food. They were chatting away, focusing only on each other. I watched them for a while, contemplating when to disrupt their conversation. When they walked away, I waited until they found a quiet spot.

They didn't see me. But I saw them. Kissing. Lila had her hands around Syl's face and was claiming her, as if Syl belonged to her and her alone. This, to me, was the ultimate sign that she was now controlling Syl.

A fearful feeling came over me. I felt anger. Sadness. And guilt. What had I done?

"And here we are," I said. *At the end of all things.*

CHAPTER TWENTY-THREE

Lila Jenkins. Freaking Gorgeous Lila Jenkins turned scarlet and stared at me as if she had seen a ghost. She let go of Syl and said absolutely nothing. Syl looked at me stoically, not at all like I had expected.

"So," I said. "How have you guys been doing?"

Lila refused to acknowledge me while I waited for Syl to gather her wits.

"Good," she finally said. "What are you doing here?"

"You two are together?" I asked, instead of answering her question.

"We are an item, yes," Syl said coldly, "but that's none of your business. You have nothing to do with my life anymore, so I suggest you move on."

Her words frustrated me. I immediately felt the old Viola popping up, even though I fought hard to ignore her.

"It *is* my business now," I said coolly. "You two, huh? Since when?"

"Some time," Syl said softly.

"How long, Syl? Since you came on to me? Or earlier than that?" I lashed out, forgetting all my self-made promises about apologizing to her.

"That is also none of your business."

"Come on, we used to be best friends, and you didn't even bother introducing me to your lover. That says a lot, doesn't it?" I went on, hitting my mark.

"We are not—"

She stopped talking and looked at Lila for support, who obviously didn't like Syl's reaction.

I smiled. Score.

"Come on, we're old friends. Don't act this way. I apologized, didn't I? Why are you so mean to me?"

"Just go, Viola," Syl said through tears.

"I don't think so."

I sat down by the pool and looked Lila in the eye. She was so nervous; it was fun to watch. This was the first time the three of us actually spent time together with me being sober enough to talk sense. Syl, realizing she had made an error, tried to squeeze her hand, but Lila seemed frustrated.

"So tell me, how's life treating you? Come on, Syl, don't be like that. I offered you a truce and you accepted it earlier, but now you are treating me like a pariah again when all I offered is friendship. Why can't we be friends?"

"You don't know the meaning of friendship," Lila said. "You're an abuser."

Look who's talking.

"I'm— Excuse me?" I asked. I eyed her up and down, holding back the urgency to throttle her right there and then. Who the hell did she think she was?

"You heard me," Lila said. "For years you've been treating Syl like garbage, using her for whatever you could. You never treated her with respect; you don't give a damn about her."

I flinched when Syl smiled briefly, showing Lila her support. What the hell was I supposed to do now? Should I tell her the truth, when she's obviously happy? But where will this all end if she doesn't know everything?

"I thought we were friends," I said.

"No," Syl said. "Friends treat each other with respect and value their boundaries. You never did. Please go away."

"I'm hurting, Syl," I blurted out, trying a different approach.

"Then find help elsewhere. We're done."

"You were always there for me."

"But you never were for me."

I stood and looked at Lila, who kept on defying me, challenging me to speak the truth. She knew I wouldn't. But I couldn't leave it like this, not when I saw all the signs in Syl's behavior that proved Lila was controlling her. I coughed while frantically thinking. And there it was: the ultimate hand I had not wanted to play.

"I came here tonight to tell you that I love you," I lied. "It took me a long time to realize this, but I am in love with you. I was ignoring my feelings, like my dad had been, but I don't want to make his mistake. Syl, I want us to be together."

Lila gasped. Syl stood, shaking, and with such fury in her eyes that I knew this was a big mistake. "Fuck you."

"Syl, come on!" I said as she reached for Lila's hand, grabbed her bag, and walked away. "Syl, *listen to me!*" I called out after her. "I know things. Lila is not who she says she is. You're being fooled. Syl!"

"No!" she screamed, turning around, coming back to me, and shoving me hard. "Stop ruining my life!"

"I'm not," I said. "I'm protecting you. Ask her what the truth is. Ask her!"

"You're crazy."

"No, I'm not, I swear. You have to trust me on this. We used to be friends. Did I ever betray you?"

Many times, I thought, listening to my own bullshit, but that could not play a factor here now.

I needed to free her.

"Yeah, right," Syl said sarcastically. "Just leave us the hell alone, or I swear I'll punch you so hard, you'll remember it for a long time."

"Syl, come on, it's me! Please hear me out, for old times' sake. You owe me that much."

"Leave. Us. Alone!" she screamed.

I let her go, but not before seeing Lila's pale, exhausted face and Syl's anger and insecurity melting into one. I had planted a seed, and it would blossom and grow into a tree.

———

The next morning Mom got me out of bed. She walked into my room, as pale as a sheet, and sat down. The first thing I thought was that Syl had done something crazy. But it wasn't Syl. It was Lila. She was dead.

I've never known for sure what happened that night after Syl and Lila left, but I didn't have to. I could figure it out for myself. That seed that had grown into a tree had done so in a matter of minutes. They must have argued about everything. Lila must have told her the truth, or Syl may have guessed it. They must have broken up, or Syl may have sent her away.

Lila died of something called SCAD, a.k.a. spontaneous coronary artery dissection. In human language: A tear formed in a blood vessel of her heart that caused sudden death. (I had to look it up.) Turns out Lila really could not afford any strong emotions. She went to therapy. She was a lot sicker than most people knew, and that night had cost her dearly. They buried her as if she were an angel. I knew she wasn't, but I kept my mouth shut.

I didn't see Syl, nor did I call her. I did go to the funeral, just like everyone else in town, and I felt as if I had murdered Lila. Perhaps I had in a way. If only I had kept my mouth shut, if only I had not planted that seed, if only I had not asked her to befriend Syl last year.

Syl spotted me and looked me straight in the eye. I was sitting with Georgina's group; she was seated behind Lila's parents. All she had to say to me was shown in her expression.

You did this. You killed her. I hope you rot in hell.

She didn't have to tell me. I knew it too.

CHAPTER TWENTY-FOUR

Life picked up quickly again after Lila's funeral. It always does.

Syl came to school, too, and went through the motions. She kept on hanging out with Lila's former crowd, who took her in and nurtured her as if she had always been one of them. I was hanging out more with Georgina's crowd now, and sometimes I would go to Steve's group, too, even though things had changed now that he was growing closer to Alicia.

I didn't care. I didn't want to get too close to Steve because that meant I would probably end up telling him the truth one day. And that was the one thing I would have to carry with me for the rest of my life. Only two people knew what had really happened that night, and we were now joined together by secrets, but no longer by friendship.

I threw myself into my schoolwork, hardly went out anymore, and dropped all other activities. NYU was on my mind and I would go for it. I had learned that Syl wanted to go to Stanford, which was a relief to me. I vowed not to get close to her again, in whatever way. She and I would never be friends again. We couldn't be, not anymore. Lila's death would forever stand between us. There was no coming back from this.

In class, we had made a silent agreement never to be paired for assignments again. It was Syl who would always voice her disdain and plead with teachers not to be paired with me.

Sometimes we would get curious gazes, but no one ever dared to ask us directly what was going on. Of course, they had all seen how we had grown apart the year before, so this only seemed to be the sum of all things.

One morning, somewhere in January, a rumor was spread about me, started by Syl. She had told one of Lila's friends how I had been snapping at Lila, and how Syl was still upset with me about this whole situation. She basically spread the word that I had been very jealous of their relationship and had done everything in my power to break them up.

Because of my drinking and drug problem last year, it wasn't so hard for others to believe that I could have done this. Even Steve, who always used to have my back and even now stayed supportive and kind when I was having a rough day, came to me to ask if this was true.

"No," I said. "Of course it isn't. I dumped Syl, remember? Not the other way around."

"Then why would she say this?"

"Because she's lost her best friend and she's in a bad place. She needs to lash out at someone, and that person is me. I get it, Steve. We've moved on, but she's still dwelling on the past, mourning her loss. I don't blame her, and I'm not upset with her."

That made Steve look at me in a new light.

"You really have grown," he said, almost in admiration.

"No," I said. "I've grown up, though."

He smiled and I laughed, and when he hugged me tight, he whispered, "You're one of the good guys, Vi. Don't ever let anyone tell you otherwise."

No, I wasn't, but he would never have to find out. There were a lot of things I'd done in life that I wasn't proud of. The number one thing being the farewell to my dad when he left. The number two being what I had done to Syl when I sent Lila after her. The number three being what I had done to Lila.

If I had known the whole story about her health, if I had taken it seriously enough, I would never have challenged her like that. I would not have seen her the way I always saw myself. The thing is, I had no idea she was really that sick. That it wasn't all just exaggerated, like so many of us had believed.

For years there had been rumors going around school about Lila, about how she abused her medical condition to get what she wanted. How she was perfectly capable of doing a lot more than she wanted us to believe. How she convinced others to do things for her because she was supposedly too lazy to do them herself.

I had believed all these rumors because they seemed logical at the time. I had never seen Lila so sick that she could hardly walk, or so weak that she would need help getting up the stairs. After her death, a lot of stories started popping up about how life had really been for her. About how Syl had always been there for her, taking most of the work onto her shoulders, and how grateful Lila had been to have someone close to her who would see things that others didn't. Lila's mother even came up to the school to give a speech about her daughter, and how she was going to found a charity for people suffering from SCAD, and she wanted Syl to become cofounder in name. Syl accepted the offer.

After that day, Syl was treated completely different at school, with a reverence she hadn't experienced before. She grew stronger after the tragedy. She became vocal about helping kids with medical needs make it through their high school years. She sat down with the school board and came up with ideas.

In May, the foundation was officially created and named the Lila Jenkins Center. A plaque was hung at the school's entrance; a small office was freed up where a counselor now resided to help those in need. I was proud of Syl, but I couldn't and wouldn't tell her. She was still ignoring me, anyhow.

In the end, I had to admit that she came out the strongest of the two of us, and rightfully so. She had grown from a weak, independent teenager into a strong and vocal young woman who was getting ready for Stanford.

After graduation, we would lead our own lives apart from each other, which was for the best for the both of us. And it would have to end like that. I had no intention of ever contacting Syl again, or to even attempt to see her. But that was not what fate had in store for us. Obviously, life had been playing a lot of tricks, and the biggest one was still to come.

That summer, I was at home alone a lot. Mom had turned her life around last year in some ways, and she was now constantly away from home to help at charity events. In other ways, though, her life hadn't panned out the way she wanted. She was still falling off the wagon on a regular basis. At least she wasn't the same aggressive drunk she used to be. She retreated to her room and didn't bother me with it.

I forgave her because she did her best. This time around, I didn't get dragged into the mud, and we strangely enough came to a quiet understanding about her need to fall back into the abyss on occasion.

Leaving me alone at the house a lot meant that I had plenty of time to start getting nervous about NYU, despite having been accepted and having done all the paperwork and preparations. I had too much time on my hands and no one to hang out with. Georgina would be in Europe all summer, and the rest of the gang was already falling apart since everyone was preparing to leave Love Hill. Steve had just come home from vacation with Alicia, making it clear that they were serious about each other.

I cleaned out my room and packed up the boxes that would be shipped to NYU, where I would be sharing a room with some unknown girl.

The radio had been tuned to some R & B station, and Travis Scott was on, bringing me back to that trip two years ago in Westport, where Syl was chatting away about him. Of course I missed my dad; I would for as long as I lived. The music brought it all back.

Dad kept those photos of our annual trips in boxes in his room. I had never asked about them since I never really cared about "real" photos, just the ones I took on my own phone.

My mom must have kept those photos, and I knew where. She had boxes of my dad's things stashed in the attic-storage room, unable to throw them out. I found them easily. Inside my dad's boxes were smaller black boxes that had been labeled with a date. I found the last one, from that trip with Syl, and settled down to look through the photos. And there I found it—*the* picture that brought me here, today, to this very point. The memory of a past I had tried so desperately to forget came screaming back to me at full force. I started crying. Then the rage started. All my good intentions to close off the past were pushed aside.

This could not be ignored.

HERE WE ARE, THEN, AT THE END OF THE LINE

Steve's phone rings. Again. It has been ringing off the hook for about an hour now, but so far, we both ignored it. This time, when he looks at his phone, he frowns.

"What is it?" I ask.

"My dad. He's supposed to be working the night shift, and he knows that I should be sleeping by now. I have to get this."

He answers the phone before I can comment and walks into the other room, mumbling things I can't understand from this distance. They're talking about me, of course. That old fear is back, the one that tells me he won't react the way I've been hoping, and I won't blame him for that. He's upset about the things I've told him, about my part in Lila's death. He should be. This isn't okay—none of it is. He comes back into the room after a while with his phone in hand.

"My dad wanted to know if I had seen you."

"What did you tell him?"

"I told him that you came by, but I kept the details to a minimum. It was a pretty vague conversation. Everyone's looking for you, apparently, so they're contacting the people you are the closest to."

That won't be too many, I think.

"You haven't told him that I'm here?" I say, surprised.

"No. I'm not sure if that's the right thing to do at this moment. I have to think about what we're going to do next, but I'm guessing that will all depend on what you have to tell me."

Steve runs his hands through his hair while looking at the other messages on his phone, and suddenly he looks like that sixteen-year-old kid again, who I had such a good time with. He is eighteen now, six months older than me, and very much looks like a young man who knows what he's doing. But now it seems I've put him through the wringer, and he doesn't know what to do with my story. I can't blame him for that. I was surprised at my own confessions, knowing all too well this had opened a can of worms I couldn't close again.

"That's weird. I received a message from Annie Jones."

I sit up, surprised. Annie Jones, the witness who was there right after my car crashed.

"What does she want?"

"She says, 'I'm looking for Viola. I have a message for her. If you see her, can you tell her to contact me at once?'"

"A message?"

"Do you know her?"

"Not personally. She's an odd character; I never know what to make of her," I say.

He puts his phone down and looks at me. "Why did you really come here, Viola?"

"You asked me that before."

"Yeah, and you lied before."

"No, I didn't. I told you I need an alibi for tonight. Someone who can vouch for my whereabouts so that they don't know I was driving."

"But that's not really true, is it?" he says. "You know all too well that it won't take a genius to figure out what happened in that car. And you obviously care enough about me not to get me into trouble. So again, why are you here?"

"Like I said—"

"Stop lying, Vi!" he suddenly roars, banging his hand on the kitchen table. "If you can't do that, you might as well go now. I'm fed up with listening to you concealing the truth. Tell me why you're here."

Tears stream down my face; I wipe them away quickly. I shake my head. God, I'm so tired.

"Haven't you figured that out yet?" I say. "It's all connected, isn't it? Syl's death, Lila's death, me being here. I'm the reason they're both gone, but twice, I haven't wanted any of this. I drove that car, yes, but I didn't hurt Syl. She did this to herself."

"Are you honestly telling me that you're completely innocent and that Syl caused her own death?"

"Yeah."

"Bullshit, Vi. Stop lying!"

"I'm not!"

"Then tell me the truth. Why are you here?"

"You're the only one who will believe me, okay? And I need someone to root for me. Not my mom, who will undoubtedly go back to binge drinking the moment she finds out what I've done; not Georgina or any other of my so-called friends, who never bothered to get in touch with me once while I was in rehab last year. There's only you, Steve, and I depend on you to explain to others what the truth is. If I tell them my story, they will call me a liar. You are the only one who has never judged me, has always believed what I had to say. I'm asking—no, pleading with you now—to help me get through this."

"I can't if there are any more skeletons in your closet."

"There aren't, I swear."

He made a face as if I were cracking a joke. "Okay, then. Let's say there aren't any left. You still haven't told me what happened in that car tonight."

"I was getting to that," I say weakly. "I swear."

"You're doing a lot of swearing, but the truth is that you are the only one who can still share her story. Syl is dead and cannot tell her tale."

I take a deep breath to begin my final confession. And then he receives another message. Again, that frown.

"What is it?"

"Annie Jones again. She's adamant about reaching out to you, apparently."

"What does she say?"

"'I know Viola was driving that car. If you protect her, you will be blamed too. Please tell her to go to the police and turn herself in, but whatever she says, don't listen to her. She's lying.'"

We look at each other.

"We need to talk to her," Steve says. "She may have seen you. If I vouch for you, we will both get in trouble. I can't risk that, Viola. I just can't. I'm sorry."

"I know," I say, placing my hand on his wrist. "I don't want you to lie for me; it was absurd to ask. We're going to see her together. I'm going to tell her my story."

"And then what?"

"Then you can take me to the police, and I'll tell them the same story. They can do whatever they want with me, but then my fate will be in their hands."

"Okay," Steve says after taking a deep breath. "Are you ready to do this?"

"I am."

He sends Annie Jones a text requesting her address. She replies almost immediately.

It's already getting lighter by the time we settle down in his car. I sit next to him, looking at the quiet streets. The rain has stopped, but the roads still glisten under the streetlights. If they were looking for me, they weren't doing it here.

We reach Annie's house in less than ten minutes, and he parks the car on the street. We walk to her front door, and Steve rings the bell. She opens after a few moments. She was obviously not expecting me to show up as well.

"What are *you* doing here?" she asks.

"I came to talk to you," I say.

Without another word, she steers me into her study, where she waves us over to a large couch. There is another chair, a strange tattered armchair that looks like it came from a garage sale. Her phone is sitting on the coffee table in front of it. Odd. I look at Steve, but he doesn't seem to care. He's nervous.

"Sit down," Annie says, waving to the couch.

Steve wraps his arm around me and guides me to the couch. We sit down and I look at Annie, who looks as if she's been up all night. She seems as exhausted as I am. "Are you okay?" I ask.

"Yes, why wouldn't I be?" she asks, surprised.

"You saw the car. You were there."

"I'm okay. I slept a few hours and woke up early," Annie says and waves at her notepad. "I'm trying to remember all that's happened. I need to go to the police station this morning for a statement. Why are you here?"

"We came to talk to you," Steve says. "We're looking for proof that Viola didn't do what people are accusing her of. She did not crash that car on purpose."

I could kiss him right here and now.

"Oh? Then who was responsible?"

"I was there," I tell her. "But it wasn't like it's being told all over town. I'm being accused of murder, but I did not kill Syl—"

"I don't know what people are saying," Annie interrupts. "I've been here the whole time, not talking to anyone."

"So you don't know anything? About how they are accusing her of cold-blooded murder?" Steve says.

"No." Annie looks at me pointedly. "Were you driving your car?"

"Yes, I was."

"Did you move her body?"

"Yes, I did."

"Why?"

"I was in a panic. I figured that nobody would be the wiser if I put her behind the wheel. She was dead already, so what would it change? I would have come clean sooner or later; I just needed time to think."

"Well, it sounds to me like you did something worse than just leave her there," Annie says. "You pinned the blame on her. Have you ever thought about that?"

I sigh, then blurt out exactly what I *didn't* mean to say. Anger, sadness, and frustration are all pouring out together, and I'm tired.

"The thing is, Syl *did* cause the accident herself. I swear on my mother's life that she did. I just need someone to believe me." I start crying.

Annie remains still. So does Steve.

"I swear it on everything that is dear to me," I whisper, and take out the photo I've kept in my pocket this whole time.

WHAT DO YOU THINK HAPPENED THAT NIGHT?

To find out the whole story, you have to read Syl's version of events too. If you haven't read it yet, turn to page 1.
    And if you're ready for the ending, then move on to page 345.

DEAD GIRLS DON'T TALK

... THE TRUTH ABOUT THAT NIGHT

HERE WE ARE, THEN, WHERE IT ALL BEGAN

(THE END)

CHAPTER ONE (VIOLA)

The photo lay in my hands. I almost crumpled it out of sheer anger. What was this? How could this even be happening? This was some sort of parallel universe, a twilight zone of a world that wasn't mine to begin with.

I frantically started digging in the black box my dad had kept labeled with the last year of his life. He always did that, always put all the pictures of that year together in one big box. Not just the ones of our holidays together, but all the ones he took on his phone or his camera and he deemed interesting enough to print and keep.

This stack went from January to August. Not July, when we had our vacation, but August, when we had already come back. The photos before the holidays were scarce and didn't seem relevant at all; they were just pictures of people at parties or pics from our family.

Then July: all photos of our vacation. And August: photos I had never even seen before, and felt so out of place here that I didn't know what to do with them, so I kept them in the box. But *that* one was the one that changed everything.

And the ones that were stashed behind it, and the ones after that. My dad, without probably even realizing it, had taken photos of something he didn't know would be so important. But if I had seen those photos back then, everything would have been so very different today.

The last one broke my heart. It was the ultimate proof of what had happened two years ago. I had two choices: either ignore them all and move on—or *do something*!

I chose the latter.

"I have to tell Syl," I said aloud.

"You have to tell Syl what?"

I looked up to find Mom standing in the attic, staring at me sitting on the wooden floor in our storage room between Dad's boxes. I stood up on trembling legs while I waved the photo that seemed to be glued to my hand.

"Did you know about this?" I asked.

"What are you talking about? What are you doing here, going through your dad's things? What gave you the right to—"

"To what, Mom? To find things that used to belong to him and are now mine by inheritance?"

"No, they're not. They're still his. And mine."

"Why, Mom? He was my dad. I have the right to see what his life was about. Look at this—there's hardly anything left of him! You threw it all away like it meant nothing."

"No, I didn't. I kept the most precious things, like those pictures you're looking at. Why are you acting so weird? What's going on? I really thought you were doing better, but looking at you now, it feels as if you've gone off the deep end again. Have you been drinking?"

"No, Mom," I said sarcastically. "I just saw the light."

She looked at me as if I were going crazy, and I realized in an instant that she really had no clue what I was talking about. She walked over and snatched the photo out of my hands, looking at the seemingly innocent picture of us in Westport. But there was nothing innocent about it.

"I don't get it," she said with a frown. "Why are you so upset?"

I wiped my face and snatched the photo back. "You wouldn't understand. I have to go."

"Go? Where?"

I left the pictures and the black boxes where they were and rushed down the attic stairs. She followed me.

"Viola, what is going on? I can't let you leave like this. Please talk to me."

I stopped downstairs, where I had to put on my shoes and raincoat. It was miserable out there, like it had been for days. I would be soaked in seconds if I went without my coat.

"I need to see Syl," I said.

My mom held her breath and reached for my arm. "Viola, please. I really don't get this. Tell me what is going on, or I won't let you leave."

I looked at her through the tears that kept on flowing and shook my head.

"All this time I've been feeling guilty over something that wasn't even my fault to begin with. But no more, Mom. I can't take this anymore. I have to talk to Syl. Don't worry about me; I'll come back soon. This won't take long, trust me."

"Then at least let me go with you."

"No. I have to do this alone," I said.

"Why now, Viola?" Mom asked worriedly. "Does this have something to do with your dad?"

"No, Mom," I said. "It has nothing to do with him leaving or his death. But it has everything to do with my life and Syl's over the past two years. Everything was a lie."

"Viola, please. I have a bad feeling about this. Don't go, okay? Please, wait until morning. Things always feel different in the morning."

I stood by the door in my coat and shoes, with my car keys in my hand, and contemplated my mom's suggestion. I shook my head.

"No, Mom," I said. "If I don't go now, I won't have the guts to do it in the morning."

I left the house and ran to my car, got in, and made the ten-minute drive to the other side of town, where Syl was still living with her parents in their mansion. Her mom and dad would probably be at work, and if her housekeeper was there, I would ask her to let me in and leave us alone.

Ten minutes later, I parked in front of Syl's house. I rang the bell frantically and banged on the door for good measure too.

Syl opened the door herself. She was so surprised by my visit that she instantly seemed to forget what had been going on between us. She didn't even ask me what I'd come here for. She stood still. I don't know, maybe she saw something written on my face that made her step back and wait for the bomb to drop, or maybe she simply didn't want to cause a scene in the neighborhood. Now that she had gained people's interest by being part of a foundation, she had to think twice about everything she said and did.

I could have wiped the smug look off her face. Or maybe she was just feeling scared. I walked into her foyer without waiting for an invite and shut the door with a bang. It was quiet—a sure sign that Syl's parents and the housekeeper weren't here. They would have shown their faces by now.

"What do you want?" she asked.

I shoved the photo in front of her and watched her expression change from slight annoyance to sheer shock and guilt. She searched for words, and my heart pounded in disappointment. So it was true, then. All this time. All this damned time.

"What is this?" she said in a shaking voice, trying to recapture some of her composure. "Is this some kind of sick joke? Why are you here showing me this?"

"It is a sick prank, but one that you set up," I said, still shaking with anger.

"I have no idea what you're talking about."

"No? Have you taken a good look at this picture, Syl? Have you seen all the details?"

In the first picture, I'm standing with my mom and Syl in the middle of the pedestrian shopping street of Westport, our arms around each other's backs like the way people who care about each other usually do.

Other tourists are walking by us left and right. It had been a crowded and typical summer day, I think the fourth or the fifth day that we were there. My dad had taken about six photos of us at that time, and he had printed them all. Not only that, but in the stack of photos of that vacation, there were plenty more pictures like it, but taken on different days and different streets.

But always, near us, either to the left or the right, standing behind us, gazing at us, watching us, was a very familiar face. Lila's. Freaking Gorgeous Lila Jenkins was in Westport at the exact same time as we were, and she was in about half of the pictures. She was even in the same hotel. The same damn hotel, in the lobby—again, watching us, or standing near us.

I'll never know if my dad had realized this girl was near us quite a lot. If he had, he would have recognized her as a guest staying at the same hotel. Maybe he had even spoken to her on the street. Maybe they'd had a nice conversation about the weather or the beauty of Westport.

And then there was the last photo. The one my dad must have taken on purpose. The reason why he *knew* that Syl had liked girls more than boys. Why he hadn't been so surprised when I told him what Syl had said to me about her feelings. In that photo, she was talking and standing close to Freaking Gorgeous Lila Jenkins.

"It was all a setup," I said. "You already knew Lila Jenkins was coming to Westport when we were there, didn't you? Why did she come? To keep an eye on you? To spend a few stolen moments with you here or there? Were you guys conspiring against me or something? Were you laughing behind my back when you tried to come on to me? Did you try to set me up to get back at me? Tell me, Syl!"

She shrugged, remaining very calm. "What do you care? You hired her to be my friend, remember?"

"Months later! Don't twist this around," I shouted. "Tell me the truth! Photos don't lie. Did you know her before Westport, and did she come to see you on purpose?"

"All right, then," Syl said, her face cold, her tone distant. "If you insist on finding out the truth now, I might as well tell you. Yes, I knew Lila before we went to Westport. Yes, we were friends, but we weren't together yet. That came later. And yes, she came to Westport to see me. But it's not like you believe any of this happened."

"Then tell me the truth!"

She took a deep breath.

CHAPTER TWO (SYL)

"Why do you let her treat you like that?"

"Sorry?" I looked up from my study book in the confines of the library, surprised that someone other than Viola was talking to me.

Viola had gone to use the bathroom, and so I sat alone at our table, math books lying open to various pages. We had a two-hour break between classes because our French teacher had gone home sick, and Viola had suggested coming to work on our math here. In other words: She needed help, and I needed to be there for her. But now Lila Jenkins was hovering over me.

"You know what I'm talking about. Viola Harrison treats you like her personal pet. You should stand up for yourself. This is not right."

"It's okay. I don't mind," I told her.

"Well, I do. You shouldn't be treated like that by anyone."

"She's my best friend, and it's really okay. She's not that bad," I said, surprised by Lila's fierce reaction. What did she care? We were classmates but not friends, even though I had always liked her.

"Well, I disagree," Lila said, sitting down in Viola's seat. "What are you working on? Math? Of course, because she sucks at it. But I don't, and you certainly don't, so you don't need to go the extra mile. Come on, let's get out of here and have some fun. It's warm out. You shouldn't be cooped up in here."

"Thanks, but no thanks," I said. "I really have to stay and help her out, or her finals will be a total disaster. Maybe later."

"Okay, then let's meet in the park after school. I'll buy you ice cream."

I was stunned again. What was going on? Lila wasn't friends with me or Viola's group. She had her own crowd. Didn't she hang out with Ellie and her gang a lot? I glanced around, almost expecting cameras to catch the joke on video. This had to be a prank, right? Perhaps Viola had set it up.

"That's really sweet of you," I said, trying to get rid of her, "but I'm supposed to go home with her. Her mom is making dinner tonight, and I really don't want to disappoint her."

That made Lila frown, and then she laughed. She seemed to get it all of a sudden, that odd relationship between Viola and me.

"Oh my God, it's even worse than I thought. You're her adopted twin, aren't you? Sitting at her parents' table for dinner, chatting about whatever television program or movie has caught their attention while trying to show your interest in it or their feelings might get hurt. Is that it? Are you sucking up to them?"

I felt myself blush, because yes, that was exactly it. I wanted to have that warm family feeling, and in order to do so, I sometimes acted like a chameleon. But Lila Jenkins, who had a good life and experienced normal parenting, would never understand where I came from or how I felt.

"I'm sorry," Lila said, turning serious when she saw my reaction. "I know your parents suck. I didn't mean to hurt you."

"It's okay," I whispered.

"No, it's not. I feel ashamed. Look, why don't you give me your number, and we'll meet up when you want to. And if you don't, that's fine too."

"Why?"

"Why not?"

"Nobody cares about me, so why should you?" I blurted out.

"I care. Why shouldn't I?"

"You're just like everyone else in this town. Nobody here cares about anyone else. If you're talking to me now, there has got to be a reason."

Lila smiled. "Well, then maybe you have found the only person in town that does care."

She scribbled down her number on my notepad and left before Viola came back. I tore the number from the pad and tucked it in my pocket. All the while, when Viola was sitting next to me, going on and on about how she didn't understand math, that phone number was burning a hole in my pocket. I knew that I would call her.

Lila and I started hanging out as friends, which came surprisingly quickly and felt easygoing. We talked about her condition, even though, as I would discover much later, she downplayed it quite a lot. She had tried to fit in but realized that wasn't possible, so she lied to others about it a lot. She lied to me at first too; I saw through those lies quickly.

We became really good friends, in secret because I didn't want Viola to find out just yet. She wouldn't like me spending time with someone else. We started hanging out in the evenings, as soon as I came home from school and having dinner with Viola's parents. It wasn't that hard keeping the secret to myself.

"Why don't you want anyone to know we're friends?" Lila asked.

"Because I want to enjoy these moments without anyone interfering. That will change as soon as Viola finds out. Trust me."

"You're afraid of her."

"Yeah, I guess I am."

At some point, I had started opening up about Viola and how I felt about her and this whole situation, how I wanted to free myself but didn't dare to.

"She's toxic," she said. "You won't be free until you've freed yourself."

"I can't. It's not that easy."

It was the end of June and a hot summer's day. I had just been asked to go to Westport by her parents, and I knew I wanted to go, despite my feelings toward Viola. I liked Viola, more than I dared to admit, and I hadn't told Lila. But she had guessed.

"You feel something for her that is beyond friendship."

I didn't deny it.

"Why?"

"I don't know. I just do."

"And what if I were to tell you that I have feelings for you?"

I looked at her, surprised. "You?"

"Yeah, me. You're not the only one in Love Hill hiding secrets, you know. There are plenty of us around who like each other more than they're supposed to—or at least, according to the rules in this town. We just don't say it out loud. A lot of us are biding our time."

That didn't make me feel any better, but at least it was something to know that there were others like me out there.

"Don't go," she insisted, but I couldn't just do that without causing suspicion. Me, the girl without a single friend, who had absolutely nothing going for her in life except her parents' money, couldn't just say no to an offer to tag along on a family vacation. It would rouse suspicion, and Viola wasn't the type of person who would accept my *no* and let it go, even if she didn't really want me there in the first place. Oh yeah, I knew all too well that she didn't like it one bit, but what could she do about it?

"I have to," I said.

"Then make her life a living hell. Get under her skin, suck up to her parents, make sure she hates having you around. She'll go pleading to her daddy about having some quality time together, which will give you time to spend with me."

"What?"

"I'll go too. I'll get my parents to go and book us a room at the same hotel and act as your ghost or something. You'll know I'll be there, and that will give you mental support."

"You're crazy! They'll see us."

"I'll make sure they don't, I promise. We'll take the train up there; my parents won't mind. My mom has been busy with this huge event, and my dad has been working all summer. They need a break."

Hanging around Westport without anyone ever noticing seemed like a crazy plan, but we both wanted to see each other as much as we could, because we already couldn't *be* without each other anymore. I wasn't stupid. Despite my feelings for Viola, I was developing feelings for Lila, too, and they were slowly taking over.

Viola had always believed I had no friends to connect with, but she never once realized that I took every single spare moment when she wasn't around to send messages to Lila, to share a gaze with her, to look at her while we were sitting in restaurants or on the beach, to think about her when I was talking to Viola and her parents, to dream about her when I was alone in bed.

We were so young and so innocent, but crazy about each other. The more time I spent with her, the more impatient I became with Viola, and the more courage I gathered to say no to her.

Lila texted me one morning.

You should tell her that you're gay and see how she reacts. Come on, that'll be the best part of this trip.

I can't, are you crazy??? What if she wants to kiss me?

She won't, she's not like us. She likes Steve, remember? Dreamy Stevie. And this will drive her into his arms much faster. She'll want to get rid of you immediately.

You're right, she will. God, this is genius!

Then do it. Get rid of her. But make her think that she is getting rid of you!

And so I told Viola half my truth.
She reacted exactly how we had predicted.

CHAPTER THREE (VIOLA)

"You disgust me," I said after hearing the whole confession. "How could you do this?"

"I did it because I was tired of being your little pet," Syl said. "How did you think you made me feel all this time? You were toxic, Viola. You used me all the time, and I couldn't take it any longer."

"You were happy enough to spend time with my parents at their dinner table. You took advantage of them too. My dad even felt sorry for you," I said angrily. "And then you dared to send me texts about how sorry you were that he left and then died? Hypocrite."

"Maybe I am a hypocrite, but so were you," Syl said. "You couldn't wait to get rid of me after Westport. Up until today, before you found this picture, you were eager to believe that it was best for me to be with someone of my own kind. You dumped me as fast as you could."

"I did," I said, "and I'm ashamed of that. But I didn't *dump* you in that sense of the word, I didn't do it because you were gay. I did it because you were a leech. How right I was, more than ever. You latched on when you didn't have a warm family to go to, and then you used me as an excuse to be with the girl you liked. Why didn't you come clean sooner? Why did you even pretend not to know Lila at school?"

"That's your doing," Syl said. "You actually did me a favor when you went to talk to Lila that day, asking her to hang out with me. Your little act with Steve gave us the perfect excuse to become best friends without arousing any suspicion. Everyone at school knew what you had done to me; word got around fast. And Lila simply took your spot while you kept on believing all this time that you were pulling the strings."

What she said was true. I had been so absorbed in my own little world, with my own issues, that I had been blind to what had been right in front of me all this time. Everyone, including myself, had commented on the sudden closeness of Lila and Syl, who had played out this whole act just to be together. How had it even come this far?

"You know what's the saddest part in all of this?" Syl said, sitting down on one of the chairs in the huge foyer she used to call the ballroom because of its excessive grandeur. "I had to lie to you for days during our vacation. I had to come up with excuses like going to the bathroom all the time, or just slipping into a store you hated so I could spend a few brief moments with her while she followed us around. How pathetic is that? And the worst of it all is that your dad had been playing this part his entire life. He let go of the one person he loved the most. Well, I decided I would never do that. I've loved Lila for as long as I could, even if that was only a very short period of time. I was happy for over a year. And then you went and ruined it for me."

"*I* ruined it? How do you see that?"

Syl didn't answer.

"Wait a minute," I said. "Hang on. You said earlier that I went to *talk* to her. You didn't use the word *blackmail*. She never told you that I *blackmailed* her, did she? She told you that I gave her permission to befriend you, to take you off my hands. That's why the two of you had that fight the night she—"

"Stop it," Syl snapped. "Just stop it, okay?"

"I'm right, aren't I? Tell me something, Syl. Your precious girlfriend lied to you about our conversation, and you know exactly why she did, don't you?"

Syl looked away.

"You didn't know about Ellie. You actually thought you were the first one she had a major crush on."

"Get out."

I started laughing.

"Oh my God, you really didn't know anything about her, did you? She did the same thing to Ellie, Syl. She practically stalked her. Ellie was scared of her, and so damned happy to be rid of her. Lila wasn't the sympathetic, kind girl you took her for. She never was."

"Get out!"

This time Syl screamed and started for the front door. I shrugged, not caring if I would ever see her again.

"You two really were a match made in heaven, weren't you? All this time you were blaming me for all the shit that went wrong in your life, but in truth, you owed everything you got to yourself. I'm done feeling sorry for you."

"What's going on?"

The front door had opened without either of us even noticing it, and Syl's dad had walked in. He was in a suit, obviously dressed for some event.

"Just picking up some things," he said before kissing Syl on her forehead. "Is everything okay?"

I didn't look him in the eye; I hadn't done so since the day my father had left, and I wasn't about to now.

"I'm done with this family," I said, and stepped into the pouring rain and walked to my car.

I got in, shook the rain off my coat, put the key in the ignition, started the car, and turned up the volume. Before I pushed on the pedal, the passenger door opened and Syl got in.

"We're not finished," she said.

"Well, that's too bad, because I'm going home and you're not welcome there," I said. "Get out, Syl. Go back inside, go to Stanford, and leave me the hell alone."

"I don't want to," she said. "We need to end this right here and now, or this will never be over."

"Have it your way, then," I said, turning the key again. "I won't drive away until you get out of the car."

She fished a gun out of her pocket and aimed it at me. "Drive."

CHAPTER FOUR (SYL)

I don't even know why I got into that car. I don't know why I took my dad's gun from his safe as soon as he'd gone to get whatever he needed for that stupid event he was attending with my mom. I don't know what came over me. Blind rage. Fury. Anger. Or sadness.

Viola visiting me, with all her accusations and spite toward Lila, drove me to a point of such anger. Lila was still dead because of her. Not because of that fight we'd had or the lies Lila had thrown in my face, or the secrets she had kept from me. Or because she was, in her own way, just as manipulative as Viola had been.

Lila was dead because Viola had messed up our lives, and I wouldn't stand for it anymore. I just couldn't have it. Or maybe it was my own part in this mess that I wanted to get rid of.

"So what are you going to do now, huh?" Viola said, her voice a mixture of anger and fear. "Are you seriously pointing a gun at me, thinking that will scare me off? You're crazy, Syl. Put that thing away before you hurt someone. You're not the kind of person to do something so stupid."

"Aren't I?"

"If you're pretending to be this crazy idiot, then I've never known you. You are not going to do anything dumb tonight."

"I want you to go where she was hurt," I said, ignoring her words. "I want you to see where she died. I want you to feel the hurt I have felt."

"I know where she passed away. I've been there," Viola said.

"Yeah, right."

"I'm serious. I've visited that area several times. What? Do you really think I have no compassion at all? That I'm this selfish, crazy bitch who doesn't give a damn about anything? Come on, Syl. I've been feeling like crap for a year, too, you know. You've ignored me, bashed me, and made sure that I was sharing the guilt you've been carrying around. Guess what? You didn't even have to do any of that. I felt bad enough as it was."

"That's not enough," I said. "It'll never be enough."

"Then what is? This?" She nodded at the weapon in my hands.

I thought about an answer. "We shouldn't be here at all."

"What the hell are you talking about?" Viola said, now clearly starting to feel nervous.

"I'm saying that we have not been punished for her death. It's never enough. Why should we be able to go to college when she never will, Viola? Have you ever thought about that? Why are we doing all these things with our lives anyhow? Do we even deserve to be happy?"

Viola snorted, for a moment acting like her old self again. "Have you ever considered the fact that Lila brought this on herself? She was the one who did most of the lying. She had enough secrets of her own. She wasn't this perfect girl you made her out to be. And she used you."

"Just like you did," I said, and felt the tears streaming down my face. I couldn't hold them back any longer. "You both used me."

"Yeah, I did. I didn't realize it at the time, but I didn't value you enough. I'm sorry about that. I've tried to make it up to you, but you wouldn't listen."

Viola drove on through the dark evening with the rain pouring down on us, a troubled expression on her face and the obvious realization that this wasn't going to end well. She felt it in the air, the unsettling feeling that tonight would change everything.

"Please, Syl, this isn't you," Viola said as she drove up the small elevated area with the curved road that led to the open space where Lila and I had our last conversation.

Dead Girls Don't Talk

There was more than one reason why I had chosen Annie's house to go to every week. It brought me past this same area every time. I had been punishing myself, without even realizing it. Of course, I didn't just go to Annie to talk to Lila. I did it because she happened to live half a mile down the road, and this was the only way to get there.

"Please put down that gun," Viola said after I'd shared this with her aloud, not even realizing I was doing so until I had already said it. "You have to listen, Syl. What are you going to do? Shoot me? Shoot yourself? Come on, this isn't the answer and you know it."

She was right, of course. The gun felt like lead in my hand, and I couldn't hold it up any longer. I didn't even know how to use it; the safety was still on. Suddenly, it felt like it was this heavy thing that could blow up at any second.

On a whim, I opened the window, threw it out, and watched it bounce against a tree, where it remained in the darkness, in the rain.

"What the h— Are you crazy?!" Viola barked. "You threw it out? You can't do that! Kids play in this area, Syl! We have to go back. I have to turn around. God, what were you thinking?"

She started slowing down and sighed in relief as we reached the open space, but then the car made this weird move, and suddenly it felt as if I were waking up from a bad dream, realizing just what I had done, and I stared at her in shock, upset by what I had caused, and I took my seat belt off, and then the vehicle jolted, skidded, and slipped off the road through the muddy ground onto the open space where Lila had passed away. The car was still going too fast, and Viola screamed and pulled at the steering wheel to avoid hitting the tree, but she didn't make it. She couldn't steady her brand-new car, given to her by her mom to drive to NYU.

And then the tree came right at me. Or we headed right toward it. I reached for the wheel.

ANNIE

They sit together in my study, Viola and Syl, but Viola doesn't even realize she's sharing the space with her dead best friend. I've heard Viola's version of events, and I've heard Syl's, and they've come together like pieces of a puzzle that fit perfectly.

"Don't tell her about me," Syl whispers. She's no longer clearly visible, but fading, fading, fading away.

I didn't have to ask Syl if Viola had been telling the truth about the events that brought on the crash. It was clear to me that she was.

"There's a gun out there somewhere, lying between the bushes by the road leading up to the open space," Viola says. "I've looked for it, but I couldn't find it, and I couldn't risk hanging around. But the truth is, it's too dangerous to stay there, so we have to tell the cops. It will have Syl's fingerprints on it. And if the police do their job right, the skid marks and other forensic evidence will show them the rest."

"You really didn't come here tonight to ask me for an alibi, did you?" Steve says, hugging Viola. "You were protecting your friend, even when she was already dead."

"Yeah, well, I really wanted to keep them from finding out that she took her dad's gun during a moment of sheer panic. I owe it to her, after all the things I said and did. And for all the times I wasn't there for her. She didn't deserve all that. Plus, she never really tried to kill me. That, I just know."

Steve smiles; I do too. Syl laughs.

"True," she says in a weak voice. "And I really didn't want to kill her."

But you did accuse her of killing you.

Syl must have read my thoughts, because she looks straight at me, and she smiles and shrugs.

"I never said I wasn't messed up. I'm sorry I didn't tell you everything. I'm sorry about dumping this on Viola. I was mad about the way she acted when I came out, and so many other things. It's this town that makes it so hard for everyone to live. And I'm sorry about Lila. I'm sorry that it all had to end this way."

I smile gently and nod. The chair empties, and she is gone. Just like that. Poof. Like she faded with the wind. Viola looks straight at the chair one last time and shivers, as if she can feel it too.

"And now what?" she asks.

"Now you have to tell the police what happened," I say. "Get your conscience cleared. And go to NYU. Get your life straightened out." I look at Steve, who still has his arm around her. "All of it."

Viola smiles.

"Maybe I should do all of that," she says. "But I need to go talk to her parents too. They need to know their daughter didn't do anything wrong. All she ever did was love someone a bit too much. Not once, but twice. Syl was one of the good guys, and I will miss her every day for the rest of my life. I just wish I hadn't done her so wrong."

"She knows that, believe me," I say.

"If I didn't know any better, I'd almost say you had a connection with her," Viola says. "But of course, that sort of thing doesn't happen—does it?"

"I guess not," I say.

I have accepted that my recordings will have no use. Nobody will be able to hear Syl's side of things anyhow, and they won't believe a word I'll have to say about it. What would the point be, when the story has already ended?

Some things just have to stay with the dead. There is a reason why they usually cannot speak.

EPILOGUE

I sigh as I get out of the SUV after the more-than-six-hour drive to the NYU campus. There's a flurry of students who seem to be going in all directions. They walk around as if they belong here, and don't look as nervous and green behind the gills as I do.

"This is perfect," Steve says as he hides a yawn. He's been driving the whole time; the car is his.

"It is," I say. "It'll be a fresh start."

He starts taking my suitcases and bags from his car and brings them into my assigned dorm building. We find my room on the second floor, where a girl named Tammy is waiting for me.

"Hey," she says. "Welcome!"

She seems quite nice and immediately starts helping me with my things. I like her already; she seems cool. I walk Steve back to his car. He will be staying on the other side of campus.

"I have to get going," Steve says. "Are you sure you're going to be fine?"

"I'm more than fine, Steve. Thanks. Now go call Alicia before she thinks you and I are together again. She'll be nervous as it is."

"She's fine with us being friends." He smiles, pecks me on the cheek, and gets in. "Give me a call; we can have dinner tonight."

"Or maybe I'll have dinner with my new roommate," I say. "And we can have a bite to eat with Alicia tomorrow?"

"Sounds like a plan. Wow, you really have changed, Vi," he says. "See you later."

"See ya."

He takes off, and I wave before heading back into the building, where I'm greeted left and right by people I have never seen before, who all treat me like their equal. It feels amazing to get this fresh start, to be away from the town that felt like it was choking me on a daily basis.

Finally, I am freed.

Freed from any accusations against me; freed from people thinking that I crashed the car on purpose that night; freed from people believing that Syl took that gun because she really wanted me dead for whatever secret I was still holding; freed from all those jerks who'd rather believe a non-truth than what had actually happened; freed from those who wanted to see me charged and punished for something I didn't do, but won't because there isn't a shred of evidence that I did anything wrong except lose control over the steering wheel of my car.

I am freed because I will never go back there to face those accusers. I will never return to Love Hill, not once. Not for the rest of my life. From now on, the world is my oyster.

I walk into the room, where Tammy is unpacking the last of her things. My suitcases are on the bed—one of them open, the other one, with my personal things in it, closed. On the floor next to the wall on my end of the room are the boxes that were shipped earlier.

I open the one I've put a mark on and carefully unpack the photos of my dad, Syl, and my mom, all taken in Westport.

Tammy approaches me.

"Your parents and your sister?" she says. "They seem nice. I hope we can be each other's family around here. People need family, you know. And family are people who care about each other."

I smile. "That would be great," I say. "I'd like that."

She gives me a small hug and goes back to her side of the room, decorating it just like she wants it. Nice, naive girl. It will be good if she's strong in math.

I look at Syl in the photo, smiling back at me. And Lila standing in the far distance, with a grim expression on her face, gritting her teeth because she couldn't be part of our little family. The photo is a bit crumpled around the edges because I'd held on to it for so long that night, but I still managed to get it framed.

Every single day, for as long as I live, I will remember what happened.

How Syl reached for the steering wheel. How I panicked, knowing she was trying to save herself and kill me. How I pushed her away and twisted the wheel hard, which made the car swerve, causing it to crash against the tree on her side and not mine. I only started remembering the details of it much later, when the police were asking me all these questions that I replied to with lie after lie. I told them how she'd pulled the wheel toward her, and they responded with sympathy.

"She must have seen it coming. She must have been trying to save you. She *did* save you."

"Yeah," I replied. "She's a hero."

I was driven out of animalistic fear for my life, but it didn't change the outcome. Didn't make the secrets easier to bear. That picture will remind me of what I did. And that will keep me straight on my feet.

"Yeah," I say as I rearrange the frame. "My family."

ABOUT THE AUTHOR

Sandra J. Paul is a Belgian author of a number of psychological thrillers for both adults and young adults, including *The Last Days of Holly Hayes* and *Dead Girls Don't Talk*, both of which have gone viral on TikTok, with millions of views. Paul is the recipient of the Aspe Award for crime fiction, among several other awards. Her work has been translated into multiple languages and sold internationally in the United States, the United Kingdom, France, Slovenia, the Czech Republic, Spain, and Italy, among others. Paul also writes under her pseudonym, Joanne Carlton. Follow her on TikTok @sandrajpaul.

Printed in Dunstable, United Kingdom